HOLY WAR

ALEXANDER M. GRACE was a career foreign service officer who was posted in numerous countries in Latin America and Europe. An expert on Latin American affairs, he presently teaches international relations at the University of Central Florida. He lives in Orlando, Florida.

AVAILABLE NOW

HOLY WAR

ALEXANDER M. GRACE

ibooks
new york
www.ibooks.net

DISTRIBUTED BY SIMON & SCHUSTER

An ibooks, inc. Book

Distributed by Simon & Schuster, Inc.
1230 Avenue of the Americas, New York, NY 10020

ibooks, inc.
24 West 25th Street
New York, NY 10010

The ibooks World Wide Web Site address is:
www.ibooks.net

First ibooks, inc. mass market printing: December 2004

ISBN: 0-7434-9331-1

10 9 8 7 6 5 4 3 2 1

Printed in the U.S.A.

To Maricruz, my best friend and one true love.

Holy War

PROLOGUE

†

By 8:30 in the morning the inbound lanes of the N-VI northwest of Madrid had reached their normal state of near gridlock. The three lanes were jammed with cars, while apparently insane motorcyclists weaved between the stalled autos at dangerously high speeds, using the white lines as their own private thoroughfares. An occasional motorist, impatient with the wait, slipped onto the shoulder and cruised ahead until a lamp post or sign blocked his way, at which point he expected to be let back into the flow of traffic. Horns would honk, and there was an occasional fistfight over the right to advance several more yards toward the city. It was the first Monday in September, and everyone was back from their traditional August vacations. The day was already sweltering as the temperature began to rise to another promised record high, and tempers were short.

Only one man in the throng appeared to be enjoying himself, a rather short man with very dark hair just flecked with grey, and a trim moustache. He was slender, but rather than appearing frail, he seemed to be constructed of twisted steel covered in leather. His dark eyes smoldered beneath bushy eyebrows. He sat in the center lane in his rented Ford Escort, drumming his fingers on the steering wheel and rocking his shoulders in time to a cheerful salsa tune on the radio. It was one of his all-time favorites, for, under the very danceable rhythm, there was a clear political message for those who bothered to listen. The song told the story of "Father Antonio and his altar boy Andres," a godly man who tried to bring peace and understanding to his people and was gunned down, along with the poor altar boy, for his troubles. You'd never guess it from the music, though, and the driver suspected that most people didn't bother to listen to the words and learn.

Politics aside, however, the driver really loved the song because it reminded him of his youth in the slums along the banks of the Rio Ozama in Santo Domingo. He had danced barefoot in the muddy streets to just that sort of music as it filtered from cracked speakers in some ramshackle bar. He could see his playmates, mostly black or mulatto, with a few of European stock like himself, mostly naked because of the heat and because of their poverty, as they swayed and jumped to music that seemed to come from within themselves. As he looked back now, those seemed to be the only truly happy days of his life. He had been poor and had gone to bed crying from hunger more than once, but his mother had loved him. Now he knew that he had been happy because he hadn't known that people weren't meant to live like that and because he hadn't known that he was the man chosen to do something about it.

Well, Lazaro Puente was happy now. He had led his people on a long journey "through the wilderness," but by the end of the day they would have earned their passage back home. Of course, this only meant that his real task was just beginning, but the preparatory work was ending, and he would now be working for his own cause, on his own soil, and at his own discretion.

He thanked God for the men and women who had followed him these long years, and he prayed for those he had lost along the way. They still called him "Padre," even though the Church had disowned him long ago. He didn't care about the title, of course, but it pleased him that in their simple way they understood that it was he, not the fossilized, bureaucratic Church, who was doing God's work. Lazaro had chosen his people well, and they had been tested more times and in more ways than any of the apostles. They had their faults. They were only human, but they knew the will of the Lord when they heard it, and they would happily give their lives to fulfill that will.

Most of his followers were among his original parishioners in Santo Domingo. He had been lucky enough to get into a seminary after his mother had literally worked herself to death, so that he didn't have to quit school and go out on the street shining shoes, selling trinkets or just begging like so many other children from his neighborhood. Lazaro had learned of the mysteries of the Catholic faith and of the power of the Church, and he had gladly gone back into the slums of his boyhood to bring that faith to his people.

He soon became a convert to "liberation theology," a movement popular among the younger priests, which stated that one could not do Christ's work in a society in which man preyed upon his fellows, living like kings while poor children starved. He had grown up with the poor, but his education had exposed him to the wealthy sector of Dominican society with their Mercedes cars and their vast mansions in Arroyo Hondo which might have been on the moon for all the contact they had with the men, women, and children of the Rio Ozama slums. He organized reading groups, first to teach the people to read, and then to direct their reading in the works of Che Guevara, Mao, Fidel Castro, and his personal hero, the radical priest Camilo Torres of Colombia, killed leading guerrillas against the oligarchy. Lazaro had believed primarily in nonviolent protest, however. With a supposed democracy and a free press in the Dominican Republic, he imagined that the hordes of voting poor would eventually make their wishes known, and the politicians would have to respond or be booted out.

The years taught him differently, however. He watched the striking workers he had helped organize being beaten by policemen in the streets when they asked for a minimum wage which would barely keep their families in food and shelter, much less clothes, medicine, and the other "luxuries" of life. There was no money in their strike funds to support the families for even a few days, and in the end the strikers were lucky if they were able to beg to get their jobs back at lower wages than when they had started the strike, because of the hordes of jobless men who were willing to do anything to earn any amount of money at all. To celebrate, the owners and their political friends took their families to Disneyworld or Switzerland, while the workers had to listen to their children crying themselves to sleep at night from hunger. The workers could only clench their powerful fists to their ears to block out the sound, or go out and spend what little money they had on cheap rum so that they could pass out and not be bothered by the crying.

Lazaro fought the good fight for five years, and nothing changed. The Church told him that his job was to give people faith in the afterlife, which would give them strength to tolerate what they were destined to suffer in this one. But he couldn't believe that Jesus had wanted the fat bishops and cardinals to cover themselves with jewels and not use any of that wealth and power to help the faithful. That was when he had taken a hundred of his young men and women off the island, to fight for the cause. He had taken them to fight in the service of others so that they could learn the ways of war and could earn the right to go home and free their own people. They had fought from Central America to the Middle East for ten long years. Now, of his original hundred, there remained only 28 hardened fighters after the dead, the crippled, and those who simply had not measured up had fallen away. Today would be their last act on behalf of others. From here on they would be on their own, and their real war would finally begin. Praise the Lord!

†

Just ahead of Lazaro's car, in the right hand lane, U.S. Navy Commander Frank Keenan sat in his Volvo station wagon and looked impatiently at his watch. His home in the suburbs was barely six miles from his office in the Spanish Air Ministry where the Office of Defense Coordination was headquartered, yet he had been on the road for over half an hour and was barely halfway there. On Tuesdays and Thursdays he had to pick up his daughter, Carol, after her dance classes, since the school bus schedule did not allow for after-school activities. Otherwise, he would take the train into town every day and forget about this traffic.

He enjoyed living in Madrid well enough. True, Madrid had become one of the most expensive cities in Europe, and the allowances he got from the Navy didn't make up the difference, but this was still the nicest post he'd had in years. Most importantly, it had been a choice of Madrid or another assignment afloat, and he felt it was important for twelve-year-old Carol to get as much of a normal family life as possible at this stage. He had stuck it out for three years in Norfolk, which had been fine for the family, even if it wasn't exactly a "career enhancing" slot for him. His wife had let him know that, after his time on the cruiser *Vincennes* in the Persian Gulf, she didn't think she could take another extended separation. He had been in Madrid for two years, with one more to go, and things were looking good. Carol was already showing signs of preferring to spend time with her friends instead of with her parents, as kids do when they hit their teens, so next year he could probably swing another ship assignment without too many tears from his wife.

Keenan stepped hard on his brakes as the jerk in the car in front of him slowed again. Keenan swore and pounded his steering wheel with the heel of his hand. He hated guys who left a fifty-foot gap ahead of them when traffic was moving at two miles per hour, practically inviting people to cut in front of him and slowing progress even further. Spaniards were not noted for leaving more than the width of a coat of paint between cars when they were ripping along at 120 clicks an hour, but it never failed that you'd find some bozo like this in heavy traffic. He would have gladly swung over into the center lane to try and get ahead of this guy, but there was a Ford Escort half a length behind him, just keeping pace, so he never had room to move. There was nothing to do but sit this one out.

Luis touched the brake of his rented Citroen again, letting the space in front of him grow, keeping the Volvo glued to his back bumper with the Padre's car alongside and slightly to the rear. This was the most frustrating part of the operation, and Luis was not particularly pleased with the plan. There was still another hundred yards to go before he reached the little roadside kiosk painted in the bright yellow of a Schweppes advertisement which was his landmark for initiating the action, but in that distance it was still possible for some idiot to wedge his way in between his car and the American, spoiling everything. After all of their work, they would have to abort again, and it might be weeks before they got another chance like this. To his mind the requirement to do the deed in the middle of a main traffic artery at rush hour seemed unnecessarily risky. If it hadn't been for the Padre's insistence that they comply with their sponsor's scenario to the letter, Luis would have just done the deed and been well on his way out of Europe an hour ago.

Actually, the hardest part of the operation had been setting up surveillance of the target's home, and Luis was proud of the solution he had found for it. The sponsors had provided them with the name of the target and his place of employment. It had been fairly easy to spot an American naval officer of the appropriate rank during their casing of the Air Ministry. Since the ministry had armed guards all about, and was very close to the Spanish prime minister's residence at Moncloa, adding further to the security profile of the area, the surveillance team had been very discreet and had abandoned the Air Ministry end as soon as they determined his home address.

That only added a host of new problems, however. The target lived in the suburbs on a street of townhomes with no commercial property nearby. With the high crime rate in Madrid, a parked car with people in it, or someone just lounging around, would certainly have attracted the attention of the police long before the team could establish the target's pattern of activity. They needed to know just when he left the house each morning, and they needed confirmation that he would be driving his car on a given day rather than taking the commuter bus or train. Lastly, they would need precise warning of when the target left home on the day chosen for the hit. All of these things demanded someone to be within line of sight of his doorway.

In the movies they could have just rented or occupied the house across the way with no trouble. They did check, not just the house across the way, but all up and down the street, but none were for rent. They were contemplating just buying one, since money was no object, but they learned that the paperwork would take weeks to wend its way through the Spanish bureaucracy, and there was no time for that. Finally, it was Luis who hit upon the solution.

The area was an upscale residential neighborhood, very domestic, so what would be more normal than someone walking his dog, letting him shit on his neighbor's driveway rather than his own? Luis went out and picked up a small mixed breed terrier from the local Society for the Protection of Animals and Plants, a name which struck Luis as odd, but it got him the dog. He had one of the women do a dry run wearing a housecoat and with her hair mussed up, as if she had just gotten out of bed to do the chore the children had promised to do when the dog was a new puppy. They drove to a spot about two blocks from the target's house where a high blank garden wall faced a vacant lot, so no one would see this strange woman getting out of a car with her dog. From there on she was just part of the scenery, probably living just around the corner as far as the local residents were concerned.

The woman could now easily spend forty-five minutes to an hour within sight of the target's door, leisurely walking up the street to the corner, letting the dog investigate every strange scent along the way, and then strolling back again. That was more than enough of a window to pick up the target's departure. As Padre Lazaro had pointed out, even officials who are sensitive to possible terrorist threats and who try to alter their times of travel and their routes, tend to set their alarm clocks for the same hour every morning, take the same time to get dressed, and head out the door at a predictable time, and he had been right. Catching a target coming home is harder, as people can get hung up in meetings, have errands to run and leave early, etc., but in the morning people are only half awake and habit takes over while they're on autopilot.

The woman's radio was in the pocket of the housecoat with the antenna running up inside the lapel. All she had to do was to hit the talk button twice if the target were leaving home on foot, which meant there would be no action that day, three times if he were in his car, with another three clicks the second the car left the driveway. That would give the heads-up to the cars parked on the main road nearby, which fed into the N-VI a mile farther on, letting them get into position, one pulling out in front of the Volvo, and one taking up station a couple of cars back.

Twice already they had gotten so far as to have their two cars rolling, but something had always occurred to cause them to abort the mission. It was three miles from the starting point to the selected site, and once the cars had simply not been able to get into position. The second time they had been in position on the N-VI, but some idiot truck driver had swung out of a gas station, cutting in front of the Volvo, nearly hitting it, and there was no way to complete the mission that day.

As Luis passed the Schweppes stand, traffic moved on another ten meters and came to a halt. Luis reflexively touched the butt of the Czech-made Skorpion machine pistol slung under his arm and then pulled the gear lever into reverse. There was no flashing of back-up lights to because Luis had disconnected them. Diana, in the passenger seat, worked the action of her Beretta automatic and slipped it back into her purse. They both braced themselves as Luis eased on the gas.

Keenan had been half dreaming when the jolt of the two cars and the tinkle of broken glass shook him awake. He instinctively jammed on the brakes, but his foot was already on the damn brake. He had let his car roll forward without realizing it and had bumped into the jerk in the Citroen, who had probably stopped again to let someone else into his lane.

The couple in the Citroen were already getting out of their car. The cars ahead were slowly pulling away, those on his left were rubbernecking, particularly the man in the Ford Escort next to him, who had stopped completely, and somewhere behind him someone was already blowing his horn. Keenan quickly climbed out of his car to inspect the damage. The driver was a short, stocky man with curly hair in his middle thirties, wearing sunglasses and a dark windbreaker. The woman was a little younger, with obviously dyed blonde hair, a long dark jacket with sequins on it, and oversized dark glasses. Overdressed in the typical Spanish style, Keenan thought.

They did not appear very angry, but the man shrugged his shoulders, stuck out his chin and gestured with his two hands, palms up, in the universal, "So what's this?" message. Keenan involuntarily repeated the two-handed gesture, pointing at the two merged autos and opened his mouth to apologize just as the man reached under his windbreaker.

Keenan thought he was taking out his wallet, or a pen to get insurance information. His brain did not register the fact that he, and now the woman, were both pointing guns at him until the force of the first bullets striking his chest spun him around with his back against his car door. He fell heavily to the ground and tried to raise himself up on his hands, his mouth still open to form the first words of his apology. The last thing he saw was a large motorcycle roaring up between the lanes of stalled cars behind him. He thought he was going to run over, but another bullet tore off the back of his head, and he thought no more.

A second motorcycle had already pulled up on the other side of the Volvo, and Diana jumped on the back. They sped to the off-ramp fifty yards ahead, the way now wide open due to the total blockage of the right two lanes. Luis strode quickly to the body and bent down. From the pocket of his windbreaker he pulled an ice pick to which was attached a clear plastic envelope. He jabbed the ice pick into Keenan's chest, and shouted, "Let's get the hell out of here," in Spanish, then hopped onto the back of the first motorcycle, and they too raced off.

Diana's bike had taken the M-30 heading south. Just out of sight of the ambush, she yanked off her blonde wig, letting her long black hair blow in the breeze, and shed her jacket, revealing a white tank top, suddenly transforming herself from a crazed matron into a clean-cut college girl. She reached around and unclipped the driver's dark face mask and tossed it aside, changing his profile as well. Luis and his driver swung back under the highway as Luis pulled off his wig, glasses and windbreaker, leaving him with a flashy red shirt and a bald pate. He also stripped a swath of black adhesive tape off the helmet of the driver, changing the color of the helmet to white. They then came right back up on the N-VI heading in the opposite direction at about 110 kilometers per hour.

†

Padre Lazaro slid his hand out from under the newspaper on the seat next to him, which concealed his own pistol, and floored the accelerator, as any sane person would do in such a situation. He had seen enough. He drove quickly, but conservatively, once he was out of the immediate area and proceeded across town, turning north on the broad Paseo de la Castellana and headed into the huge La Vaguada shopping center. He parked in the underground garage and tossed the keys onto the floormat, pausing only long enough to slip his pistol into a carryall bag and to wipe his fingerprints off the steering wheel with a handkerchief. He closed the door, also using the handkerchief, and walked away, noting with satisfaction the flecks of blood on the passenger side door. The car had been rented under an alias that he would not be using again. By the time the car was discovered, assuming it wasn't stolen first, he would be out of the country.

He wound his way up various escalators into the mall itself. Exiting from the south side of the building, crossed the street and walked through a small parking lot on the other side. At the end of the parking lot, there was an open staircase which obliged him to turn sharply left and switch back, giving him a good view of the path he had just taken as he climbed. He then wove his way through a series of interlocking public patios and walkways which connected a dozen or more lower-middle-class apartment buildings. The only people about were a few mothers watching their kids play in the patios, and no one was moving with him. He emerged near a metro stop and travelled to the Puerta del Sol, with several changes of lines. There he climbed up to the street and turned south along a narrow street until he came to the small Plaza de Angeles where the Gran Hotel Victoria was located. He nodded pleasantly to the doorman as he entered and went downstairs to the coffee shop.

A dark-skinned man with a prominent nose and fierce moustache was already sitting at a corner table. He had arrived that morning via Geneva from Teheran and was Lazaro's current contact with the *Etelaat-e Sepah-e Pasdaran*, sometimes just referred to as the Sepah, the intelligence unit of the Iranian Revolutionary Guard Corps. Lazaro privately wished these Iranians would learn to wear something other than old dark suits with white, collarless shirts, and no tie. At least this one didn't have a beard and smell of goat meat.

Lazaro smiled broadly as he sat down. "The deed is done, brother," he said in Farsi.

The Iranian grabbed Lazaro's extended hand in both of his and said grimly, "It is the will of Allah, and you have been a faithful servant of the Lord. When I see the coverage on the television news tonight, the money will be transferred immediately to your accounts, as you directed."

"While the money will serve God's purpose in the end," Lazaro answered in a low tone, "my heart rejoices that we have been able to exact some small retribution for what they have done to your people. I will be going now to begin the fight to free my countrymen the way the immortal Ayatollah freed yours. May God go with you." Lazaro rose quickly, politely waving away the waitress who was just coming to take his order.

"And with you, brother," the Sepah man said, bowing solemnly.

†

That evening Lazaro bounded up the stairs to the safe apartment in Barcelona. Luis was already there, watching television, waiting for the evening news to start. The two men embraced warmly as Lazaro entered, following his signal knock on the door.

"I saw the whole thing," Lazaro exulted. "It went perfectly. No one followed you or Diana from the scene. This is a great day for the movement."

Luis's smile stretched from ear to ear. "It certainly is, Padre. Diana should be in London by now with Paco. Pedro's, in the bathroom, and the surveillance team's plane left for Tenerife before lunch. They should be well on their way to Brazil."

An overly tall young man came out of the bathroom, wearing nothing but boxer shorts, rubbing his stringy hair with a towel. He also gave the Padre a warm hug and moved his motorcycle helmet off one of the chairs to give Lazaro a place to sit.

The happy chatter and backslapping stopped suddenly when the theme music for the television news began. All three men sat down and stared intently at the screen. The top story on the headline news was a car bomb outside a Guardia Civil barracks in Burgos, probably the work of the Basque ETA terrorist organization, in which three Guardia Civils and half a dozen innocent bystanders had been killed and over twenty seriously wounded. The film footage showed rescue workers gently lifting the bloody corpse of a girl, who must have been seven or eight years of age, onto a gurney. She had been wearing a brightly colored sun dress and still clutched a towel in one hand, all now stained with dark splotches of blood. She had apparently been on the way to a public swimming pool.

Padre Lazaro's face became beet red and his eyes bulged as he shook a clenched fist at the television. "Why do those news vultures have to show that? Don't they think that little girl has parents? Do they need to see that? It's a shame her little head didn't fall off right there. Now that would have been NEWS!"

Luis and Pedro both knew better than to say anything when the Padre got in this mood. They just continued to stare at the screen and nod mutely. Luis was only upset that his own story had not been at the top of the news. Of course, the Spanish were always going to be more concerned when the victims were Spanish, but still this ETA stuff happened a couple of times a week, so he questioned whether it was really the most important news item of the day.

The picture shifted to a section of the N-VI. Cars were stopped now on both sides of the median strip, with an ambulance with flashing lights and several Guardia Civil cars and TV news vans lining the shoulder of the highway. Men in dark green uniforms were trying to wave cars by the obstruction without much success. Luis smiled.

The camera zoomed in on the corpse next to the Volvo. It paused for a moment and then continued to close in on the plastic envelope stuck to the man's chest.

The newscaster was talking a mile a minute. ". . . this morning. The killing was apparently the work of Iranian extremists, as the note they left with the body identified the victim as the gunnery officer on the American cruiser *Vincennes* and as being responsible for the July 1988 shoot-down of the Iran Air passenger plane over the Persian Gulf in which over 200 people died. The note stated that the killing was in revenge for that tragedy, which was described as "a calculated act of imperialist genocide." A spokesman from the American Embassy stated that, while Commander Keenan had served on the *Vincennes* some years ago, his position was that of ship's supply officer and that he had nothing to do with the mistaken firing of a surface-to-air missile at the Iran Air plane . . ."

Pedro's mouth dropped open. "You mean we killed the wrong man?"

"Shut up, you idiot!" Luis hissed. "He was American, wasn't he? He was military, wasn't he? That's all that matters."

Padre Lazaro held up his hand. The news headlines had gone on to a story about continued skirmishing in Bosnia, so he turned to Pedro with a serene look on his face. "The identity of the man doesn't matter. It certainly doesn't matter to us, and I doubt that it matters to the Sepah either. He was on the guilty ship, which was enough for them, and if any mistake was made, they made it. We did the operation to serve the cause of our own people, and that cause has been served. We now have the money we need to go back home and start our own work, and we have paid our hosts back for all that they taught us. We have done God's work today."

Pedro was about to answer something, but Padre Lazaro lowered his head in prayer, a sign that both the others should do the same and that the conversation was at an end.

The news broke for a commercial for Nescafe on ice, which appeared to be the perfect refreshment for an attractive young couple without much in the way of clothing, after a furious night of lovemaking. Pedro noticed that Padre Lazaro turned his head demurely to one side, while Luis watched intensely. After the commercial the news went into the detailed stories of the day.

Apart from seeing the same footage of the ambush site and shots of the Air Ministry, some American warship supposedly representing the *Vincennes*, and the American embassy, there was not much new to add to the recap until the end of the clip. ". . . and a spokesman for the Guardia Civil stated that a close watch is being kept on all airports, ports, and border crossings in the search for the four suspects." They gave a rough description of Luis and Diana, before they had doffed their disguises, and described Pedro and Paco only as young men on motorcycles. ". . . while it is assumed that the Iranians were responsible for this act, one witness heard one of the gunmen shout to his accomplice in Spanish with either an Andalusian or Caribbean accent."

Lazaro shot a look of rage at Luis. "You weren't supposed to open your mouth!"

Luis's proud grin vanished in an instant. "But I didn't say anything."

Pedro mumbled something.

"What?" Lazaro asked, softening his tone just slightly.

"Yes, you did, Luis," Pedro stammered. "You said something about getting out of there."

Luis just glared at Pedro, and Lazaro cut in. "Well, it's been done now. No point in whining about it. There's still no way they can use that information to any advantage, and it will only lead them down a dozen false trails until they assume that it was the witness' imagination." He patted Luis gently on the shoulder. "It just would have been better if they had no idea that non-Iranians were involved at all."

The news continued. ". . . Iranian President Rafsanjani denied any connection to the attack, but the White House has cancelled the planned trip by the American secretary of state to Teheran where the possibility of easing economic sanctions on Iran was to have been discussed."

ONE

†

The L-1011 airliner touched down at the airport in Santo Domingo just before dusk, but the wall of thunderheads rolling in from over the Caribbean to the south promised to cut off what little daylight remained. As the plane descended, William Featherstone smiled at his wife, Anne, who had been staring out the window at the waves crashing against coral cliffs with a look of contentment he had rarely seen in her eyes. Of course, this time they were travelling first class, which was nice even for the short flight from Miami, as compared to their traditional 14-hour purgatories jammed into "cattle" class en route to previous posts. But he suspected she was really looking forward to the post itself.

After more than twenty years of service in one unpleasant post after another, to say nothing of the physical risks he had been put through, he had finally been honored with an ambassadorship. Santo Domingo might not be exactly the hub of world affairs, but that suited Featherstone just fine. It was a rather small embassy, with a staff of only about 70 Americans and as many local hire Foreign Service National employees (FSNs), but the country had a reputation as a picture postcard kind of place, with white sand beaches, crystal clear waters, waving palm trees, and lively salsa music.

Still, the fact that he would be in charge at last made the difference. Of course, he would still have to answer to Washington and would have to watch his step with the local government to stay in their good graces, but Washington was far away and impersonal, and relations with the Dominican government were traditionally quite warm. Over the years, Featherstone had learned to accept serving a string of imperious and often incompetent superiors and to let their snubs and pettiness roll off his back, just as he ignored the inconvenience of shifting his family around the world every couple of years, living in rented housing, and surrendering all of his worldly possessions to the

14

"Royal Congolese Moving and Salvage Company" with little hope of seeing them again for months, if ever. It had always been Anne who had taken these things harder, particularly what she perceived as a lack of appreciation by Washington. She did her share of complaining about their gypsy lifestyle, but he suspected that this was just window dressing for her deeper resentment over the lack of recognition in terms of promotions and assignments. But now he was the ambassador, the biggest fish in a small diplomatic pond, and things would be different.

Featherstone had known some diplomatic wives over the years who let their husbands' positions go to their heads, alienating everyone by haughty and humiliating behavior, but he knew that Anne was not like that. She had had to put up with it on the receiving end, but rather than wanting to get her turn to do the same, Featherstone knew that Anne wanted to show everyone how it could be done right.

Being in first class, they didn't have to claw their way through a mob of rabid tourists to off the aircraft. The stewardesses selflessly threw their bodies in the path of the unwashed hordes while the front cabin emptied out. Featherstone could feel the heat and humidity of the place press against him like a giant hand as he stepped out onto the portable stairs, and he wondered if he had been destined never to be assigned to a country where they actually had those enclosed jetways to the aircraft. He could feel a fresh breeze coming up, although he suspected that it was the forerunner of the storm he could see building on the horizon.

There was a small knot of people waiting at the foot of the stairway, and as Featherstone descended, a very tall, very angular man shot a long arm out to him from what seemed to be about ten feet away. The man's clammy fingers were so long that they seemed to wrap all the way around Featherstone's hand and overlap on the other side as the man shouted above the noise of the dying airplane engines.

"Welcome to Santo Domingo, Mr. Ambassador," the man said. "I'm Dane Stileforth, the chargé, or your DCM, I should say now," he hastily corrected himself.

"Pleased to meet you," Featherstone shouted back. Stileforth, a man of about forty, was well over six feet four, but Featherstone doubted that he weighed 150 pounds, most of that taken up by lanky arms and legs which appeared to have four or five joints in each. He had thinning reddish hair, swept severely back from his forehead, and this combined with a beak-like nose to give the impression of a face observed in a soup spoon at close range. His cold blue eyes did not seem to be connected to the immense grin which spread over his face. "My wife, Anne," Featherstone said, stepping aside and disengaging his hand from Stileforth's, thrusting Anne into the breach.

"A tremendous pleasure, ma'am" Stileforth gushed. "You can't imagine how much the embassy has missed having someone to take on the female side of the representational duties, lo, these many months."

Anne smiled grimly. "I hope we'll be able to pick up our luggage before the first obligatory coffee clatch, Mr. Stileforth," she said half jokingly. Stileforth had been minding the store as chargé for six months since the last ambassador had been withdrawn for medical problems, and it was not entirely convincing that he was relieved to be turning over the top post in the embassy.

"Not to worry, Mrs. Featherstone," Stileforth said guiding the couple quickly across the tarmac as a phalanx of sturdy porters grabbed their carry-on bags for them. "We've purposely arranged an easy schedule for you both until you've learned the ropes, what?"

Anne gave Featherstone a sidelong glance, arching one of her eyebrows toward her hairline, but Featherstone just shrugged his shoulders slightly. Stileforth was fully aware that Featherstone was a career Foreign Service Officer, not some political appointee from Kansas who had achieved his position by raising seven jillion dollars for the winning presidential contender, and he knew the ropes as well as any. Still, Featherstone understood from his own experience that every new ambassador needs to deal with a certain sense of trespassing on the incumbents' turf until he has a chance to establish himself, so there was no need to make an issue of it so soon.

Stileforth ushered them into the VIP lounge of the airport, which at least was air conditioned. A young steward with many, many shiny white teeth served them cool drinks while invisible hands were searching for their luggage. After a few moments, Featherstone noticed a husky man, dressed in a comfortable-looking guayabera shirt and sports slacks, in contrast to Stileforth's severe suit and tie, who was standing by himself and grinning at him, apparently trying to work up courage to introduce himself. He looked to be about 35, with medium brown skin, and he wore some sort of plasticized ID badge clipped to his shirt pocket. Featherstone had just made up his mind to go over and break the ice, on the assumption that anyone who dressed decently and had access to the VIP lounge was probably not a terrorist, when the man steeled himself and marched across the room and stuck out his hand.

"Claude Lafeur, Mr. Ambassador," the man said. He had a firm grip but not the kind that implied that the owner was desperate to prove his manhood by crushing the smaller bones in your hand. "I'm with the embassy . . ."

"Time enough for introductions later, sir," Stileforth said, briskly sliding in between the two men and guiding Featherstone by the elbow toward the door. "The luggage is loaded, and the cars are waiting. There's a storm a-brewing, so we want to get you home before it starts to rain, what?"

"Uh, yes. See you in the halls, Claude," Featherstone called back over his shoulder. The man's smile had turned into a grim, straight line, and Featherstone suspected that he did not "hang out" with Stileforth much.

Anne strolled up to Lafeur and offered her hand. "I'm Anne Featherstone, Mr. Lafeur, and I hope you'll forgive the rush some of us seem to think we're in."

Lafeur dropped his head shyly and grinned again. "I'm very pleased to meet you, Mrs. Featherstone. Thank you, but I suppose you'd better be going too."

"I don't think they'll leave without me," she said, staring him in the eyes with an open, friendly look, "and I've been rained on before."

Stileforth was standing in the doorway, frantically waving with one hand, the other indignantly planted on his hip.

"Won't you be riding back to the embassy with us?" Anne continued.

"No, ma'am. I'm here to meet another flight, but I thought I'd come early to meet you both. I know how hectic the first few weeks at a post can be."

"Well, thank you, Mr. Lafeur," Anne said as she turned very slowly toward the door. "I hope you'll come and visit us as soon as we're settled. I'm sure that my husband will want a chance to talk with you in private about your work, whatever it might be." She smiled again.

"Political, ma'am. I'm in the political section," Lafeur stammered. "And I certainly will take you up on that." He waved as she swept past Stileforth who lasered Lafeur with a vicious glare, but Lafeur studiously kept the same amicable grin on his face and kept waving until Stileforth slammed the door.

"Same to you, Dane" Lafeur said under his breath.

†

The ride into the city was one of the prettiest Featherstone had ever seen, ranking right up with the George Washington Parkway along the Potomac in early autumn. There was still plenty of light to see the brilliant blue of the Caribbean off to the left of the highway, just beyond a strip of parkland covered with delicate palm trees. The waves spewed foam over the coral cliffs as they hit, and geysers shot up through blowholes in the coral. Now this is what diplomacy is all about, he thought.

Featherstone held Anne's hand in the back of the bullet-proof sedan, while Stileforth sat in the front with the driver, giving him an endless stream of instructions, since the man had probably driven this road only 500 times in the last year.

"Well, Mrs. Ambassador," Featherstone said. "How do you like it so far?"

"This is beautiful, Bill," Anne said, patting his knee. They watched the scenery roll by, the waves, the trees, young men selling piles of green coconuts or large pink conch shells by the edge of the highway. Traffic was light, and Stileforth called back to them that they should be at the residence within half an hour.

After about fifteen minutes, they began to enter the city itself. First a number of tumble-down shacks, the kind squatters frequently set up on the fringes of cities in Latin America, made of a random collection of bricks, planks, pieces of cardboard, and corrugated tin. Then came what appeared to be working class suburbs with two or three-story concrete apartment blocks with bars or stores on the ground floor and endless strings of drying clothes hanging from the upper windows. The streets off the main highway were unpaved and piles of trash adorned each vacant lot or street corner. Featherstone noted larger and larger clusters of men, mostly black or mulatto, all wearing just a T-shirt and shorts, no shoes, standing around in idle conversation, watching traffic flow by. Featherstone had the impression they were all just waiting for something to happen.

Stileforth guessed at their thoughts. "You know that unemployment in the city is close to forty percent, by official figures, sir. We suspect, of course, that the actual total is much higher, with the economy in a nose dive and all."

"You can call me Bill, you know, Dane," Featherstone said.

"Thank you, Mr. Featherstone, I certainly will," Stileforth called over the static of the driver's two-way radio.

"Is there any chance that things will pick up in the near future? The word in Washington is that investment money is becoming more accessible for the Caribbean."

"It's not a question of money alone, sir," Stileforth continued. "It's a combination of corruption, lack of basic infrastructure in the country to make use of the money, and just plain laziness. I know you'll think I'm an awful bigot for saying so, but I think you'll share my opinion inside of six months' time. The Dominicans just don't work."

"You obviously never hired a contractor in the States to work on your home," Anne chimed in, "or you wouldn't be so quick to judge the Dominicans."

Stileforth turned all the way around in his seat so that he could throw Anne a cold look. "I don't have a home in the States, Mrs. Featherstone, as it happens. The Foreign Service has been my home for two decades, but I suppose you're right and I'm wrong."

A silence fell between them for a moment, while Featherstone was conveniently distracted. As dusk and the coming storm gathered, and as they entered the urban area, the lights of the city had been coming on, when everything outside the car was suddenly plunged into darkness. The lights over the highway and on the street corners, in the shops and homes all around, simultaneously went black. It was an eerie feeling, as if the world had suddenly shrunk to the tiny patch lit by the headlights of cars on the highway, the rest disappearing in an instant.

"An *apagon*, a blackout," Stileforth said. "You'll get used to them. They hit various sectors of the city all the time."

"What's the problem?" Featherstone asked. "Did a transformer blow up or something?"

"No, it's not like that at all. The power company simply shuts off grids from time to time. They only produce about half the electricity the city needs, so this is their form of rationing. They know that no one is going to take seriously any energy conservation measures, so they just let people plug in whatever they want, and arbitrarily shut them off at the source when the strain gets too great."

"That's odd, we haven't encountered anything like that on a regular basis before, and we've been to some pretty underdeveloped countries in Latin America," Featherstone said.

"Of course," he continued in a condescending tone, "YOU won't have to worry about that much. Being next door to the embassy, the residence is hooked into the embassy generator which kicks in automatically. In fact, most of us have generators. They make a hell of a racket, but it's better than sitting in the dark."

"I don't suppose anyone's thought to build more generating capacity," Featherstone said, looking at the window but being able to see only his own reflection.

"Oh, they've got the capacity," Stileforth went on, warming to his subject. "There are plenty of hydroelectric plants, most of them constructed by Americans, some as far back as the "occupation" of the 1920's. The trouble is that the dams for the generators create lakes, which attracts the small farmers, who cut down all the trees to plant their crops and toss the trees into the lake. Then the rains come and wash the topsoil into the lake and then all those trees and all that mud end up in the turbines, which tends to reduce their longevity, what?"

"You know the old saying," he went on, " 'If it's not broken, don't fix it.' Well, here the theory seems to be, 'If it's not broken, don't touch it, don't oil it, nothing.' There are projects underway to build new plants, but they're stalled for lack of funds."

"One would suspect that it would be cheaper to fix the existing plants than build new ones," Featherstone commented unenthusiastically. This place was starting to sound less like a picture postcard spot all the time.

"Well," Stileforth sighed, resting his chin on his arm on the back of the front seat, "one gets a much bigger hunk of graft with the contract for a new plant than for the repair of an old one, and that's a prime consideration. But the bigger issue is that there's no money for repair either, because no one pays for their electricity anyway, except perhaps our embassy."

"And just how do they get away with that?" Anne chimed in, with obvious scepticism.

"You'll see as you drive around town. In the poorer neighborhoods, people just hook a wire over the high tension line, a rather dangerous practice which roasts one or two locals every month. In the rich neighborhoods, they have a real electrician come out and simply install a conductor around the meter box."

"Doesn't the electric company catch them?" Anne asked, as Featherstone gazed wistfully out the window, letting the others carry on the conversation.

"Certainly. They send an inspector out, he rings the doorbell. The man of the house comes out and gives him fifty dollars, and the inspector goes away for a couple of months. These are, without a doubt, the dumbest and most corrupt people on God's green earth."

Featherstone and Anne immediately stiffened at this remark, exchanged a quick look of surprise, and then glanced at the Dominican driver next to Stileforth, staring fixedly at the road ahead. No need to wonder where the "Ugly American" had gone. He was alive and well and sitting in the front seat. Featherstone suspected that Stileforth believed the driver did not speak English, but it had been his own experience that virtually all of the local hire employees at an embassy, understood English perfectly well, whether they chose to inform their employers of the fact or not. On second thought, it occurred to Featherstone that Stileforth was the sort of man who simply didn't care what the help thought. They were furniture, machinery that one spoke to only in the manner of turning the "on" or "off" switch, nothing worth being concerned over.

Just then the driver jammed on the brakes a little too hard, and the car rocked to a sudden halt in front of a tall wrought iron gate. Stileforth lost his balance briefly and had to grasp the back of the seat to avoid being hurled against the dashboard.

"Sorry, sir," the driver said in Spanish. "The brakes have been catching. We're here." That answered Featherstone's question about his understanding English.

Stileforth glared briefly at the driver and turned around to face forward as two uniformed guards peered in the car and then ran to swing the gates open. Where they had been driving through a cloud of darkness, pierced only by the thin headlight beams of their car, they now entered an oasis of light, as powerful outdoor lamps revealed a broad expanse of lawn, carefully tended flowers, and a curved driveway which led to the front of a sprawling Spanish colonial mansion.

Anne leaned way over Featherstone to look out his window and gasped. "It's beautiful, Bill! Just beautiful!"

Stileforth smiled as if to take credit and leaped out of the car as soon as it came to a halt under the portico. He slipped in front of the Dominican butler, immaculate in his white jacket and black trousers, who had obviously been waiting along with a pair of crisply uniformed maids, and opened the rear door of the car.

Anne and Featherstone ignored Stileforth's grand, sweeping gesture toward the house for a moment, pausing to nod politely to the assembled servants and to take in the view of the yard. The front garden alone occupied the area of two or three good-sized house lots, Featherstone thought, and he suspected that caring for the carefully trimmed shrubs and the riot of flowers which tumbled out of their beds in calculated confusion must provide full-time employment for several gardeners. Anne sighed contentedly, clasping her hands in front of her as she looked around. Featherstone smiled at her. It had been worth it. She had earned this moment. The first drops of rain started to patter against the hood of the chase car which had pulled up behind them in the driveway, and the bodyguards discreetly climbed back in to get out of the wet. Somewhere behind the house they could hear the grumbling of the electrical generator.

Stileforth finally managed to escort them into the house itself. Anne stopped again and put her hands to her mouth. They were in a two-story entry hall, glowing with sparkling tile floors and heavily polished wood, and dominated by a vast crystal chandelier overhead. An immense floral spray erupted from a round table in the middle of the room. They had been in ambassadors' residences before, of course, and most of them had been pretty nice, but the sensation had always been one of touring the White House. It would have been difficult to imagine anyone actually shuffling around in in their bathrobe and slippers of a Sunday morning. This time, this was their home for the next two years, and Anne took some time, walking through the living room, dining room, kitchen, reception rooms, and finally up to the bedrooms, touching the tables, pulling open the odd closet door, just convincing herself that she was really there.

The effect was enhanced by the fact that the house was fully furnished and ready for occupancy. The butler and other servants were already racing in and out from the car, shuttling the luggage upstairs, desperately attempting to make the transfer appear to have occurred by magic, as good help always trie to do. Everything else was in place, from the tables and chairs and beds to linens, cutlery, and dishes with the crest of the U.S. government embossed in gold. Their personal possessions were coming, which would make the house truly theirs, but this time there would be no long weeks of sitting around a hotel room, eating in the cafeteria every day, or living in a spartan "transient apartment" that looked as if it had been furnished out of a Salvation Army Thrift Store. They were home already.

Featherstone turned to Stileforth, who was proudly, smugly, supervising their exploration of the house, and this time it was Featherstone who grasped Stileforth's hand. "Thank you very much, Dane, for coming out to pick us up. It sounds like quite a storm brewing out there, so you'd better be getting on your way home."

Anne also walked up. "Yes, Dane. Thanks for everything, and I hope you won't insist on an invitation just to stop by whenever you like." Anne reached up and pecked him on the cheek.

Stileforth looked disappointed, even hurt. He had apparently looked forward to a rather longer spell as instructor and guide, but he bowed his head and forced a thin smile. "I'll see you then in the morning, sir. Have a good night's rest."

He turned briskly and brushed past the butler, who held the door for him, both their faces masks of cool indifference. After closing the door, the butler bowed again to Featherstone and suggested that a light dinner could be served in about an hour, if the ambassador so desired. He did, and the butler glided out of sight.

"I can't say I like him very much, Stileforth, I mean," Anne finally said. "And did you hear that absurd semi-British accent he tries to affect, what? Talk about cheek!"

Since Anne was British, she always took affront at any American who aspired to the same status. She was more than ready to admit that American accents, as a rule, sounded unbelievably boorish, and that the world would be a better place if everyone talked as she did, but she could not abide people who tried. Featherstone knew that he had been very lucky that she hadn't made this a major topic of discussion with Stileforth.

"Let's not be too quick to judge," Featherstone soothed. "You know how it always is with a new boss arriving. Stileforth was chargé for quite awhile, so there's some natural resentment. I'll agree that I don't much like his manner of dealing with subordinates, but it takes all kinds."

"Well, I don't care," Anne said finally, throwing her arms around his waist. "The house is beautiful. The garden is beautiful. And you're ambassador, master of your own fate at last." She looked up into his eyes. They had been married just over a quarter of a century. They had two grown children, who were old enough to have children of their own, although neither was married yet. But he couldn't really say that she looked much different from when they had been married. Her blue eyes still glowed with a kind of inner light, and her smile still made him feel as if she were doing him a special favor just by looking at him. Her blonde hair was cut stylishly short now, where it had been long when they had met, but that made her look even younger. She had even kept her figure quite nicely, where his had transformed from long and lanky into well-padded, although he could still see his feet. His hair had thinned on top, and he had compensated by cultivating a short, bushy beard. He had contemplated shaving it off when it started to come in grey in spots, but he was saving that for some time when he really wanted to take off a few years suddenly. Right now, as ambassador, this just added to his "presence." He loved Anne very much, even if he could never fathom what it was exactly that she saw in him.

†

Lafeur paced languidly up and down the covered walkway along the edge of the tarmac at the airport. The rain was coming down in sheets now, lashed by a vicious wind, so that sprays of water occasionally reached him even here, but at least it was cooler than in the stuffy terminal.

He hated pulling embassy "duty," which came around twice a year and lasted for a week. During that week the duty officer was on call 24 hours a day for whatever emergency might arise. After hours and on weekends, it was the duty officer who fielded the barrage of phone calls from American tourists who lost their passports and wanted a new one NOW, or some local bigwig who was travelling to the States in about an hour and not only didn't want to wait in line for a visa but wanted one NOW.

Apart from emergencies, the duty officer also got stuck with routine jobs like meeting the diplomatic courier, and the rules stated that he had to meet the airplane, escort the courier to his hotel for the night and then bring him to the embassy in the morning. That was what he was doing now. The courier's plane had been due in at seven, and it was after eight now, with no word on its new arrival time. An Avianca plane had come in just before the storm had reached its peak, at no small risk to the lives of its passengers, but Lafeur couldn't believe anyone would try to land in weather like this.

Suddenly, there was a loud pop!, and everything went black. The lights in the terminal went out, as did those on the runway and everywhere else. The only light around was coming from the cabin of the Avianca plane about 200 yards away, barely visible through the curtain of rain. This was typical, Lafeur thought, no emergency lights, no nothing. He looked into the immigration area, where people were groping around in the blackness, the only glimmers of light coming from tiny flashlights or cigarette lighters some tourists had wisely brought with them. The airport officials, of course, had no such equipment and just sat there in the dark, waiting for their shifts to end. He would wait a moment and then go looking for one of his airport contacts to see if the place was officially "closed" so he could call it a night. If he just left now, and the lights came back on and the storm slackened, the plane might come in. With no one there to meet it, he would be up shit creek.

Just then, an airport official he knew scuttled by, and Lafeur was able to confirm that the airport was officially closed until dawn. Apparently the thought of a large passenger aircraft plowing into the terminal had finally convinced the tower that discretion was the better part of valor. That was good enough for Lafeur, who hurried to the restricted parking area, his little chalkboard with "U.S. Embassy" written on it, held over his head as a futile protection against the buckets of rain which washed over him. In fact, the rain was falling with such force, that it was literally bouncing a foot or two after striking the pavement, so he would have ended up soaked even had he had the foresight to bring a proper umbrella.

He raced across the parking lot, leaping over puddles, threw open the back door of the Embassy Blazer, and jumped inside. The driver, who had been dozing comfortably on the front seat, jerked awake, tossing the clipboard he had been pretending to study against the windshield.

"That's it, Jose," Lafeur announced. "Let's go home."

The driver didn't need to be told twice. He quickly started up the engine and pulled out into the glacial flow of traffic as all of the taxis, buses, and private cars that had been waiting for arrivals or departures attempted to wedge themselves through the two exit turnstiles at the same time. Lafeur mopped his brow ineffectually with a scrap of used paper towel he had found on the floor and then lay down on the back seat.

Lafeur dozed briefly during the ride back to the embassy. When he awoke, he found himself already well into the downtown area. The lights in this sector were on, and the rain had slackened considerably. He could see some of the slum residents taking advantage of a broken rain gutter to grab a quick shower in the resulting waterfall. One man, dressed only in gym shorts, was lathering up, while two other people were waiting in the shelter of a store's awning with their towels.

By the time they pulled into the embassy parking lot, the lights in this neighborhood were also back on, and Lafeur began to hope that this would be the case at his own house. He signed the form on the driver's clipboard, acknowledging the mileage for official use of the car, stopped to check with the marine that all was quiet, and climbed into his own car.

On the way home he toyed with the idea of stopping to pick up a couple of *cubanos*, the local equivalent of the submarine sandwich, made with sliced pork, sausage, and cheese with tart pickles, but he really didn't feel like standing in line, so he just trusted that there would be something in the freezer at home. He pulled up to a stoplight that happened to be functioning at a major intersection, and a dark-skinned boy of about eight, with another child, possibly a girl of maybe two years of age, hanging on his back like a koala cub, came up and tapped on his window. The two children rolled their eyes plaintively, and each held out a small hand. Lafeur was fully aware that local racketeers ran begging as a thriving business, hiring children to work the cars while the adults sat in the shade, or in a bar in the evenings, drinking up their earnings. Even so, he couldn't help himself, and rolled down his window a bit, dropping a few coins in each hand from a small pile he kept in his otherwise unused ashtray. He quickly rolled the window back up as a dozen other kids, drawn by the scent of blood, converged on the car in a feeding frenzy. As the light changed, and he drove on, he wondered whether the first two kids were on the level and whether they would be able to hold onto their few pesos against the onslaught of their peers.

Normally, the beggars didn't bother Lafeur much. He didn't present a very attractive target, which suited him fine. He drove a six-year-old Datsun, the paint job of which had seen better days, and he used local, not diplomatic, license plates. More importantly, he looked like a Dominican, being approximately two thirds black, and almost always wearing the traditional, loose guayabera shirt. He liked the guayabera, not only because it was cool in the hot sticky weather which dominated during the two wet seasons, each of about six months duration, but because it also conveniently camouflaged the respectable roll which surrounded his waist and overhung his belt. The beggars and the thieves wanted rich, stupid tourists, and he looked like a lower middle class homeboy, not worth bothering with.

When he finally reached his own neighborhood, his spirits drooped to see the near total blackness, disturbed only by the dim light of a hurricane lamp faintly glowing through someone's front window. He pulled up to his gate and gave the horn a short tap on the theory that it would scare the rats that lived under the large spikey bushes on either side of the gate, although he doubted that anything much he could do would scare a rat the size of a cocker spaniel. He jumped out, opened the gate, drove the car into the carport and raced back out to lock up again. This, of course, was the most dangerous moment in terms of thievery, and on a night when there was a power outage *and* a storm, everyone knew that no policemen were about to be coming to the rescue, as if they ever would.

He stepped up to the front door, opened that iron gate, then the two locks on the door itself and let himself in, moving as quickly as possible to get the gate and doors locked again, now concerned less about thieves than about the forms of multi-legged life which might like to take the opportunity to move in with him.

Inside the dark front hall of his house, he reached up and found the flashlight with the magnetic clip that he kept stuck to the front door hinge plate and used it to guide himself to the kitchen. It was nearly ten o'clock now, and he had a general rule about not using his generator after that time, as his house was flanked by two large apartment houses which did NOT have generators. He could easily imagine that the one thing worse than sitting, sweating in the dark, was sitting, sweating in the dark and listening to the roar of your neighbor's generator all night long. Of course he knew that no Dominican would think twice about running his own generator, but he also didn't want to be taking sniper fire the next morning. Tonight, however, he was very tired, very dispirited, and hungry, so the neighbors would have to live with it.

He wove his way through the living room and into the kitchen. He pressed hard on the large button mounted on the wall and heard the generator coughing to life in the backyard. He let it run for a moment, getting up to speed, and then threw the large switch which disconnected the house circuitry from city power and connected it to the generator. A couple of lights flickered on elsewhere in the house, and the motor of the refrigerator began to hum. He grabbed a package of frozen fried chicken, dumped the contents onto a cookie sheet, and started up the gas oven.

He grabbed a lukewarm beer from the fridge into his bedroom, turning on the lights as he went. He turned on the air conditioner to at least cool things down while he had the generator running and flicked on the TV. One of the few advantages of the Dominican Republic was that you could get stateside cable TV. He doubted that the hook-up was totally legal, but he didn't much care.

He switched through the local channels, most of which featured salsa bands consisting of about twenty guys in shiny shirts and baggy, zoot suit-type trousers playing drums and brass, while the lead singer poured his heart out in a song suggesting that things would be great if only all peoples of the world would spend more time dancing.

He finally found a feature film on one of the American cable channels and sat on the edge of the bed, sipping his beer. He had seen the film before, but it had lots of action. He would watch while he ate, then turn off the generator and just pray that he didn't get called in on this last night of duty.

Then he saw the cockroach scuttling across the tile floor. Actually, he heard it first, since the cockroaches here were easily big enough to make audible scraping noises as they ran, and even to require license plates in some states. He had his shoes on, fortunately, so he stomped the bug into the hereafter with a vengeance. It was unusual to find cockroaches in the house, as, unlike the American variety, they were largely outdoor creatures here and relatively easy to keep out with screening, the judicious plastering up of overflow drains and other odd chinks, and the habit of keeping sink drains plugged when not in use.

Lafeur was just wondering how this one had gotten in when a second cockroach scraped under the bathroom door, a tight squeeze, even though there was a gap of nearly half an inch, and made a mad dash toward the dresser. Lafeur squashed this one too, and grabbed a can of Raid from his nightstand.

Thus armed, he jerked open the bathroom door and was greeted by the sight of a virtual carpet of cockroaches scattering across the floor, while others raced up the walls. A glance at the bathtub told him what the problem was. The heavy screen which covered the drain was attached by only one screw, and could thus pivot away from the hole. He must have inadvertently kicked the screen to one side when he showered that morning, for now there was a layer of bugs a solid inch deep in the tub and approximately three million more spread around the room. He managed not to scream, spraying insecticide wildly all around himself while he beat a retreat toward the door. He slammed the door shut and emptied the can coating the doorframe and the floor. He then grabbed a cardboard box from his closet, folded it to the right size, and wedged it under the door. Lastly, he conducted a detailed inspection of the room, especially under the bed, looking for escapees, but found only a couple. At last, he collapsed on the bed, staring blankly at the television.

As much as he hated bugs, it was a good thing that his wife hadn't been the one to discover that mess. Of course, he reminded himself, he didn't actually have a wife anymore. The living conditions in Santo Domingo had finally been too much for her, and she had packed up and left for the States two months ago. That was why he was living in a house with only embassy furniture in it and perhaps the contents of two suitcases of his own possessions scattered about in a haphazard manner.

Lafeur knew in his heart that the conditions in Santo Domingo had only been the pretext for her leaving. It had started earlier, probably just before they had gotten married four years before. Part of the problem was that she was white. At the time, it seemed like the ultimate liberal statement and was roundly applauded by all of their fashionably liberal friends. As the novelty wore off, however, Lafeur began to see the truth in that part of "Fiddler on the Roof" where the Jewish father, confronted with his daughter's desire to marry a Gentile, says something to the effect that, "A bird may love a fish, but where could they build a home together?" It had been that way with Lafeur and Clarisse. No one likes the feeling that people have suddenly changed the subject of their conversation when one enters the room. Going through life like that, in every room you enter, is just too much. Not that many people were openly hostile to them, just the opposite. Most people bent way over backwards trying to be "open-minded," but that was even worse.

Oddly enough, he thought, his own family had been the hardest on them. His father, a professor of Romance languages at Tulane, had simply been rather cool, but then he was rather cool toward everyone. His mother, showing her Haitian roots more clearly than his father, had bemoaned the marriage from the first and had refused to attend the ceremony. Lafeur suspected that the fact that he and his wife had not had any children had further aggravated the situation. Lafeur was an only child, and his mother had made it quite clear that his principal function on earth was to provide her with grandchildren. One of Lafeur's uncles had speculated that his mother might have obtained some expertise in the occult arts back in Haiti, before coming to the States in the 1930's, and that both the childlessness of the marriage and its ultimate dissolution were simply results of her work.

Lafeur doubted that, at least he thought he did. While his wife had sacrificed her own career in real estate to travel overseas with him, first to Mexico City, then to Caracas, she had never been very contented. She had really wanted a posting in Europe, some place nice, like Paris or London, and when he was offered Santo Domingo, and nothing more, she had been upset. When the island proved not to be the tranquil land of resort hotels (which were mostly located on the more hospitable northern and eastern coasts of the island), she had shut out the rest of the embassy community, and they were left to face each other. And when it came right down to it, they really didn't get along. It had been all right in the States where they each had their own circle of friends to escape into, but they had been alone here, and all of the frustration finally came to the surface one particularly steamy night, with no electricity, of course. In the morning, she had announced her decision to leave. Lafeur had expected it, and he hadn't tried to stop her or to get her back thereafter, but he certainly missed her now, especially as he faced a night alone with an army of cockroaches on the other side of the door.

He went and got his chicken, not bothering to take it off the cookie sheet, and placed it on a towel on top of the nightstand he had dragged around to the foot of the bed to serve as a table. He sat cross-legged on the bed and ate while he watched TV. When he had finished, he brought three large battery-powered lamps into the room and placed them on the floor around the bed, which he dragged a few inches away from the wall, and finally felt safe enough to turn off the generator. Then he sprayed a thick line of Raid around the bed itself, being careful to pull up the loose ends of the sheets, so as not to provide easy access to any resilient roach who might run the chemical gauntlet, and lay down, coughing a bit from the fumes, and eventually drifted off to sleep.

†

Padre Lazaro's flight to Santo Domingo had been turned back by the storm, and he didn't arrive until later the next day, after a weary night in Miami International Airport. Since he and most of the other passengers coming from Europe didn't have American visas, they were not allowed out of the international transit area and had spent the night sprawling across their luggage and the stiff plastic seats especially designed not to let the user get too comfortable.

Being unable to sleep anyway, Lazaro had spent his time telling Bible stories to several Dominican children who had been scrambling over everyone and generally making themselves unwelcome. The parents were more than happy to let someone else watch them while they dozed, especially a man of the cloth, complete with his black shirt and white collar. Lazaro had a way of breaking down the complex Bible parables into children's language without losing the moral of the tale, and he kept the children enraptured until, one by one, they nodded off to sleep in each other's arms. Talking to the children made Lazaro feel warm inside, and it also served the purpose of preventing the other priest and the two nuns also waiting for the flight from entering into conversation with him and asking difficult questions about the parish he was going to, since he wasn't going to any.

Diana met Lazaro at the airport in Santo Domingo and drove him to the safe apartment the advance party had rented. He dropped off his bags, but even though he hadn't slept for more than forty-eight hours, he insisted on walking around the city before he would consider taking a rest.

The apartment was in the unfashionable part of town between the touristically restored colonial section with its expensive shops on the southeast and the more upscale commercial area, where most of the government ministries were also located, to the northwest. They walked east first, toward the slums where Lazaro had been born and raised. The buildings had all changed, of course, since most of these ramshackle structures were not designed to last more than a year or two, but, in essence, they had not changed at all. They were all painted with the most outlandish colors possible, partly because these unusual colors were probably cheaper than the more popular white, but Lazaro suspected that it was also a subconscious effort by the owner to scream out the fact of his existence, to get the world to notice him. Naked black children still played in the muddy streets, and the same rhythmic music still wafted from unseen, cracked speakers in some bar or brothel.

It had been over ten years since Lazaro and his flock had left the shores of the Dominican Republic. It was necessary that he get back in touch with the people he was going to save. First, after a brief stopover in Cuba to receive some basic military training, they had gone to Nicaragua. They had been part of the "literacy campaign," supposedly designed to teach the Nicaraguan peasants how to read and write after the downfall of the dictator Somoza, but actually spent their time fighting against the Contras as part of a light "hunter" infantry battalion in the hill country north of Jinotega. They had fought hard and well, losing over a dozen killed and even more wounded. But Lazaro had become disillusioned with the Sandinistas, whose first act had been to take over the mansions of Somoza and his cronies, so he began to look for a cleaner source of support.

It was in Managua that he met the representative of the Iranian Revolutionary Guards. This was a man he could respect. Their religions might be different, but they sprang from the same source and derived their strength from faith in the one God, not like the filthy Sandinistas with their mixture of poorly understood marxism, castroism, and maoism. The Sandinistas would fight for power, but the Iranians would fight *and die* for their beliefs. Whether they won or not didn't matter, it was the act of faith which led them to the fight that was important. The outcome was in the hands of God, and *that* was what attracted Lazaro.

He convinced the Iranian of his sincerity and of his willingness to prove his devotion to the idea of taking the world back from the godless capitalists and communists and giving it to the true believers of the two great faiths, Islam and Christianity. He traveled to Iran with less than fifty of his original hundred, after the losses and desertions along the way. They fought in the trenches against Iraq for four long years as common foot soldiers, charging across frozen fields into storms of Iraqi shrapnel and wasting away in the swamps of the Fao Peninsula. When the war ended, they continued to work with the Revolutionary Guard's internal security service, known and feared simply as the Sepah, hunting down members of the communist Tudeh Party and the Mujaheddin e-Khalq. Having earned the respect of the Sepah and having placed them in his debt, he had now returned with his 28 survivors, hardened and cleansed by the fire of battle, to free his own country.

Lazaro and Diana passed a vacant lot in which the foundations for a building were being dug, and they could smell the breakfast of cooked bananas, rice, and eggs which a very fat woman was preparing in a little hut for the workers. Lazaro gestured with his chin to Diana, indicating for her to continue on her way a bit, and he slipped through the open gate in the chain link fence surrounding the work site and joined the line of workers waiting for their breakfast. He had taken the time to change out of his priestly garb and now wore only a simple dark T-shirt, well-worn blue jeans, and cheap canvas tennis shoes with no socks, so he could well have been one of them.

"How goes it, brother?" Lazaro asked a stocky man with hairy arms who stood in front of him.

The man turned slowly and looked Lazaro over from head to toe. "There's no work here, if that's what you mean, and the cook only takes cash for her food," he said with a sneer.

"Oh, I'm not looking for work yet," Lazaro said off-handedly. "I just got back from two years in New York, and I just missed the cooking."

"You shouldn't have come back if you were lucky enough to get to the States, friend," the man said over his shoulder, having returned his attention to the progress of the line.

"It wasn't my idea. The 'miga' raided the place I was staying, and, well, you know . . ."

The man just chuckled and nodded. With a population of only six million, the Dominican Republic has nearly one million of its citizens living in New York, many of them illegally, and many of the islanders had made the trip at least once. "Well, I hope you made a bundle and saved it, because there's no work around here."

"Why's that?"

"Oh, it's the fucking *apagones*, for one thing. The factories can't run without electricity. Most of them tried to hang on, since we stupid Dominicans work so fucking cheap, but then their emergency generators would blow up, BANG!, and they'd just fold up and go home. So everybody's out of work or fighting for what jobs there are." The man spat contemptuously on the ground.

"What's the new government doing to fix things?"

"Ha!" the man guffawed and looked around at Lazaro to see if he were joking. "They're fighting poverty all right, stuffing their pockets as fast as they can. You probably didn't hear about the big scandal at the national lottery last month. You know how poor people will go out and spend every penny on lottery tickets. They figure that they'll starve for sure with the little they've got, so why not gamble and at least have one chance in 10,000 of hitting it big? So it now comes out that the money for the lottery is just . . . *gone*. The bastards didn't even take the trouble to rig it. They just walked into the vault, filled up a bag, and went to Switzerland. So here are people with I don't know how many millions of dollars worth of winning tickets trying to collect, and there isn't a dime in the lottery account. And look down there on the corner," he said, pointing to a man leaning against a building with long strips of colored paper hung round his neck. "They're still selling the damn tickets for next week! It's not enough that they steal the food out of peoples' mouths, now they have to steal their little fucking dreams as well."

Lazaro accepted a steaming bowl of food from the vendor and dropped some coins into her hand. The stocky man had shuffled off to sit with some friends, so Lazaro sat on an overturned paint can against the rubble of an old brick wall. He closed his eyes as he ate the sticky, sweet rice, and was transported back to his mother's kitchen. He always returned to his youth when he wanted to look into his own heart, because that was when his heart had been pure.

He had been happy at first to hear that things were as bad as he had imagined. After all, it would have been a terrible waste of the last ten years if a way had been found for the masses to enter an earthly paradise without having to pass through perdition. He had had a pretty good idea of the state of things from his followers whom he had been feeding back onto the island as much as three years ago, but this was seeing things on his own. Now his happiness was replaced with a burning anger which welled up inside him. He would sweep the pigs from their mansions into the sea, and he would teach the people to "take up their beds and walk" as Jesus had done, but instead of a bed, they would take up a gun, and he would teach them to use it.

He finally opened his eyes. The workers had mostly finished eating by now and gone on to work. The fat cook was starting to "wash" her plates and bowls in a bucket of brown water, and two scrawny children, a boy in a bib overall with only one strap, and a girl in a little sun dress that had probably been white once were leaning against the fence, watching him and sucking their thumbs. He got up and handed them his unfinished meal. They didn't thank him. The girl grabbed the spoon and dug into the rice, while the boy snatched the banana and tried to cram it into his mouth at once. As Lazaro walked away he thought, they don't have to thank me. *I* should apologize to them for letting them live in a world where hunger is the only sure thing in their lives. They can thank me later, when their bellies are full, and their backs are straight, and then I'll tell them not to thank me anyway and teach them how to thank God.

Diana didn't speak to Lazaro as she rejoined him, walking back to the apartment. She knew better. His head was up, and his dark eyes were focused straight ahead, but he wasn't really there. He was where he got his orders, and it was her job now to watch his back, so she clutched the handle of the pistol in her shoulder bag a little tighter and followed a few paces behind him. He walked straight back to the apartment, entered his room, and slept for 24 hours.

When Lazaro emerged from the bedroom, refreshed and smiling, Angel Santander was sitting with Diana at the kitchen table, drinking coffee. Angel bounded to his feet and ran to Lazaro. Before Lazaro could even say a word, the tall, white-haired man had kissed his hand reverently and then enveloped him in a fierce bear hug.

When Angel finally released him, Lazaro took a step back, grasping the taller man firmly by the shoulders. "So, how have you been keeping, Angel? We have missed you these three years."

"Very well, Padre," he gulped. "You just don't know how I have prayed for this day to come!"

"We have all been praying for this day, and our prayers have been answered. Now, tell me what you have been up to." "I took the liberty of setting up a meeting with Melgarejo for later this morning, if that's all right, Padre. I know you must be tired."

"I'm tired of waiting, Angel," Lazaro said soothingly. "You did exactly the right thing."

"I suppose you read all my reports about him and his people."

"Yes, Angel, they were excellent. You have done a fine job." Angel bobbed his head enthusiastically at this, smiling broadly. They made an unusual picture, the raggedly dressed dark man being catered to by the taller one with a very patrician air, neatly pressed guayabera and slacks, which passed for formal attire in Santo Domingo, and the carefully coiffed hair of a successful businessman. "Let's go," Lazaro finally said.

The three climbed into a shiny new Toyota sedan parked at the curb, and Angel drove a circuitous route around the city to an isolated house in the western suburbs, near where a number of idled factories sprawled in the direction of San Cristobal. An unseen hand opened the driveway gate, and they drove directly into a garage which closed as soon as the rear bumper was inside.

Seated in the living room of the sparsely furnished house was an overweight man with very pale skin, for a Dominican, and a very bald head. In fact, it appeared that he had given up trying to cultivate hair on top and had concentrated on creating a luxuriant crop of greyish eyebrows which splayed wildly outward, and a thick coat of grey fleece which encased his beefy forearms. Although he wore a large guayabera, his rolls of fat pulled the material tight across his chest and stomach, revealing large diamonds of pink skin between straining buttons.

Next to him on the couch sat a younger man, about thirty, with an exaggerated hairdo which would have been fashionable in the fifties, coated with grease and swept up into an impressive ducktail over his forehead. Despite the heat, the younger man wore a turtleneck sweater and a sports coat, which did not quite conceal the gun in his shoulder holster. Neither man rose to receive their guests.

"So this is the famous Padre Lazaro!" roared the fat man with superficial congeniality. "Angel has been telling us all about you and the wonderful things you are going to do here."

Lazaro bowed deeply. "I'm very grateful that you could take the time to meet me Don Emilio," Lazaro said, using the respectful tone of a peasant speaking to his patron. "I've been getting the newspapers from home occasionally, and there isn't a one that doesn't have an article about Emilio Melgarejo, President of the MIR." Lazaro didn't mention that the articles about the radical Revolutionary Movement of the Left (MIR), were usually about two inches long and clipped from page 16, just below an ad for detergent. "And you must be Pablo Baca. I believe our paths crossed briefly back in Nicaragua."

Baca straightened up somewhat, apparently unused to having his fame trumpeted in the presence of his superior. "Yes, and I heard a lot about your group, Guerra Santa, wasn't it?"

"Yes, or Santistas for short, the Holy Warriors."

"One thing I've always wanted to ask you, Padre," Baca continued. "When I was in Nicaragua, the Sandinistas split all of us 'internationalists' up into different groups and mixed Dominicans with Chileans, Argentines, whatever, so there were never more than two or three men from the same country in a platoon. How did you manage to get them to let you keep your people together? You must have had a full company."

Lazaro just waved his hand. "That was just the deal we made at the start. Most of you others went over on your own, we went as an organized unit, and I just told them, take it or leave it. They needed fighters, so they took it."

Baca was about to say something else, probably to reminisce about some forgotten battlefield, but Melgarejo, the fat man, who had never fired a weapon himself, was not about to participate in an old soldiers' reunion. "Let's get on with this!" he said in a voice several decibels louder than necessary. "I've got municipal elections coming up, and plenty to do without sitting around here chatting."

"I'm sure you do, and we won't keep you longer than we have to," Lazaro quickly said. "I have a simple offer to make, and you can accept it, reject it, or think it over, as you wish."

Melgarejo sat back and folded his arms, just barely, across his broad chest, sticking out his chin for emphasis.

"Your party has done good work for the people, for democracy, but it seems, from the election results of the last few years, that the capitalists and the imperialists, are not about to let you win any elections peacefully. I suggest that it's time to up the stakes a little."

"Our vote total went up nearly ten percent in the last election," Melgarejo interrupted.

"Yes," Angel said, reading from a notepad in his lap, "from 0.8 percent to nearly 0.9 percent. Still short of a majority."

Melgarejo glared at Angel and then at Lazaro. Lazaro went on. "You have another strength that you have let lapse in recent years. Yours used to be a revolutionary party."

"It still is!" Melgarejo bellowed.

"In ideology, yes," Lazaro said, pointing his finger at the fat man. "But not in action. You used to send your young men to Cuba and Nicaragua, like Pablo here, but no more. It's time to shake this country up, and you need to put people into the street to do that. Then the recruits, the militants, and the voters, will come flocking to your banner as the vision of a chance for a new world."

"We still have our share of fighters," the fat man said, but he was already losing heart in the debate.

Angel consulted his notes again. "You have exactly 12 men who have had some kind of paramilitary training and who are not in prison. Only three of them, including Pablo, have actually been in combat." Pablo's chest swelled a little, even as his face wore a mask of impassivity.

"So what are *you* going to do about it?" Melgarejo whined. "Revolution is dead. The fucking Russians ran out of Eastern Europe and Afghanistan. The fucking Sandinistas managed to lose an election, an *election*!, to that old whore Chamorro, and even the Cubans are so busy kissing the Americans' butts that we have nowhere to turn. We can't beat the American marines all by ourselves. What can we do?"

"Let me help you," Lazaro said. He paused, forcing Melgarejo to beg for more.

"How?" he asked finally.

"I have a sponsor, a sponsor that has spit in the Americans' faces and still laughs about it, a sponsor that has people who don't just kill for a cause. They *die* for it. I'll tell you who later. Right now, all you need to know is that I've got 28 fighters, all combat veterans. They can use every weapon from a T-54 tank, to a Stinger anti-aircraft missile, to any kind of small arm you can name. They can lay mines, set booby traps, run communications networks, conduct interrogations, every skill a guerrilla needs. What's more, they can train people to do all of those things."

"That's still nothing," Melgarejo scoffed, getting back some of his bluster. "Thirty people total? What country are you going to take over with that?"

"I said that they could train people, an army," Lazaro hissed, and Melgarejo uncrossed his arms, and the corners of his mouth turned down like a little boy who had failed to learn his catechism. "We also have a thousand assault rifles coming, a million rounds of ammunition, machineguns, hand grenades, mortars, enough to massacre this comic opera Army they have here. And we have ten million dollars in cash, and more where that came from, if we need it."

"If you have all this," Melgarejo whimpered, "what do you want from us?"

"Your name. Your party. Your people. We could start from scratch, but it would set us back months, years. You can still get enough people out into the street to start things rolling. Open your eyes!" Lazaro was on his feet now, looming over the fat man, screaming at him like a fire and brimstone preacher chasing devils out of his tent. "There's an army waiting for you out in the street, waiting for something to happen, waiting for someone to lead them. They know your face and what you have been fighting for, and they believe it. All you have to do is give them a chance to believe that it's possible to win, and they'll smother you with kisses and run singing against the army's machineguns. And if you convince them that there's a chance, then there *will* be a chance, and all the power on earth can't stop us!"

Pablo let out a primal scream of emotion and jumped to his feet, his fists balled and tears forming in the corners of his eyes. He stood there waiting for Melgarejo to say something, and Lazaro could tell, without turning his head, that Pablo was his already.

When Melgarejo spoke, his voice was soft and trembling, as if he feared that Lazaro would scream at him again. "I'll be in overall command, of course. All decisions will come through me." He looked at the floor.

Lazaro sat next to him on the couch, throwing his arm around his shoulder. "That's what I said. We want to put *you* in power. Just let us help you. That's all we ask."

Melgarejo raised his head, his jaw set grimly, but with a smile playing around the corners of his mouth. "What are we waiting for?"

TWO

†

Featherstone was pleased to see that the rainstorm of the previous night had completely dissipated, leaving the sky a brilliant blue, with just enough clouds along the horizon for artistic effect. He hefted his new briefcase, a present from Anne, and set off for the office.

It was hardly like going to work at all. In the morning, after a leisurely breakfast served by the attentive and numerous domestic staff in starched white uniforms, Featherstone simply strolled out the back door of the residence, and down the flagstone steps to the pool. Some young embassy staffers were playing mixed doubles tennis on his court, as was allowed from eight to nine in the morning and from six to seven in the evening on weekdays, the other 158 hours of the week being reserved for the ambassador himself. Featherstone waved at them and smiled, and one of the girls stopped in mid-swing to wave back, letting the ball bounce past her undisturbed. He made a mental note that he would have to open up the courts, as he didn't play tennis anyway. He understood that his predecessor hadn't either but had kept the restrictions on, just for principle.

He continued across the well-tended lawn, watching the lizards, who glided over the grass like wind-blown leaves at his approach, and let himself through the low iron gate onto the embassy grounds. He walked around to the front entrance, and there he was, at work. The embassy looked rather more like a four-star tourist hotel from the fifties than a working embassy. It was a rambling one-story stucco affair with one of those long green curved awnings which stretched down the steps from the front door to the circular driveway.

The parking lot in front of the building was dominated by two immense trees, whose gnarled trunks sent complex networks of roots out over the ground and whose branches extended over twenty yards in all directions. From the branches hung yard-long green gourds, and

Featherstone hoped not to be standing under one if it should decide to fall.

Standing with his back to the embassy, he paused a moment to survey his new realm. The compound was surrounded by the same high iron fence, with menacing points on the top, which protected his residence. Across the street to the left was another compound which, he remembered from his chat with the residence domestics, housed the garage and maintenance facilities. Beyond that would be the embassy warehouse and the small commissary, where the American employees could buy corn chips, salad dressing, or any other American delicacy they couldn't live without. To his front was an ugly brown, four-story building housing the USAID mission with the embassy cafeteria on the top floor.

A large silver tanker truck was filling up from the embassy well in preparation for delivering water to American diplomats' homes, since there had been no city water available for several weeks. He knew that the consulate, which had its own building, was a couple of blocks away, and he would have to make an official visit as soon as he could.

He turned and walked up the steps into the embassy. He waved his diplomatic passport at the young, uniformed woman security guard at the door as he entered the reception area. Inside his bulletproof booth, the Marine Security Guard snapped to attention. Featherstone waved and walked up to the booth.

"Hi, I'm Bill Featherstone, the new ambassador," he said.

"I know, sir. We've been expecting you. I'm Sgt. Larry DeSoto," the short, muscular marine answered. "If you'll just wait a second, I'll get the Gunny. I know he'll want to meet you."

Featherstone nodded. He had always made it a point at his previous posts to get to know the marines personally. They were all very young men, some just kids really, and a long way from home. Actually, he suspected that they were clones obtained from some central warehouse, since they never seemed to change from post to post, and never to age from year to year, while he got greyer, and broader, at an alarming rate. He could not help admiring their uniforms, certainly the most attractive of the armed services, with their blue jackets, high collars, Sam Browne belts, and their smart white caps. Someone had made a wise decision years before to make them the guards at our embassies. They made an excellent impression on visitors, and Featherstone knew from experience that they were worth their weight in gold if there were ever a threat to the embassy.

A moment later another marine, this one dressed in freshly starched fatigues, strode into the reception area and extended his hand.

"Gunny Mike Besserman," the marine said, giving Featherstone's hand two very military shakes. He was of average height, and his hair, which was cut to "regulation" length, just a shade longer than "bald as an egg," was flaming red. His skin was rather pale for someone who obviously spent a lot of time out of doors, but this was largely disguised by an impressive display of freckles, which started at his nose and went right down to his fingers. "Welcome aboard, sir." It was apparent that his voice had been trained to issue commands across a parade ground, and the effect in the confines of the small reception area was resounding.

"Proud to be here, Gunny," Featherstone answered. "Say, I suspect that I'm going to be terribly busy over the next few days, but do you happen to have a TGIF party or something scheduled at the Marine House for the near future? It would give me a chance to meet all of your men and maybe some of the locals on neutral turf."

"Funny you should ask, sir," the Gunny beamed. "We've got one on for this Friday at 1800 hours."

"I'll be looking forward to it. Now, maybe you could introduce me to our lovely receptionist."

The gunny made a sweeping gesture with his hand toward another bulletproof booth which flanked "Post 1."

Just as Featherstone was approaching the smiling young woman in the booth, Stileforth swirled into the room like a hurricane, although not quite as subtle.

"Thank goodness you're here, sir," Stileforth gasped breathlessly, as he grabbed Featherstone by the elbow and attempted to propel him through the doorway as he awkwardly held the heavy plexiglass door open with one long, skinny leg. "I'd already called the residence and was just about to send out the dogs, what? You know the Country Team meeting is due to start in about two minutes."

Featherstone suddenly dug his heels into the thick carpet and came to an abrupt halt. "Just a minute, Dane," Featherstone said in his most official-sounding voice. "In the posts I've been to previously, the Country Team meeting didn't start until the ambassador arrived."

"That's quite right, sir. That's just the way it is here," Stileforth stammered, as he still was attempting to haul Featherstone through the doorway. His original simpering smile had now been replaced by a stormy frown, the wrinkles of which cascaded down between his eyebrows and threatened to overflow onto his nose. "But everyone's waiting."

"So," Featherstone continued, ignoring Stileforth's remarks and disengaging his arm, "since the ambassador isn't there yet, there's no hurry, is there?"

Without waiting for an answer, he turned back to the receptionist.

"This is Carmen, sir," Besserman said. His face was a strict mask of neutrality, but the corners of his mouth had begun to twitch, a sign that there was a horse laugh somewhere that had been filed for future reference.

"Pleased to meet you, Carmen," Featherstone said softly, as the young woman quivered with nervousness and contentment. "I've heard nothing but good things about you from Ambassador Middlehouse in Washington, and he sends his regards." Actually, Featherstone's predecessor had said nothing of the kind, but Featherstone opined that he probably should have. A good receptionist can save the ambassador many headaches, and a discontented one could make life hell for him without ever leaving a trace.

Then Featherstone turned quickly on his heel and whisked past Stileforth, who was still painfully holding the heavy door with his foot. "Come on, Dane. We don't want to keep everyone waiting." He called back over his shoulder, "See you Friday, Gunny, if not before."

"Ooh-rah, sir!" the Gunny shouted, clicking his heels and throwing a wink at Carmen, who giggled uncontrollably after Stileforth had disappeared through the door.

"Hey, Gunny," deSoto called through the metallic-sounding speaker of his booth. "What's this about a TGIF? We don't have anything on this week."

"Flexibility is the key to victory, son," he answered as the marine buzzed him through the other door to the "working wing" of the embassy. "Now get on it. I'll watch the door. You get over to that computer and whip us out some flyers!"

Passing through the hallway into the "front office" of the embassy, Featherstone paused again to greet two secretaries who were waiting by the desk in the reception area between the ambassador's and the DCM's offices. The first introduced herself as Elaine Watson, who would be Featherstone's secretary, a fifty-ish woman with her hair pulled back in a severe bun. Despite her cool appearance, the fact that Featherstone stopped to speak with her with a roomful of embassy executives waiting obviously met with her approval.

The other woman was much younger, perhaps twenty-five, and far more attractive. A Dominican named Maripaz Zuñiga, she served as social secretary for the ambassador. Since a Dominican citizen could not handle classified materials, her work was limited to extending and receiving invitations from and to the ambassador, handling his social calendar, and supervising the many receptions and other functions which the embassy hosted. She had dark brown skin, set off by even darker eyes and short, curly black hair. While Featherstone was no expert on fashion, he noted that her clothing was impeccable and perfectly color coordinated, with coral and peach predominating, her hem line just high enough to be fashionable and low enough to be business-like, and he believed that her blouse was home-made, although very well done. Her ample lips and warm smile were in stark contrast to the almost nonexistent lips and guarded attitude of Ms. Watson. Featherstone finally succumbed to Stileforth's sighing and impatient twitching and passed on into the conference room.

As was customary, all the members of the Country Team, the heads of the various sections of the embassy staff, rose as the new ambassador entered the room. Stileforth's face brightened involuntarily, as he had entered first, until he remembered his changed status, and his frugal mouth returned to its usual short, straight line. After Stileforth had made a cursory run through of the names of those present, Featherstone made a brief speech focusing on his pleasure in being at post and on the warm feelings held by the highest dignitaries in Washington for each and every member of the embassy.

To compensate partially for his conscious snubs of Stileforth in retaliation for mistreatment of his subordinates, Featherstone announced that Stileforth would continue to chair the weekly Country Team meetings for the next month or so, while Featherstone would merely sit in and throw out any questions which came to mind. Stileforth was visibly pleased with this, and began to go around the table, receiving the report of each section chief in turn.

Jim Vernon, head of the political section, was an intense little man with the high forehead, wire-rimmed glasses, and sharp eyes that one normally associated with college professors. He had been on island for over a year and had served on the Caribbean section at the State

Department before that, so he was intimately familiar with Dominican politics. He gave a knowledgeable rundown of how the new government of President Juan Selich, which, rather than concentrating on the massive economic and social problems which threatened to overwhelm the nation any moment, had spent its first few months in office busily granting profitable contracts for highway construction and other projects to faithful supporters of Selich's Christian Democratic Party (PCD) who had no engineering expertise. They would turn around and sell these contracts to real construction firms after extracting an appropriate "finder's fee" for themselves.

Vernon also gave a brief recap of the disintegration of the so-called political parties upon the recent death of the octogenarian Joaquin Balaguer and his equally ancient rival Juan Bosch. The votes were currently split more or less evenly between Selich's PCD, the rather more leftist Dominican Revolutionary Party (PRD), and the substantially more leftist Party for Dominican Liberation (PLD), with the PCD having won a slight plurality and the presidency, but hardly a mandate for any kind of meaningful change, even if they had had the desire. There were also a few splinter parties on the radical fringe, the rightists feeding on racist feelings against Haitians who came across the border illegally to work the sugar harvest, and the leftists still vainly trying to sell the discredited philosophy of Marx, Lenin, and Castro. None of these groups had any electoral backing and, more importantly, none had engaged in any significant acts of violence for over a year.

Marine Colonel Avery Miller, the Defense Attaché, came next. His steel-gray hair was cropped very short, and his neck, what there was of it, was essentially the same circumference as his bullet head. Featherstone was about to mark him down as some sort of military android, when the Colonel buried his face in his hands, his shoulders heaving with mock sobs, as he described a field inspection he had just completed with a Dominican Army infantry battalion.

Overcoming his "grief," the Colonel related how, on the firing range, seventy-five per cent of the men couldn't get their rifles to go "bang." Since the officers in alleged command of the battalion could not be found, Miller and the Dominican liaison officer who escorted him began checking the weapons and found most of them fused with rust. Taking charge of the situation Avery rounded up a couple of dozen rifles which did not appear likely to explode upon firing and ran the men through the range in relays. Unfortunately, this only revealed that most of the men didn't know how to load or clear their rifles either, much less aim them. He added that, unlike most of the armies in Latin America, the Dominican Army was not composed of conscripts but of long serving professionals. The Colonel was just starting a further tale of woe, recounting a trip he had made along the Haitian border where isolated Dominican Army outposts were reduced to spending all of their time raising vegetables since they hadn't received any rations in months, when Featherstone interrupted him.

"On balance, then, Colonel," Featherstone said, "I guess you wouldn't invest a lot of money in Dominican War Bonds."

"Well, let me emphasize that these are extreme examples," he cautioned. "The units I saw on this trip were from the 2nd and 3rd Brigades, based in Santiago and Barahona and those *are* basically worthless. On paper the 1st Brigade, which covers Santo Domingo is the same size, but it really has all of the fighting power of the army, all the best troops, the few armored vehicles they've got, and the best officers. I'd say they've got about 3,000 troops that are worth their salt out of 15,000 total. The trouble is the massive level of corruption among the officers. They steal the army blind, and the few officers and troops who are serious about their work are left without the means to do it. The Presidential Guard Battalion is about the best of the lot."

"How about the other services?" Featherstone asked, making notes on a yellow legal pad.

"Neither the air force nor the navy have the kind of equipment necessary to make a difference. The Air Force still flies old P-51 Mustangs from World War II, and the navy has a few coastal patrol craft and some landing craft of dubious reliability. The air force also has a small battalion of paratroopers who are pretty good, and the navy has a battalion of marines, although, with all due modesty," he said placing his hand on his breast, "they're really *not marines*, if you get my drift. Just glorified gate guards."

"And the police?"

"That's a little better. They've got a 1,000-man counterinsurgency unit just five clicks out of town which is fairly impressive. Not exactly U.S. Navy SEALS, but adequate. They also have a good riot control unit, the "Black Helmets," kind of unsubtle, but they can break up a mob quickly and with minimal bloodshed."

Featherstone nodded, and the floor passed on through the representative of the U.S. Information Service, who talked about exchange students, the Econ Counsellor, who talked about interest rates, the General Service Office chief who complained about not being able to get the local repair contractor to come and fix copier machines, the Consul General who noted that the number of visa applicants had risen nearly 30 percent over last year, and the Regional Medical Officer who talked about an outbreak of "pink eye" among some of the mission children. It was then the turn of the CIA Station Chief.

Featherstone had recognized Lafeur from the airport, although he hadn't realized *which* "political section" he had been referring to at the time. He was also aware that Lafeur was only acting COS, the previous one having been evacuated for "medical problems" which apparently had to do with overexposure to the contents of liquor bottles. That had been six months before, and no one had thought it necessary to replace him yet. As usual at these large meetings, the CIA man had little to contribute. If he had any information of value, it would be for the ears of the ambassador, DCM, and maybe the political counsellor alone.

Lastly, all eyes turned toward the Admin Counsellor, Peter Rambling. He was the closest thing the Embassy had to a political appointee, having served with distinction on the personal staffs of two Secretaries of State, apparently having been largely responsible for hors d'oeuvres and airline scheduling. This was his last tour before retiring, and he had lobbied for an overseas posting, his first in twenty years, with a hardship differential to boost his salary during his "high three" pre-retirement years. According to Featherstone's sources in Washington, during Rambling's two years on the island, he had spent a total of over nine months either in Washington on "consultations," in Miami on leave, or at his family home in Georgia on "medical evacuation" for illnesses not fully understood.

Rambling announced that the summer turnover of personnel was largely completed and that the biggest challenge facing the embassy at present was to survive on the remaining funds for the rest of the fiscal year. He was outlining a money-saving scheme which would limit water deliveries to the homes of American staffers to once per week and eliminating afterhours and weekend emergency repair service for the generators supplied to employees living in privately leased quarters. Featherstone immediately realized that this last stipulation would have left the "working level" people without their generators for days on end, but not the section chiefs, DCM, or the ambassador, who were all in quarters leased by the government.

Before Rambling could continue on to his second sheet of suggestions, Featherstone interrupted. "Peter, before we get into any more budgetary matters, I wonder if you could give me a read-out on morale at the embassy."

"Morale?" Peter said with a quizzical look. He shuffled through his notes, as if hoping to find an answer there.

"Yes, morale. I believe that, as head of personnel, this is in your bailiwick. I've been talking this over in Washington, and this post has the highest proportion of med evacs of any in the world, that includes places like Beirut and Chad. We've also had two resignations of first tour officers and four divorces. There have been several complaints to the inspector general, and one has reached formal grievance proceedings."

"These things happen," Stileforth chimed in. "Conditions are difficult, and not everyone can deal with them." Rambling stuck out his lower lip and nodded emphatically.

"I can see that things are difficult," Featherstone said calmly, "but they are certainly not more difficult than in Bogota, for example, where all embassy dependents had to be evacuated due to terrorist attacks. What I am referring to is why the morale at this post seems to be so much worse than these other places."

Rambling continued to fumble with his papers, and Stileforth apparently decided to let him figure his own way out. So Featherstone continued.

"My personal philosophy is that people will put up with a lot if only they feel that everything possible is being done to satisfy them and if the burdens are being shared more or less equally. Therefore, I think we should begin at the top, eliminating all travel except for change of post, for one thing. I notice that there are several conferences coming up in Washington for various section chiefs. While I'm sure that they'd be worthwhile, I think we can muddle through without attending them. I'm also going to cut the staff at my residence and forego the traditional redecorating of the place that all new ambassadors like to indulge in. I'll take time to talk to you, Peter, about this later, but I do want to make it clear that, while I don't plan a revolution here in my first week, neither will I be bound by policies from the past. We're about 20 percent short of personnel here right now, and no one

seems to want to come. We've got to do something about that."
Featherstone could see that neither Rambling nor Stileforth were particularly pleased with his statement. Glancing around the table, most
of the other section chiefs were smiling discreetly, except for Lafeur,
who was grinning broadly, and Featherstone could see how the battle
lines would be drawn. Despite the oppressive heat and humidity outside, both Rambling and Stileforth were wearing nicely tailored suits,
button-down shirts, and silk ties. Everyone else, except for the Colonel,
who was in uniform, was wearing the local guayabera, as was Featherstone. This implied to Featherstone which of his subordinates probably intended to venture outside the air conditioned comfort of their
offices sometime during the day. Clearly, it would take some time to
whip this embassy into shape, but time was something Featherstone
had plenty of right now, and for the first time in his career, the embassy
would become just what he made of it, no blaming it on anyone else,
and he relished the challenge.

†

Lafeur was driving toward the west end of the city in his "ops
vehicle," a very old, not very reliable, Opel Kadet which he normally
kept in a small rented garage about six blocks from the Embassy. The
car was registered in the name of a Dominican businessman who, for
a modest consideration each month, performed minor support functions like this for Lafeur. Lafeur was nominally under cover as a State
Department political officer, but since his job involved a good deal of
direct liaison with both the Dominican police and the military, he was
only really hiding from local civilians and the press. Even the Dominican employees at the Embassy knew very well what agency of the
government ran the office with all of the extra locks that they weren't
allowed to enter.

In fact, the only thing that Lafeur was particularly interested in
keeping secret was the identity of the few bona fide Dominican agents
he ran. For that reason, he didn't drive his own car to meetings, and
made a habit of running lengthy "surveillance detection routes" to and
from his meetings. He knew from experience in trying to arrange
training for the Dominican police in surveillance work that he really
didn't have much to worry about, but he felt it was always wisest to
"play the game."

Actually, he only did these routes because it gave him a good excuse for getting out of the office. It was virtually impossible to run a meaningful SDR without being able to use a combination of car travel, public transportation, and walking to drag any suspected surveillants through a series of traps which would reveal their presence without tipping them off. In Santo Domingo, public transportation consisted of a handful of decrepit buses and private cars which functioned as taxis, into which twelve or more passengers would cram themselves, neither of which would be of much use for Lafeur's purposes. So the best he could do was drive around and see if the same car popped up more than once in his rearview mirror.

Lafeur hated driving in this city. From his previous tours in Latin America, he was used to creative interpretations of the traffic code, but no one drove as badly as they did here. He would pull up at a stop sign, waiting for an opening to cross a major avenue. The car behind him, obviously unable to fathom why he would be stopped like that in the middle of the road, instead of waiting behind him, would pull up next to him, in the lane meant for oncoming traffic. Of course, the same thing would happen on the other side of the avenue, so you would have four cars facing each other, two on each side, and when the cross traffic did clear, it was always exciting to see who would end up on which side of the street.

There was, however, another problem. Almost everyone here went armed. Lafeur did not, as was the rule for Agency personnel everywhere except, perhaps, Beirut. In Santo Domingo, there was hardly a car on the road that did not have a pistol under the front seat, and most men took great pride in how poorly they could conceal the large automatic jammed inside the belt in the back of their pants. This could turn the average traffic infringement into something like the landing at Omaha Beach. Elsewhere in Latin America, you could tell the really important people by who had an armed guard on their house. Here, everyone had a sleepy looking man with some kind of uniform and a shotgun. Even the casual day workers who roamed the city looking for employment sweeping a driveway or painting a fence invariably carried a vicious three-foot machete, which came in handy for chopping weeds, but the prominent scars one could see on bare arms and faces in lower class bars implied that weeds were not all that got chopped.

Ordinarily, it would not fall to the same individual to handle both the liaison work of the COS and deal with unilateral agents as well.

Unfortunately, for the same reason that Lafeur's superiors had not found it necessary to replace his old chief, they had also not replaced the single case officer normally assigned here when the last one left the year before and the candidate for his slot got cold feet and decided to return to his corporate job in Burger King instead.

Lafeur had to admit he didn't really do very much that should cause the local government any concern. He reported regularly on the internal workings of the various political parties, from right to left, and occasionally was able to provide information on the laundering of drug money through the island, but that was about it. In fact, Lafeur suspected, that was why he was chief now. Santo Domingo was a "safe" post for a black COS.

Certainly, the Agency paid lip service to general equality of opportunity, but he found the practice fell far short of the theory. He had only to look around him to see how few black case officers there were, and virtually none of those in management positions. He also knew full well that, like many other federal agencies, the CIA made up its minority quotas by staffing the more mundane branches in headquarters, such as personnel, supply, and even the char force, almost exclusively with minorities. There was even an Agency joke that a case officer who failed in the field would be put in charge of "black ops" in headquarters, a phrase which usually referred to illegal border crossings, but in this case involved supervising the cleaning crews as they mopped the bathrooms after hours.

Lafeur had learned to live with a certain amount of racism as he grew up, but he had been somewhat sheltered by the academic circle of his father's friends. He didn't even have a proper "black" accent, or even an identifiable Louisiana one, having largely lost it when he studied at Columbia University and then in the army. Within his group of friends, he was a very acceptable black, just the kind you'd want to invite over to your white neighborhood to show everyone how multicultural you were, but without running any risks.

Consequently, Lafeur had not been equipped to deal with the more subtle racism that he found in the Agency. It was nothing you could point to, nothing to base a complaint to the Inspector General on, but it was there. When he had first joined the Agency, he had planned on specializing in the Middle East, but the Near East Division people had told him that, frankly, he wouldn't do well because the Arabs were so racist that they wouldn't take him seriously. You see, it wasn't NE

Division that was racist, it was the damned Arabs. He had heard the same thing from East Asia Division. Africa Division wanted him badly. He already spoke good French, and being black would have been an absolute boon for an officer in Brazzaville, but Lafeur didn't want to follow that road. Also, he noted, the divisional management for Africa was still predominantly white. Finally, he had settled on Latin America Division, where they didn't want him for his color, but they weren't going to turn him away because of it either. Since LA Division covered the Caribbean, the population of which was largely black, as well as Brazil, there were plenty of good posts, the living was decent, and the work seemed interesting, so he made his choice.

His promotions had come fairly regularly, about what he would have expected given his good but not spectacular performance in the field. Now, with a significant period of management under his belt, he could expect something meaty either back in Washington, or maybe he would take a tour in Africa now, on rotation.

Things at least were looking up at the embassy here. The new ambassador seemed like a decent sort. After the Country Team meeting he had visited each of the sections of the embassy. He didn't call the section chiefs to his office to receive their obeisance, like his predecessor and other ambassadors Lafeur had known. He had talked to Lafeur for half an hour about his operations, not probing to identify his sources, but getting a feel for the kind of reporting he could expect. He had also promised to lean on Washington to send out another case officer, not a real COS, implying both that he didn't want to replace Lafeur and that he thought Lafeur's work was important enough to merit some support. A very interesting guy, Lafeur thought, and he doesn't seem to like Stileforth much either, another point in his favor.

Lafeur finally pulled around the back of a lower middle class apartment building and parked the car out of sight of the street. He realized that, despite his extensive SDR, if he happened to be seen casually by one of his police contacts sneaking into this building, that alone might be enough to burn his agent.

As Lafeur got out of the car, he glanced up at a second floor balcony and noted the presence of a red mop handle casually propped against the railing, his signal that all was well and that his agent was in the apartment.

Dominican police Lieutenant Federico Quiroga was sitting in the darkened apartment when Lafeur entered, the red eye of his cigarette bobbing in lethargic greeting. The two men mumbled their hellos, and Lafeur turned up the volume on the radio to cover their conversation. He knew that a serious intelligence service could easily pick up a conversation recorded against a background of music, but he was much more concerned about the little old lady sitting on her balcony next door than he was with any high-tech snooping, and it was too damn hot to close the windows.

Quiroga was substantially shorter and thinner than Lafeur, and at 32 somewhat younger. Although he was a couple of shades darker than Lafeur, Quiroga referred to himself as "European," while Lafeur would have classified himself as undeniably black. He was a tremendously energetic man with a lively sense of humor. Lafeur marked this down to the fact that, although stuck in the files and records department of the police, an area not considered prime ground for obtaining extra cash, he had had the good fortune to have let himself be "recruited" by Lafeur's predecessor as an "investigative asset," someone who could trace a license plate, phone number, or criminal record unofficially. Lafeur was proud that he had turned this useful but unspectacular asset into the head of an embryonic surveillance team. He had even groomed him to be a regular handler of sub-agents, who would not be aware they were working for anyone other than some mysterious branch of the Dominican government. Lafeur particularly liked the touch that Quiroga was a real cop who could flash a badge if anyone questioned his activities.

"So, how did the surveillance go?" Lafeur asked, pocketing a bunch of flimsy papers on which Quiroga's detailed report had been typed. He would read it over when he got back to the office, where the lights worked, but he wanted at least a foretaste. Quiroga became very enthusiastic about the past two days during which he and a new recruit, a young police lieutenant named Walter Arce had followed a Palestinian businessman from his arrival at the airport until that afternoon. Quiroga didn't know that Lafeur had picked the name at random from a travel manifest that he had obtained from a contact at the airline and had meant this merely as a training exercise. He had, however, recognized that the man's activities were out of the ordinary.

"On the first day," Quiroga began, "he did just the sort of thing your average Arab businessman would do. He registered at the Hotel Lina in a nice suite. He stopped by a couple of banks and a warehouse. Then he did some tourist shopping for coral jewelry at the Plaza Criollo, had dinner at La Fromagerie, went back to the hotel and had a nubile young waiter up in his room for a noisy session. I taped some of it from in front of his door, if you want to hear." Quiroga pulled a small tape recorder from his gym bag.

"That won't be necessary," Lafeur said, waving his hand wearily. There were a lot of Palestinian and other Middle Eastern businessmen in the Dominican Republic, many of them descendants of immigrants over the past century. Others were current residents of the Middle East who did business in import-export, tourism, and a host of less well-defined and less-legal enterprises. Lafeur supposed that this was just another one of them, but at least Quiroga had been on the job. He would check later to make sure that the man actually had registered at the Lina.

"It was all so ordinary that I considered breaking off," Quiroga continued, "but there was something *wrong* about the guy. You know what I mean?"

"No, what do you mean?" They had been talking in Spanish, but Quiroga, who like so many other Dominicans had had a strong dose of Americanization, inserted the "wrong" in English, something he had picked up from American police movies.

"Well, for one thing, he was looking for surveillance, and he was pretty slick about it."

At this Lafeur cocked his head slightly. Quiroga might be new to the business of international espionage, in fact he wasn't really in it yet, but Lafeur was more than willing to believe that this cop could tell when a bad guy was acting strange on the street.

"You know," Quiroga went on. "He'd drag us through different kinds of areas, working class, residential, business, just to see if anyone stuck out in a different environment. If we had been in New York, it would have worked fine, but here you'll find gardeners and construction workers walking past mansions, and businessmen wear guayaberas just like everyone else. Still, if we hadn't had our bags with changes of clothes, he would have made us for sure. What was really creepy about it was that he didn't do anything obvious like using store windows as mirrors or ducking around corners and then stopping to tie his shoes. He was looking, but he was slick. I had Arce hang way back. We figured it was better to lose him than to be spotted. We could always pick him up again at the hotel."

Quiroga paused with his bright white teeth gleaming in the dim light from a street lamp outside, and Lafeur gave him the thumbs-up signal to show that he had done the right thing.

"So anyway, about 0400 I get this call at home from Arce, who had the watch until six, when I was going to take over again. He had followed the guy out of the hotel about two hours before and had just managed to find a working pay phone to call me. Instead of taking a taxi right at the door, the way he had before, he took off on foot across a vacant lot and walked all the way downtown. Arce was able to keep tabs on him with his moped, sprinting ahead a block or two and watching the guy pass by, then riding ahead again. I still figured at this point that he was probably into drugs or something, but guess who he met with."

Lafeur just sighed and frowned at Quiroga who quickly raised his hands in surrender.

"He met two guys in a bar about two blocks from the Cathedral. I don't know the first one, but the other one was Pablo Baca, number two man of the MIR." Quiroga rubbed his hands together rapidly in excitement.

Lafeur had been staring off into space when Quiroga began his talk, but, as the name registered, he leaned closer to Quiroga, who did likewise, in a conspiratorial manner. "Now what do you suppose Baca would have to do with a Palestinian businessman?" Lafeur wondered aloud.

"I was sort of hoping you could tell me," Quiroga said in a flat tone, and Lafeur realized that the policeman was waiting for him to tell him why the Palestinian had been a target for surveillance in the first place. He considered for a moment simply telling the truth, explaining that it had merely been a training assignment, but that would set a bad precedent. No, a lie would be much better.

"He was reported to have been a front man for Hizballah in Lebanon, and we were curious what sort of business he would have in this part of the world. He set up support structures for them, renting apartments, cars, that sort of thing, for their terrorist hit squads." Lafeur forced himself to stop before he embroidered too much.

Quiroga nodded emphatically. "Well, the big question is who the third man was. Their meeting only lasted half an hour, and they were gone by the time I was able to get there, so I told Arce on the phone to follow the unknown man. I've got an address and a license plate that I'm tracing right now. I'll have an answer for you in the morning."

"Good man," Lafeur said sincerely. Quiroga had proven that he could think on his feet. Even if this Palestinian thing turned out to be nothing after all, he had seen Quiroga in action, and he liked what he saw. Lafeur would run full traces on the Palestinian with Washington when he got back to the office and see if there really was some sort of file on him.

"Oh," Quiroga said, reminding himself. "I had a meeting with that guy from the phone company, my wife's cousin. I think he's the man we want."

From a really routine administrative session, this was turning into something of importance, Lafeur thought. "What's his exact position?"

"He calls himself an 'engineer,'" Quiroga said. "What he is is a shift supervisor in the main telephone exchange downtown. He's just one step up from a lineman, actually, but that means that no one's going to question seeing him running around the cable racks with a pair of pliers. From that exchange, he can do any number in the Santo Domingo area." Quiroga paused briefly. "And he needs money. His daughter has some sort of eye problem, and he wants to get her to the States for an operation. If we can convince him that it's officially authorized, he'll do whatever we want."

"He sounds perfect," Lafeur agreed. "Get me his full bio data, and I'll check him out." Lafeur had been dreaming of setting up a means of doing telephone taps unilaterally, that is, without the coop-eration of the local authorities. He would have to be careful, since most of the juicier political figures' phones would be tapped by the govern-ment already, and he didn't dare risk tapping the phone of some senior government figure or military officer, as much as he would like to. There were, however, plenty of radical fringe types whose conversations might prove interesting. The main thing anyway was to be able to tell Washington that he had created this capability for his Station, an important feather in his cap which would far outweigh any actual value derived from the operation.

"You'll find it in with my surveillance report," Quiroga said, in-terrupting Lafeur's thoughts. "If that's all, I've got to get out and meet with Arce. Once I've got a name for the third man, I'm going to surveil him for awhile and see what other contacts he has. Assuming that's all right with you."

"Yes, of course," Lafeur said distractedly. He winced at not having been quick enough to say that first. Quiroga was a good man, but Lafeur would have to be on his toes all the more for that.

Lafeur left first, theoretically to draw off any surveillance he might have brought with him to the building, leaving Quiroga to wait another half hour before going on his way. Lafeur knew that if he had been under surveillance by someone as good as Quiroga, the watchers would simply let him go and wait for Quiroga, but there was no helping that.

†

A Friday night party at the Marine House tended to be either a tremendous snore, where few people showed up and those who did stumbled around, engaging in shop talk with the same people they had worked with all day, or it turned into a bacchanalian revel with head thumping music, free-flowing liquor, and riotous celebration by all. This night leaned more toward the latter extreme.

The Marine House itself was a one-story home, obviously built for a large family. The bedrooms occupied by the marines were off in one wing to which guests were theoretically denied access, although an occasional female guest had found the rules waived for her benefit from time to time. The heart of the complex was what had been the living and dining rooms of the house plus an enclosed patio. Here the Marines had installed an oak bar from which to dispense the necessary lubricants for smooth social interaction. The bar was now jammed three deep as both American and Dominican employees of the embassy tried to attract the attention of the tall black marine who was supposed to be serving drinks but who appeared more interested in gyrating his hips to an M.C. Hammer tune on the stereo to the delight of several young Dominican secretaries clad in breathtakingly tight lycra mini-dresses. Off in a side room, a couple of Marines were shooting pool with another pair of young ladies who seemed to lean much farther over the pool table in their low-cut blouses than absolutely necessary. No one seemed to mind, however.

Featherstone and Anne were standing at opposite corners of the bar, each engaging a tight circle of embassy employees and their spouses in animated conversations. Featherstone was pleased to note the surprise with which each new arrival perceived his presence at the bar. He was talking now to Maripaz, whom he found to be a delightful young woman with penetrating eyes and a daring, playful smile. Although Featherstone was concentrating on not letting his gaze drift any lower than her chin, since Anne was keeping a close watch on him from only a beer bottle's throw away, every other man in the room was ogling the gentle curves of her delicate body, attractively draped in a brightly colored sun dress which left one shoulder bare with just enough of her legs exposed to confirm their perfection. Featherstone was most taken by her casual expression which seemed to say, "Yes, of course I'm beautiful, but let's talk about something else."

He learned that she had come from a poor family but had finished high school and was within a year of obtaining a college degree in English language and computer sciences. She had been at the embassy only five years, but she had managed to land this prime job, which normally went to some old matron who had been in place for decades, solely on the basis of her remarkable efficiency and charm with any kind of visitor. She told Featherstone how she was raising her baby daughter alone, after her husband had been killed in an automobile accident about a year before.

He was impressed with her long-range plans, for someone of only 25 years of age. She expected to work at the embassy for another ten years. Then, with the immigrant visa to the United States which was offered to all FSNs after fifteen years service, she would move to New York where she had relatives, get a job at the UN, and see her daughter through American high school and college.

Featherstone had other questions for her, but he noticed that Anne had struck up a particularly warm conversation with a marine whose muscles were in a constant state of warfare with the constraints of his T-shirt. The message was clear. It was time to "mingle" elsewhere.

Just then someone yelled, "Limbo!" The cry was taken up around the room to the accompaniment of rhythmic ooh-rahs from the marines. Gunny Besserman popped a new CD in the stereo, and the strains of "Limbo Rock" came throbbing through the speakers. The floor was cleared, and Lyle Fiore, head of the DEA office grabbed the hand of Elaine Watson and began wriggling under a broomstick held up by Colonel Miller, against Elaine's rather feeble protest. The bar was only just below shoulder level, and the pair easily made it through to the wild cheers of the crowd.

Then Featherstone leaned way across the bar, grabbed Anne by the wrist, and they took their position.

"Lower! Don't be a pussy!" a loud masculine voice shouted from behind the bar. The last word was clipped off, and the speaker had decided to check the inventory of the bottles under the bar by the time Featherstone and Besserman had a chance to look in that direction. But the bar was lowered to about chest level in any event. Featherstone and Anne began half-hopping, half-sliding under the bar, knees first, then the belt. Featherstone was desperately trying to keep from toppling over backwards as the bar neared his chin, but the good Colonel mercifully lifted it an inch at the crucial moment, and they both shot through gratefully. The applause was deafening. As Featherstone came up, laughing, he caught a glimpse of Stileforth and Rambling, still in their suits, slipping out the front door.

Another shout went up, this time for Maripaz to come "front and center." She demurely climbed down from her stool and stood in front of the bar, while Lafeur appeared at her side and gallantly took her hand. She smiled at him, and gently pushed the bar downward with one finger until it was below the level of her delicate waist. Lafeur swallowed hard but met her stare, and the crowd began clapping in time to their movements.

"This has the makings of a real show-stopper," Anne said in Featherstone's ear, and delicately put her hand over his eyes.

Lafeur's ample thighs were spread wide apart as he inched them under the bar, and some of the cruder marines had gone down on their haunches ahead of the couple for a better view. However, Maripaz just smiled and swung her knees, chastely locked together, side to side, steadily moving under the bar, first bending far forward and then, at the last moment arching her back and slipping underneath, just as Lafeur did the same. Maripaz raised her arms like a showgirl, and they both bowed, Lafeur pausing to kiss her hand with a flourish.

Featherstone shook Lafeur's hand.

"About the only good thing to come out of my tour in Kingston," Lafeur panted, "was the ability to do the limbo."

"Well, then it wasn't a total loss," Featherstone laughed.

†

The baby generally had been sleeping all night since she was three months old, but Maripaz still had a mother's sense of trouble which could bring her out of a deep sleep even before the first wail or cough.

She sat upright in bed and listened first. The baby's crib was in the living room, the only room besides her own bedroom and the kitchen. That had been her mother's idea, saying that the baby would actually learn to sleep alone faster if she didn't hear Maripaz in the same room all night.

At first there was nothing, and Maripaz was about to lay back down when she heard the soft gurgling and cooing which told her the baby was awake. She probably needs changing, Maripaz thought, and it would be better to give her a little milk and see her well asleep again rather than be reawakened an hour from now. She glanced at the luminous hands of her bedside wind-up clock, the only kind that worked in a country with irregular electrical supply. It was three o'clock, and she had only gotten in about two hours before. At least it was Saturday.

She pushed her hair back out of her face and shuffled into the living room without turning on the light. She bent over the crib and put her hand in gently. She touched the flat mattress and felt around, but the baby wasn't there. She gasped when a hand suddenly was pressed over her mouth and, at the same time, someone switched on the light.

She was panting for breath, her eyes wide with terror. The owner of the hand now had an arm around her waist pressing her back against him with incredible strength. Seated calmly on her couch were a man and a woman. The woman was a little older than she was, but the hardness around her eyes made her look much older. In her hand she held a pistol. The man had burning dark eyes but looked at her with a peaceful expression on his face. He cradled the baby in the crook of one arm. In his free hand he held a machete, the blade resting across his knees next to the baby.

They stayed like that for what seemed a long time. Maripaz was able to make only little whimpering noises as she struggled weakly with the man who held her, afraid that if she were to break free, they would hurt the baby, but just as afraid to remain immobile.

"Hello, Maripaz," the man with the baby finally said. "I'm sorry we had to come to you this way, but we have very important work to do and very powerful enemies who would prevent us from doing it."

He paused and looked at her for another long while. "We want to talk to you. We want your help. We want you to *want* to help us, but we will have your help one way or the other. I will tell my friend to uncover your mouth now so that we can talk. If you make any noise or try to get away, we will kill you, and we will kill your beautiful little baby. Please believe me. I have lost count of the men I have killed, and the women, and the children, in doing my work." He paused again. "Now, will you be quiet?"

She nodded vigorously. The man uncovered her mouth, but when she lunged toward her baby, she found his arm still wrapped tight around her waist. The man on the couch raised the machete just slightly, pointing the edge of the blade at the side of the baby's head. He cocked his own head as if to ask if she understood, and she let out her breath.

"That's better," the man said. "You don't know us, but we know you. We know that you work in the American embassy. We know where your desk is, your extension number, your salary, where you have lunch and with whom. We can come into your home whenever we want, or your mother's, or your aunt's in Santiago. If you talk to the police, we will know. If you talk to the Americans, we will know. Then we will come and find you and your baby, and your mother, and your sister, and we will kill you all, because you will have chosen the side of the rich Americans against the poor of your own country. We do not blame you for working with the Americans. You were a poor girl and have done well for yourself by your own hard work, but now you have been chosen to do something for a cause bigger than yourself. You will be a tool in the hands of God and will serve the welfare of all the people."

His voice was monotonous, hypnotizing. She thought of herself as a little girl again, listening to the priest in catechism class. She had to shake her head to keep her thoughts straight and to keep from fainting.

"Who are you and what do you want me to do?" she asked, her voice still husky with sleep and fear.

The man smiled, just as a priest would when a child came up with the right answer to a Sunday school question about the Virgin Mary. "Who we are doesn't matter, but you will hear of us as the santistas, which is short for holy warriors. We have fought against imperialism and injustice for many years in many lands, and now we have come home to *our* land, to free it from oppression. What we want is simply that you report to us on all of the movements of the American ambassador, William Featherstone. That is all."

"What do you want to know that for?" she asked, knowing in her heart what they must have in mind.

The man behind her tightened his grip, and she looked up at his reflection in the mirror behind the couch. He was slightly taller than she, balding, with a dark moustache, and his teeth were showing in what might have been a grimace or a smile. The man on the couch continued to talk calmly, but there was a hard edge to his voice, the way the priests talk when they tell you of the hell which waits for sinners who do not repent.

"Don't ask a question unless you really want to hear the answer, Maripaz," the man said. "You already know what you need to know. You know what you must do, and you know what will happen if you don't do it or if you talk to anyone. Do you understand me?"

She nodded her head without taking her eyes from him.

"Good." The man rose, handing his machete to the woman who had neither moved nor spoken, never turning the barrel of her gun away from Maripaz. He lifted the baby and kissed her head gently before placing her carefully in the crib. He watched a moment as the baby made herself comfortable and then dropped off to sleep. "Then I can leave you now with Luis. He will tell you just what you must do and how you will provide your information until we tell you that we don't need it any more."

He made a little bow to her, and then he and the woman walked softly to the door and let themselves out.

Maripaz' breath was still coming in short gasps, and she became conscious of her breasts pressing against the silk of her night shirt. They stood like that for a moment, and then the man brought his free hand up, running it first over her breasts and then down her stomach and between her legs. At first she gritted her teeth, but finally half shouted, "No!"

The man's hand shot to her hair as he jerked her head back and spun her around to face him, still pressing her close to him. He held her face next to his for a long moment, letting her try to push away from him and then squeezing her all the tighter, pulling her hair until it hurt.

"The first thing you will have to learn is obedience, sister," he hissed. He breathed hard on her face, and there was a strong odor of heavily spiced food which made Maripaz want to vomit, but she controlled herself with every ounce of her will. "Get down on your knees."

She resisted vainly as he pushed her down in front of him. He held tightly to her hair with one hand while he undid his pants with the other.

"No," she sobbed quietly, casting a sidelong glance at her sleeping baby only a few feet away.

"You will learn to do everything I tell you without question, little sister," he said. "Or you will watch your baby roast alive."

The tears began to flow so fast that she couldn't see, but that was just as well.

Luis threw his head back and closed his eyes. This was what he adored. Not the sex. It was not often that Padre Lazaro left him alone like this to enjoy it. Luis wondered whether Lazaro was too pure to understand Luis' drives and desires or whether he just didn't care as long as Luis did his work. And Luis was so very good at his work. It was the total power over people, the ability to make them do whatever you wanted. That was even better than sex.

He had thought Lazaro was crazy when they were fighting in the hills of Nicaragua and Lazaro had come to them and said that they were finished fighting for the godless Sandinistas and that they were going to Iran, of all places! After a while though, he began to see the logic of it. The Iranians, especially the Revolutionary Guards they worked with, were people of God, just like the santistas. He hadn't much liked the fighting in the marshes of the Fao Peninsula, always up to his knees in stinking muck. After serving their time at the front though, the santistas had graduated to work against the internal enemy, the communist Tudeh and the Mujaheddin e-Khalq guerrillas, learning their trade from officers of the Sepah. They had learned to follow people undetected, their Latin faces blending in well enough with the Iranians when they wore local clothes. When they found a suspect, they would swoop down on his house in the middle of the night, just like this. Then they would make him talk about his contacts, arms caches, whatever. And they always talked.

He remembered torturing one man in front of his family, a wife and two young children. He couldn't remember now whether the children were boys or girls. The man wouldn't break. Oh, he named all of his neighbors and the men he worked with as Tudeh Party members, but he was lying. He wouldn't reveal the arms cache they knew he had somewhere, which would have proved his story, of course. Finally, Lazaro had had Luis douse the wife and children in gasoline and burn them to death in front of him. Still he wouldn't talk, so they had killed him. The Iranians had taught them to do that. They had explained that the Tudeh and Mujaheddin did the same to pro-Ayatollah informers and their families, but they didn't have to rationalize it to Luis. The look on the peoples' faces was enough justification for him. It was like food, sex, wine, everything. Sometimes he let a suspect live, first to enjoy the grovelling thanks, and then returned the next day to finish the job, getting the whole benefit all over again.

Now they had paid their dues to the Sepah and the Sepah would back their play in the Dominican Republic with money, guns, false documents, whatever they wanted. And Luis knew this would be better. Dealing with Iranians had always left him a little flat. They were too alien. These were his own people. He could relate to them. He could picture himself in just this same pose in some rich woman's house in Arroyo Hondo. This was worth dying for, and he thanked Padre Lazaro for making it possible. If the man wanted to be a president, or a god, Luis would die trying to make him one, as long as he could do this while he lived.

The woman had finished by now, and Luis let her go to the bathroom to throw up. When she returned, he took her into the bedroom they would share for the coming days, and he explained to her just what was expected of her, both by the movement and by himself.

†

Lafeur had been more than a little surprised when his trace cable came back from Washington identifying his randomly selected Palestinian as none other than a contact of the Hizballah after all. He had fabricated this story on the spur of the moment for Quiroga's benefit, but it had proved largely accurate. The headquarters trace, however, was more specific. The man was something of a grey arms merchant, rather a darker shade of grey than even that unscrupulous bunch normally included. His specialty had been supplying arms for various terrorist and guerrilla groups around the world. He had been behind the shipment of American-made weapons from Vietnam to the FMLN in El Salvador in the early 1980's. He also purchased weapons around Europe which had a habit of turning up in the aftermath of terrorist incidents. Since the collapse of the Warsaw Pact, he had been very active in Eastern Europe buying up blocks of everything from small arms to tanks and jet aircraft for resale to poor but belligerent Third World nations at discount prices. Most recently, however, the man had been reported in Iran, doing no one knew just what.

Lafeur passed this information on to Quiroga at their next meeting. What Quiroga had had in return was equally interesting. Arce had followed the third man from the meeting with Pablo Baca and had finally been able to identify him as Angel Santander. Santander was essentially unknown in Dominican police files, but he had turned up in Lafeur's files as being among a group of leftists who had gone to Nicaragua in the early 1980's and who may have had paramilitary training in Cuba. It had been reported that this group had left Nicaragua as long ago as 1985. A CIA contact in the new Nicaraguan government had provided information that at least some of these Dominicans had gone to Iran. Nothing further had been heard of them. "This Santander character is also very shrewd about detecting surveillance," Quiroga had reported. "He does things that, if you sat down and analyzed them, seem entirely normal, a regular businessman going about his daily routine and stopping for occasional errands, but when you stand back from it, every move seems calculated to give him a chance to check what's around him. What's more, I can't really say what he does for a living, although he seems to have plenty of money, drives a nice car, rent paid up three months in advance, in cash. Yet you don't actually see him do anything. Not that that's all that strange in this country, but it just looks funny to me."

"How about his other contacts?" Lafeur asked.

"Well, apart from several leading MIR types like Baca, he only meets with other Dominicans whom we can't identify either. The strange thing is that once, in a cafe, Arce got close enough to overhear the conversation he was having with some woman, and they weren't speaking either Spanish or English. Arce said it sounded weird, like Arabic or Russian or some other language he'd never even heard spoken before."

"What else did you learn about the Palestinian?"

"He left the country about an hour ago for one thing," Quiroga continued. "I checked his alleged company's records with customs, and found that they had brought in a shipment of something, claimed it was several refrigerators, about a week ago. That went through customs so fast that you know he had to have paid someone off. There's another shipment, a bigger one, coming in later this month, supposed to be twenty more refrigerators. I've got a friend down at the port keeping an eye out for it. With luck we might be able to get a peek at it unless you want to tip the Dominican authorities and let them have it."

Lafeur didn't really want to bring the Dominicans in on this. If it turned out to be nothing, he'd look like a fool, and if there really was some sort of connection between the MIR, this Palestinian gun runner, and some other mysterious Dominican radicals with Iran, he kind of wanted to get all of the credit himself. "No, let's just see what we can find out first. After all, maybe they really are refrigerators."

THREE

✝

Padre Lazaro stood on the balcony of a small apartment sipping a bottle of mineral water. Melgarejo stood next to him, nervously fingering the railing with one hand and rubbing the other back and forth across his fat stomach. Lazaro noticed that the role of a true revolutionary seemed to have an unwelcome gastric effect on his brother in arms.

They were overlooking a spot where Avenida 27 de Febrero emerged from the jumble of shabby stores and offices of the downtown area, swung around a gentle bend, and spread out into the six-lane divided boulevard which was the main east-west axis of the city. The avenue led straight from the lower class districts into the costly commercial sector of town where most of the government ministries were located, and this was the traditional route for marches by the workers. This was the first point on the avenue which offered the police room to maneuver, and the bend in the road offered an element of surprise when the marchers discovered the police barricades. Even more important, because the police would have respectable middle class residents behind them, rather than potentially hostile slum dwellers, this was the place usually chosen by the police to stop a demonstration.

The protest itself had started spontaneously, the best kind to Lazaro's way of thinking. An elderly blind woman had won over $100,000 in the state-run lottery, and her extended family, along with a mob from her squalid neighborhood had accompanied her to the lottery office to collect. There had been a good deal of hemming and hawing at the lottery office, since there really wasn't any money in their coffers. When the embarrassed officials tried to escort the lady and her followers to the door, her strapping young son had slugged one of them. A security guard for the building had taken it upon himself to step in, cutting the young man in half with a blast from his shotgun. This, in turn, had set off a melee in which over thirty people had been injured and several killed. All of this had been captured on national television.

Upon Lazaro's advice, Melgarejo had finally been persuaded to send some "organizers" to the lady's neighborhood. The result was the protest march, ostensibly the funeral cortege for the son, which was now forming some blocks away. The police had heard of the plans, since Angel Santander had called them anonymously with the information. The police were unloading sawhorses from a truck to block the street, and platoons of other ragged-looking policemen in an odd array of uniforms, some with helmets and some without, were forming up in the grassy space which divided the boulevard. All of the policemen, however, were equipped with batons about three feet long, and some were swinging them, just to get the feel.

Angel came out of the apartment's kitchen bringing a mixed drink for Melgarejo. "It shouldn't be long now," he said.

"I'm not at all sure this is a wise move, Padre," Melgarejo said in a low voice, carefully avoiding looking directly into Lazaro's eyes. "The police are already onto us, and we haven't had time to train our people yet. I really think taking any steps this year is rushing things too much."

Angel's face was a mask of neutrality, but Lazaro could read the disdain in his eyes. Lazaro walked over to the larger man and put a comforting hand on his shoulder.

"Trust me, Emilio," Lazaro said, turning Melgarejo and forcing him to look him in the face. "If we don't take some step to bring our movement to people's attention, we will never be ready. We have spent the past two weeks giving refresher training to your people, and the word I have received is that they are really quite good. That gives us forty men and women. The weapons for the first phase are here and have been distributed. We have also begun training another twenty of your young men, and they will be able to support today's work. Then, you must not overlook the fact that there will be a crowd of a thousand or more angry people out there on our side, even if they aren't actually taking our orders."

Melgarejo shook his head uncertainly. "It's just that, if the police react quickly, we could be crushed before we're strong enough to defend ourselves."

Lazaro smiled warmly. "Just look at those policemen down there," he said waving his hand toward the avenue. After their initial formation, about half of the police had drifted off to nearby stores and coffee shops to get refreshments. Others were sprawled under the shade of the trees or playing slap and tickle among themselves. There were no officers in sight. They had retired to several sedans parked half a block farther back, with the engines running for the air conditioning.

"Can you say you're really afraid of those clowns?" he asked.

"There are other police who are better," Melgarejo stammered. "What about the Cascos Negros?"

"Even if they come," Lazaro said soothingly, "they won't be expecting what we have in store for them, and my people will go through them like a hot knife through butter. We have fought far tougher men and won."

Melgarejo said nothing more. He just pulled at his drink and frowned down on the scene. In the distance, one could hear the rhythmic chanting, still unintelligible, of the marching crowd and the steady thumping of their feet on the hot pavement. The policemen began to rouse themselves from the grass and to scuttle back to their positions from the shops nearby, some still taking a last swig from a can of soft drink. Reluctantly, the doors of the officers' cars opened, and one or two of them leisurely sauntered over to where the ragged lines of police were forming.

Luis was walking along the right edge of the street, keeping pace with Pablo Baca, who was on the opposite side. They were about fifteen yards behind the leaders of the march, and spread out between them were six other santistas and two of the paramilitary miristas. Each of them carried either a plastic shopping bag or small workman's satchel slung over his shoulder. Luis estimated that there were between one and two thousand people in the column thus far, and more were joining at every intersection. He was aware that many were probably ignorant of the purpose of the march and were merely going along out of curiosity, but that was all right with him. What they wanted right now were simple numbers, solid mass. He figured they had another three hundred yards to go until they reached the police barricades.

Over a block behind them Diana led another small group of santistas along with all twenty of the new MIR trainees. This would be their baptism of fire. Diana's job would be to herd as much of the crowd as possible back into the center of the action after Luis and Pablo had kicked things off. The demonstrators would be like sheep, and Diana and her troops would be the sheep dogs, or the Judas goats, she thought.

The column was led by a group of MIR political workers, one of whom was pushing the old lady lottery winner in a wheelchair, since she had been injured in the scuffle at the lottery headquarters. Behind them came a coffin borne on the shoulders of six of the taller demonstrators. Actually, the woman's son had been buried the day before, since bodies did not keep well in the humid atmosphere, and the coffin was only symbolic, but this was all the better, since a loaded coffin would certainly have become a burden. Their banners called for "accountability" for the missing lottery funds and prosecution of the guilty parties. The marchers were mostly young people, with a smattering of rollicking children and a few slow-moving older folks. The mood was generally pacific, with rather muted replies to the chants of the MIR agitators over their crackly bullhorns. A few veteran demonstrators, those from the more belligerent labor unions in particular, carried flimsy cardboard signs fastened to stout wooden handles, which could rapidly be transformed into weapons in any confrontation with the police. A number of the men also carried the ever-present machete hanging loosely from their belts.

The head of the column finally swung around the bend and came within sight of the police barricades, which were backed by four rough squares of policemen, probably a hundred men total. Progress slowed and then ground to a halt fifty yards in front of the first barrier, but the body of the column continued to advance, pressing the leaders forward and massing the people tighter and tighter. Insults were shouted from the crowd. One police officer, standing on the hood of a jeep, tried to make himself heard over the chanting, probably telling everyone to return peacefully to their homes. He didn't have much effect.

There was the sound of breaking glass which rang out over all the other noise. Again and again, unidentified individuals in the crowd hurled stones at the windows of shops or homes along the street where the owners had not been fast enough to get their steel shutters down. The police moved closer to their barricade, and the crowd involuntarily recoiled, but the marchers still coming from behind inexorably pushed them closer together.

Suddenly, a lone hunk of brick arched out from the middle of the crowd and struck the pavement next to a formation of policemen. It was followed by a hail of stones and bricks and one or two molotov cocktails which burst into flame on the sidewalk. The police had no shields or other protection, and more out of self-defense than in response to any order, they fired a volley of tear gas canisters and charged the crowd. There were some scattered screams, and a few people split off down narrow side streets to escape, but the bulk of the mob wasn't cowed. The signs were torn from their staffs, and a wild melee ensued with sticks, stones, and fists arrayed against the police batons and tear gas guns.

From their vantage point, Lazaro, Angel, and Melgarejo saw the thin line of gray-clad policemen crash into the brightly colored mob. The column was pushed back a few yards, but then the sheer weight of numbers began to tell. From two blocks away, Lazaro could hear the crunch of wood on bone and the terrifying roar as the policemen were gradually pushed back. Another squad or two of police rushed in, but the momentum was with the demonstrators now. Here and there a single policeman would break and run, or would go down in a flurry of fists as the crowd swarmed over him. Melgarejo was half crouching down behind the railing of the balcony, wiping his eyes furiously as the first wisps of tear gas wafted up to their level.

From somewhere behind the police line, a steady throbbing sound emerged and began to dominate the scene. The fighting and yelling along the front line tapered off for a moment as both policemen and demonstrators paused to listen, trying to locate and identify the sound. At that moment, from a side street emerged the head of a neatly formed column of uniformed men, with guidons waving, black helmets shining in the sunlight. They jogged forward in time to whistle blasts and slapped their batons into their hands rhythmically as their left feet hit the ground. They came in a column of eight and split into two columns, four abreast, swinging smoothly into line, perpendicular to the avenue, and came to a halt with a shouted command which they echoed, their voices reverberating off the neighboring buildings.

The combatants had frozen as they stood, watching the maneuvers of the approaching Cascos Negros. The policemen came to their senses first and quickly broke contact with the demonstrators and ran for the protection of the new line. Several truckloads of regular police had also pulled up, and they now formed up with the more than 200 Cascos Negros and the survivors of the initial battle to form a solid phalanx across the width of the avenue.

The Cascos Negros were not all equipped the same. Half of the men were provided with long batons with a short additional piece inserted perpendicularly just above the handle by which the weapon could also be held, permitting the bearer to twirl the club or to hold it parallel to the forearm to help deflect a blow. They also had tall clear plastic shields and face masks on their helmets. Every other man in the line, had no shield or club but was armed with a massive looking shotgun tipped with a long, wicked bayonet. They held out these in front of them with the bayonet just above the horizontal, the butt braced against the hip. In this way they lunged forward progressively, protected by the shield bearers on either side from thrown rocks, while their bayonets remorselessly advanced, driving the crowd back before them. The regular police units scattered around the two Cascos Negros companies would cover their flanks and provide volleys of tear gas canisters fired over their heads into the crowd.

Colonel Antonio Palacios, commander of the Cascos Negros, proudly watched his men advance, grunting loudly with each lunge and step. He could see the crowd wavering already. A few rocks continued to sail overhead, but with little spirit, and they dropped harmlessly to the ground. From his training and experience, he knew that his task was to get the crowd moving the way he wanted, then to split it up down one side street after another. This would give the faint hearted the chance to run off, and deprive the mob of the courage which comes from the anonymity of the group. As the group became smaller, each participant felt himself stand out more and more, and would eventually break and run. He held back half a dozen six-man "assault squads" whose job was to rush out ahead of the advancing line and grab any apparent leaders in the mob who would be identified by spotters he had placed atop buildings nearby with binoculars and radios. When the mob was thus decapitated, it would only remain to mop up the remains. His tactics were flawless and had worked a dozen times in as many months. He took considerable pride that, while the police and army were often reduced to opening fire on disorderly crowds, his Cascos Negros had not been accused of a single death since he had been in command, although they had cracked more than a few heads and ribs. This job looked no tougher than any other.

The police line advanced slowly, for the psychological effect, allowing the mob time to think things over and run away. The crowd dropped back step by step with them, keeping a margin of about twenty yards between them. Occasionally a young buck would stand out into the margin and bare his chest at the policemen or shout some insult, but he would eventually return to the crowd, his honor satisfied, well before the points of the bayonets reached him. Most of the people had covered their lower faces with handkerchiefs soaked in water or vinegar to cut the effect of the tear gas, but all were coughing, eyes red and streaming.

The police had now rounded the bend, compressing the crowd back down the narrower portion of the avenue whence it had come. They advanced another twenty yards, fifty, a hundred, the crowd always moving ahead of them but not yet beginning to break up. At a signal from Baca, one of the MIR agitators stepped out into the no-man's-land between the two bodies and began to chant through his bull horn. At the same time a huge dump truck rolled precipitously from a side street onto the avenue about 200 yards ahead of the police line, scattering demonstrators in its path. It stopped, blocking most of the road and trapping the bulk of the crowd between it and the police.

One of the "assault squads" rushed through a gap in the police line at the sound of a shrill whistle, heading for the mirista with the bull horn. He hurled the device at them and several young men charged forward to help defend him. A wild fight broke out and another squad of Cascos Negros rushed ahead as their line continued to progress slowly. Only six or eight demonstrators were now struggling with a dozen policemen, and several had already been beaten to the ground. The front edge of the crowd undulated for a moment and then resumed its rearward movement.

Luis, Baca, and their supporters with the various bags now moved up to the front line of the crowd. Luis carefully pulled a small cylindrical object from his pocket and held it up. It was a pocket-sized air horn which ladies sometimes carry in their purses to ward off muggers. He pressed the button, and the noise of battle was pierced by the shriek of the horn, causing the combatants to pause and look up.

At that signal, he and the others pulled Uzis from their bags and fired a long burst into the leading rank of policemen. The bullets tore through the plastic shields, flipping men over backwards, cutting off legs, and shattering skulls. Luis and his men continued firing in short bursts now, butchering the "assault squads" which had been out front. The rattle of their fire was joined by the throaty cough of an M-60 machinegun firing over their heads from the dump truck which blocked the street, cutting down still more policemen.

For a moment the policemen with shotguns or pistols were too surprised to react, but they soon began firing wildly into the crowd.

The santistas had taken cover in doorways or even behind the bodies of the dead or wounded, so most of the rounds tore into the mass of the marchers as they screamed in terror.

The resistance of the police only lasted a moment, however. After a couple of volleys, they turned and ran, Cascos Negros alongside the regular police. This was not what they had expected. They were hopelessly outgunned, and they needed time to regroup.

As soon as the retreat was on, Luis and his men stopped firing, as did the machinegunner. In the eerie silence which followed, Diana and her detachment began screaming at those around them that the police were murderers, that they were on the run, and that the people should go in for the kill. Diana's group had formed a long line across the street and, aided by the body of the dump truck, had prevented several hundred of the marchers from escaping. They now succeeded in turning these marchers around and spurring them into a headlong charge after the fleeing policemen.

The screams of the crowd were now of pure rage as first a few, then a dozen, then almost all of the men and women began to run pell mell over the sprawled bodies in the street. Some of those with clubs or machetes paused to finish off a wounded policeman or merely to mutilate a corpse. Others stooped to pick up a shotgun or pistol and then continued the chase, firing wildly in the air.

Luis, Pablo, Diana, and their people didn't follow. There was no need. The twenty trainees did jog along behind the crowd, mostly to get the experience of a little more combat, but the job of the santistas was over. Luis looked to a light head wound one of the women fighters had received, and then he and the others split up and melted into the working class neighborhood. Just before leaving the area, however, Luis took care to toss his Uzi down next to the body of one of the demonstrators.

Colonel Palacios heard the firing before he had reached the bend in the avenue. At first he was furious and rushed forward to find out what policeman had begun the shooting. Suddenly it occurred to him that this was automatic weapons fire, and that none of his men had any automatic weapons. He skidded to a halt, and then saw the first uniformed refugees running for their lives. The first ones he saw were regular policemen in their sloppy gray uniforms, which didn't surprise him, but then he saw some of his own men, in their neat olive green uniforms, come racing toward him, some without their weapons or helmets, some with bloody foreheads or arms.

He reached out and grabbed one of his sergeants as he came tearing by. He held the hysterical man by his shoulders and shook him hard.

"Machineguns," the man spluttered. "They cut us down with machineguns. I don't know how many dead."

"Shit!" was all Palacios could say. He continued to hold the sergeant while the man's breathing slowed. "Try and gather some of our men by the trucks back there. We'll have a hundred yards of open space and mow them down as they come across." The sergeant nodded, then saluted raggedly.

Palacios drew his own gun and gradually began walking backwards himself, pulling together a small knot of his men. The first of the rioters, not demonstrators any more, came screaming around the bend, waving a bloody machete over his head. Palacios took a two-handed grip and put two rounds through the man's chest at forty yards. Another man came running, then more, and Palacios dropped back to where several police trucks were parked at angles across the broad part of the avenue and dividing strip.

He had about fifty men with him, all Cascos Negros, the other policemen having long since headed for home and different careers. They had a dozen shotguns, the remainder were armed only with automatic pistols. He quickly spread them out, using the trucks for cover, while one of the continued to pump tear gas canisters at the advancing mob, filling the area with drifting curtains of bluish white smoke.

"Hold your fire until I give the order," Palacios shouted to his men. "Then pick your shots, two rounds to a target for the pistols. Aim low . . ." He paused for a moment. ". . . and shoot to kill." Several men turned to look at him, but their expressions were not of disapproval or even fear, just grim determination.

The rioters came roaring over the wreckage of the first skirmish, the broken bottles, burning trash cans, and dead bodies. Palacios had a long silver whistle in his mouth, both of his hands clasped on his pistol. He waited until they were fifty yards away, then forty, thirty, twenty. He let out a series of shrill blasts on the whistle, at the same time firing at the chest of an immense, shirtless man, who was charging at him with a two-by-four raised over his head. The man crumpled to the ground, and the entire line erupted with the flash of the shotguns and the crackle of rapid pistol fire.

The first wave of rioters went down in an instant, but others now had weapons and began to blaze away at the policemen. The sergeant Palacios had stopped first, who had been standing at his side next to a truck, staggered backwards, his face torn away by a charge of buckshot. His scream turned to a gurgle, and he splayed on the ground. Palacios emptied one clip, ejected it, and loaded another in one swift motion.

"Go for the men with the guns," he screamed, picking off a man who was shooting a pistol from behind the false cover of a low bush.

Through the tear gas and the smoke from burning cars and piles of rubbish, Palacios could hardly see fifty yards ahead of him, but he noticed the fire slackening from his men. He looked up from the sights of his own weapon and saw that there was not a person left standing in the open area before him. He could still hear shouting, banging, and the breaking of glass coming from the poorer neighborhoods beyond the veil of smoke, but that wasn't his problem now. He had stopped the wild assault by the blood-crazed rioters. It would remain to someone else to try to pacify the eastern half of the city now.

Without holstering his sidearm, he wearily led his men forward in a rough skirmish line to pick up any weapons left lying around, and to count the dead. In the distance he could hear ambulance sirens growing steadily louder, but he could see that for those policemen who had gone down where the rioters could get at them, ambulances would not be necessary. He wiped tears from his eyes which were not due solely to the pockets of tear gas still floating over the battlefield.

Melgarejo was grasping the railing of the balcony with both hands, crouching down as low as he could, his knuckles white, and his eyes bulging out of his head. He remained in this position long after the last shot had been fired. Lazaro and Angel looked at each other without speaking, then Lazaro went forward and took the larger man by the shoulders.

"Everything went perfectly, Emilio," he said in a quiet voice. "You will see. Starting tomorrow we will have more recruits than we know what to do with, and there will be hundreds of young men out in the streets fighting the government on their own as well, which will divert attention from us."

"I-I've never seen anything like that," Melgarejo said without moving or taking his eyes from the street below.

Lazaro forcibly spun the man around, revealing the raw strength in his wiry arms, and he stared in his eyes. For a moment he abandoned his soothing tone and let his voice take on an icy edge. "Well, you had better get used to it, because this is what a revolution looks like." The fat man just stared at Lazaro, his mouth hanging dumbly open.

"Now we will wait for the reaction of the government, which will certainly not be long in coming," Lazaro continued.

"But they will know that the MIR was involved. So many of our political people were seen down on the street. Our name was on the banners. They will know just where to come."

"No they won't, because you aren't there any more," Lazaro said, smiling. Melgarejo just cocked his head with a confused look on his face. "Starting today the MIR is an underground party, just like the Guerra Santa which is its strong sword arm. When the police hit your old headquarters, they will find nothing but the old political tracts you used to spend your time printing and distributing. When they look for your people they will only find a handful of the most public and junior ones. We have already taken steps to secure the key members of your party, and we have prepared a brand new headquarters for you in what will become a virtual fortress of the revolution."

"Where could that be that the army can't just walk in and crush us?"

"They won't be able to walk in because they won't know where it is, but even if they did, they would have more trouble getting to us than the Nazis did getting into Stalingrad." Lazaro shook his head. "All of your years as a 'revolutionary' and you have never learned to value the fighting qualities of the common man. You haven't taken the time to analyze the weakness of this feeble military machine which supports the oppressor government. Today we gave them their first push, just a taste of what's to come. They will react and we will turn and hit them harder than ever. They will react again, and we will increase the violence to levels they never dreamed of, and you will see these fat generals stuffing their Mercedes with suitcases full of money and heading for the airport before the year's end."

"But what if you're wrong?" Melgarejo whimpered. "Remember, you've been out of the country for years. Maybe you don't understand how this system has been able to survive for so long."

Lazaro dropped his quiet tone again and fairly screamed at the quivering old man. "They've survived because no one had the balls to challenge them before." Even Angel raised his eyebrows. It was the closest he had heard Lazaro come to swearing in over a decade. "Well, *we've* got the balls, and if I'm wrong, I'm ready to die for it. There isn't any more a man can do in this world."

When Melgarejo failed to respond, Lazaro warmly put his arm around the man's flabby shoulders and hugged him. "But don't worry about that. We are winning now, and we'll keep winning. I think you'll agree when you see the new headquarters we've prepared for you."

†

The television news was just starting, about ten minutes later than the scheduled time, as usual. Featherstone had arranged for a large TV to be set up in his office. The heads of the political, CIA, and Defense Attache's Office (DAO) were seated around the room, along with Stileforth and Rambling, who happened to occupy the honorary position of Post Security Officer.

There had been a TV film crew on the scene of the march, and there was some footage of the initial skirmish between the police and the demonstrators. It was obvious that the newscaster was unused to dealing with serious news stories on short notice. After a few introductory words, he simply stopped talking and let the video speak for itself. The scene cut to a segment showing the Cascos Negros driving the marchers out of sight. The picture on the screen then bounced wildly, showing first blue sky, then a piece of littered ground, but one could clearly hear the clamor of automatic fire close at hand. The cameraman had apparently left his unit on while he prepared to run for it, and there was a brief but clear view of a street cluttered with more than a dozen bodies. Several policemen were seen running toward the camera, but two of them were cut down in a matter of seconds. Beyond the bodies, one could make out eight or nine dark figures, crouching, firing in the direction of the camera. There was a scream, and the camera jerked skyward, and the picture settled into a view of a patch of sky with the corner of a roof jutting in at a crazy angle.

The video clip ended, and the commentator came back on, announcing grimly that viewers had just seen the last footage shot by the late Channel 5 cameraman Jose Arguedas. The official death toll was 39 policemen killed and another eight wounded. The government had announced that more than twenty of the demonstrators had also been killed, but unofficial sources claimed that several hundred had actually died, and local hospitals were swamped with gunshot victims, many of whom were in serious condition. A call had been put out by the Red Cross for blood donors. The government had declared a midnight to dawn curfew for the downtown area where looting was reportedly continuing.

"It was a fucking ambush!" Colonel Miller announced, shaking his head gravely. "Those men firing weren't just local thugs. That was a regular infantry urban street fighting deployment if I've ever seen one. There are some very bad people wandering around out there gentlemen."

"I'm frankly a little surprised that the government let this candid a report on the air," Jim Vernon, the political counsellor said. "My guess is that they're in a state of shock. Once that wears off, you'll start to hear all sorts of disclaimers, downgrading the number of killed on both sides, blaming it on foreign agitators, Chinese communists, who knows what."

"It's just what we should have expected," Stileforth said, his arms crossed and his legs entwined tightly as he sat far back in one of the Ambassador's wing chairs. "At least when Trujillo was running the country, he knew how to keep the rabble in line. He might have stolen the country blind, but at least you could walk the streets."

Featherstone just looked over the tops of his glasses at Stileforth without commenting. He had been jotting down notes on a yellow legal pad on his desk during the broadcast. "One thing strikes me as odd," he said. "Usually, when there's some kind of combat, you have 'x' number of killed, and several times as many wounded. Here we have nearly 40 cops killed and just a few wounded. What does that mean?"

"It means you have some very pissed off folks out there," Lafeur said. "It means that they slaughtered the wounded policemen, and the only ones who lived were the ones who could still run away. Poverty is nothing new in this country, but Dane's right in one sense. Under Trujillo, and even for years after, there were poor people, but the big man, whether Trujillo or old Balaguer, took pains to see that the worst off people got some of the pie. The middle class took it on the chin in that they paid their taxes while the poor got a free ride and the rich got all the graft, but the middle class isn't about to overthrow the regime. The new politicians don't do any of the old barnstorming. They're taking *all* of the money, and don't give any of it back to buy off the poor. I can remember when you would never have a power outage if you lived next door to a minister or if you lived in a slum. Now it's only the minister whose lights work. This lottery thing is just the last straw, taking away that faint hope that by a stroke of luck the poor slobs can climb up out of the gutter. That's what set them off."

"Let it be duly noted," announced Stileforth sarcastically, "that the legendary CIA saw this one coming too."

Featherstone raised his hand. "History is a hobby of mine, but what we need to know now is what's going to happen next. Any ideas?"

"Five'll get you twenty that we're going to see a lot more blood before this cools down," Miller said. "In the past, the government has sometimes turned attention away from itself by provoking what you might call pogroms against the Haitian immigrants. I don't think that'll work this time. Unless I miss my bet, the police and army will do some serious lead slinging. If they do a 'good' enough job, they'll scare the shit out of people, and things will calm down. If they don't, we're in for a long hot summer."

Lafeur and Vernon nodded in agreement.

"I'm not really trained to be a security officer in a situation like this," Rambling said, raising his hand timidly. "I noticed there's a course starting at the Foreign Service Institute next week in 'Handling Crisis Situations,' and I think it would be worthwhile for me to take . . . in view of the circumstances."

Featherstone looked over the tops of his glasses again, and everyone else in the room took an intense interest in either the ceiling or the rug. "Thank you, Peter. I'll keep that in mind, but for the time being I think we should make do." He let out a long sigh and looked over his notes. "I know there haven't been any indications yet that any of this has anti-American implications, but you all know that it is never far below the surface when times get tough." He turned to Vernon, whom he knew had three children at the American School. "Jim, I'd like you to do an informal survey of the security procedures out at the school. Who's allowed on the grounds, what sort of guard force they have, that sort of thing. I don't want anything nasty happening out there."

Vernon nodded emphatically. "Not to appear alarmist, Mr. Ambassador, but I'd go so far as to suggest that we circulate word unofficially among the American employees and throughout the American community that this would be a good time to keep the kids home from school and off the streets for a few days, at least until we see just how far things go."

Featherstone leaned back in his chair, making a little tent with his fingers and balancing his thumbs on his chin. "I know that the kneejerk bureaucratic reaction at times like this is to avoid panic at all costs, and thereby to avoid doing anything until after it's too late. However, in this case I agree. We just don't have any concept of the scope of this problem, and I think a little low-key warning might spare us all a lot of heartache later on. Do it."

Featherstone then turned back to Lafeur. "This is all so out of character for the Dominicans. Do your sources have any inkling as to what's so different now or whether anyone in particular is behind all this?"

Lafeur leaned forward in his chair, spreading his beefy arms. "Other than what I already mentioned, the regular political sources don't have much to contribute. They're as much out of the loop as we are. I had another source out cruising the poor neighborhoods, and what he's seen points to the MIR as having a whole new life. There's also a lot of fresh graffiti on the walls either calling for a "holy war" or about some group that calls themselves that. I'm not sure whether that's part of the MIR, a statement of their policy, or what, but it's definitely something new. You know that the police picked up one of the Uzis used in the ambush, and we're running traces on the serial number now. Unfortunately, those guns can be found all over the world, and this particular one is rather old, so it could have been obtained anywhere. The initial reporting, though, is that *all* of the attackers had Uzis, which implies some kind of central organization, not some slap-dash operation. I'll know more by tomorrow."

"But the MIR is a joke," Vernon chimed in. "They couldn't pull more than a thousand votes in an election, and all of their revolutionary ideology up til now has been pure talk."

"The 'up 'til now' part might just be it," Lafeur continued. "Old Melgarejo still runs things, but maybe some young turks are taking over. Then again, maybe some other group is doing it all and putting the MIR out as a stalking horse. I just can't tell yet."

"Thank you, Claude," Featherstone said wearily. "Well, I think we're going to be very busy for the next few days, so let's get to work."

As the others rose to leave, Featherstone pressed the buzzer on his desk and asked Maripaz to step into his office. He would have to cut out some of the less important appointments for the rest of the week and try to get meetings with more of the government people. When she entered, Featherstone noticed that she did not smile. He had begun to detect a lack of attention to her normally immaculate appearance. He supposed that even good secretaries catch cold once in awhile. As he dictated his schedule for the next several days, he didn't notice the tear which fell on her notepad, smearing the writing.

†

When Lafeur went to meet with Quiroga that evening, the latter had the door of the apartment open before Lafeur was halfway up the stairs. Ordinarily, Quiroga was quite a dapper fellow, his clothes always neatly pressed, even in the soggy humidity of the city, his hair always slicked back, Rudolf Valentino style, and a cloud of "Brut" surrounding him wherever he went. Now, however, he had obviously not shaven since the day before, his shirt was stained with sweat, and he had a wild look about his eyes.

"I've just come from police headquarters," he said even before Lafeur could get the door closed. "It was a massacre, and the police are ready to do one of their own."

Lafeur forced Quiroga to sit down and took a couple of beers out of the refrigerator, without taking his eyes off the slender man twitching nervously in his chair. He knew that Quiroga undoubtedly would have lost friends in the riots, and he had no doubt that anything that Quiroga told him would be colored in favor of the police view, but he was Lafeur's only pair of eyes inside the police, and he was also a trained observer. With a little care, Lafeur should be able to piece together an accurate picture from him.

"Let's start from the beginning," he said quietly, handing Quiroga a beer. "How accurate are the numbers of dead we're hearing on the news?"

"That's bullshit, as usual," Quiroga spat. "It looks like there were over sixty killed from the Cascos Negros alone, and maybe twenty or thirty other cops. Colonel Palacios had to be physically held down to keep him from going down to the Ozama and burning the place out himself. I can get you a list of the names, before it disappears, if you don't believe me." Lafeur looked away from Quiroga for a moment so that the man couldn't read quite so clearly in his eyes that this was just the case.

"Listen," Quiroga went on. "The government can't hope to hide the fact that a lot of policemen were killed, and keeping that number large will tend to justify any reaction that the police decide to undertake. But if they let on to the true extent of the massacre, the police are going to look pretty limp, and the bad guys will get a propaganda windfall."

"How about civilians?" Lafeur fully expected Quiroga to downgrade the number of innocent deaths.

"Nobody knows for certain. The police, obviously, weren't about to go into the poor neighborhoods and look for people to help, but I figure close to fifty dead and maybe twice as many wounded." Lafeur raised his eyebrows. This was already more than double the official government figure. Quiroga saw his quizzical look. "Listen, if anything, the police are embarrassed that they didn't kill more. Almost all of the dead civilians got it *after* the ambush, when Palacios kept the mob bottled up in the workers' districts. The truth is that the police were caught flat-footed, and I'd be willing to bet a lot of money they didn't get even one of the guys with the guns who opened up on them, just a few idiots who got caught in the crossfire and some others who got juiced up to settle old scores with the police after things got going."

"And do the police have any information about who was behind this?"

Quiroga just squinted his eyes and cocked his head as if to ask, are you kidding? "Those idiots don't know shit. All they can see is that the MIR had some signs out during the march and that there is a lot of graffiti about this 'holy war' stuff." He paused for a moment. "They don't know anything . . . but *I* do."

Lafeur leaned closer, and Quiroga continued. "I just met with Arce. He had been following the mystery man, Santander just before the march got started, and he was led to an apartment building at the edge of the commercial district, just off Avenida 27 de Febrero."

"Where the riot started," Lafeur interjected.

"What a coincidence, huh? Well, he found himself a shady tree where he could watch the entrance and he was just waiting there when whom should he see come out onto the balcony of one of the apartments but Santander, in the company of Melgarejo and another guy. They were just standing there, looking out over the city, and Arce was just sitting there eating an orange when all hell broke loose with the riot. Arce had to bug out of there, because he was sitting almost in the middle of the battlefield, but it was obvious, in hindsight, that those men were there waiting and watching the riot just like they were in a reviewing stand."

"So it *was* the MIR that masterminded it," Lafeur said. "I always thought of Melgarejo as an old fart who didn't have the balls to do more than talk. I guess I was wrong."

"I don't think so. Arce was able to work his way back to the building as soon as the shooting stopped, and he caught the group just as they were leaving. Santander and this other guy practically had to carry Melgarejo to his car, which is no little job, by the way," he added, smiling. "This new guy was giving all the orders, even to Melgarejo. I think we've definitely got a new team in the league. What's more, I've got a line on who they might be."

"Well?" said Lafeur impatiently as Quiroga downed the rest of his beer.

"Arce thought he recognized the new guy. He couldn't put a name to it, but remember that Arce is an Ozama River kid himself. He says that the new guy looked an awful lot like this young priest he had seen around years ago, a real radical. The last time he saw the priest was when he took a bunch of young Dominicans off to fight in Nicaragua. That would have been the group Santander was in."

"So?" asked Lafeur.

"Well, this is just my own speculation, mind you, but we have this radical priest show up, and the MIR gets a new lease on life all of a sudden. 'Holy war,' get it? Then add to that the story that this group of Dominicans might have gone from Nicaragua to the Middle East. What do the Arabs call just about every fight they get in? Holy war, right?"

Lafeur made a grimace. It made some sense, but Quiroga was clearly stretching things. "I don't know. That liberation theology stuff is kind of out of style now, you know. The radical priests mostly dropped out of the guerrilla business years ago, and they've pretty much limited themselves to talking up the success of the Cuban revolution and trying to organize labor unions, peasant unions, renters' unions, unemployed people's unions, anything to make life difficult for any government, that didn't happen to be communist. What with the collapse of the Sovs in

Eastern Europe, the fall of the Sandinistas, and all that, they've pretty much dropped off the screen."

"No, I don't think it's a rehash of the old stuff. This is something new. I don't know why, but this whole thing smells to me more like something out of Beirut than El Salvador. It's something really new. I can't explain it. It's just a hunch." Quiroga slouched back in his chair, turning out the palms of his hands.

Lafeur pressed his knuckles against his lips and thought for a moment. He hadn't known Quiroga that long, but he was coming to have an increasing respect for the man's hunches.

"So, anyway," Lafeur continued. "What's next?"

"I don't know," Quiroga said flatly. Lafeur looked into his eyes and knew that he was lying. He had come across this before in his career. A military man might tell you all sorts of things about other people's coup plans, but not about his own. A politician would tell you about the corruption in other parties, but not about what he was up to. This was a matter of "them against us," and, in this situation, Lafeur didn't count as one of "us." If Quiroga told Lafeur, Lafeur would have to tell someone else, and something would have to be done. So there was no point in pushing this any further.

†

Maripaz could tell that Luis had been involved in the street fighting that day. He had been practically living in her apartment since that first night, always arriving shortly after her mother had gone home, and staying until just before dawn. Normally, he would first debrief her on all of the personnel in the embassy, their personal habits, their work, everything. She suspected that he had most of this information and was merely using it to check her, and she didn't try to hide anything. He would then go over the copy she made of the ambassador's schedule, noting any changes for the coming week. Then he would put away his notebooks and take her into the bedroom. He always made her do something different, something humiliating, sometimes several times a night. She wondered when he ever slept.

But tonight he had burst into the apartment like a wild man. He had simply stuffed the copy of the schedule into his small leather attache case without looking at it. He was covered with sweat and panting with energy and excitement. His eyes were red, as if he had been crying, but she found it hard to believe that this man ever cried like normal people do. He had taken her right there in the living room, in front of the baby. That was the night he began to talk to her.

After he was through, he took her to bed and began to talk about Padre Lazaro and their movement. He had talked about the "revolution" before, but only in general terms. She had supposed that he was trying to convert her, but had no idea of how to go about it. He had only talked about the sorrow of the poor and the power of the wealthy and how things were going to be so much better *after*. She imagined that even he realized how hollow all this sounded coming from a man so brutally doing to her what he claimed the "imperialists" were doing to the rest of the world.

But this night was different. He wasn't so much talking to her as he was talking to himself with her simply a mute witness. He terrified her with endless stories of the battles he and his people had fought in Iran and their merciless persecution of anyone the "Sepah" identified as enemies. He told her about how Padre Lazaro had a gift for inspiring people with the spirit of God so that a young man would strap explosives to his body and then hurl himself under the treads of an Iraqi tank with a smile on his face. He said that Padre Lazaro had found the formula for convincing Christians of what the Moslems had known for centuries; that someone who sacrifices himself in the service of God would receive an everlasting reward and, just as importantly, that Padre Lazaro was the legitimate messenger of God's will.

He told her all about the fight in the street. How the policemen had had such comical looks of surprise on their faces when he and his men opened fire. He giggled as he described how he had shot one man right in the mouth. She knew he was crazy, but he talked very lucidly about how this was the first encounter in what would be a total revolution. He said that it would all be over before the end of the year, with the current government and its army and police gone, the Americans gone, and even the MIR and its flabby leadership gone, all gone. She didn't understand this last part, as she had been under the impression that Padre Lazaro and the MIR were allies, but she made it a point never to ask him any questions. He could coerce her into providing information and into being his plaything, but her mind was her own, and she had no intention of sharing that with him.

She had thought about telling someone in the embassy about Luis and Padre Lazaro. She had some friends who had worked for the Americans longer than she had. There was Ramiro Escobar, the husky head of the ambassador's bodyguard detachment. She had even been out with him once or twice, although she had finally decided that he was too shallow for her. If they were planning to do something to the ambassador, his life would be in danger too. Then there was Claude Lafeur. While he had never done more than speak casually to her at the odd embassy social function, she had a feeling that he liked her, although he was evidently rather shy. It was widely rumored among the FSNs that Lafeur was the CIA station chief, since they all knew who worked in those offices in the back, so, if anyone could do something, he probably could. But in the end, the thought of Lazaro's blood chilling threats, against her, the baby, and her whole family, had kept her quiet. She liked the new ambassador very much, but she had troubles of her own and her family to protect. The Americans would have to look out for themselves.

†

At about two o'clock the next morning, a dozen men strode through the administrative offices of the Central Correctional Institute on the outskirts of Santo Domingo. The men were all wearing identical blue jogging suits and motorcycle helmets, their faces covered with mirror-like windscreens. There was no one in the offices, and the guards on both the outer and inner doors were strangely absent. The leader of the group had keys to all of the doors. The men were all armed with shotguns with folding stocks.

They moved silently up to the top level of the four-story structure and passed through the gate which led to the walkway which circled the central courtyard. The leader of the group consulted a notepad and signalled to the others to open one cell door after another. The prisoners inside were sleeping soundly, and the first few men that the intruders dragged from their bunks were too groggy to protest. They were used enough to surprise searches for hidden weapons and drugs not to make a fuss. Each prisoner was taken out and handcuffed to the railing along the courtyard side of the walkway. They looked at each other, trying to make some sense of this unusual procedure. Some of them may have figured it out, but it did them no particular good.

After eleven men had been selected, the leader stopped and nodded to his men. Each one stood behind one of the prisoners, placed his shotgun at the base of the prisoner's neck and pulled the trigger. One of the prisoners managed to let out a scream as his executioner was a little slower than the others. The other prisoners in their cells began to shout and bang on the bars. When the echoes of gunfire had died out, each of the corpses was lifted over the railing, to dangle by its hand-cuffed wrists over the courtyard below. The intruders silently filed down the stairs and out of the building.

When the bodies were "discovered" later that morning by the guards and newspeople flocked to the scene, the warden disclaimed all knowledge of the incident. It seems that the guard staff had declared a six-hour walk-out strike in protest over the government's lack of decisive action in response to the bloody killings of policemen during the riot, leaving only the tower guards on duty. Thus, no one had seen these alleged intruders enter the building. He admitted that it was certainly "strange" that none of the doors through which the killers passed appeared to have been forced, and he announced that a "full investigation" was underway. In response to reporters' questions about the identities of the victims, the warden stated that their names could not be released until their next of kin had been notified. But he could report that all of the men were members of, or had been members of the MIR at some time, although all had actually been in jail for petty crimes, rather than for political activities, he hastened to add. He also added that one of the victims had no connection with the MIR, but happened to have the same name as another prisoner who did, opining that the killers had apparently made a clerical mistake. The warden indignantly denied suggestions that the killers could have been policemen.

Just as the warden indicated that the news conference was at an end, and the reporters were pressing forward to get in one last question, and perhaps an answer that was not well thought-out, the driver of one of the news vans came running in to announce in a loud voice that there had been a flash over the radio that a car bomb had gone off in front of the MIR headquarters, destroying the building and killing two passersby and a part-time secretary at the MIR office. The tide of reporters suddenly turned, and there was a crush of men and women at the door of the warden's office as the journalists fought each other to get out and cover this new story.

At the barracks of the Cascos Negros battalion, Colonel Palacios spent the morning overseeing the disposal of a cardboard box of garbage, which he assigned one of his trusted NCOs to take out to sea in a motor launch and dump overboard. The box contained the charred remains of zippers and globs of congealed, melted plastic, the only parts of the jogging suits and motorcycle helmets which had not been totally consumed by a fire in an oil drum the night before. Into the box he dropped the keys to a small van that one of his men had "borrowed" several hours earlier. The keys were no longer necessary since the ignition and door locks which they fit no longer existed.

†

Melgarejo's face was ashen and pale as he sprawled, breathing spasmodically, across the back seat of the large Toyota sedan. Pablo Baca was wedged into the corner of the back seat that was not occupied by Melgarejo's sweaty bulk. Angel was driving, and Lazaro was twisted around in the front seat to talk directly to Melgarejo.

"I never bargained for this," Melgarejo was moaning. "In all my years as head of the party, I've never seen anything like this."

"That's because you didn't take over the party until long after Trujillo was dead," Lazaro counselled him. "The difference between an outright military dictator and the lap dogs of imperialism you have in power now is that the dictator goes after you, these limp buffoons will only bother you if you make trouble for them."

"Oh, and *you* certainly made trouble for them," Melgarejo went on, looking directly at Lazaro. "Things were fine before, but now we're a threat to them, so they're coming after us."

Lazaro would have preferred to have had this conversation in a more controlled, quiet environment where he could bring the full force of his personality into play, but Melgarejo really didn't require the full force. You need a hammer to kill a steer, but your thumb will do to squash a roach. He locked Melgarejo in his magnetic stare. The fat man seemed to shrivel the way a snail does when a child pours salt on it.

"Things were fine for *you!*" Lazaro screamed, sticking his accusing finger within an inch of Melgarejo's eye. "The time has come for you to decide whether you want to lead a revolutionary party or to cut a deal with the fat cats and get yourself a condo in Miami Beach at the expense of the workers whose children will starve or die of the simplest diseases. We are in a war now, and in a war people get killed." He paused as Melgarejo wriggled uncomfortably. He could tell that the fat man wanted to drop his eyes, but he knew that Melgarejo simply couldn't break the lock imposed on him by Lazaro's stare.

"I will only tell you this once," Lazaro said in a deeper voice. "We have reached a point already that your tragic death at the hands of the powers of evil would only provide the movement with another valuable martyr and would not hinder our long-term plans in the slightest. Is that quite clear?"

Melgarejo's eyes went wide with terror. He turned his head frantically to look at Baca, but Pablo was staring impassively at the back of Angel's head, his jaw set. Lazaro smiled inwardly. He had gauged Baca correctly. He was a doer, not a talker. He had seen combat before in the only cause which appealed to him, and he had only accepted the post of arm twister for this fat slob because nothing else seemed to offer itself. Now that there was a road open to glory, he belonged to Lazaro body and soul.

Melgarejo stared forlornly at his expensive Italian shoes. "It's just that, all those people killed . . . my people. I feel responsible for them. I don't like being in a situation where I can't protect them as I've always done."

Lazaro knew that he had won. Melgarejo didn't care about the lives and welfare of his people any more than he cared about the life and welfare of the roasted chicken he had just devoured at lunch. What he was worried about was his own life, which for the first time in his "revolutionary" career, seemed now to be in jeopardy. And it was, but not from the police.

The car travelled east along Jorge Washington Avenue, the broad street which led along the shore, otherwise known as the Malecon. They passed the luxury hotels, the Sheraton, the Jaragua, and the fancy restaurants with their spectacular views of crashing waves. They passed the tiny replica of the Washington Monument, only about fifty feet high, and turned off into the narrow streets of the old quarter of town. The car was rather large by Dominican standards, a full-sized sedan, and Angel had to bounce up on the low curb more than once to slip down some of the streets. The few pedestrians had to step into doorways as the car passed, its sideview mirrors just barely clearing the flower boxes and grillwork of the windows of the bordering houses. They finally came to a stop in a small interior courtyard, completely surrounded by three- and four-story buildings. Wires criss-crossed the courtyard overhead, hung with bright-colored clothing. The sound of tinny, conflicting radio music issued from different apartments, competing with the wailing of babies and the sound of a heated argument between two women for dominance.

"What's this?" Melgarejo asked uncertainly as he eased his bulk out of the car.

"Your new party headquarters, a clandestine one," Lazaro replied.

Melgarejo made a sour face. He had recovered some of his composure, and it was apparent that he had expected something a little more luxurious from these people who claimed to have virtually unlimited funds. They walked up an interior staircase of one of the buildings. The doors of all the apartments had heavy grills over them in addition to two or three sets of locks, a sure sign of a high crime rate neighborhood. There was a heavy odor of cooking, washing, and bathroom plumbing that did not work especially well. They climbed to the third floor of the four-story building, and Melgarejo made another face. He would not have even the relative prestige of the "penthouse" suite even in this dump.

Angel had gone ahead and opened the grill and door to one of the apartments. Melgarejo entered like the venerable squire inspecting his estate and made gruff, snorting sounds. Inside, what had obviously been several apartments had been gutted and combined into a single, massive suite. It had been freshly painted in glowing white. There was lustrous tile on the floors, and stylish modern furniture was tastefully arranged around the room. Melgarejo poked his nose into the shiny, fully equipped kitchen and nodded curtly to the woman, dressed in a simple maid's uniform, who was stirring something on the stove. There were several bedrooms, including a massive one with a king-size bed and silk coverlet, certainly designated for Melgarejo himself. There was also a "command post" with two computer terminals, a radio set, and several television screens, manned by two young men Melgarejo did not recognize.

"This is your 'bunker,' Don Emilio," Lazaro said, resuming the more respectful title and tone which he knew Melgarejo craved.

"No windows," Melgarejo grunted.

"No, there aren't, for security reasons," Lazaro explained. "You see, you'll be safer here than the American president in his White House. From the outside it looks like this place has windows like all the other apartments, but we've walled up the openings on the inside. We've also reinforced the walls, floors, and ceiling, and what appears to be a regular, wooden door is actually steel plated on the inside. We've installed fluorescent lights to help take the gloominess out of the place, however.

"But the real strength of this place comes from what's outside." Lazaro led Melgarejo over to the couch and sat next to him, pulling out a rolled-up diagram of the entire city block. "We've wrapped this building like a cocoon with layers of protection. The top floor and the lower ones of this building are occupied by families of your own trained MIR fighters and those of the newly trained ones we've put through our paramilitary course. You will always have several bodyguards on duty. No one can get in here without making a full-scale assault."

Lazaro could see that all this talk of combat wasn't comforting Melgarejo much, so he went on with his presentation. "In any case, by the time any enemy could reach this room, you won't be here." He pointed to the center of the diagram. "You can see that this building is surrounded by other apartment buildings just like it. Well, we've spotted other mirista families all through those buildings, and on every street leading here for blocks in every direction. We've set up a network of watchers and informers throughout the working class district so that a single policeman can't get within half a mile of here without our knowing it, and if someone tries . . ."

Lazaro led Melgarejo over to a corner of the room. Angel slid a large chair out of the way and rolled back the edge of a throw rug, revealing a trap door in the floor. Lazaro lifted the trap door, which concealed a staircase leading downward.

"This passageway was built to lead between the interior walls of the apartments below, down to the level of the basement. From there it connects with the sewer system, so, at the cost of getting a little damp and dirty, you can pop up on the other side of town before any attackers could find the entrance."

"But what if the police already know about all this," Melgarejo whined. "I mean, it would only take one informer."

"We've been rather more careful in screening people than you have been," Lazaro said, smiling. "Most of them only know the little part of the task assigned to them, such as watching for police and pressing a little button if they see one. As far as getting all this property, we've been at this for more than two years, bit by bit, renting, buying, whatever, and the secret parts of the construction were done by my own people whom I've been filtering back into the country for many months now."

Lazaro could see that Melgarejo was duly impressed, but he had saved the best for the last. Beckoning with his hand and smiling warmly, Lazaro led the way to what appeared to be a closet door. He opened it, revealing another downward spiraling staircase.

"What's this?" Melgarejo asked.

Lazaro just held up his index finger and crooked it invitingly. Melgarejo followed him down the narrow staircase, his ample flanks brushing both walls. They went down one, two, three floors, Melgarejo estimated, although there were no doorways or landings.

Lazaro was talking over his shoulder as he descended. "There's no way down here except through your apartment, so you have total control," he said. Melgarejo was already pleased, even though he didn't yet know what it was that he was controlling totally.

They finally reached the bottom of the stairs, and Lazaro punched a number code next to a dark metal door. He opened it, reached inside to flick on the lights, and stepped back to let Melgarejo squeeze by.

Beyond the door was a large room, what had apparently been the basement of this building and then some, carved into the rock and coral which comprised the island's base. Along the walls were racks of M-16s, glistening with oil. There were sniper rifles with fancy-looking scopes, long wooden crates with stenciled writing on the sides identifying the contents as "machinegun, calibre .50" and others labelled, "mine, anti-personnel, claymore" or "grenade, rocket-propelled." The labelling on some of the boxes was in Cyrillic script or Arabic writing which Melgarejo assumed were weapons as well. There were also boxes and boxes of ammunition and explosives. Melgarejo put his chubby fists on his bulging hips and nodded approvingly.

"This is the egg from which your liberating army will spring," Lazaro said happily.

Melgarejo just looked around for awhile, strolling up one crowded aisle after another, taking down a rifle from a rack and hefting it, as if he knew weapons. Finally, he stopped and turned to Lazaro, the confrontation in the car apparently forgotten.

"Is it wise to concentrate everything in one place?" he asked. "I mean, I appreciate the security measures you've taken here, but still, putting all of our eggs, so to speak, in one basket . . ."

"There's more than this," Lazaro said. "This is just the principal cache."

"Shouldn't it be out in the country somewhere," Melgarejo pursued as he peered down the sights of an M-16. "The old guerrillas in the mountains approach."

Lazaro didn't mind humoring the old fool for a while. This was all part of the script. "No, we're really safer here, surrounded by our allies, than we would be off in the jungle where the army or the air force could blast their way in to us. Meanwhile, we're right at the heart of the action and not putting ourselves in solitary confinement in the middle of nowhere. Remember that Castro won his revolution only because Batista ran away without fighting. There were no big battles like in Vietnam, or even Nicaragua. The Vietnamese and the Sandinistas won because they had sources of steady outside support and because their opponent's support was eventually cut off. Neither of those things is going to happen for us. We have a source of money and arms, but not on the scale of Vietnam. And there's no indication that support for the government is going to be cut off, yet," he added significantly, "although we're working in that direction as you'll soon see. The deaths of your colleagues in prison will serve the cause in that regard. Although I sincerely expect this government to cut and run sooner rather than later, we can't expect to win without a fight. We can't follow anyone else's formula. This is a unique situation and calls for a unique approach."

Melgarejo just nodded again. Lazaro doubted that he had been listening. His head was too full of visions of glory. Seeing real military power in his hands for the first time must be exhilarating, Lazaro admitted. Melgarejo still thought getting a new mimeograph machine or a scholarship to the Soviet Union for one of his followers was a big thing. He was certain that Melgarejo had not thought seriously about seizing power for many years. Now it was being placed before him on a silver platter.

†

Featherstone and Colonel Miller sat uncomfortably in the reception area of the President's office, not far from the embassy. Featherstone was not looking forward to this meeting. He had only just presented his official credentials a week before, and now he was faced with dealing with what promised to be an impossible list of requests (read, demands) from the Dominican government to help them deal with the current crisis.

Unfortunately for the Dominicans, the world had changed a great deal in recent years. In the 1960's, 70's, and 80's, Third World countries could present their aid requirements to the appropriate superpower with the thinly veiled threat that, if their needs were not met, they would take their business, along with their military basing rights and UN votes, over to the competition. Well, there was no more competition.

For that reason, Featherstone knew that, no matter how minimal and reasonable the Dominicans' requests might be, they would be received with a withering barrage of complaints about the tight budget. In the old days, they used to kill ambassadors who brought bad news. Now they just made the ambassadors wish they *had* killed them.

After having kept the gringos waiting an appropriately dignified period of time, an aide to the President opened the double doors leading into his office. The room was furnished in a slightly gaudier version of Louis XIV style, with more gilding on the furniture and busier murals on the walls. Even so, Featherstone could not help but notice that the material covering some of the chairs was worn rather thin in spots, and he could hear the air conditioning unit rattling rheumatically through the vents.

Featherstone and Miller were greeted "coolly but correctly" by President Juan Selich, his Minister of Interior Geronimo Diaz, and Army Commander General Aurelio Tamayo, plus the ministers of social welfare, economy, and commerce, with a few well-dressed aides posted along the walls behind them. They were directed to seats close to the president. Trays of rich, dark coffee in tiny cups were brought around. Featherstone would rather have been offered a cold beer right from the can, but coffee was at least a sign of cordiality.

After exchanging a polite bit of small talk, with Featherstone expressing his and his government's sincerest regrets about the recent tragic events in the Dominican Republic, General Tamayo produced copies of the "wish list" for the American government. While Featherstone read, Selich talked about the Dominican Republic's long history of alliance with the United States and his personal conviction that these recent events were the work of foreign agitators, paid and trained by some outside power.

The list was pretty much what Featherstone had expected. Several thousand tear gas canisters, five hundred sets of anti-riot body armor, shields, helmets, etc., and several light armored cars equipped for crowd control work. All that was on an immediate basis, requested to be flown in within 24 hours. Longer-term items included training for 1,000 men in riot control tactics and another fifty in counter-terrorist SWAT operations. None of it was unreasonable, and the United States had provided this kind of equipment and training and more to countries in the region in recent years.

Unfortunately, Featherstone was obliged to inform the president that, while he would pass on the text of the request itself immediately to Washington, he had received only two hours before, a telegram from the Department stating that Congress had passed a resolution suspending all but strictly humanitarian aid to the Dominican Republic until the investigation into the deaths of the MIR prisoners had been fully resolved. He added that at least two of the victims appeared to have had valid American green cards and were thus being considered as "U.S. persons" by Congress.

General Tamayo, not surprisingly, came off his sofa like a rocket and seemed to remain suspended several inches off the floor while he ranted and raved at American perfidy. He brought up the millions of dollars in military aid sent to the "nun killers" in El Salvador and to the "bandit" Contras in Nicaragua. He marvelled that a government which had 32 policemen murdered (seven of those included in the official death toll of the previous night apparently having gotten much better, Featherstone noted), a democratically elected government, could not get a few non-lethal items from its closest ally with which to defend itself from foreign agitators and terrorists just because there happened to be an unsolved murder on the books. The president echoed these themes, although in more diplomatic language, having served as ambassador in Washington in the course of his career.

Featherstone always enjoyed it when Congress, in its wisdom, chose to make use of its control of the governmental purse strings in the international arena to gain press time and to exercise their political muscle. He explained cautiously that drawing parallels to other times and places was a futile endeavor, adding that he fully supported the request being made by the Dominican government and would use whatever influence he possessed to have it attended to. He pointed out, however, that the issue of the prison killings was not a frivolous one, having almost certainly been the work of individuals with at least access to police facilities, and that the failure of the government even to identify suspects could not be viewed by the world as evidence of a serious investigation. The interview was terminated quickly and curtly, without the usual round of handshaking.

On the way back to the embassy, Featherstone hoped they wouldn't have to ask the Dominicans for any favors real soon.

He didn't notice a taxi that had been parked a block from the President's residence and which followed them for several blocks before turning off, to be replaced by a small pickup truck which was, in turn, replaced by a young man on a motor bike, who didn't even turn his head when he passed the ambassadorial motorcade as it turned into the embassy parking lot.

†

The exclusive neighborhood of Arroyo Hondo, on the northern outskirts of the city, boasts some of the most opulent mansions in the Western Hemisphere. The walls of some enclose acres of carefully manicured lawns, helicopter pads, tennis courts, and olympic-size swimming pools. The more modest ones occupy less than a city block, but tend to make up for it by parking three or four Mercedes, BMWs, or Porsches within sight of the gate. All are surrounded by high walls topped with broken glass or razor stripping and, as a matter of course, have uniformed guards lounging by the driveway to discourage intruders.

The most striking thing about the area is that some of the poorest slums in the hemisphere can be found, literally, within a stone's throw of their gates. They are the same clapboard and cardboard shanties that line the Ozama River, with their hordes of dark-skinned, hollow-eyed men and women standing about in the heat and mosquitoes, just waiting for something to happen.

At just after 10 that evening, a weeknight, there was normally little activity in Arroyo Hondo, unless one of the local worthies happened to be having a birthday bash at which the goal was to consume as conspicuously and noisily as possible. The only sound now was the steady throbbing of the large private generators which kept the floodlights shining on all of those acres of manicured lawn. The streets were pitch dark, as were the slum neighborhoods which crowded up around the mansions like waves bordering a rocky coastline. Several cars and trucks, without headlights, were winding through the dark streets, but that was not unusual in Santo Domingo. What was unusual were the groups of dark-clad figures, four to six in a group, which rolled silently out of the moving vehicles and gathered in the shadows under the lee of the garden walls.

The first gate guard on the street never knew what hit him. He was sound asleep, his metal folding chair propped back on two legs against the garden wall. A hand clamped down over his mouth, and at the same instant a knife plunged into his throat. He was hurled into the nearby bushes where he bled to death without ever coming fully awake. There were eight homes, estates really, which had gates within about 300 meters of each other along a narrow cul de sac, and the guards at each were dealt with silently. At one gate, the guard had been flirting with his employer's maid. Both of them died in a hail of sub-machinegun fire, but the silencer on the weapon made the shooting no noisier than the spattering of gravel from a passing car's tires. The guards had keys to the gates, which each group of attackers recovered and began working its way toward its target house.

Altogether there were some forty men and women slinking through the darkness toward the brightly lit homes from which the sound of televisions or stereos could now faintly be heard. Luis' group contained two other santistas, an experienced mirista fighter, and one of the more promising new recruits.

Luis crawled along the edge of some decorative shrubs bordering the long driveway up to the house. He knew from his reconnaissance over the past week that there would be only one guard, but it always paid to be careful. A chance encounter with some butler or child could warn the owner, who might turn out to be a gun collector, which could cause problems. It wouldn't stop Luis, of course. He had faced more serious threats than a startled civilian with a shotgun, but he was a professional and took pride in a neat job. It took Luis' group nearly ten minutes to reach the edge of the veranda which surrounded the house, where he still had to wait, lying in the cover of the green leaves as lizards nervously skittered around him, for the appointed time to move.

Luis looked at the luminous dial of his watch. When the second hand finally crept around to the twelve at H-hour, he snapped his fingers twice loudly and lunged to his feet. He carried a short-barrelled, semi-automatic 12 gauge with a folding stock and a laser sight mounted above the muzzle. He had already flipped the laser on, and a tiny red dot materialized on the first object directly in the line of sight after he sprinted across the patio and up to the large sliding glass doors.

The family was gathered together in the recreation room, watching a video tape. The father, a man of about fifty, who was still wearing his dress shirt and slacks, although he had removed his coat and tie, was lounging in a big recliner, a tall glass of beer in his hand. The wife was sitting near him on the couch, knitting while she watched the television, and two teenage girls were sprawled on the floor, looking alternately at the TV and at fashion magazines they had spread out in front of them. Despite the floodlights on the lawn, it was still far brighter inside than out, so the family didn't see Luis until the glass of the door shattered with his first shot.

Luis was smiling broadly behind his ski mask at the shocked looks on their faces as he came leaping into the room. This was the part he liked the best, wrenching the fat, satisfied people out of their comfortable lives and into his world of death and violence at one jolt. He blew apart the father's chest before he could even rise from his chair. Then, according to plan, he stepped aside and let the other two santistas, a man and a woman, finish off the others with their machetes.

Meanwhile, Luis sent the other two team members racing through the house. There would be two maids, a dog, and a driver somewhere. The dog was not long in appearing, a black Labrador which had apparently been in the kitchen when he had heard the screams. A huge black shadow came hurtling over a low railing and caught the hand of the man with the machete as he was about to finish off one of the girls. Luis smiled to think that the girl must have had a split second of hope that she had been rescued by her beloved pet, but then Luis sent a charge of buckshot into the dog, throwing it against the wall in a bloody heap. The machete man had to switch to his other hand, but he went on with his work.

There were screams and shots coming from other parts of the house, so Luis knew that some of the domestics had been found. One of the attackers appeared by the stairs and flashed a hand signal indicating that the two maids were dead. That left the driver, and Luis didn't like having the one relatively young man still on the loose. He raced through the kitchen to the servants' quarters and was greeted by the figure of a stocky young man, wearing only boxer shorts and a sleeveless undershirt who suddenly emerged from a doorway. He had a revolver in his hand and got off the first shot, but he was scared, and his shot went wide, splintering the door jamb next to Luis' head. Luis was not scared, and his shot took off the man's head.

By the time Luis returned to the rec room, the other members of the team were busy placing small charges of C4 plastic explosive around the house. They put one by the stereo, another by the TV and video player, one under each of the three cars' gas tanks, and one in the master bedroom, where the jewelry was bound to be. They rejoined in the middle of the bloody wreckage for Luis to make a quick head count, and then dashed off into the night. When they reached the gate, Luis pulled a small radio transmitter from his pocket, extended the antenna, and pushed the button. The remaining windows in the house were shattered by a series of loud explosions, and a small fire started in the upstairs bedroom, but the house remained relatively untouched. Luis was satisfied. They had sent their message that this was a political matter, not a robbery. As he passed the guard's body, he pulled an ice pick from his other pocket and jammed it into the man's chest, fixing with it a plastic envelope enclosing a brief "statement of responsibility."

The pickup truck was already there, and the team leaped into the back, taking with them the guard's shotgun. Luis thought it was time to begin gathering up the spoils for the long war ahead.

Throughout the city those who had electricity tuned in the eleven o'clock news. They saw the face of the usual anchor man, but instead of his carefully coiffed look and overly heavy make-up, he had an angry blue bruise running diagonally across his face. Part of the normal backdrop behind him had been broken down, and the legs of a man could be seen protruding from the hole at a crazy angle.

His voice was as resonant as always, but it quavered as he read a "proclamation." Anne was already watching, dumbstruck, when Featherstone walked into the room from taking his shower.

". . . tonight the armed forces of the movement "Holy War" have struck a blow of vengeance against the murderers of the people. In retaliation for the assassination of 11 members of the MIR in prison and for the massacre of over 500 unarmed demonstrators on the streets of Santo Domingo, a number of individuals have been executed by peoples' vigilantes. These individuals had been found guilty by a people's tribunal of belonging to the oligarchy which daily is responsible for the deaths of hundreds of poor men, women, and children in this country by starvation and neglect. The message of the "Holy War" Movement, of which the MIR is an integral part, is that such murderers are no longer safe behind their walls in their mansions, no matter how many armed guards they hire. The message also implies that anyone who supports these parasites by serving them or guarding them, will receive the same justice. The road to the airport is open. Take it while there is still time."

A man in a dark ski mask walked up behind the newscaster, who did not divert his gaze from the camera. The man raised a pistol and fired, directly into the lens of the camera. The picture dissolved into a flurry of static.

Anne looked up at Featherstone, who was still holding a towel to his wet hair. "Uh-oh!" was all she said.

FOUR

Normally, an embassy conducted an orientation session for all new arrivals, giving the new American employees and their spouses a series of briefings on the organization of the embassy, with each section chief giving a short talk about his work. There would also be helpful hints on getting settled in the country and information on how to make the tour a pleasant and productive one. That, at least, was the theory. Featherstone had come to the conclusion that it would be more accurate to call the meeting a "*dis*-orientation program." Nevertheless, he complied with the spirit of the concept and called a meeting.

Since Featherstone's predecessor had not bothered to conduct any such meeting for over a year, the small auditorium of the embassy was jammed with sixty or seventy officers, secretaries, communicators, and their spouses. More than half the total staff had arrived in the past year. All of the section heads were seated on uncomfortable folding metal chairs on a small raised platform at the front of the auditorium. The air conditioning was working, but was far from adequate to deal with the combination of sweltering heat and humidity outside and the press of humanity inside. That certainly didn't help keep tempers under control. A number of people had made little fans out of the agendas, and these fluttered futilely in the stale air.

Featherstone had taken the coward's way out and had let Stileforth make the opening statements. Considering the situation, this should have fallen to the Post Security Officer, Rambling, but the events of the preceding few days had so unnerved Rambling that Featherstone knew he could never have handled this crowd. In fact, Featherstone had found a "request for leave" slip from Rambling shuffled in among a bunch of other papers awaiting his signature. He had been obliged to call the man in and tell him that, while he would accept a letter of resignation, he would not consider leave for any of his senior officers at a time like this.

Stileforth might be a lot of things, Featherstone thought, but he was not cowardly. In fact, with his patrician bearing and coolness, he was dealing well with his presentation. Intentionally, he had begun his talk with a canned presentation, without making reference to the current crisis, but that approach was starting to wear rather thin.

Featherstone was taking the opportunity to evaluate the audience. He looked around the room and saw the tension on the faces. The embassy staffers, both new arrivals and senior officers waiting to make their presentations, were decidedly uneasy, particularly those with families. They knew enough about the growing violence around them to appreciate the danger but felt helpless to do anything about it. They were all clearly praying that something he would say would make it all better.

The wives, spouses, he corrected himself, since he had a couple of female officers who had husbands as dependents, weren't scared. They were angry. They knew very well that they were at the low end of the food chain when it came to information. Of course, the senior embassy officers had access to everything any section of the embassy learned, officially or unofficially. The "working level" employees generally knew only snippets and rumors picked up over lunch. The spouses at home, however, got only what their mates picked up, less whatever the mate decided to conceal so as not to worry them. This lack of information caused frustration, and frustration bred anger. Right now the wives were like mother bears protecting their cubs, growling and slashing at this invisible danger which now seemed to threaten their families. The husbands were restrained by their desire not to appear cowardly in a tense situation, and fear for their jobs, but the wives had no such compunctions. They wanted action and they wanted it now.

He had seen these women before, Foreign Service wives. He had seen them sitting on top of piles of luggage in a crowded, sweltering airport, trying to keep an eye on two rampaging kids, while she held a third one, with a fever, in her arms, waiting for the privilege of boarding an airplane, tourist class, for a fourteen-hour flight to another crowded, sweltering airport. All too often, the husband would be too indispensable at work to accompany the family, so the wife would have to fend for herself. In times like these, it looked as if someone had tightened the skin at the back of their heads an extra turn, pulling the corners of the eyes and mouth and making both into unyielding slits. And that could be something as "simple" as a normal change of post, with no danger thrown in for good measure.

Featherstone was getting ready to take the plunge and start his own presentation, or more exactly, to discard his prepared presentation and to open a discussion of the issues everyone was interested in today. Hands were beginning to shoot up around the room, and, although Stileforth was doing a masterful job in deflecting questions not directly related to the immediate topic of protocol at official receptions, things were starting to get out of hand, and Featherstone knew it was time to step in.

He sympathized with these people, both employees and spouses, and his job was not going to be made any easier by the telegram he had just received from Washington in response to his own report of the previous night's massacre. A total of seventy-two people, men, women, and children, had been found murdered in their homes, many of them hacked to pieces with machetes. The police could point only to the MIR as the culprits based on the declarations made on television at the time of the attacks and leaflets left at the scene. What made it worse was there had been no survivors, no one left for dead, no one who had escaped or hidden under the bed. They were all just gone. The fact that over half of the victims had not been the rich oligarchs who were the alleged targets of the attack, but poor servants working for minimum wage or less, seemed to have been lost on most people.

He had known from the first moment that the cry from his own little community would be for some sort of protection or for a chance to get the hell out of Dodge. The cable from the Department, obviously written by some politically astute observer, was to the effect that, any overt action, such as the evacuation of dependents, could be construed as a lack of faith in the Selich government and could not be authorized at this time. The cable went on to point out that no Americans had been targeted, and, in fact, no Americans had been victims of any violence.

Yet. That was the word that was looming large in the minds of everyone in the room. They knew that decisions made in Washington were being concocted by people whose children were safe in Fairfax County schools and whose wives were happily shopping at Tyson's Corner. The day a dozen crazed fanatics did go rampaging through the American School in Santo Domingo, hacking teachers and children with machetes, those people would put on their "serious" faces, deplore the incident, and *then* organize some sort of evacuation of the surviving dependents.

Featherstone rose, moved to the small podium, and put his hand on Stileforth's shoulder. Featherstone leaned over the microphone, which squealed the way microphones always seem to do.

"Thank you, Dale. I think it would be appropriate to drop our planned agenda and address the problems which I know are on everyone's mind right now. Later, if we have time, we'll get back to telling you about the nurse's office and the size limitations on mailing packages."

With a relieved sigh, Stileforth shuffled back to his seat, throwing a defiant glare at the audience as he did so. As Featherstone straightened up and squared his shoulders, the hum of conversation which had been growing in the room quickly died out, and only the fluttering of the little paper fans disturbed the silence.

"What we're all really concerned about at this moment," he began in a loud voice, choosing not to trust the sound system, "is the bloody killings which have taken place here in the past week."

There was a growl of approval and emphatic nodding of heads. Featherstone knew that attempting to sugarcoat the issue was not what they wanted. They were afraid of death and wanted to know that he understood.

"Unfortunately," he went on, "it's even worse than what you've already heard." The murmur of talking ceased abruptly. "It hasn't been made public yet, but we have information that over a dozen Dominican policemen have been killed, in separate incidents, in working class areas down by the river in the old part of town. The result has been that the police have pulled out of that area and are unwilling or unable to go back into it. We assume that this is the part of town where the terrorists have their stronghold, but now that part of the city is essentially off limits to the Dominican authorities." There was another frantic buzz of conversation. He saw Lafeur looking at him in surprise. Lafeur had just brought in this information himself for the Country Team, and Featherstone had taken it on his own authority to pass it along to his people. Since Lafeur had said it was already widely rumored in the city, the source of the information was not in danger.

Over the heads of the crowd, he could see Anne, standing against the back wall amid a tight circle of some of the youngest wives. Almost as if he were speaking in a foreign language, she was busily "interpreting" to them in a low voice, while she held the hand of a very pregnant woman who was trembling noticeably.

Featherstone held up his hand and raised the volume of his voice a notch to get their attention again. "*And* I have just been instructed by Washington that there will be no formal evacuation of dependents since there has been no indication of a risk to Americans per se."

"Yet!" several voices rang out in unison from somewhere in the room. There was a little nervous, not very amused, laughter at this, but Featherstone talked over it.

"Those are my instructions, and, in principle I agree with them. The purpose of these horrendous attacks appears to be to undermine the authority of the Dominican government and make it appear powerless."

"Which isn't far off the mark," Vernon said, half rising from his seat. He sat back down almost immediately, and Featherstone could see he hadn't meant to say that out loud, but the thought of his children living in danger had obviously gotten the better of him.

"Those are my instructions, and I must obey them," Featherstone continued. "*However*," he said emphatically, and the word cut through the noise of whispers and shifting chairs, "my view is that, if Washington wants to run things from hundreds of miles away, I will abide by the letter, but not the spirit of those instructions." As he said this, he saw Stileforth out of the corner of his eye, cast him a sinister look, but Stileforth was the least of his problems. "Now, this is what I am authorizing, and I want each section chief to take note and to pass the word along to any members of the staff who are not present here today."

At this, several people took out notebooks and pens in a reflex bureaucratic reaction, forgetting for a moment their intense personal concern. "First, there are a few employees whose families either have not come to post yet or who are away from post for some reason. They should be told to remain away for the present." He saw one young, first tour officer from the commercial section, whose wife and baby were due in later that week, clench his fist next to his chest, as if to say "Yes!." Now he would not be put in the position of sounding like a whiner by asking it himself.

"Next, 'liberal leave policy' will be in effect for all employees who have not yet taken their R&R or who simply have accumulated leave time and wish to use it." This was the sort of announcement they usually made in Washington on bad snow days when the bureaucrats couldn't make up their minds to close government offices, so there was a legal precedent here. "I will be going over with section chiefs the bare minimum crew we can get along with, with an emphasis on single people over families and volunteers welcomed at all levels."

"Lastly," he said, looking at the sea of increasingly hopeful faces, "I'm aware that not everyone can afford the expense of airfare to the States and a hotel stay for days or even weeks, so I am instructing the Regional Medical Officer to err on the side of caution and to advise medical evacuation for anyone with any actual or potential health problem, since we certainly cannot count on local hospital facilities being available for the immediate future." He looked over at Anne again. The pregnant woman was now holding Anne's hand to her cheek, and sobbing softly, but with a smile on her face. Medical evacuation meant that the trip would be paid for and that the evacuee would receive hotel and food costs.

"Oh, one more thing," he added. "In anticipation of a general exodus of wealthier Dominicans from the island, I've made arrangements with one of the American carriers to reserve us 100 seats on flights to Miami and San Juan over the next couple of days." He didn't want to remember what he had had to promise the local airline manager in terms of visas for his extended Dominican family in return for this favor. "And one other, very last point," he said, turning back as if he had been just about to leave the podium, "I'll be staying, as will my wife, Anne, and we'd certainly welcome the company of any of you who volunteer to join us." Anne gave him the thumbs up sign, and spontaneous applause broke out across the room as he walked to the door. I'll pay for that eventually, he thought, but one way or another one always did end up paying for doing the right thing.

†

General Tamayo had made it quite clear to Miller that he was only being invited to the planning session of the Dominican High Command on the basis of the personal friendship which had developed between them, and not out of any sense of obligation the Dominican military felt toward the American government. Although approval for the shipment of at least some of the equipment requested by the Dominicans had finally come through, two days after the massacre in Arroyo Hondo, this had been due less to sympathy with the Dominican government's cause than to the revelation that the Uzi recovered at the site of the first street battle had come from Iran. The serial number had been checked and corresponded to a lot sold by Israel to Iran just before the revolution. The fact that all of the attackers had been similarly equipped implied official sponsorhip. That was enough to label this an "international terrorist" incident, which always played well in Washington. The Dominicans were still irate, however, at the initial rejection by Washington and the fact that two California congressmen were still pushing an investigation into human rights violations by the police.

Tamayo and several of his staff were bent over a large map of Santo Domingo discussing the deployment of army units. Miller was seated against one of the walls of the conference room, just listening. He was pleased to note that the army had effectively taken charge of the situation, partly to bring its greater manpower to bear, and partly to avoid repetitions of the prison incident in what was becoming a blood feud between the police and the Holy War movement.

The First Brigade had been placed on full alert, although Miller noticed that it was being represented by the unit's executive officer, Colonel Leon Calvo, since the brigade commander had deemed this the appropriate time to undertake a fact-finding mission to Western Europe related to Army procurement policies. He was not expected back for several weeks, but since he was a political appointee without military experience, he was not particularly missed. The brigade had set up a loose cordon around the southeastern portion of the city, with well-armed checkpoints backed by mobile mechanized infantry units in case of trouble. Without totally cutting off traffic through the city, these checkpoints would be used to search for weapons in passing vehicles and to examine identity papers in hopes of rounding up more miristas to add to the eighty or so who were already in jail. While this was a good first step, Miller speculated that, given the planning and execution of the terrorists' actions thus far, they would have anticipated such a thing and probably had all of their people and weapons exactly where they wanted them already.

More importantly, the Military Intelligence Department, unfortunately referred to by its Spanish initials of DIM, had established a network of informers in the suspect area. The DIM representative reported on vigorous recruiting efforts being carried out by the santistas, primarily among the urban poor, but also among restless middle class university students who traditionally make up the bulk of terrorist movements. The fact that the santistas were not depending on the usual collection of pseudo-intellectual radicals, preferring instead the hard-handed workers was a change in style which Miller suspected the analysts in Washington might appreciate.

DIM sources had also identified an area, about four blocks square in the center of old town, which appeared somehow isolated from the rest, with discreet guards who prevented anyone not "belonging" there from snooping around. At least two of the men who had been sent to investigate had not come back. A raid by a company of the police Special Operations Group, the special counterinsurgency force, on the old MIR headquarters and on the residences of MIR President Melgarejo had turned up nothing, implying that the MIR and Holy War, whether they were one and the same or not, had moved, probably to this forbidden part of old town.

Tamayo announced that he was bringing in a military police company and a motorized infantry battalion of the Support Command, normally stationed at San Cristobal, to reinforce the 1st Brigade and was beefing up security at the airport as well as throughout the rest of the country, against the possibility that the santistas' next move would be to strike outside Santo Domingo to spread the government's forces thinner. Guards would be augmented on the president's residence, the legislature, all government ministries, and on the homes of leading political figures. Roving motorized patrols would cruise the city in irregular patterns, to make the terrorists' plans more difficult. Tamayo raised his head from the map briefly and added, that there would be extra guards on all major embassies as well.

Miller nodded in return, but was not really satisfied with the planning. He was not being asked to contribute and did not want to close off this source of information by intruding, but Tamayo seemed to be taking a very predictable, traditional approach to deal with a very unpredictable, radical threat. He was busy protecting symbolic places and public figures, while the santistas had thus far shown no interest in attacking either. Miller mused to himself that at least the protection of government officials would be made easier by the fact that no fewer than four ministers and thirty legislators had chosen this time for junkets abroad.

Tamayo was also laying plans for a major assault on this apparently forbidden area in old town, but, since this could easily involve a wild firefight in a heavily populated part of the city, he would need more to go on than the fact that intelligence sources couldn't get in there, so the main focus right now was on gathering more information.

At this point, Miller chose to offer the one bit of aid he had at hand. He stood up and eased toward the table, opening the large portfolio he had been resting against his chair.

"These might be of use," he said, laying out a series of black and white photographs on the conference table. They were overhead imagery of the city taken on a satellite pass a day or two previously. "Satellite photos are usually better for spotting ICBMs and tanks than guerrilla fighters, but they will at least give your tactical planners the very latest look at what buildings are where, new construction, etc."

Helping hands quickly arranged the photos, which overlapped to provide a picture about four feet square, of the city from east of the Ozama River to the ends of the urban area to the north and west. The pictures were a little grainy, since, even in times of crisis, the U.S. government was unwilling to provide state-of-the-art material to the Dominicans, but you could pick out individual figures on the ground, even identify the make of cars, and certainly locate all walls and obstacles around the city.

"This is great!" one officer exclaimed. "I've been up in a helicopter reconning the area, but it's not the same as having it photographed in such detail. Thank you, Colonel"

Tamayo only grunted. "By the way, Colonel," he grumbled. "I should mention to you that we have been able to meet most of our munitions needs through private purchases in Europe." He smiled superficially. "I was able to persuade some of our wealthier members of government to dip into their 'personal expense budgets' to finance the buys."

Miller accepted the snub in good grace, since it was no more than the U.S. deserved. "These photos are just a sample," he went on, talking directly to Tamayo. "And I have several sets, so you can feel free to mark them up." Tamayo whipped a red grease pencil from his pocket, and began to do just that, marking off the Army cordon with its checkpoints and then circling the suspect area in old town.

"This is where we suspect they've holed up," he said, jabbing the center of the circle with his pencil.

"For your planning, then," Miller continued, "I have something extra for you." He gestured to a corner of the room in which he had been permitted to set up a strange piece of furniture. At his signal, a

U.S. Air Force enlisted man turned a switch, and fluorescent lights under the low table flickered on.

The table looked like a normal drafting table except that the surface was now a sheet of white light. On top of the table were arrayed two identical photographic transparencies, each about a foot square, and over it was an unusual set of lenses, one poised over each photograph and connected to a binocular eyepiece in the center. The enlisted man peered through the eyepiece and slid first one photo, then the other, slightly until he was satisfied. Then he stood up and offered his chair.

Tamayo took a seat, looked through the eyepiece and gasped. The two views of the city came together through the lenses into what appeared to be a three dimensional model of the city in infinite detail. His reaction, like that of most people viewing stereo photos for the first time, was to reach out a finger and touch one of the photos, half expecting to be able to insert his finger between the buildings and bend the trees over.

"This is unbelievable," he gushed.

There was a brief shoving match as the other officers tried to get into the chair. Miller had taken care that the photos on the light table were of rather better quality than those of the prints, and when seen through the magnifying lenses, the viewer could literally "fly" around the city at treetop level.

"When you get down to tactical planning for an assault," Miller explained, "with the help of the specialist here, we can actually measure the heights of walls and buildings, tell you where you can place snipers to get good fields of fire. You name it." He didn't add that this would mean that the Americans would also have advance warning of any operation, but, there is no such thing as a free lunch.

Tamayo only nodded. That was as much of a thank you as Miller was likely to get, but it was enough. He would be in on any future planning, which was all he wanted.

†

A man with a full, black beard, a dark suit and a high-necked white shirt with no collar or tie stood with Angel just inside Padre Lazaro's room, waiting. Lazaro was on his knees, his back to them, his arms extended to the sides in the form of a cross, his eyes closed in meditation. Angel had seen Lazaro hold this position for hours and knew better than to disturb him. Angel didn't know, in his heart, whether Lazaro really communicated with God during these sessions, but the clarity of thought and purpose with which he emerged from them made it appear as if he did, and that was all that mattered. Like most of Lazaro's followers, Angel had been taken from the squalor of the Santo Domingo slums and given a sense of mission. After growing up being able to hope for nothing more than an occasional full stomach at the end of the day, until some easily preventable disease snuffed out his life, this was a feeling worth dying for.

Abdol Reza Hashem-Zai-Nehbandan would not have considered interrupting a man at his prayers. This man might not be a Moslem, but he was a man of the book, a devout man, fanatically devout, and that was a quality all too lacking in most Christians Abdol had met. Lazaro did not automatically ostracize believers of other faiths, a very Islamic, un-Christian way of thinking to Abdol's mind. Like all rational people, this man reserved his deepest hatred for those who believed in nothing spiritual at all, just in money or power, like the communists and the capitalists.

Abdol had not seen Padre Lazaro since that morning in Madrid weeks before. It had been another successful operation by this strange band of Latin Americans who fought on behalf of the Iranian Revolution. Abdol, a major in the Etelaat-e Sepah-e Pasdaran, had worked with Lazaro for nearly five years, off and on. Together they had hunted Tudeh party radicals and Mujaheddin-e Khalq guerrillas in Shiraz and Esfahan, and he had been impressed with both the dedication and the ferocity of these foreign infidels.

Lazaro finally lowered his arms to his sides and rose to his feet. He turned toward the two men, his eyes still closed. When he opened them, there was an angelic smile on his face, and he warmly embraced Abdol in the Middle Eastern manner.

"Everything is going very well, thank God," Lazaro said as they sat on the couch.

"Yes," Abdol said. "We have already been receiving word that the Americans have connected your movement with Iran, but, as expected, they assume it is the government rather than ourselves, who is behind it."

"We're ready to go on to the next phase of the plan, which will simply fuel their paranoia all the more." Lazaro paused. "I assume that the rest of the money has been deposited, and that the arms will be delivered on schedule."

"Check with your bank," Abdol said, raising his hands. "It's all there. The final shipment of arms should be arriving within the next 24 hours, as agreed. I have to tell you that there was some displeasure in Teheran about your decision to 'use up' your first delivery in the way you propose."

"You'll have to trust me that those weapons will do more good in that way than they would in the hands of an army of commandos."

"We're also a little concerned," Abdol said in a soft voice, "about your grand strategic plan, as you've explained it to us. You'll have to admit that, while it's easy to start some civil strife and to kill a few policemen, it's quite another thing to claim to be able to seize power in a country in a matter of weeks as you do."

Lazaro turned his burning gaze on Abdol, who met it with one of equal intensity. "You must understand that our society is as corrupt and feeble as that of the Shah was. How many divisions did the Ayatollah have when his revolution started? He was up against the best-equipped army in the world after those of the United States and the USSR. Did that stop him? Did anyone calculate his chances of success? No! God was with him, and that was enough. Our enemy doesn't have the power of the Shah, and he will collapse all the faster, not because of that, but because God is with us. I can feel it! I can feel Him guiding my hands. I'm so certain of it that I am willing to die to prove it."

Abdol bowed slightly. "This is your war, and your decision. May Allah favor your arms."

The two men clasped hands. Lazaro resented somewhat having a watchdog over what should be a purely Dominican operation, but he was not in a position to argue, yet. But Abdol was not intrusive, and his long years of experience in various sorts of clandestine operations might actually come in handy. Still, it was something of a slight to Lazaro's pride, and he reminded himself that he must always be on guard against the sin of pridefulness. He was doing the will of God, not merely advancing his own situation.

†

Quiroga was rather uneasy at the meeting that evening, but Lafeur couldn't see why. Thus far, he and Arce had performed far beyond all expectations, keeping him informed of the situation on the street, giving some insight into the atmosphere within the police, if not providing their actual plans, and, most importantly, turning up the original connection between the santistas and Iran. This last could prove to be the one clue which would explain the whole series of events in the Dominican Republic, to say nothing of getting a nice promotion for Lafeur himself. So, if Quiroga had some problems with all of this, Lafeur really didn't want to hear about it.

Quiroga leaned far over in his chair, resting his elbows on his knees as he flexed his fingers together. "This may sound stupid," he said finally, "but it's just too easy."

"Too easy!" Lafeur roared. "You guys are out until all hours, running around like crazy, hiding in shadows, watching guys we know have lots of guns and know how to use them, and you call that easy?"

"That's not it at all," Quiroga said, shaking his head. "I'm a cop. I know that the big cases usually break, if they ever do, because of some dumb, lucky stroke, not because of brilliant detective work. Some crook gets drunk and tells a snitch where the loot from the bank job is hidden or where the body is buried. What bugs me is that I get this feeling we're just seeing a little piece of the picture, and it's a piece someone wants us to see. How else do you explain that Arce has been able to saunter into this 'forbidden zone' and back out again when half a dozen other cops, most with more experience than Arce, have been murdered trying in the last few days?"

"He's been into the zone?" Lafeur almost shouted. "When did this happen?"

"Last night. I've got the report right here," he said, drawing several roughly folded sheets of paper from his back pocket and tossing them to Lafeur, who snatched at them greedily. "He says that block you were interested in is the 'nucleus' all right, and that the apartment building in the center of the block is definitely some kind of headquarters. Lots of people coming and going at odd hours, and lots and lots of guns around."

Lafeur could hardly believe it. Here he was in this jerkwater post, forgotten by the world, particularly by Langley, and now he was about to be rich and famous. All the papers were full of the massacres committed by both sides and mysterious references to who might be behind it, and here it was right in his hands. He could walk into the briefing room and draw a damn ring around the heart of the problem with his pen, and all the army had to do was clean it out. He was mentally dividing up the information into neatly packaged intel reports, which would boost his production for the month and send shivers up the spines of the analysts in Washington. After this tour he could write his own ticket for his next assignment. Paris might be nice, he thought to himself. After all, somebody has to go there.

"This is fantastic, Quiroga," he gushed. "Really fantastic! There'll be a bonus for you this month, and for Arce too. You can bank on that."

He looked up from the papers and saw the weary look on Quiroga's face. He forced himself to fold up the papers and address his man's concerns head on.

"Anyway, that doesn't prove anything about the validity of the information," Lafeur argued, already starting to put together the kind of vocabulary he'd have to use if anyone in Washington raised the same questions. "Maybe he was lucky and the others weren't. Maybe he's better on the street than they were. Who knows? What really matters is that who the hell would want to give us this kind of stuff? It's the fucking crown jewels, for Christ sake! Those people know that the strength of any guerrilla or terrorist movement is its mobility and its clandestinity. When government forces can pinpoint them, they can squash them like bugs. No, I think your paranoia glands are working overtime. Maybe it's time to switch to decaf."

Lafeur chuckled half-heartedly, wishing that Quiroga would just relax and enjoy it as he was doing and stop with these stupid questions. Quiroga just looked at him quizzically, and Lafeur realized that no Latin American could visualize the concept of decaffeinated coffee, so he let the matter drop.

"I signed up the telephone guy for you, too, by the way," Qurioga added without much enthusiasm. "He can hook up any number we want. All we need is an apartment with a phone line installed where we can put the LP."

"Great!" Lafeur exclaimed. This was unbelievable. Another recruitment, just in time for the end-of-fiscal-year reporting, and the opening of a significant technical operation. He'd have to think of a way to tie it in to this santista terrorist thing to give it added punch with headquarters. "I've had my eye on a place about six blocks from here. If it's still available, I can have it rented by the end of the week, and we're in business."

Quiroga didn't have any more news, but Lafeur felt obliged to sit around and have a couple of beers with him, "building rapport," as they liked to call it. The reports were burning a hole in his pocket, and Lafeur was barely paying attention to Quiroga's talk about baseball, a national passion in the Dominican Republic and something which interested Lafeur about as much as reading train schedules. He mentally crafted each report and filed it away so that he would only have to type them up back at the office. Not a bad day's work, he thought, draining the rest of his beer at one gulp.

†

Late that night, Colonel Manuel Zamora, commander of the Dominican 10th Motorized Infantry Battalion, returned to his home. His battalion had been transferred from its base at San Isidro out near the airport, where it formed part of the Armed Forces Training Center, which was actually a fourth brigade of the army. Its task in the city was to screen the northern side of the "forbidden zone" and to provide roving patrols for that part of the city.

Zamora found this new level of activity highly annoying, exemplified by his having actually to work until nearly midnight, making certain that his units were in place and that officers were monitoring the troops. In all the years of his career, Zamora had only been concerned with buttering up the right superiors to ensure his promotion, and then milking that position for all it was worth. He had begun small, as a lieutenant, carrying discharged soldiers on the books as being on active duty, collecting their pay himself and selling their rations on the black market. As the commander of a battalion, he had far greater scope for his "commercial" activities, which included receiving half of the first month's pay for each new recruit, the other half going to the brigade commander. The recruits were glad to pay this bribe, since a job in the army was one of the few which guaranteed a paycheck, a place to sleep, medical care, and three meals a day. He also supervised the sale of "spare" tools and supplies provided by American military aid, which brought in a tidy sum.

Zamora had invested his money wisely, building a small shopping center in the eastern suburbs. He had used his troops as general laborers and trucks from his unit to transport construction materials to the site. His profits were safely banked in Miami, where he also owned a comfortable condo with a new American car in the garage for his frequent vacations there. Until the outbreak of this unfortunate rash of killings, his major concern in life had been buying a choice piece of real estate in Arroyo Hondo, currently occupied by poor squatters. He had planned to use his troops to evict the tenants, but, after the Arroyo Hondo massacre, he was glad that he had not yet settled on a firm price with the owner. The owner had called him several times that day, pressing for a meeting, hinting at dropping his price, but Zamora now thought that the money would be better spent on a nice home in Coral Gables, and his wife definitely agreed.

Zamora was dropped off by his driver in his command jeep. Normally, he would much prefer using his air conditioned Mercedes, but he didn't want to risk it on the street now, so he had to make do with the admittedly martial image he struck, racing up and down the avenue in full battle dress. It was kind of fun really. He instructed the driver to be back by 0700 hours the next morning, earlier than he would have liked, but the damn American defense attaché was making a nuisance of himself, prodding the General Staff to make repeated visits to battalion headquarters, and he couldn't afford to be caught at home if they came by early.

Zamora was greatly displeased to find the soldier assigned to guard his gate (and to mow the lawn while he was at it) was not at his post when he arrived, and he vowed to make the man's life pure hell as soon as he found the corner he had crawled into to take his nap.

It wasn't surprising that the power was out in his neighborhood. It was always that way, but he wondered why his wife hadn't cranked up the generator, since those of their neighbors were chugging away happily in their back yards. He had a momentary pang of fear that he had let the fuel supply run out, and he would be in for a severe tonguelashing when he got through the door.

It was with great caution, therefore, that he opened the front door of his house. All was quiet inside, and he hoped everyone was asleep. He could then see if the generator would crank over, and, if not, he would have all night to think up a good excuse. He felt his way to the kitchen, since no one ever took his advice about leaving a flashlight where you can find it. He finally reached the generator switch, tripping and stumbling all the way, cursing under his breath. He threw the switch and the generator rumbled to life. The lights in the kitchen flickered briefly and then came on strong.

He turned to head for the bedroom, wondering what the problem had been. Probably, the power had just gone off after everyone was asleep. As he reached this conclusion, he tripped and fell flat, swearing a blue streak at the maid who had probably left her mop in the middle of the floor.

Then he sucked in his breath to stifle a scream. The obstacle he had tripped over wasn't a mop, it was the extended boot of his gate guard, who lay sprawled on the kitchen floor, his throat slit, and his unseeing eyes staring blankly at Zamora. Amid the puddle of blood on the floor were the shards of a broken beer bottle and a plate with the half-eaten remains of a sandwich scattered about. Evidently the man was being entertained by the maid here in the kitchen when he was killed.

Zamora scrambled to his feet, slipping on the blood-slick tiles, and raced for the bedrooms. There was the harsh rasp of static on the TV, where someone had been watching a video, and the "12:00" on the VCR was flashing stupidly. His .45 was in his hand now, but in the excitement he hadn't bothered either to chamber a round or remove the safety.

He kicked in the bedroom door, which flew open with a crash since it had not been locked. He let out a gasp, which softened immediately to a sigh of relief at what he saw. Lying side by side on his bed were his wife, ten-year-old daughter, and five-year-old son, all bound and gagged, their eyes wide with terror, but alive. At the foot of the bed lay the body of the maid, who had been shot in the back of the head at close range. Blood and bits of her brain and face were splattered over the expensive oriental rug on which she was crumpled.

His first impulse was to rush to his wife, but he stopped short, wondering whether this might be a trap. He spun around, pointing his useless gun with both hands at the various corners of the room.

"Are they gone?" he shouted, turning to his wife. She nodded her head frantically, almost choking as her chest heaved with great sobs which were blocked by the rag tied over her mouth.

He holstered his pistol and sat on the bed next to her, his trembling fingers fumbling with the stiff knots of the ropes. It seemed to take a long time to get the three of them untied, after which they all just clutched each other, crying. His wife still couldn't talk, but she pointed at her vanity table.

The usual collection of women's accoutrements, perfumes, and creams had been swept onto the floor in a heap, and in their place was a single, typewritten page, neatly situated in the middle of the table. Zamora bent over it, afraid even to touch it. It read:

Good Evening Colonel:

As you will have noticed, we visited your beautiful home tonight and got to know your fine family. We don't plan to return just now, but we could drop by any time. If you would prefer that we didn't, you will follow these instructions. By the way, you will be thinking about getting your family out of the country about now, which is fine. If, however, you think that their being at your prestigious condominium in Miami will put them beyond harm's reach, you are mistaken, and, if you fail to follow our instructions faithfully and discreetly, we will find them, and you, and kill them . . .

The letter went on to instruct him to return to his battalion headquarters immediately and order his unit back to their base "for reorganization." He was not to discuss this order with anyone, and, if he were to receive countermanding orders from his superiors, he should simply ignore them. The letter commented that, assuming he got his troops moving by dawn, and kept them off their station until afternoon, his purpose would be served, and he could then bring them back into the city at his discretion. It concluded with the observation that the worst that Zamora's superiors could do would be to fire him, implying that the people who had visited his home that evening could do far more than that.

"Get out the suitcases," he said to his wife in a flat voice. "Pack what you and the kids will need in Miami and will fit in two suitcases, no more. There's a flight out at six thirty in the morning, and you're going to be on it."

"Aren't you coming with us?" she sobbed, although she had already untangled herself from her children's arms and was pulling two large leather suitcases out from under the bed.

"I'll be coming along tomorrow. Believe me, I'm not hanging around here any longer than I have to, but I've got to do something so these people don't come after us. Maybe they're just bluffing, but we can't take that chance. If I do what they want, they'll leave us alone, and then this fucking island can sink into the sea for all I care."

Zamora re-read the letter while his wife grabbed armloads of clothes out of the closet, dumping them, hangers and all, into the open maw of a suitcase. "There were four of them, with ski masks on. They just shot Maria," she said, wiping her nose with the back of her hand as she spoke, "right in front of the children. They said that this is what we could expect if they weren't pleased with our 'cooperation.' There was one man who seemed to be the leader. You could see his mouth through the opening of the mask, and he was smiling all the time." She broke down and began sobbing again.

†

Lazaro could see that Luis was not pleased with the way his mission had gone the night before. He was aware of Luis' attitude toward his job, and normally this attitude helped him perform the tasks Lazaro gave him with great efficiency and elan. It tested Luis' discipline to the utmost, however, when he was required to stop short of total destruction of the enemy. Lazaro had assigned Diana to the team which hit the Colonel's house with this in mind, and with special instructions to "deal with" Luis if it appeared he was getting out of hand. He was pleased that Luis had carried out his orders to the letter. Now it was time to hone this weapon a bit, to make sure it was razor sharp for the coming confrontation.

"Our man out at the airport informed us that Colonel Zamora's family left for Miami this morning," Lazaro began sitting on the sofa where Luis was hunched over, contemplating his shoes. "Apparently the flight was fully booked, as all of them seem to be lately, thanks to you," he added, and Luis smiled a little. "The Colonel tried bribery, but he was evidently not as rich as some of the other passengers, so he had to take the ticket agent into a small office of the customs police and shove his pistol halfway down the man's throat before the agent 'remembered' three seats they had been reserving for late-arriving VIPs."

"The most important thing," Lazaro continued, "was that the 10th Battalion was on the road before dawn, roaring back across the Ozama bridge toward San Isidro, and the coast is clear for us to continue with the operation. So, you see, a live enemy can sometimes be of more use than a dead one."

Luis turned his eyes on Lazaro, and Lazaro saw a certain light of

sincerity in his eyes, somewhere behind the ferocity. "It's just that
people like that don't deserve to live, not one minute more." The veins
on his temples were bulging as the intense little man struggled to
express himself in mere words, when action was his usual language.

"There will be time enough to settle accounts," Lazaro soothed,
"but first we must take power and give it to the people. Only then can
we afford the luxury of our righteous vengeance. If you had killed the
Colonel's family, he might just as easily have turned into our most
fanatical enemy instead of a trembling coward. If you had killed him,
his second in command would have taken his place, and that battalion
would still be in our way. We just don't have enough people to kill all
of the enemy one by one." Lazaro waved his arms as he searched for
an explanation. "We're like cavemen fighting a giant mammoth. Nothing we have can simply kill the beast. We have to drive it mad, terrify
it, enrage it, and then lead it to charge over a cliff to its destruction.
Then we just climb on down and carve up the meat." He patted Luis
on the knee as the latter bowed his head and nodded meekly.

"You have the new schedule?" Lazaro asked, deciding it was time
to get Luis focused on his next task.

"Yes. It looks like 1100 will be our best opportunity."

"Let's take it. We have no word that the 10th Battalion is heading
back to the city yet, and it probably couldn't do so at least until noon,
but we can't take a chance on any other unit taking its place in the
meanwhile."

"We're ready," Luis said, rising slowly. Lazaro rose with him and
gave him a firm embrace before seeing him to the door.

"Remember . . ." Lazaro began, but Luis cut him off with a wave
of his hand.

"I know. 'Take him alive or die trying.' Don't worry. Either you'll
next see me with him in tow, or you won't see me again at all," he
managed a tired smile, turned, and disappeared through the door.

†

Manolo Cuesta was fidgeting nervously in the chair in his office,
glancing up at the clock on top of his filing cabinet every few seconds,
waiting for ten o'clock to roll around. Although the morning shift had
officially begun nearly two hours before, he knew that many of his
technicians also held down other jobs, either working on those jobs

until late in the morning or leaving early to work in the afternoons. The handful of men who did come to work at eight naturally felt entitled to a lengthy coffee break, having done the work of the full shift thus far, and when they drifted back, they would probably be accompanied by the bulk of the other technicians covering their own late arrival. As a manager, Cuesta should have disapproved of this practice, but everyone did it. It was the only way to support a family on the miserable wages paid by most employers. That was why he had welcomed the offer of an added salary from Lieutenant Quiroga, and he didn't even have to leave work to get it.

Today, in particular, Cuesta had no problems with the double employment system, since it would mean that he would be virtually alone in the telephone central from ten o'clock until nearly eleven. There would be a couple of tellers out in the offices where people paid their bills, and maybe a secretary covering the phones, but back in the rack rooms there would be only one technician on hand to deal with catastrophic breakdowns until everyone else came back, and, if no such breakdown occurred, he would be lounging in his own little office, reading the newspaper.

Cuesta fiddled with paperwork on his desk, waiting for the minute hand to crawl around the face of the clock. Finally, he could hear the shuffling of feet and the discreet opening and closing of the street door as people began drifting off to their coffee break. Glancing out his window, he could see a couple of technicians jogging across the street to the little cafe which was the traditional watering hole for telephone company employees. He waited a few more minutes until the sound of the migration had faded. Then he dipped under his desk to retrieve a small leather handbag with his personal set of tools, and headed toward the racks.

The racks were where the thousands of telephone lines for this sector came together and were routed through the central network. The phone system was one of the few things in the Dominican Republic which performed reliably. While not as sophisticated as the system in the United States, the Dominican phone system worked.

Cuesta had a three-by-five card in one hand as he quickly walked along the ends of the tall metal racks with their cascades of multicolored wires. He kept looking around furtively, although he had a yellow work order in his pocket for a fictitious repair he was allegedly making for some bigwig. On the card there were two telephone numbers, the first that of the "target" phone, the second that of the listening post (LP) where the call would be monitored. He checked the prefix labels on each of the racks until he finally found the one corresponding to the target and ducked down the row.

About halfway down the row, Cuesta stopped in front of one particular bundle of wires. Checking the number labels carefully, he finally selected a light blue one. Glancing up and down the row one last time, he zipped open his tool bag, pulled out a pair of wire snippers and deftly spliced the blue line with a red "carrier" line from the tray which ran along the base of the rack. He then wedged the target line back into the thick bundle, grabbed his bag, and ran swiftly out to the end of the row. He ducked into another row, corresponding to the LP's line, found the correct cable and made a similar connection. He then ran back to the central panel at the end of the row, selected two of the carrier lines and spliced them, again slipping his handiwork underneath a tangle of other wires.

For all intents and purposes, he had just made the LP telephone an extension of the system in the target site. His great worry was that, if Quiroga chose to tap a line that happened to be targeted by another security service, and if that service were to make the connection here in the central as opposed to at some neighborhood connector panel, they might discover his own tap. Cuesta had done this a couple of times before on behalf of powerful patrons, although in those cases, they were actually tapping their own home phones to check on cheating wives. The problem here was that he didn't know who the target was, and if it turned out to be someone in a position of power, maybe someone who was paranoid enough to have his line physically checked, the tap might be discovered, and it would only be a matter of time before they traced it back to him. Of course, that was what he was being paid for, and rather well paid at that.

That done, Cuesta slipped out the back door and jumped into his car. Quiroga would be waiting for him to monitor the first few calls on the target line. If everything worked as it should, he would be paid on the spot, a thought which made him smile to himself. There were some things he had been wanting to buy for his house.

At this time of the morning, the streets of Santo Domingo would normally be a happy chaos of too many cars constantly defying the law of physics which states that no two bodies can occupy the same space at the same time. Since the violence had begun, however, the traffic situation had improved. There were still cars on the road, but not nearly so many, although Cuesta had heard that the road to the airport was constantly jammed these days, with people even abandoning their cars along the highway in their desperation to get off the island. Of course, the abandoned cars didn't stay there long, as there were plenty of people left who knew how to hot wire a car. He noticed that a lot of businesses, especially chic boutiques and jewelry stores, were closed. Those businesses which remained open frequently had three or four armed guards conspicuously patrolling out front. A couple of homes along this street had apparently been looted and then gutted by fire as the residents of the small shanty towns scattered around the city had decided that the time had come to settle accounts. The police had harshly suppressed such actions, with many reported killed, evidently taking out their frustration for not being able to deal with the "forbidden zone" by crushing any signs of uppity-ness in the more accessible poor quarters.

Cuesta found the door of the small office unlocked and let himself in. The sign on the door said "ENTECA, S.A.," which meant nothing to anyone, but it sounded very much like the other company names on the building registry. The office was a simple room, about ten by fifteen feet, with only a battered old desk, a single swivel chair, and a small wooden credenza upon which a phone sat. Quiroga was slumped in a swivel chair, looking at the credenza, the open doors, revealing what looked like a small stereo outfit inside.

"Shut the door and lock it," was all Quiroga said by way of greeting, and Cuesta could see that he probably hadn't been getting much sleep lately. "It seems to be working, but we haven't had a call yet."

"I just made the connection, give it time," Cuesta added, sitting down cross-legged on the floor in front of the credenza.

Inside the cabinet were three devices on separate shelves. On the bottom was a simple tape recorder. Cuesta flipped the switch from "mute," where it would rest during most of the operation, to "speaker," to permit them to listen while the conversations were taped. Above the recorder was a simple metal box called an actuator. It had a couple of knobs and a voltage meter on the front, and its purpose was to register the drop in voltage when the receiver of the target phone was lifted. It would then complete an electrical circuit which would route the call through the tape recorder, cutting off when the receiver was replaced in its cradle. Above that was another plain box with a digital display on the front. Its purpose was basically to count the "clicks" when the target phone was dialed, displaying and recording the number called.

As Cuesta checked the cable connections and adjusted the knobs, the needle on the actuator's voltage meter suddenly jumped, and the sound of voices came over the speaker.

"Here we go," Cuesta said happily.

It was an incoming call, so all they had heard at first was the click of the receiver being picked up and a scratchy female voice answering, "American embassy, good morning."

Cuesta raised his eyebrows and turned to Quiroga. "You're tapping the American embassy?" he asked in surprise. He had rather expected the targets to be drug traffickers, which would naturally interest the police, or maybe some corrupt government officials making their shady deals, which would interest just about anybody with an eye to clean government or a share of the take.

Quiroga just raised his hand wearily. "This was just a test. I didn't want to have to listen to an hour of taped conversations or make a pretense call myself to see whether you had hooked up the right line. Of course, I couldn't tell you that in advance. I've got our first target number right here," he tapped his shirt pocket. "If this works properly, you can hook it up today or tomorrow, whenever you have time. Let's just listen a bit longer. I want to get an outgoing call to see if the digital readout works."

Cuesta turned back to the machines. The tape player had kicked in as advertised, and everything seemed to function properly. "Everybody knows the phone number to the U.S. Embassy in this country," he said. "We've all been there looking for a visa at one time or another, and this isn't it."

"I know that," Quiroga said quietly, apparently debating whether he needed to satisfy Cuesta's curiosity. "This is the ambassador's direct line, right to his secretary, not through the switchboard. This was just my own idea, no big deal."

Cuesta nodded and fiddled some more with the knobs. There were several more incoming calls, mostly very important people demanding the ambassador's personal intervention because they had been denied visas for some reason. The secretary had obviously dealt with this sort of thing before and parried each request with the skill of a fencer.

Cuesta and Quiroga had to chuckle as she easily deflated each windbag in turn, although Quiroga noted some tension in her voice. She was still a great secretary.

Finally, the needle on the actuator jumped again, and they heard the rapid clicking of the phone being dialed. Red numbers began appearing in the digital display above the actuator. From force of habit as a policeman, Quiroga began writing them down on his pocket notebook. One, two, three numbers appeared. Then there was a pause, and it seemed as though it was taking an awfully long time for the caller to dial. Four, five, six numbers. Cuesta touched one of the knobs, and suddenly the display went blank.

"Shit!" Cuesta said.

"What did you do that for? You damn techs are all the same. You can't help tinkering with things even when they're working fine."

"I was just trying to adjust the brightness of the display. There must be a loose connection or something. It's back on now. We'll just have to wait for the next call."

There was the sound of a phone ringing. It rang several times before a man's voice answered. The secretary was talking.

"He's leaving now."

"Tell me when the car leaves the gate," the man answered in a flat tone.

There was a pause of several moments, and then she said, "There he goes," her voice cracked as she said this, and she slammed the receiver down hard.

"What was that all about?" Cuesta asked curiously.

"You know how the bigwigs like to have doors open magically when they arrive somewhere, right on time. That was probably some aide trying to calculate when the Ambassador would pull up to some gate."

Cuesta just shrugged, and they sat back to wait for the next outgoing call.

†

Featherstone had been pleased with the way his mini-evacuation had worked. There had been no mention of it in the press thus far, and Washington snored on in blissful ignorance. He had managed to get everyone out of the country who wanted to go, but it hadn't been easy.

Lafeur had chosen to stay, being single, and you couldn't have blasted Stileforth out of the country with dynamite. Featherstone would almost have preferred that Stileforth had gone. Although his knowledge of the country and its political leaders was useful, it was so prejudiced that anything Stileforth said had to be taken with a large handful of salt. Moreover, Featherstone had the sneaking suspicion that Stileforth was keeping a careful log of every word, action, and decision he made, with an eye to using it against him if anything did go wrong. Although, Featherstone figured, if things really went wrong and people started dying, Stileforth's bureaucratic back-biting would be the least of his worries. Most of the other section chiefs had stayed, along with a skeleton staff of young single officers, and Jim Vernon seemed about ready to lay down his life for Featherstone in gratitude for getting his family out of harm's way.

The only question mark had been old Rambling. Featherstone had decided that he had made the man suffer enough, but he wanted to try to harness his seemingly inexhaustible supply of energy when it came to serving his own interests. Despite the promises of the airline manager, Featherstone knew very well that it would be a dog fight at the airport, since it was that way on a perfectly normal business day in Santo Domingo. He had sent Rambling out to the airport with Lyle Fiore from DEA with the order that Lyle would give Rambling his airline ticket only after the other forty Americans in their little convoy, mostly women and children, were safely checked through customs, immigration, and had boarded the plane.

Featherstone and Fiore had enjoyed a good laugh over a cold beer when Fiore got back. Rambling had become a veritable lion, leaning halfway over the ticket counter, screaming at the besieged airline employees, hauling bags, even carrying a hollering two-year-old in one arm as he bullied, cajoled, and tricked his way past every obstacle amid the mob of terrified would-be passengers. To hear him barking orders and hustling people about, Fiore said, you would have thought you were watching John Wayne in action, especially after he lost his bow tie to one of the luggage conveyor belts. He had promised visas, or threatened their revocation, to half the airport staff before he was done. And when Fiore had finally handed over his ticket and boarding pass, you would have thought he was Sir Galahad being handed the Holy Grail. Fiore pouted comically, adding that Rambling had forgotten to say good-bye as he tore up the stairs and into the plane.

That had been the only contingent of Americans able to go out by commercial flight, but fortunately the DAO maintained a small propeller aircraft at Santo Domingo to shuttle bigwigs around the Caribbean. Miller had placed it at Featherstone's disposal, and the remaining dependents had been hopped over to San Juan, a few at a time, with the last batch having left the night before.

Featherstone had been grateful to Miller for stretching his own authority in this way, so, he was in no position to argue when the colonel had requested that he join him for a visit to army headquarters at eleven o'clock. Apparently, the army deployments which had been going so well just the day before, had begun to unravel, with units wandering off on their own for no apparent reason. Miller was going to talk to General Tamayo about getting his act together, and he felt that having Featherstone's presence would give added horsepower to the play. It had taken some last minute shuffling of his schedule, but Maripaz had handled it beautifully, with just a few phone calls, and a minimum of ruffled feathers. Featherstone was still concerned that Maripaz was not well. She had drastically lost weight in the past couple of weeks, but her work was top notch. After all, who wasn't under a lot of pressure in this country these days?

The motorcade was waiting in the embassy driveway as Featherstone came bounding down the steps. The door of his own "armored" car was being held open by his regular driver, Jorge. The chase car, manned by his police bodyguards, the burly Ramiro Escobar and the small and wiry Lucho Ayala had its engine running just behind. As an added precaution, one of the marines, Sergeant Larry DeSoto, would accompany Featherstone in his car.

Featherstone didn't really like this semi-martial convoy. His car had thick sheets of plexiglass behind the regular windshield and side and back windows. The roof, floor, and doors all had extra metal plates, sufficient to stop small arms fire or shrapnel from most mines, and the gas tank was self-sealing, to limit the danger of explosion. The engine had been souped up to handle the extra weight and still put out 120 miles per hour if necessary. Jorge had received State Department Security officers called "defensive driving" training.

The bodyguards carried their service revolvers, and Ramiro, the more experienced of the two, also had an Uzi under the dashboard. Jorge was also qualified as a bodyguard, at least theoretically, and carried an automatic pistol. DeSoto, who wore civilian clothes for this duty, had his own .38 in addition to a pump action Remington twelve gauge next to his feet.

All of this hardware should have given Featherstone a feeling of warmth and security, but he also knew that there were people running around the island who had "kicked butt." As Jorge closed the door, Featherstone caught a glimpse of Maripaz standing at the window of her office, watching him with a sad look on her face. He smiled and waved casually to her, but she must not have seen him, since she quickly pulled the drapes and disappeared from view.

The trip to the offices of the Corps of Military Aides wasn't long, about four city blocks. Because most of the streets in this neighborhood were one-way, the little motorcade would have to take a detour of several blocks to the south, before heading west to the main Avenida Maximo Gomez, and then north to the meeting site. Although traffic was decidedly lighter these days, it was still totally undisciplined, and Featherstone estimated the journey of a mile and a half would take some twenty minutes, so he made himself comfortable, stretching out crosswise on the back seat, and settled down to look over his briefing papers en route.

The driveway gates slid open as they circled the parking lot, and the heavy roll-up barriers, designed to foil mad truck bombers, rotated back into the ground. One of the gate guards stepped out into the street to stop oncoming traffic in a slight usurpation of local police authority, but Featherstone still appreciated the gesture, particularly since the man was clearly risking his life to accomplish it.

They turned south on a quiet residential street, and waited for a chance to turn right through the cross traffic on the much busier Calle Abraham Lincoln. Jorge's view was partially blocked by a mini-van, which passed for public transportation in Santo Domingo, was engaged in discharging passengers and wedging in new ones on the corner to his left, but he found a gap and accelerated into it. At that moment, however, the mini-van driver decided to continue on his way, sprinting away from the curb, spilling one heavyset woman onto the ground.

The van driver was obviously concentrating on the flow of traffic coming from behind him and not looking ahead, and he plowed into Featherstone's car just back of the front wheel at about ten miles per hour, shoving the Cadillac bodily against the curb, and spilling screaming, swearing passengers out of the open side door and onto the street.

Featherstone was thrown onto the floor by the collision but was unhurt. By the time he had raised himself up to look over the front seat, Jorge was already out of the car, arguing with the van driver and his helper, whose job is to cram passengers into the vehicle. The chase car had taken up an officially recommended position, angled across the street behind them, blocking open a space of about twenty meters. Both Escobar and Ayala had gotten out and were marching up to the scene, preparing to flash their police IDs and scare the van driver, who probably didn't have a license. Featherstone supposed he could move over to the chase car to continue on his way, since he doubted that his own vehicle would be driveable after such a jolt.

He was about to make this announcement, when DeSoto, who had been standing, halfway out of his door, his shotgun held out of sight down below the level of the dashboard, suddenly collapsed onto the front seat. Jorge's door was open as well, and a husky man wearing a sweaty tank top thrust himself into the car, shoving a pistol in Featherstone's face.

"Out of the car, or you're dead," the man shouted in very passable English.

Featherstone looked around him frantically. DeSoto had been clubbed on the back of the head, and another man was dragging him out onto the ground by his feet. Escobar and Ayala had their hands in the air and were surrounded by four or five "passengers" from the van, all of whom had shotguns or submachineguns. The driver of the van and his assistant had also drawn pistols, and one of them had smashed his into Jorge's face. Jorge now lay on the street, blood streaming from his nose and mouth.

"Get out of the fucking car!" the man screamed again, reaching in and jerking open Featherstone's door from the inside. Calloused hands and strong arms appeared in the open doorway and hauled Featherstone bodily out of the car. A delivery truck had angled across Calle Abraham Lincoln, completely blocking traffic, and a large American sedan sat in the middle of the street, next to the wrecked van, its engine running and the trunk standing open.

Featherstone looked at his two bodyguards as he was hustled toward the waiting car. Ayala simply stood there, a look of calm resignation on his face, but Escobar was twitching nervously, his eyes bugging out of his head and his temples bulging red with rage and frustration as he looked helplessly from one attacker to another, as if calculating his chances in a fight. Those chances weren't good, as one of the attackers had the barrel of his shotgun pressed up against Escobar's thick neck, while the others stood back several meters, covering him with their weapons.

Someone yanked Featherstone's hands behind his back and he felt a sharp pinch as handcuffs were roughly fastened. He was shoved head first into the trunk of the sedan, and as he squirmed around to look back, a hand clamped a cloth impregnated with a strong, hospital kind of smell over his nose and mouth. Ether, probably, Featherstone thought placidly as his eyes rolled back in his head and he lost consciousness.

Even before the sedan pulled away, one of the remaining attackers stepped up to each motorcade vehicle and blasted the two-way radios with submachinegun fire. They then fired bursts into the radiator grills and at the tires. The van, which had a reinforced bumper on the front, made of welded steel pipes, as did many of its kind in Santo Domingo, was still functioning and, with a screeching of twisted metal, pulled away from the ambassador's car and angled itself to continue down the avenue. The half dozen attackers still remained on the scene, retreated slowly to the open door, their guns still trained on the two bodyguards.

Ayala stood like a statue, his hand gently resting on the thick forearm of Escobar, who was still trembling with rage. The last terrorist, a short, balding man with a dark moustache, stepped onto the running board of the van grabbing hold with his free hand, while his other kept his Uzi pointed at Escobar. He smiled and said something to his companions which made them laugh as the van sped away.

Tears were streaming down Escobar's face. He had never been so humiliated. He had been relieved not to have been killed outright, but he realized that the attackers could have killed him at any time, and now waves of shame washed over him. Worse, the terrorists had not even bothered to disarm him and Ayala, and his big .357 was still bouncing uncomfortably under his arm as he ran to the corner to watch the van disappear around a curve. It was as if they did not consider him and Ayala as a serious threat like the young marine DeSoto, still lying unconscious halfway out of the ambassador's car.

He ran back to where Ayala was standing.

"Get to a phone and call the police," he screamed, pointing to a small pharmacy down the street which would certainly have a telephone.

"For all the good that it'll do," Ayala mumbled as he casually began walking toward the store.

"Move, you asshole! And call for an ambulance too," Escobar shouted, as he started running back toward the Embassy. Of course, Ayala was right. What were the police going to do anyway? The terrorists had been right. He was a clown, and so was Ayala. He hadn't even tried to draw his gun. He was a typical bodyguard, paid a salary to protect someone, but when it's a question of your own life, that salary doesn't look so large after all. He had been doing this job for years, taking advantage of his huge bulk to cow people into getting out of the way when they had to move through a crowd, but never really considering what he'd do in a real showdown. Now he knew. This ambassador was better than most, too. He had treated Escobar and Ayala like professionals, not like domestic servants the way the last ambassador did, and he deserved better than this. Well, at least Escobar could see that the Americans got the report as quickly as possible.

The sweat had soaked through his shirt and through his suitcoat as well by the time he had jogged the two blocks back to the embassy. He was already out of breath, and had to bang his gun on the iron gates to get the guard even to peek out of his little booth. The guards had apparently heard the gunfire and taken the wise precaution of making themselves scarce, just in case the trouble was heading their way.

He shoved the guard out of the way as soon as the gate was open enough for him to squeeze through, and staggered up the driveway to the embassy entrance. Gunny Besserman was already standing in the doorway, wearing camouflage fatigues and a flak vest, a shotgun discreetly held behind his back, the barrel concealed behind his leg.

"It's the ambassador!" Escobar gasped. "They got the ambassador! Kidnapped!"

"What?" Besserman shouted, grabbing Escobar by the shoulder with his free hand.

"Ten . . . twelve men and women," he panted. "Submachineguns, shotguns . . . dark, four-door American sedan, . . . white van . . . heading west on Abraham Lincoln. . . . DeSoto and Jorge hurt, but not dead." Escobar could see the look in the marine's eyes that said, but you weren't hurt at all, were you?, and he had to look away.

"Was the ambassador hurt?" Besserman asked as he half-dragged the beefy guard into the reception area and dropped him into a tastefully upholstered armchair by the door.

"No, I don't think so. They put him in the trunk of the sedan and took off. They only shot up the car engines and radios . . . I sent Ayala to call the police," he added, knowing how feeble a contribution it had been.

"Stay right here," Besserman said, rushing toward the door which led back to the offices where Escobar knew both the defense attach and CIA people sat. A tall black marine had appeared in the reception area, apparently called by the one in the bulletproof booth. This one also wore fatigues and a flak vest and carried a shotgun. "Watch him," Besserman said to the marine. Escobar noticed that it wasn't "take care of him," or "stay with him," but "watch him," as if he were the enemy. Well, he couldn't blame them.

Escobar sagged backward in the chair. He happened to look toward the door to the ambassador's office and saw Maripaz standing there. He had always thought she was so pretty, but she certainly wasn't right now. She was pale as a ghost, which was far from her natural color, and the make-up around her eyes was badly smeared.

FIVE

†

The reduced country team, now occasionally referred to as the "war cabinet," was seated around Featherstone's office early that evening. The group consisted of Jim Vernon, Lafeur, Colonel Miller, Lyle Fiore, and Colonel Palacios, who had come to provide the latest police report on the kidnapping. Stileforth, who was again charge d'affaires, had been there but had excused himself to take a secure phone call from Washington.

The faces around the room were grim. Lafeur had been pleased to see Palacios placed in charge of the operation. He had been closely involved in sealing off the "forbidden zone" in old town since the survivors of his Cascos Negros had been incorporated into the police counterinsurgency force, of which he was now the executive officer. He had a good reputation and had received considerable American training, so he was about the best the country had to offer. However, the news he brought was not heartening.

Palacios had admitted candidly that the kidnappers had almost certainly emerged from the "forbidden zone" in the early morning hours at the time that the 10th Motorized Infantry Battalion had abandoned its positions without orders. Palacios said what they had all been thinking privately, that this movement was not coincidental but had somehow been engineered by the santistas. This view was reinforced by the fact that the battalion commander's family had departed the country in a hurry that same morning, and Zamora himself was now reported to have taken a plane to Venezuela. Palacios commented that the Dominican government had made a formal request of the Venezuelan government to arrest Zamora as a deserter and return him to Santo Domingo for questioning, but he doubted that the request could be acted upon before Zamora disappeared, as evidently was his plan.

Palacios had also mentioned that, while neither of the vehicles used in the attack had been recovered, as everyone expected, abandoned in some deserted spot, a report had just come in from a police patrol which might bear on the case. About half an hour after the kidnapping of the Ambassador, a police patrol had made a routine stop of a van fitting the description of the one used in the attack. The incident occurred in the zone of responsibility of the 10th Motorized Battalion, and the van had been heading toward the "forbidden zone."

According to eyewitnesses, the jeep full of policemen had been attempting to cover the gap left by the 10th Battalion until reinforcements could arrive. Almost as soon as the van had stopped, the policemen were cut down in a hail of automatic weapons fire. One of the policemen, who had been manning a machinegun mounted on the back of the jeep, had managed to squeeze off a burst before he died, and blood stains found at the scene indicated that at least one of the terrorists had been hit. The van continued on toward the "forbidden zone," followed by a sedan, which had stopped a block up the street, and which also fit the description of the one from the kidnapping.

Palacios apologized for the tardiness of the report, but, since all of the policemen on the scene had been killed, and most of the eyewitnesses had disappeared immediately, it had taken some time to piece the story together. The police could now confirm that the blockade of the "forbidden zone" had been reestablished and that an assault group was being organized, which Palacios himself would lead, to go in after the Ambassador as soon as he could be located.

"That shooting incident with the van would explain this," Miller said, pulling some large black and white aerial photographs from his briefcase and spreading them on the low coffee table in the center of the room. "These are some hard copies of film from the latest aerial photography of the city, taken less than an hour ago. We've got a couple of old U2s staging out of Florida, providing almost continuous coverage with cameras by day and with infrared by night. They're old birds, but plenty good for this kind of work and a lot more timely than satellite passes. The quality isn't very good, since these were just faxed here from Washington. A courier is on his way with the real thing for the High Command, but you can still see some of the things their specialists highlighted for us."

The men crowded closer, bending over the table. There were several red circles on one photograph which showed the entire "forbidden zone" area in large scale. One centered on the city block area which the police had identified as the probable headquarters of the santistas, with a smaller circle inside of it. Another circle was on a street somewhat to the east of the headquarters area. The other photographs were enlargements of the circled areas.

"Here's the suspected headquarters complex," Miller continued, pointing to the large circle, "but look at these enlargements. This one off by itself is a light colored van, parked near one of the known entrances to the headquarters. You can't make it out from this print, but the folks in Washington say that the windshield has been shot out, at least it doesn't have one."

"That would jibe with the story of the shootout at the checkpoint," Palacios interjected.

"Exactly," said Miller. "Maybe it's just a coincidence, maybe not." He then pointed to a blowup of the small circle within the headquarters complex. "This one is supposedly the back end of a dark colored, American style sedan just protruding from a covered parking spot within the courtyard in the center of the complex. It just looks like a soft blur to me. They also say that the trunk is standing open."

There was a slight buzz of conversation, but Miller continued. "Lastly, they say that neither vehicle was in that location at the time of the last satellite pass, about six hours before, nor at any time previously. Again, it's not conclusive, but it sure is interesting."

"As I was saying," Palacios said, "we have an assault element ready of over one hundred men, trained in urban combat and in hostage rescue operations. If we're convinced that the ambassador is in that building, we can be in there within one hour from start time."

"I'm happy to say that that won't be necessary," Stileforth announced breezily as he strode into the room. "I've just gotten off the phone with Washington, and the Delta Force is already being activated. A C-130 will land out at San Isidro just before dawn day after tomorrow, and we'll be taking care of things from here on in."

Palacios straightened up with a grim look on his face. "I would like to remind you that this is a sovereign country with its own armed forces and police, and we are perfectly capable of taking care of security matters on our own soil."

Lafeur looked anxiously from Stileforth to Palacios and back. In principle, he had to agree with Stileforth that the Dominican security forces hadn't exactly outdone themselves so far in dealing with the Holy War phenomenon. But he also understood what a blatant slap in the face it was for the Americans simply to storm in and take charge of things.

"I quite agree, my dear fellow," Stileforth continued, quite unperturbed by Palacios' comment. "This is a sovereign country with its own president, and President Selich has agreed wholeheartedly to my plan and has authorized the Delta Force to intervene in this situation."

Palacios let out a long breath, and Lafeur could imagine jets of steam issuing from his nostrils. Lafeur wondered what that presidential agreement had cost the U.S. government, probably a big aid program, or maybe just plain cash for Selich himself. In any event, it was another insult for Palacios to be told this by an American official and not by his own government.

"The Dominican forces," Stileforth was continuing, "will have a very important support role, securing the perimeter of the 'forbidden zone,' and mounting a diversionary action well away from the target area. After the ambassador has been rescued and safely withdrawn from the country, President Selich proposes taking advantage of the disorder our own commando operation will undoubtedly have caused in the rebel ranks to overrun the entire suspect area by open assault." Stileforth blessed all of the officers present with the glow of his triumphant smile.

"But this is Dominican soil, not the United States," Palacios interrupted, increasing the volume noticeably. "I don't care what kind of private arrangement you've struck with President Selich. The Dominican Armed Forces will take a very dim view of any military intervention by the United States in this incident." Palacios stood there, his chin thrust out, his fists clenched, staring defiantly at Stileforth.

Stileforth fixed Palacios with a gaze one might use on a cockroach who had survived the first swat of a bedroom slipper. In cold, measured tones he began to "explain" things to Palacios. "I know the Colonel has been very busy in the last ten or twelve hours following leads to the disappearance of Ambassador Featherstone and coordinating with our officers, for which I am sure we are all deeply grateful." He paused briefly as if to imply that maybe he wasn't. "Consequently, he did not attend the most recent meeting of the Dominican High Command this afternoon, which was essentially cancelled because, of the ten permanent members, only four showed up, the others being occupied either in arranging air travel for themselves out of the country or in supervis-

ing the establishment of strong guards on their own homes and prop-
erties. For that reason, as much as any other, President Selich has
chosen to entrust the primary mission of the rescue operation to forces
from the United States."

Lafeur watched as Palacios almost literally deflated in front of his
eyes, his arms dropping limply to his sides. Lafeur's stomach churned
with rage at this revelation. First, it was the product of a highly classified intelligence report he had provided Stileforth only a couple of
hours previously, sourced to one of his contacts who had been present
at the High Command meeting and who would now very likely break
off all contact with someone who could not keep a secret. Worse,
Stileforth had opted to score debating points over an issue that had
already been decided by President Selich and had, in the process, totally
alienated and demoralized a local official upon whom they might have
to depend in the near future. Palacios did not make any effort to resume
the conversation, and Stileforth treated himself to a long, slow gaze
around the room, savoring his victory, while the other Americans found
somewhere else to look.

Lafeur took advantage of the pause to raise a question that had
been bothering him. He turned to Palacios. "Colonel, about how long
had that police patrol been in position when they were shot up by the
terrorists?"

Palacios didn't look up from the table. "About five to ten minutes
we estimate," he mumbled.

"Hmmm," Lafeur mused, leaning over a street map of the city
laid out on the table. "It just strikes me as odd that the kidnappers
would take nearly half an hour between the time they seized the ambassador to reach a point where they ran into the patrol, which is
barely ten minutes' drive away. Add to that the fact that the road into
the "forbidden zone" was open all during that missing time, we have
to assume according to their own plan, and you have a bit of a mystery."

"What are you suggesting, Claude?" a feminine voice asked.

All heads in the room turned toward the door, and they saw Anne
standing there. She was very neatly dressed, as became an ambassador's wife, her hair nicely coiffed, but there were taut lines around her
eyes, and her usual smile was gone, replaced by the thin straight line
of her mouth.

"Anne, dear!" Stileforth oozed. "What are you doing here? You
should be resting, what?" He shot a harsh glance at the secretary

Elaine, who had apparently violated his instructions by letting Anne interrupt the meeting. Elaine, however, merely met his glare with a raised eyebrow which asked if, heaven forbid, this incident was going to be reflected in her annual performance evaluation report.

"Fatigue is not my problem right now, thank you, Dane," she said in a calm voice. "I'm sorry to barge in on your meeting, but I think you'll agree that I have an interest in the proceedings." Ordinarily Anne would never have taken advantage of her husband's rank to insinuate herself into the functioning of the office, as some ambassadors' wives were wont to do. However, she had noticed that Stileforth was bearing up extremely well in the face of the bad news about her husband, and she wanted to be certain that something was being done for Bill. She didn't give a damn about the pecking order at the office or about anyone's promotion. She just wanted her husband back, and was not about to sit around the house with her hands folded in the hope that someone was going to deliver him for her.

"You were saying, Claude," she continued with a firmness in her voice which made it clear that her presence was not open to discussion.

"I was just speculating," Lafeur began to stammer. He wasn't sure just what he meant yet. "It seems almost as if they wanted to be certain that they were seen heading into the 'forbidden zone,' as if they hung around until the police showed up so that they would *have* to shoot their way past them."

Lyle Fiore of the DEA cocked his head and pursed his lips as he contemplated this. He was used to dealing with rather devious, unscrupulous types, and this kind of thinking was right up his alley.

"That's absurd!" Stileforth snapped. "There could be any number of reasons why it took the kidnappers as long as it did to go from point A to point B in this city. The place is in a virtual state of war. They could have had a flat tire, taken a wrong turn, anything. Aren't you being just a little too machiavellian? I know it's an occupational hazard of your agency, but aren't you being just a bit silly to think that this group would risk everything on such a stunt? What if the policemen had been a little quicker on the trigger? It could have all ended right there."

"It's just pure speculation on my part," Lafeur said, defensively raising his hands. "It just seems that this group has done nothing so far that wasn't intentional. They don't make many mistakes, and they don't seem to have any fear about being able to dominate any situation.

All of these little indicators of their location . . . It's just too nicely packaged."

"Well, they've made a mistake now," Stileforth said. "We know where they are, and we have the means to deal with them in no uncertain terms."

"I only raise the point," Lafeur went on, his palms still held up in front of him, "because, if we accept the theory that the terrorists somehow intentionally staged the shootout with the police, it must have been for a reason. It would then appear that they wanted us to know, or at least to believe, that they had gone to this headquarters area in the 'forbidden zone,' which would mean that maybe they've laid some kind of trap for us."

"Well, I for one certainly don't accept your theory," Stileforth said, "and, what's more, if these backwoods terrorists think that they can trap the American Delta Force, they'll find the jaws of their trap slamming shut on a very hard nut indeed."

†

Featherstone became aware of his aching limbs first. His eyes were still shut tight, or maybe he was still locked in the trunk of the car, he thought. For a moment he tried to force himself to believe that he was actually home in bed, but he was lying on something hard, cold, and damp which killed that fleetingly comforting idea. He opened one eye a crack and saw that he was actually in a glaringly bright room, lying on a cement floor inside what appeared to be a cage constructed of chain link fencing.

He slowly turned over and sat up. He found that he had been stripped down to his underpants, and he almost chuckled to himself when the thought struck him that this was why his mother had always told him to put on clean shorts every morning. The sight of the young man with the dark eyes who sat on a metal folding chair outside the cage with an Uzi cradled in his lap froze the chuckle in his throat.

Without acknowledging the presence of the guard, who also showed no reaction to Featherstone's movements, Featherstone began to examine his surroundings. "His" cage was about four feet square and six feet high, not quite high enough for him to stand upright. It was made of chain link supported by a stout metal frame anchored firmly in the floor. The only furnishings consisted of a plastic bucket in one corner. The room outside was apparently part of a basement, perhaps fifteen by twenty feet, with a heavy metal door next to the guard's chair, and no windows at all. Featherstone was still a little woozy from the ether or chloroform or whatever they had used to knock him out, and his throat felt sticky and sore.

"Could I have a glass of water?" he asked the guard. He did his best not to make it sound like a plea, trying to adjust his tone to imply that the kidnappers had committed a grave social faux pas by failing to anticipate his thirst, but he wasn't at all sure it had come out that way.

"You'll have to wait for Padre Lazaro," the guard replied. "He should be here shortly."

"And he didn't give you the authority to issue water?" Featherstone sniped sarcastically.

"No, he didn't." The guard had been staring more or less blankly ahead, but now he turned and stared Featherstone full in the face. "His purpose might be for you to die of thirst, and I wouldn't want to set back his timetable." Featherstone assumed that this was meant as some kind of cruel joke, but he saw no humor in the young face, only the tired look of someone who had probably carried out even worse orders. He saw that the man held his Uzi very casually, not toying with it or posturing with it. It was like an extension of his arm, like a carpenter with his hammer or a plumber with a wrench.

"What's your name?" Featherstone asked. "I suppose you know mine." He had read the testimony of many hostages over the years, since this was a topic which American diplomats tended to take rather seriously. He vaguely recalled that it was good policy to try to get on personal terms with one's captors, to show them that you were not just the official representative of Yankee imperialism but a human being. The theory was that establishing such a relationship would make the kidnapper more reluctant to kill you. It was just a theory, but it was worth a try.

The young man, however, just returned to his blank gaze, and Featherstone could see that he had tuned him out. Nonetheless, Featherstone was about to try again, if only for the comfort of hearing his own voice, when the door to the room swung open.

Three men entered. Two were burly mulattos, probably Dominicans, wearing blue jeans and the traditional tank top of manual laborers, each carrying a black baton, about three feet long. The third man was smaller and very lean, but not what you would call skinny. He must have been in his early forties, a light touch of grey in the short curly hair at his temples. He had leathery skin like a campesino farmer, or a soldier. But the most striking thing about him was his intensity. It was not just the burning look in his eyes, but every movement was like part of a carefully calculated plan aimed at a distant goal.

The two larger men took up positions on either side of Featherstone's cage, and the guard, who had risen when the group entered, had now quietly shut the door and stood in front of it. The intense man stepped up to the cage and stood there, rocking slightly forward on the balls of his feet like a karate expert about to enter into combat. Featherstone, too, had risen unconsciously, and now was trying to stand erect, something which the roof of the cage prevented him from doing, forcing him to bow his head slightly. He suspected that this was a psychological ploy to put him in a subservient posture, and he hoped that the fact that he recognized it as such would prevent it from having that effect.

"Who are you, and what do you want with me?" Featherstone asked, again trying to keep his voice flat and emotionless. He quickly decided that empty threats and indignation would get him little with these obviously very professional people, and they might actually respect his getting down to business directly.

"My name is Padre Lazaro," the man replied, "and I am the leader of the group popularly known as the santistas. As to what we want with you, I believe we already have it, thank you."

"If you're hoping to obtain some kind of political concessions from the United States government, or a ransom," Featherstone stated, trying to look and sound as distinguished as possible while standing half hunched over in a cage in his underwear, "I should advise you that the American government has a strict policy of not negotiating with terrorists."

"And a very wise policy it is," said Lazaro in the same kind of pleasant, understanding tone the beloved village priest might use in dealing with a young boy's confessions. "I certainly wouldn't expect them to deviate from it on my account, although we both know that the American government has negotiated, made concessions, and even paid out substantial sums of money to terrorists when it suited their fancy. Of course, then you come to the more difficult problem of defining just what you mean by 'terrorist.' If you can bend the definition enough, you can deal with just about anybody."

The man's coolness and sarcasm were infuriating, and Featherstone could feel his own fear welling up inside him and coming out in a wave of rage. "Then what the hell do you want with me? Are you just some sort of tinpot little tyrant who gets off on killing and terrorizing . . ."

Featherstone didn't get to finish his thought, as one of the husky men reached through the mesh of the cage and jabbed him in the ribs with the end of his long black baton. The jolt of electricity from the cattle prod shot through Featherstone's body, sucking the air out of his lungs.

"Jesus," he screamed as he bounced off the far wall of the cage. The other man was waiting there with his prod and gave Featherstone another shot from that side. There was nowhere inside the cage that Featherstone could stand to be out of reach of their weapons.

"Oh, God!" he shouted, doubling over on the floor in the fetal position.

Lazaro raised his hand, and his two men stepped back slightly from the cage.

"I'm very sorry about that, Mr. Featherstone. Can I call you Bill?" Lazaro smiled down at him in a benign way. "I don't personally take offense at your outburst. I understand the situation you're in and how you must feel helpless and frustrated, but I'm afraid my followers do demand a certain level of respect from others in dealing with me. I can't very well be angry with them for that, can I?"

Even as he lay on the floor, overcome with a coughing fit and with his muscles still twitching uncontrollably, Featherstone noticed that Lazaro hadn't exactly set any speed records in stopping his men, and they had, after all, come into the room equipped with cattle prods in the first place. This must be some sort of warped version of the "good cop-bad cop" thing.

Featherstone finally regained his composure and rolled up to a sitting position. "Then what *do* you want? I don't have any information that would be of use to you that you can't read in the newspapers."

Lazaro let out a long, friendly chuckle. "My dear Bill, I assure you that, if I had wanted information from you, you would have been begging for the opportunity to tell me by now." Lazaro stopped laughing and locked Featherstone's eyes in a burning stare. "I've done that sort of thing before."

At first Featherstone had been indignant at the presumption of this man, but there was a kind of cold fire in his eyes which sent chills down Featherstone's spine. Like most people, Featherstone had sometimes wondered, usually when watching some celluloid hero undergoing torture and making his foes shake their heads in disbelief at his endurance, how he might stand up to it. Now that he was confronted with a man he had every reason to believe dished out pain to his fellow human beings as part of his daily work, all he could think of was that he didn't want to be hurt. His mind was racing with how to give this man whatever he wanted while sacrificing the minimum of his pride.

"No, Bill," Lazaro continued. "It's your presence here that I want, and that's all I need from you for the moment."

"And how long do you intend to keep me here?" Featherstone was desperately trying to keep the whining tone out of his voice, but he doubted whether he was fooling Lazaro.

"I'm afraid I can't put a specific time limit on it," Lazaro said airily. "You see, it all depends very much on the actions of other parties which I can only affect indirectly. It could be as little as a few days. It could turn out to be months, or even years. You may or may not be aware that I have spent a good deal of time in the Middle East where the holding of hostages for such periods is not unheard of."

"If you don't plan to negotiate or demand anything, and if you don't care about anything I might know, what exactly are you trying to accomplish?" Featherstone asked again.

Lazaro sat on the metal chair the guard had vacated, but he didn't even appear to take the weight off his feet. He sat poised on the edge, leaning slightly forward, as if always ready to spring.

"I like that," he said expansively. "This is the first question that seems to come from genuine curiosity and not out of a sense of fear for yourself. It shows that you have some character, Bill."

Featherstone just sighed. "I'm happy you're happy. Now, would you mind answering the question?"

"Not at all. And it's not that you'll never live to tell anyone, as they say in the movies. Actually, I would have thought it pretty obvious. You see, our kidnapping you, just like our attacks on the homes of the rich, the temporary seizure of the television stations, and the drubbing we have been giving the police, are all just evidence that the government has lost control of the country. In your particular case, we have you, and they won't be able to get you back. That will be a message for the rich and powerful that we can get at anyone we choose, no matter how well protected he seems to be, and the government can't do anything to save them, no matter how hard they try. While I'm sure that our methods appear very bloody to you, my real purpose is to avoid a wholesale civil war by scaring the wealthy exploiters out of the country. When the money men go, the handful of mercenaries who have been keeping the people down will go too, and we will simply take over, not unlike what happened in Cuba back in 1959."

"Haven't you been reading the papers?" Featherstone asked incredulously. "Communism's dead. It doesn't work. I really didn't think that anyone gave that Che Guevara ideology a thought anymore. You might be able to seize power, but you can't run an economy, and you can't hope to keep the people down any better than the KGB in Russia."

"Oh, no, no, no," Lazaro said, holding up his hands. "I was afraid you'd get that impression. In fact, if our campaign were going to last any longer, I'd have to take steps to see that this wasn't a common misconception. We're not communists, Bill. We favor the common man over the rich. We favor the good of the many over the good of the few, but I really don't think that Marx invented any of that. We don't believe in a strong centralized state with its secret police and command economy. If you had to classify us in political science terms, I guess you could call us anarchists in the sense that we don't want to wait for the state to wither away. We want it gone right now."

"But who's going to run things?" Featherstone asked, for a moment letting his fascination in the beliefs Lazaro clearly held with such sincerity push out of his mind the fact that he was sitting in his underwear in a cage surrounded by armed terrorists.

"God's will," he answered simply.

Featherstone rocked back, suppressing a laugh. "And whom, may I ask, has God designated as his spokesman here on earth? You, by any chance?"

Lazaro raised his hand as the two men with the prods took a step closer to the cage. "No, not me. I have been designated, as you put it, as the one who will open up the door to freedom for my people, but, like Moses, I do not expect to set foot in the promised land myself. We will drive the men who have butchered the poor from this country. They have butchered them through their neglect and their greed, letting them die far worse deaths from hunger and disease than quicker deaths from bullets or gas. Believe me, I have seen both up close, and I don't have any doubts about the one I would prefer for myself. When these exploiters are gone, the people will choose their own leaders from among themselves, and they won't need us anymore."

"Ah, but that's what they all say," Featherstone said, wagging his finger in the air. "Once you're in power, then there'll be the question about whether *all* of the enemies of the people are gone, and you'll have to have some kind of security organization to weed out the survivors, and anyone else who challenges your vision of the future."

Lazaro locked Featherstone in his fiery gaze again, and the smile faded from Featherstone's lips. "I will not keep power, and I will kill anyone who tries to subvert the will of God for his own selfish purposes. I have seen the Church corrupted to serve the rich. I have seen communism corrupted to serve the powerful. That is why I sought my allies in Islam. They are not perfect either, of course. They have their corrupt and their power hungry, but the fundamentalists alongside whom I have fought for years are the only 'fanatics' left. They are not fighting for what they can amass in this world, but are storing up values that will be of use in the next. That is what we Christians have forgotten how to do. There are no Crusaders any more. My people have learned this level of belief anew with me, and while we stand together there is no force on earth which can stop us. God is with us, and we will triumph."

With that Lazaro rose, his eyes glazed over with the vision of things unseen by mere mortals. He turned toward the door, and the three guards prepared to follow him.

"Wait a minute!" Featherstone almost shouted, jumping to his feet and grabbing onto the mesh of the front of the cage. "Can't I have my clothes back? And something to drink? And maybe a newspaper or something to read?" He hadn't meant it to come out like that. He had read that in hostage situations, the captive can help put pressure on the kidnappers by making demands for reasonable things, usually things that had simply not occurred to the captors. He had planned to make a list of demands during the course of his conversation with Lazaro, but his sudden departure brought it home to Featherstone how badly he wanted these things. It had sounded like a frightened child pleading instead of an outraged diplomat insisting on the Geneva Convention.

Lazaro turned slowly at the doorway, as if just waking up from a deep sleep. "Oh, yes. We'll be leaving you a bottle of water shortly. As for the clothes, I think you'll find it more comfortable dressed just the way you are. It gets very warm down here in the afternoons. And, no, I can't allow you any reading material. I think it will do your soul immeasurable good to appreciate the mind-numbing boredom that the poor, whom you do not teach to read, have to endure all of their lives." With that he strode out the door, followed by all three guards. The door shut solidly behind him. There was a small window in the door, and Featherstone got a glimpse of the first young guard, taking a peek at him before the light in the hallway beyond was extinguished, and the face disappeared.

Featherstone remained standing, staring at the door for a long time. He had been in situations before that either were dangerous or could have become so, as many diplomats had, but this was the first time he had been so totally alone. He supposed that something was being done to rescue him or to arrange his release. He supposed, but he didn't know. He couldn't help but think about the hostages in Lebanon who had been held a year, or two, or more, and about that CIA station chief in Beirut who apparently had been tortured to death after long months of imprisonment. Whether that would happen to him was completely out of his hands. It would be decided by this Lazaro character, who was obviously completely out of his mind, and there wasn't a damn thing Featherstone could do about it.

He had already made the decisions that had put him in this position, Featherstone reminded himself. After his last tour he could have easily taken assignments in Washington for the rest of his career. He had a house with a modest mortgage payment, and Anne could have even gone back to work, so the normal economic crunch of returning to the States would not have been a problem. But then they had offered him this ambassadorship. He had seen so many bad ambassadors in his time that he had longed for the chance to do the job right, and he had wanted to give Anne the reward of the status and prestige of being the ambassador's wife. At least it had seemed logical at the time.

He had known that any American diplomat always stood the chance of being the target of terrorists. He had known that was why they gave you bodyguards, because you might need them, although, he reflected, having them seemed not to have done him much good. He had made the same mistake of every victim since Abel, thinking it couldn't happen to him.

He sat down cross-legged on the cement floor. He looked around him again, as if new things might have appeared in his sharply reduced world since the last time he had looked. There was nothing, no bedding, no food, nothing. He had never been able to sleep properly without a pillow, but he supposed that he would have to learn. What he really missed most was having something to do. He had read about prisoners making little chess sets or decks of cards out of scrap paper, but he didn't have even that. He thought of what it would be like to spend a whole day staring at blank concrete walls, then another day, a week, a month. He feared he might go mad.

He had no idea what time it was, but he was tired. He rolled over stiffly and stretched out on the hard floor. He lay his head down on his forearm, and he quickly felt the circulation to his hand being cut off. He glanced over at the bucket in the corner. Urinating wouldn't be much of a problem, but he didn't look forward to doing anything serious other than in a proper bathroom, which was why he had never enjoyed camping. Well, he would put that off as long as possible, and maybe they would lighten up on him a little in time.

He closed his eyes to shut out the bright fluorescent light and tried to go to sleep. He wondered if they would kill him, or torture him. He just wanted to go home, get his wife, and get the hell out of this damn country. He wanted to be in their "two-story colonial" in Springfield, on the Virginia side of Washington. It had been a long time, years maybe, since Featherstone had done more than shed an odd tear at some movie, but now his shoulders heaved, and he turned his face toward the wall, away from the door.

†

"Delta Force, my ass," Colonel Palacios grumbled as he slapped a magazine into his M-16. "We don't need a bunch of gringos to come down here and wipe our butts for us. We know where the bastards are, and we've got the balls to go in and get them ourselves."

The police counterinsurgency commando sitting next to him on the bench, busily cleaning his rifle, simply looked over and nodded dumbly, not having the vaguest idea what the Colonel was talking about. They were sitting with about thirty other commandos in a large warehouse in the small 27 de Febrero Navy Base on the eastern side of the Rio Ozama, opposite Santo Domingo. All of the men were wearing dark camouflage fatigues, and were preparing their weapons, strapping on equipment, and marking up each others' faces with black camouflage paint sticks.

Palacios leaned his rifle against the bench and stepped up to a mapboard which was propped up on an easel at one end of the warehouse. He pulled a bayonet from its sheath at his belt to use as a pointer and tapped it against the mapboard loudly.

"Listen up, everyone!" he shouted, waiting for the rustling and clicking of equipment to die down. "You've all had your individual briefings from your section leaders, but let's put the big picture together one more time so that you understand what your own part means in the overall scheme."

He turned toward the map covering the southeastern portion of Santo Domingo and a stretch of the bordering river. "At 0400 hours we will be towed up the Ozama in three inflatable assault craft by the patrol boat *Cambiasco*, which has been making runs up and down the river every few hours to establish a pattern. It's a moonless night, and we've seen to it that the power is out in the area, so we should be able to cut loose from the starboard side of the *Cambiasco*, away from the city, and drop astern without being noticed. We'll then make a landing at this old quay here," he said, pointing with his bayonet to the map. "Half a dozen Navy attack swimmers will have gone ashore first in order to secure our assembly area in the so-called 'forbidden zone.'" Palacios hated that expression. No one could "forbid" him to go wherever the hell he wanted in his town. "There's nothing moving in the zone at that hour according to our reconnaissance posts, so, as soon as we have formed up, we should be able to move quickly along this street, making maximum use of cover and avoiding contact with the enemy, to this point, a small square with tree cover right next to the suspected enemy headquarters complex, arriving on target at 0435 hours."

Palacios swung over to the other side of the map and shifted his bayonet-pointer to his other hand. "At that time, an armored column will crank up, here, on the western edge of the zone. It will consist of four V-150 armored cars and half a dozen half tracks filled with infantry belonging to the First Armored Battalion. The orders for the rest of the armored battalion will be to make a noisy demonstration just as we hit the headquarters complex walls with satchel charges, blasting our own doorways. Our mission will be to secure the buildings and rescue the American ambassador, who is reported to be inside. Then we hold until relieved by the armored column, which will barrel right to the headquarters area and laager with us. With any luck, between our attack and theirs, we'll decapitate this fucking terrorist movement in ten minutes' time, and open the way for the rest of the 1st Brigade to sweep through the zone and mop up."

He sheathed his bayonet and locked his hands behind his back, rocking forward on the balls of his feet. "I have to tell you men that there's a weather front coming in tomorrow night, and I normally would have waited for that to help cover our move. But I have reason to believe that the Americans will be sending in their own forces to attempt to accomplish this same mission, at least to save their ambassador, so we need to move first. I say this, not because I want to hog the glory. I say this because we need to act for the good of our country. If the Americans come in, they'll save their man . . . maybe. They haven't had a very good record of hostage rescue over the years. But then they'll pull out and leave us with the stigma of having knuckled under to the Yankees, let them run wild on our soil, and we'll be no closer to eliminating these damned santistas than we are now. Only we'll never be able beat them then, because the people will have turned away from us, we'll look like fools."

There was a grumble of agreement from the assembled men. "So we're going in there, and we're going to get even for all of our friends who have been murdered in the line of duty, and for all the women and children these animals have slaughtered across the city." There was a shout of approval. "And I don't want to be slowed down with any fucking prisoners!" The men let out a cheer.

"Sir, what are our orders for dealing with any civilians we run across enroute to the target?" a senior sergeant asked over the din.

Palacios paused for a moment, setting his jaw grimly. "Your rifles are equipped with silencers. We cannot afford to be spotted by anyone before we reach the target and the diversionary movement starts. We must assume that anyone we encounter in the 'forbidden zone' is there because they support the santistas. Do you understand me?"

"Yes, sir!" Thirty men roared in unison.

†

It was still pitch dark when the three Rigid Raider assault boats cut loose from the *Cambiasco* as it growled north up the Ozama River.

As the 160-foot gunboat pulled ahead of the bobbing craft, Palacios could see the dark silhouette of the disused quay off to his left. There were a few points of light among the buildings where residents had kerosene lanterns lit, but the entire quarter of the city seemed to be engulfed in darkness. As had been its pattern on previous passes, the *Cambiasco* switched on two powerful searchlight and played them along the shore to help blind any watchers to the commandos' approach.

The muffled motors of the assault boats could not be heard over the low rumbling of the *Cambiasco's* engines. They bounced over the larger boat's phosphorescent wake and moved smoothly toward the shore, while the men in the boats lay low to limit their profile. Palacios could make out a flashing red light, the safety signal from one of the advance swimmers.

They quickly moved into the lee of the docks and made the boats fast. The well-trained commandos climbed up to street level with agility and took cover among the scattered crates and pilings of the dock. Palacios hoisted himself up and found himself face to face with the leader of the Navy swimmers. The man wore a black wetsuit, still dripping, and in his hand carried an automatic pistol with a long silencer attached to the barrel.

"Any trouble?" Palacios asked in a whisper.

"Just one night watchman, probably working for that warehouse company over there," the Navy man answered, gesturing with his pistol to where a pair of feet clad in dirty sneakers stuck out from behind a stack of boxes.

"Good work," Palacios. "Have your men hold here until the *Cambiasco* comes back to you with word that we've completed the mission. They'll take you off."

The Navy man nodded and moved off silently through the shadows. This was evidence for Palacios of the only real weakness of his plan, the lack of reliable communications. He couldn't help but grit his teeth at the thought of how, in the armies and police forces of wealthier nations, each man on a mission like this would have a small, individual radio to provide instant, encrypted communication. His force would have to depend upon two bulky backpack PRC/77 sets, since, during their pre-operational equipment check, those were the only two sets which worked. He would take one radio operator with him, about four men back from the head of the column as they moved toward the objective, and his executive officer, Captain Vega, would have the other near the tail of the column. To communicate with the relieving armored force, they would have to switch frequencies, and to call the *Cambiasco*, should they run into real trouble and have to bug out, they would have to change again.

Palacios gave a hand signal and his two snipers dashed across the open street to the nearest buildings, each with his assigned assistant/ spotter. They reached the buildings, and one team adeptly scaled a rain gutter while the other scrambled up a fire escape to take positions on nearby rooftops from which they could cover the team for most of its half mile approach to the objective.

The snipers each carried an American M-14 rifle, equipped with a long silencer and an even bulkier starlight scope mounted over the barrel. Palacios again grimaced at the thought that a modern counter-terrorist force would have fancy night vision goggles, but those two scopes, plus the one carried by his point man were the only functioning units in the Dominican military inventory. Still, they would give his men a decided edge over the santistas who would have nothing more sophisticated than the good old "eyeball, Mark I."

When the snipers had had time to get into position, Palacios signalled his point man to move out. The man dashed up to where the street opened onto the quay and paused at the corner to sight down his rifle, using the starlight scope to check out the first leg of the route. He gave Palacios the thumbs-up sign and rushed up the street to the first doorway, while the number two man took up his position to cover him and another took up a similar position on the other side of the street. In this manner, in lunges of ten or twenty yards at a time, the entire group of some thirty men were fed down the narrow, darkened street toward their goal.

Although the streets were dark and deserted, the city was not totally quiet, which suited Palacios just fine. As the men paused in recessed doorways or alleyways, they could hear conversations coming from within some of the buildings. In the distance one could make out the roar of an occasional truck engine on the highway a couple of miles to the north, and there were always a few faint strains of music coming from some unseen radio or record player. The men could also hear odd whistles, meaningless shouts, and catcalls from somewhere among the darkened roofs, the sounds of any poor neighborhood on a hot, humid night when not everyone could sleep.

It was hot and sticky, as it usually got just before a storm blew in, but Palacios was sweating far more than the weather would account for. They had advanced about 300 yards up the street in a series of very rapid spurts which left Palacios panting for breath. He was grateful that the column hadn't come across even the odd drunk on the street. Although he wouldn't bat an eye at killing just about anyone he found in this "enemy territory," he much preferred that everything go exactly according to plan, leaving nothing to the discretion of his men. Once they reached the jump-off point for the actual assault, he could give the orders directly again. On the other hand, the tension of this near total quiet was driving him insane, and he had half a mind to just have his men rush ahead to the objective, relying on speed instead of stealth for success, but he held back. Just another ten minutes, and they would be there.

†

Padre Lazaro and Pablo Baca had taken direct command of the forces which would oppose the armored battalion on the west side of the zone, since it appeared that they were gearing up for something. Luis, meanwhile, had set up his large NOD (Night Observation Device) on its tripod on the narrow balcony of a fourth floor apartment with a view of the narrow street leading back to the docks.

His many lookouts who were living throughout the zone had quickly reported the commandos' landing and their route of advance. Looking through the large cylindrical device, the image looked like a black and white film of the street at high noon. The commandos who thought they were invisible in their black face paint and camouflage in the shadows looked almost comical as they crouched in what was plain view to Luis.

"I make at least twenty-four of them with one radio man near the front and one near the back. There's another man with each radio, which would make them officers," he said in the dull voice of a radio announcer reading off commodity prices.

Young Pedro Delgado knelt by his side, sighting through the thermal imaging device attached to his Soviet-made Dragunov sniper rifle. "I've got at least that many plus two pairs on the rooftops on either side of the street, snipers."

Luis nodded and cupped his hand to his ear momentarily. "The teams are in position on both sides now," he said. Then he keyed the mike of his radio headset and mumbled a few words into it.

Where the commandos had to move through the streets banking on darkness which had not been any protection against low light magnifiers and thermal imagers, the santista forces had set up an elaborate network "through" the buildings of each block, knocking holes in walls connecting adjacent apartments, which permitted them to move invisibly, day or night. They were now in position in the apartment buildings and stores all along the street, with fields of fire all along the opposite side of the street.

"Go for the rear radio operator first," Luis said drily.

Pedro snugged the rifle up to his cheek and began to take slow, measured breaths. His finger tightened gradually on the trigger, and then the weapon kicked slightly, the only noticeable sound being the bolt sliding home.

Palacios thought he heard something behind him, but it was time for another rush, and he and his radio operator scuttled forward, hugging the side of the building for fifteen yards to a garage doorway which offered about eight inches of concealment.

Captain Vega only heard his radio operator fall. He assumed the man had stumbled under his heavy load, but when he grabbed the man's arm to help him up, it was limp. He stooped to turn the man over when something hit him hard at the base of his skull, flipping him over the body and blowing out the front of his head. His rifle clattered to the ground.

The man across the street from Vega saw both the radio man and the captain go down and hissed, "Sniper! Freeze!" as loud as he dared. Other men up the column passed the word, but it took agonizing seconds before the news reached Palacios. When it did, his radio man instinctively stuck his head out to look back down the column to see what was the matter. Just as Palacios grabbed hold of his collar to drag him back, something smacked into his neck, just above Palacios' fingers, and the man sagged to his knees and leaned against the metal of the garage door.

"Jesus Christ!" was all Palacios could think to say.

"Now!" Luis shouted over his headset mike. He grabbed a German G-3 assault rifle and began firing into the night. He didn't need a night vision device anymore, he merely fired a burst into each shadowy doorway where he knew a commando to be hiding. Pedro was being more precise, picking his shots with care, just as he had learned to do in the marshes of the Fao Peninsula when the ammunition rafts had been blown up behind them. They had held out for three days against repeated Iraqi assaults with what they had carried into battle with them. Old habits die hard.

All along the street the shuttered windows of second floor rooms burst open and the muzzles of automatic weapons emerged, spitting fire. Half-a-dozen commandos went down in the first seconds. There were shouted curses and commands as men dove for whatever cover they could find, but those that survived at least now had something to shoot at and fought back with cool savagery, spraying the windows with gunfire, occasionally to be rewarded with the sound of a scream.

"Pull back!" Palacios screamed, as he continued to hold onto his radio man's collar with one hand while he fired his M-16 with the other, cutting down a young woman wearing a white T-shirt and blazing away with an Uzi as she emerged on a balcony opposite him. "Back to the docks!"

Without relinquishing his slender cover, Palacios was able to get ahold of the radio handset. He tried to call Vega, but there was no answer. He fumbled with the frequency knob and called the *Cambiasco*, ordering her to put about and cover their withdrawal. Lastly, he tried to contact the armored column, but he couldn't raise them. He suspected that he had the wrong frequency settings, but every time he tried to twist the radio man around to get a better look at the dials, he was covered with a shower of plaster and cement chips as bullets tore up the edge of the garage around him. Well, they would have to take care of themselves. Anyway, he assumed that First Brigade Headquarters would be monitoring all of the frequencies and would advise them of the aborted mission.

He finally released his hold on the radio man, who slumped over into the street, snatched up his rifle again and made a break for it back up the street, bullets kicking up dust and asphalt around his feet as he ran. It looked as though his men on the left side of the street had had better luck in silencing the terrorists opposite them than had those on the right, so he screamed for everyone to cut over to that side of the street for the run back. A couple of men tried it, but they were cut down halfway across by a machinegun apparently set up to fire down the length of the street.

The man who had been walking point caught up to Palacios as

they both crouched in a narrow alley. The man was trembling with fear. Even in the darkness Palacios could make out that one of his sleeves was glistening with blood from a wound in the shoulder. Palacios traded weapons with the man and hurried him back down the street.

Armed with the night scope-equipped rifle, Palacios peeked around the corner of the building and could see the muzzle flashes from the machinegun as it put down a withering fire, sweeping the length of the street. Glancing the other way, he could make out more than a dozen bodies scattered along the street and the gun flashes of his men and their opponents as they worked their way toward the docks. Taking a deep breath, Palacios switched the rifle over to fire left-handed, taking advantage of the little cover the building afforded him, and sighted on the machinegun. In the eery greenish image of the scope, he could see three figures, the gunner, his loader and another figure who appeared to be directing their fire. He aimed at the gunner and squeezed off a round. He saw the figure jerk up and then drop down. A burst from the machinegun arched off into the night sky. The other two figures dropped out of sight before he could take aim again, but that was good enough. He ducked out into the street and ran for it. He stopped to nudge a couple of the bodies of his men, sprawled in the street. Most had been cut to ribbons and were obviously dead, but he had to check. He didn't want to leave any wounded behind. Those who weren't riddled with bullets all seemed to have clean head shots, however, and were just as dead.

Just ahead of Palacios, a man stepped out onto a narrow, wrought iron balcony and fired a burst from an assault rifle at some of the commandos sheltering on his side of the street. Palacios didn't even bother to aim, just stitched a burst up the length of the man's back and watched him jerk over the railing and fall to the pavement. Palacios felt exhilarated enough that he momentarily thought about turning his men around and charging back to their objective, but a quick glance up the street disabused him of that. There were well over a dozen guns flashing at him from the direction of the terrorist headquarters, forming a skirmish line which seemed to be working its way down the street toward him. Now his men had not only been ambushed, they were also outnumbered.

As Palacios finally emerged onto the docks, he could see that his few surviving men had formed a tight perimeter with the Navy swimmers along the waterfront. As he darted across the open area to the barricade of boxes his men were using, one of his snipers' assistants landed hard on the ground next to him, having leapt from a height of over twenty feet. The man groaned with pain and grabbed his ankle. Palacios ditched his rifle and ran back. He pulled the man's arm around his neck and hauled him to his feet.

"The fuckers were already up there waiting for us when we got into position!" the soldier yelled as they hobbled as fast as possible to cover. "They got Alvarez and his partner before they even got a shot off. I was lucky to have stumbled on one of their men and got him before he got me."

The two men dove over some crates to safety, and Palacios immediately raised his head back up to survey the situation. He counted about ten of his own men left, plus the six Navy men, but they only had pistols. Meanwhile, he could see the flashes of thirty or more automatic weapons coming from the buildings along the dock, with more dark figures coming down the street he had just escaped from.

The growl of the *Cambiasco's* engines had turned to a roar, and she had her siren wailing as well as she churned the muddy river water into foam and pirouetted to head back downstream. As she came closer to where the commandos were gathering, she began to rake the shoreside buildings with fire from her two 3-inch and three 20mm guns, blasting bits of masonry into the air and shattering the few remaining windows. The trapped men cheered and poured fire into the approaching enemy, firing off their last rounds.

The *Cambiasco* was now only about one hundred yards upstream and about fifty yards from the docks. The men got ready to make a dash for the ship as soon as she pulled close enough for them to jump aboard. Suddenly, however, a finger of fire reached out from the roof of one of the buildings and smashed into the superstructure of the ship near the pilot house. Another round exploded amid the crew of the forward 3-inch gun. Then another and another hit the ship, starting fires and killing crewmen.

"Missiles!" Palacios shouted. "The bastards have anti-tank missiles! Fire at where the missile comes from, and try to distract the firer." But most of his men only pulled the empty magazines from their weapons and held them up to Palacios.

"Shit!" Palacios cursed, waving his fist furiously in the air. The *Cambiasco* was ablaze now in several places and had slowed to a crawl.

He could see some of the crewmen diving overboard. No more help from that quarter, he thought.

The sound of small arms fire was increasing from the shore now, and he could see dark figures working their way closer. Clearly, they couldn't wait here much longer.

"Get to the boats!" he shouted. He pulled his own service revolver and fired a couple of rounds at a shadowy figure. "Those who still have ammo, give covering fire."

Several men jumped down to the rafts and manned the engines, others helped some of the wounded down. In a moment, only Palacios and the leader of the Navy swimmers were left on the dock, firing their pistols until they were empty.

"Let's get going!" Palacios shouted, but the Navy man took a bullet in the throat just then and crumpled to the ground. Palacios leapt into the water and came up spluttering just as one of the rafts floated past him. He was too tired to pull himself aboard, so he just grabbed onto one of the floats for dear life as they pulled away from the shore.

The boats picked up speed slowly, terribly slowly it seemed to Palacios as he clutched a line running the length of the float. He looked back and could see silhouettes standing atop the docks now and firing at the retreating boats. The bullets threw up little geysers of water around the boats and occasionally thunked into the body of the raft or the flesh of one of the men. Finally, they pulled past the floating hulk of the *Cambiasco* and were able to use it as cover until they were out of range. One of the men then reached over and pulled Palacios into the boat. He lay there gasping among the few survivors. The boat's quiet motor purred as it drove them away from the enemy. Palacios was streaming water, serving to hide his tears of rage.

†

On the other side of the "forbidden zone" Captain Frias, commander of the armored column, heard the heavy firing coming from within the zone. They still had not received any radio message from Palacios and his men, but the firing was about on time for their assault on the terrorist headquarters, and he didn't feel that he needed additional orders. He had been to brigade headquarters several hours before. Only a couple of orderlies had been on duty, most of the officers having excused themselves to see to the security of their families.

This disgusted Frias, who was a bachelor, but he was delighted with the prospect of leading this hell-for-leather charge through the heart of bad guy country to rescue the commandos and the American ambassador. His four V-150 armored cars would lead the way, blasting any resistance with their 20mm cannons and machineguns. The half-tracks would follow with the infantry, helping to hose down the avenue of advance with their weapons. He really didn't expect much resistance to an armored force of this power, but it would make things that much easier if the bastards did show themselves and allow him to blast them into eternity.

Frias stood tall in the turret of his armored car and waved his hand in a circle over his head and pointed toward their objective in the traditional cavalry style. The drama was marred somewhat when the lead car dropped out of the column when the bottom of its oil pan fell out, spilling lubricant all over the road. Frias cursed and guided his driver around the disabled vehicle, taking over the lead himself. He vowed to have the sergeant in the platoon's maintenance section up on charges when he got back.

Padre Lazaro had made a personal visit to each of the positions along the expected route of the armored column. Although he had decided to leave Pablo Baca in tactical charge of the defense as a demonstration of his confidence in him, he wanted to make certain that Baca's lack of recent combat experience might not result in disaster. In the event, he had found the dispositions to be excellent, and he returned to the rooftop from which he planned to watch the battle. He knew that he couldn't always count on a deserter providing him with the outline of the enemy's offensive plans, but he thought he might as well enjoy it when he had the luxury.

The santistas' main weapons would be German-made Armbrust (crossbow) anti-tank rockets. Like the older American LAW rocket, the Armbrust is a single shot, disposable weapon, the firing tube being discarded after use. Because the Arbrust didn't have a back blast, it could be fired inside a closed space. Most recoilless weapons essentially fired a rocket-type projectile from a tube, with the rearward force of the rocket being expelled out the back, but the Armbrust expelled a countermass of small plastic flakes which absorbed the force of the rocket launch harmlessly. It also produced very little visible flash. Since its short range, about 300 meters, would not be a problem in an urban environment, it was an ideal weapon for street fighting. They would soon see if it lived up to its advertisements.

Since the santistas possessed only a few Armbrusts and would have to save some in case of further armored attacks, they would be supplemented with piles of the traditional Molotov cocktails which had been stashed at strategic points all around the perimeter of the zone.

Soldiers pulled aside a sawhorse barrier, in front of Frias' vehicle, and his armored car picked up speed, crossing the line into the "forbidden zone." He and the other vehicle commanders rode "unbuttoned," standing halfway out the top hatch of the turret for better visibility. If there were trouble, he would simply drop down inside, pulling the hatch shut behind him and hose down the suspect buildings with the fire from the 20mm gun. Meanwhile, he manned a .30 calibre machinegun mounted on the turret and kept careful watch on the darkened windows and rooftops as the column moved down the narrow street. The vehicles rode with all lights blazing, since there was no attempt at surprise, and Frias would need all of the visibility he could get if the column were attacked.

They passed one block, then another, and still there was no sign that the enemy was even aware of their presence. Frias began to feel very confident. There had been reports from the intelligence section speculating that the santistas actually had very limited manpower, and it now appeared that, from the volume of fire he could hear coming from the direction of the suspected headquarters complex, they were fully occupied trying to fend off the commandos. If so, his force would have a cakewalk right into their objective. It might even be that they, not the commandos, would be the ones to rescue the American ambassador by a coup de main.

Frias was easing back against the hatch cover, one hand resting casually on his machinegun, when there was a roar behind him. As he turned, a large hunk of jagged metal flew through the air past his head, and he saw the second armored car in the column burst into flame. He screamed in his headset mike to his driver to stop as he dropped down inside the turret, just having time to see the third car go up in flames as well.

He frantically worked the joystick to swing his turret around, pressing down on the trigger of the 20mm, sending a stream of shells randomly into the walls of the adjacent buildings. He looked through the narrow vision block for targets, but all he could see was a shower of flaming arcs as molotov cocktails rained down on the halftracks stalled behind the disabled V-150s. He fired blindly at the edges of the buildings from which the molotovs had come, but already he could see blossoms of flame erupting from the open-topped halftracks. There were muzzle flashes from darkened windows and soldiers who were not immediately incinerated in their vehicles were cut down in the street.

It suddenly occurred to Frias that he was doing little good where he was, other than providing the attackers with a stationary target. He screamed at his driver to get rolling. The three infantrymen sitting in the back of the car were firing their weapons through the gun ports at nothing in particular, and the noise was deafening. Frias had never actually been in a firefight before, and the smell of cordite, smoke, and fear almost made him vomit. Perhaps he could turn at the next corner, double back on a parallel street to the starting point, and come up from behind to try to rescue any survivors of the column.

The driver, however, had panicked, and instead of making the turn, had overshot and plowed into the building on the corner. He worked the gears desperately, but couldn't get the car to go into reverse.

Baca shouldered the Armbrust himself. One of the newer men had missed his first shot at the lead vehicle, but there was time now to take careful aim. The rest of the army vehicles were already afire, and only a small knot of men had managed to get out and were fighting their way back to their lines. Baca had left orders to let them go. The terror-filled stories they would tell their comrades would do more damage to the army than would killing them.

The armored car was stuck in the rubble of the building it had just smashed into, and Baca lined up the sights carefully on the deck plate just behind the turret. The armor on the top of the car was the weakest, and he had a clear line of fire from his third story window. He squeezed the trigger, and the weapon rocked in his hands. There was an explosion followed shortly by a rapid series of smaller ones from within the vehicle as ammunition cooked off. A man had thrown open the top hatch of the turret and was trying to drag himself off. His clothes were on fire, and he appeared to have the use of only one arm. Baca picked up his rifle and aimed at the man's chest. He fired a single three-round burst, and the man slumped over the hatch, his helmet dropping off his head and clattering to the street. There was no point in letting the poor bastard suffer, Baca thought to himself.

†

When Lafeur worried, he tended to treat himself to food with high caloric content. From his growing girth, one would assume that he worried a great deal, but he also tended to treat himself when things were going well. He considered this a "win-win" arrangement. Today's intake, however, decidedly fell under the worrying column. He had stopped at "Giorgissimo's," the one really decent ice cream parlor in town, and had bought a pint of his favorite mixture, called "Caribeño," chocolate ice cream with hunks of semi-sweet chocolate, coconut, and something like rice crispies. Actually, by American standards, the ice cream at "Giorgissimo's" was pretty poor, more like ice milk, but it was refreshing, and one had to make do.

Lafeur had spent a late night at the Embassy, helping to plan for the arrival of the Delta Force people, scheduled for the next day. Then he had been awakened early by a call from the Embassy duty officer reporting rumors of a major battle taking place around the fringes of the "zone." He hadn't been able to get hold of any of his regular sources, most of whom had already left the country. By the time he reached the Embassy, around eight o'clock in the morning, the word was out on the radio and television of a significant defeat of the government at the hands of the rebels. There had been film clips of the burned out hulks of armored cars and halftracks, with charred bodies hanging out of them, taken from the news helicopter. He had noticed the subtle change in the newscasters' reference to the bad guys as "rebels" as opposed to "terrorists," a decided upgrade in status.

Things were hectic around the office as everyone was busy preparing "sitreps" and "critic messages" for Washington, but that was finally accomplished by about noon, and Lafeur had been just about to slip out for a sandwich when he received a beeper message from Quiroga calling for an emergency meeting. Since they already had a meeting scheduled for that evening, this implied something serious, and Lafeur was relatively certain that it wouldn't be good news. There seemed to be decided shortage of that commodity at present.

Lafeur arrived at the safehouse ahead of Quiroga. Instead of coming back later, and waiting for Quiroga to place the safety signal as he should have, Lafeur went on into the apartment and was wolfing down his ice cream under the cool breeze of the ceiling fan when Quiroga finally burst through the door.

"Want some ice cream?" Lafeur asked, making a half-hearted effort to reach for a bowl on the kitchen counter.

Quiroga just waved his hand nervously from side to side. "No time now, thanks." Lafeur looked enviously at Quiroga's lean torso and reluctantly put the half-finished container of ice cream aside, wiping his mouth with a paper napkin.

"What's up?" he asked, with the distinct implication that it had better be important.

"Two things," Quiroga said, plopping down in a chair opposite Lafeur. "First, the teltap has been installed and is functioning fine."

"That's great," said Lafeur unenthusiastically. Lafeur had known that this was in the offing, but, considering the nature of recent events, it certainly could have waited a few hours.

Quiroga just smiled at Lafeur's impatience. "The second thing is that you have a fucking spy in your Embassy working for the santistas."

Lafeur dropped the spoon, which he had been licking absent-mindedly, to the floor. "What? Who? How did you find out? Are you sure?" He fired the questions at Quiroga without waiting for any answers.

"It was an accident, really," Quiroga began. "You see, I had the technician hook up the ambassador's private line as a sort of test, to see if he could do it and to be sure that it was the correct line . . ."

"You did what?" Lafeur shouted shrilly. "Do you have any idea how fucking illegal that is? You had better get that line disconnected immediately and burn any tapes you made. No, better yet, give me the tapes and let me burn them myself. Jesus Christ!"

Quiroga just smiled benignly at Lafeur's outburst and let him finish. "Sure. I know how you Americans are about civil rights, or whatever you call it. I had never intended listening to the tapes, but . . ." He pulled a small tape player from the gym bag he carried and pressed the play button.

"He's leaving now." Lafeur heard Maripaz' voice on the slightly raspy recording. Her voice was strained, but there was no doubt about who the speaker was.

Another voice came on the line. "Tell me when the car leaves the gate." This was a man's voice, unfamiliar to Lafeur. There was a pause, and then Maripaz said, "There he goes," and the tape cut off.

"What the hell does that have to do with anything?" Lafeur asked, trying to restrain his temper.

"Well, at first I didn't think it meant anything either," Quiroga went on calmly, "until I heard about the kidnapping of your ambassador and the time it took place."

"And . . . !" Lafeur said impatiently.

"That which you just heard was the entire conversation," Quiroga explained. "No 'Hello. How are you?' Nothing. Just those three words, and the party on the other end of the line didn't say anything either. That sort of reminds you of the kind of conversations we have when we talk on the phone, doesn't it?"

Lafeur had to admit that it was an unusually cryptic telephone call.

"But the significant thing is that the call took place approximately four minutes before your ambassador was ambushed. He was the one who was just leaving. Makes you kind of stop and think, huh?" Quiroga just smiled again.

Lafeur was holding his head in his hands. This wasn't the kind of evidence that would stand up in a court of law, but it would in the spy business. It hurt him to think that Maripaz could have committed such an act of treachery. Not that they had ever been close, but here he was, the supposed resident expert on espionage, and there had been a real spy sitting primly just a few yards from his own desk, and he hadn't had a clue.

"Where was she calling to?" he asked in a subdued voice, not wanting to look Quiroga in the eye.

"That's the problem," Quiroga said, spreading his hands. "We had a technical glitch and only got the first six numbers of the call. Actually, it was a fluke that I even bothered to note that down before the machine erased it."

"But with six numbers, that leaves a maximum of ten possibilities, doesn't it?" Lafeur said with renewed interest.

"Seven, actually," Quiroga said. "I got the tech on it right away, and he gave me three of the numbers. He's getting me a list of the subscribers and addresses now, and Arce and I will start checking them out immediately. But you know that this isn't the States. You have to buy a phone line here, and they're hard to come by, so people transfer them around, and it might take time to find the actual place the phone we want was located. Even then, if these people are sharp, it might turn out to be a bar or a pay phone anyway."

"It's the only lead we have, so get on it."

Quiroga got up and touched his fingers to his right eyebrow in mock salute as he headed for the door.

"And Federico," Lafeur said, rising and putting out his hand, "thanks. You've done a hell of a job, and I'll see that you and Arce and the tech, too, are rewarded for it."

Quiroga winced a bit at this, and Lafeur realized immediately that he had stuck his foot in it.

"I'll pass that along to the others, *hermano*," Quiroga said, "but, just so we understand each other, this has gotten bigger than just part-time employment for me. My country is on the ropes, and from where I sit, you and I are about the only two guys on our side who have their heads screwed on straight. It's a long shot, but if we pull together, we might just win this one yet."

"I . . . know that, I just . . ." Lafeur stammered.

Quiroga smiled again. "I know what you mean, *hermano*. Don't sweat it." He paused at the door. "And I wouldn't have refused the extra money myself." And he was gone.

Lafeur reached for his container of what was now ice cream soup. He had some more worrying to do before he got back to the office that afternoon.

SIX

†

At some point, Featherstone had drifted off to sleep. When he awoke, he found that they had turned off the overhead light, or there had been a power outage, he reminded himself. Everything had been plunged into total darkness. He recalled a time, years before, when he had taken his family on a guided tour through the Skyline Caverns in the Shenandoah Valley. At one point in the tour, the guide had flicked off the electric lights along the cavern walls and announced that this was what total darkness looked like. The darkness now was just as total as it had been that day in the caverns. He had to touch his face to reassure himself that his eyes were open at all.

Featherstone began to wonder if this was part of his captors' plan, to play with his mind, turning the lights on and off at irregular intervals, or delivering meals, in a way to make him lose track of time. He had read somewhere that this was part of normal brainwashing tactics, and he had to admit that it was working. He didn't have a clue as to whether he had been in this hole for two hours or two days. He felt his face and found the stubble of a beard growing, which would imply that it might be the morning after his capture.

He was suddenly overcome with an urge to urinate, and had to crawl around the edges of his cage, looking for the plastic bucket. As he felt his way, his fingers brushed against something small that skittered out of his way. Either that, or he thought he had touched something which wasn't there at all. Given the dampness of the place, finding bugs about would not have come as a great surprise, but finding them in total darkness, made Featherstone's skin crawl, and he pulled his hand back in fear.

However, the call of nature became increasingly strident, and he was soon forced to resume his search, finally finding the bucket in the corner. Kneeling on the ground, he managed to accomplish his purpose, blind, apparently without making too much of a mess. He might well have to spend a great deal of time here, and fouling his own nest would not make the time pass any more quickly. When he had finished, he slid the bucket to the farthest corner of the cage and sat cross-legged on the floor, with its smell already starting to bother him.

As he sat there, waiting for something to happen, Featherstone was plagued by two thoughts. The first was related to another article he had read about hostage situations entitled the "Stockholm Syndrome." According to this theory, it is natural for hostages to begin to identify with their captors, at least to the extent that they want the captors to get whatever it is that they are after, thus earning the captives' release. They begin to see the government security forces as posing just as much of a threat to themselves as to the kidnappers. Over time, this coincidence of interests tends to lead the captives to see the kidnappers as the good guys and the security forces as the bad guys. This explained why Patty Hearst supposedly joined the Symbionese Liberation Army after she was kidnapped by them.

Featherstone had given up any thoughts of being a hero when the first cattle prod had touched his ribs, but he was adamant that he would never give these bastards the satisfaction of even remotely sympathizing with their goals. In the mood he was in at the moment, he would gladly have been cut down in the crossfire if all of his tormentors went with him.

The other thought dated back to his college days when he had read the works of Alexandr Solzhenitsyn, when Solzhenitsyn had won the Nobel Prize, and he was still considered fashionable. One of the points that had stuck with Featherstone was Solzhenitsyn's resentment, as a prisoner in the Gulag, of how prison officials would expect, and receive, obsequious gratitude from prisoners for the restoration of some minor privilege which no one had any right to take away in the first place, such as receiving mail or a full ration of food. "It's not the ocean which drowns you. It's the puddle," Solzhenitsyn had said, desribing how men could survive the most brutal torture only to be brought to heel by the offering of small crumbs once their resistance had been broken.

Featherstone made up his mind that he would not use the words "thank you" as long as he was a captive. He would take whatever they gave him, and from the looks of it that wouldn't be very much. He would be correct but distant, and he made a silent vow that, if there was ever anything that he could do to disrupt their plans or strike back at them, he would do it, even if it meant his death. He didn't envision wrestling a gun from his captors, but at least he wouldn't make it any easier for them.

As he sat there in the darkness, constantly swatting at his body whenever he imagined that something with more legs than he had was approaching him, Featherstone was listening intently to try to identify where he was. He could hear nothing, no sounds of passing traffic, no voices, no sounds of plumbing. He sat that way for a long time, listening so hard that he almost jumped when the door latch turned, sounding like a rifle shot in the silence. When Featherstone looked up, blinded momentarily by the light of the kerosene lantern the man with him.

It was the same young man who had been guarding him when he had first awakened, whenever that had been. Apart from the lamp, he carried a plate of food and a bottle of mineral water.

"We've had another power failure," the man said, almost apologetically. "I would have brought the lamp down sooner, but we were busy last night."

"Not that there's a lot to see down here," Featherstone said flatly. So much for the psychological warfare theory of the lights being out, he thought.

The man approached a cross-shaped slot in the mesh. Horizontally, the opening was about three inches high and perhaps a foot wide, large enough to pass a plate through. The vertical portion was about eight inches wide and perhaps ten high, just the right size for him to pass his bucket through upright. It was located about a foot up from the bottom of the cage on the side facing the door. The opening was sheathed in thick sheet metal, riveted all around, as if they feared that Featherstone could unravel the mesh of the cage, with his bare fingers, and escape.

"Step back against the far wall," the man said, not taking his eyes from Featherstone. When he had complied, the man reached through the mesh and placed the plate and bottle on the floor, then stood back. "Put your bucket next to the hole." Featherstone did so gingerly and stepped back again, and the man pulled the bucket through. "I'll empty it and bring it back later."

"Is there any chance of getting to use a proper bathroom, and possibly take a shower?" Featherstone asked. "I can't really believe that all of you people with your machineguns and cattle prods are afraid that I'm going to overpower you and escape."

"Sorry," the man answered, but without the note of hostility that

Featherstone had detected earlier in his voice. "We can't be escorting you around like your bodyguards. Besides, you'll get used to the bucket. At home when I was growing up, about five minutes' drive from your residence, that was all we had until I was sixteen. Someone had to show me how a flush toilet worked when I finally got into a school when I was eight." Featherstone half expected him to start into some sort of tirade about the exploitation of the working classes, but the man just smiled shyly, and Featherstone realized that this was not meant as a parable for his political ideology, but was an innocent anecdote of his life.

Just then the overhead lights popped on. Featherstone was relieved that he wouldn't have to ask the man to leave him the lamp.

"What's your name?" Featherstone asked on the spur of the moment. "It doesn't have to be your real name, of course, but I would like to be able to speak to you properly."

Featherstone hadn't planned this out, but he was pleased to notice that the question seemed to take the young man somewhat aback. He thought a moment and answered. "You can call me Pedro . . . and that is my real name. If you get out of here, the odds are that I'll be dead anyway, so I don't see that it can cause much harm."

Get to relate to them as individuals Featherstone's mind was repeating the lessons of his hostage briefings back in Washington. He was just searching his brain for some other inoffensive topic of conversation when the door to the room opened again, and Padre Lazaro came in, flanked by his two guards.

"Good morning, Mr. Ambassador," Lazaro said lightly. Featherstone noticed that Pedro looked away when Lazaro had appeared, as if he had been caught doing something without permission.

"I'll have to take your word for that," Featherstone retorted. "One time of day is pretty much like another in here. Now, what can I do for you?"

Lazaro laughed, and Featherstone thought for a moment that, if he hadn't been a deranged killer, he probably would have made a good guest at dinner, like the other younger priests he had known throughout his career in Latin America. "I like your attitude, Mr. Ambassador. It's almost as if we had come to visit you by appointment."

"Fortunately, my calendar is clear at the moment."

Lazaro laughed again. "How lucky for us. We wouldn't bother you with this, but we had a little excitement last night. The army tried to storm into what the press calls the 'forbidden zone,' and I'm afraid we had to kill quite a few of them. Other than that, there was no real harm done, but it occurred to me that your people might be concerned about your welfare after all of the shooting, so I thought that we'd send them a photograph of you holding up the traditional newspaper, just to show them that you are alive and well as of this morning."

Featherstone brightened at the prospect. Of course Anne and the others at the embassy would have had no firm proof that he was still alive, and this would at least reassure them on that score. His brain raced as he thought of the clever things that American POWs in Vietnam had done to get messages across during their filmed "confessions," such as blink in morse code, but nothing brilliant came to mind. In fact, other than that he was still alive, he couldn't think of any piece of information he had to provide the outside world.

"No problem," Featherstone said haughtily.

Lazaro took a folded newspaper from under his arm and handed it through the slot in the mesh. Featherstone opened it to the front page and held it up in front of him, under his chin, hoping to disguise the fact that he was without clothes.

"About like this?" he asked.

"Perfect," Lazaro said, taking a Polaroid from one of the guards, opening it, and sighting on his subject.

Featherstone bent his knees slightly, so that he could keep the upper part of his body erect in the cage and put on his most defiant, proud look. Anne would see this picture, he thought, and, on the off chance it was the last one she ever saw of him, he wanted it to make her proud. As an afterthought, while Lazaro was lining up the shot, Featherstone discreetly curled back the index, third and fourth fingers of his right hand as he held up the paper.

The bulb flashed, and the camera whined and rolled out the picture. Lazaro watched as the image developed. The guards strained to look over his shoulder, just like when they take photos at a baby shower or family reunion, Featherstone thought. He consciously tossed the newspaper into the far corner of his cage as if offended by the entire spectacle, praying that Lazaro wouldn't remember it.

"This is fine!" Lazaro said, holding up the photo carefully by the edges for Featherstone to see. Featherstone was pleased that the picture showed only his face, hands, and the newspaper. There was no need for Anne to know how humiliated he felt, standing there in his underwear. "I'll leave you to your breakfast now," he added, moving toward the door, still admiring the photo. "We'll get this to your people within the hour."

As Lazaro reached the doorway, he called back over his shoulder, "And the finger was a very nice touch, a note of defiance that I'm sure will inspire your colleagues and family. Well done!" He and the guards laughed as they filed through the door, closing it firmly behind them.

Well, at least it didn't earn him a jab in the ribs with the cattle prod, Featherstone thought. He sat down on the floor and picked up his plate, keeping an eye on the window in the door. The plate was filled with a mound of mushy rice and beans with a fat cooked banana sitting on top. No meat, Featherstone thought, but at least there weren't any living things crawling around in it, and he had read somewhere that the combination of rice and beans actually provided more protein than meat. And no utensils, he noticed, but he scooped up the food with his fingers. He took his first mouthful and suddenly realized how ravenously hungry he was. He gulped down the entire plateful in the blink of an eye, licked the plate clean, and guzzled some of the water. He stopped then, thinking the water might have to last him quite a while.

Since there was still no sign of life beyond the cellar door, Featherstone reached over and pulled the newspaper to him. It was the local *El Diario* of that morning. He glanced at the headlines about government talks on how to deal with the terrorist problem and a photograph of a police checkpoint at the edge of the "zone," with a policeman carefully examining the papers of a man with a horse-drawn cart full of vegetables. He was a little surprised to see that nothing remotely like a siege existed around the "zone," with people and goods still apparently moving back and forth. He also noted that, if there had been a battle the previous night, it had apparently happened after the paper's deadline, because there was no mention of it. There was a long article on the front page referring to his kidnapping, but he chose to save that one for later.

After flipping through the entire paper to check for items of urgent interest, Featherstone then started back at page one to read everything word for word. If there was one thing that drove him nuts, it was getting stuck waiting for something or with nothing handy to occupy his mind. For that reason, he habitually carried a book in his briefcase, had one stashed in his office, and another in the glove compartment of his car. Fortunately, after many years experience in Latin America, he read Spanish almost as well as English.

He turned back to the story on his kidnapping. There was a photo of Stileforth, who appeared to be taking the disappearance of his ambassador very well, and another of himself, his identity carnet photo actually, and not very flattering. He was pleased to learn that no one had been killed or seriously injured in the assault, although a Marine had been taken to the hospital with a mild concussion. There were no real "clues" revealed in the article, although it was strongly implied that he had been cached somewhere within the "forbidden zone," which was pretty much what Featherstone had assumed. The rest was the usual pablum of how the Embassy and the United States Government was working closely with the local authorities, etc., etc.

He read all of the international news articles which interested him, then the local news. Then he started on the society pages and entertainment section, then sports, and of no earthly use to him, the weather. When he finally put the newspaper aside, he stretched out again on the floor to take a nap. All things considered, compared with his situation when he had awakened in the dark, things had improved markedly. He had a full stomach, an empty bladder, and something to read. There was a photograph on the way to his wife which would at least tell her that he was alive, and he had made a little progress with this Pedro character, not enough to matter yet, but it was a start.

†

Lafeur was nominally attending another session of the "war cabinet" in the ambassador's office that afternoon, but his thoughts were elsewhere. The photograph of the ambassador had been left at a hotel reception desk as a message for a non-existent guest, and then called in to a local radio station with an explanation of its location. Everyone was relieved that the massacre of the night before had apparently not affected the ambassador, but it heightened the level of tension. It was clear now that any action that would be done without the cooperation of the Dominicans. Stileforth had been livid at Palacios' unilateral action, and President Selich had reportedly placed the man under house arrest pending an investigation. Stileforth himself was not present, and Lafeur wondered absently where he had been for the past hour or so, since meetings were Stileforth's lifeblood.

Lafeur couldn't really be too upset, however. Palacios had made a series of mistakes, and it could have ended even more tragically, not just for himself and his men, but for Featherstone. Still, the man was out there trying, instead of conducting one pointless meeting after another.

Lafeur's thoughts, however, were on Maripaz and how to handle the explosive piece of information that Quiroga had dumped in his lap. When he had entered the Embassy, Lafeur had taken a hard look at Maripaz. She had lost weight in the last couple of weeks, and appeared to be very nervous. She had looked up, seen him staring and had dropped her eyes, not coquettishly, as she might have a month ago, but, it seemed to Lafeur, out of shame. But maybe that was just his imagination.

As an FSN, Maripaz was not allowed to handle classified material and did not even have permission to enter the inner office area, so there was little more damage she could do at the moment. Her primary function apparently had been to advise the kidnappers when they could make their hit. They might now be keeping her around just to see what else she might pick up, but the focus of the terrorists had probably shifted to the local military.

Lafeur's problem was that, if he simply came out and told the assembled officers what he knew, he would also have to admit that one of his agents had tapped the ambassador's phone. The mere fact that he had not ordered it would be of little consequence. There was already a certain amount of bad blood between the State Department and the Agency, which did much of its overseas work under State Department cover. There were always turf battles over whose contact a particular local official was, and State was justifiably jealous of the Agency's fund for "representational entertainment." State officers either ended up sitting at home or paying for lunches with their contacts out of their own pockets. Something like this would not only screw him for all time with this embassy, it would reverberate throughout the government, and he was certain that his superiors would remember clearly who was responsible. Even if the information itself could somehow prove vital to a happy resolution of the kidnapping, the damage would linger on long after the applause died. That was the way of government.

Lafeur was ruminating on this unhappy theme when he heard a loud stomping in the outer office. He looked up and found himself staring at a veritable statue of a man, or at least a man who seemed to be posing for a statue. He was an American army officer, wearing heavily starched camouflage fatigues, but festooned with various fluorescent paratrooper, ranger, and other badges, the sort of contradiction common among headquarters types, Lafeur recalled from his own time in the military. He wore jump boots polished to a mirror-like shine, and his greying hair was either cropped very close, or he had not shaved his head in the past day or two. He stood rigidly, his feet set apart, his weight poised forward, a short swagger stick lodged firmly under one arm. His pale blue eyes stabbed into every corner of the room as if about to begin a white glove inspection.

"Gentlemen," Stileforth announced, peeking over the soldier's shoulder, "I would like to present Brigadier General Xavier Pennington, commander of the Delta Force."

Colonel Miller had already leapt to his feet and snapped to attention. Jim Vernon and others around the table broke out into broad smiles, apparently confident that things were well in hand now that the cavalry had arrived. Lafeur thought to himself that it would have been better if the guy hadn't shown up here in his combat gear so that anyone would see that the American military was about to do something big, when it hit him. "Anyone," particularly santista moles who happened to be sitting in the reception office when the General waltzed through.

"Holy shit!" Lafeur said under his breath as he jumped out of his chair and squeezed past the two men in the doorway. Another Army officer in fatigues was standing at attention just outside, a large portfolio under his arm.

"Where are you going, Lafeur?" Stileforth asked in a shocked tone.

"Excuse me," Lafeur panted, brushing past Stileforth's rather limp restraining hand. "There's something urgent I have to attend to. I'll be back in five minutes."

From his expression it was apparent that Stileforth was not satisfied with this explanation, but Lafeur was in too much of a hurry to bother. He rushed down the hall to Maripaz' small office. He burst through the door and stopped. She was sitting at her desk, blankly staring at some papers in front of her. He was relieved to see that she was not on the phone. She looked up as he loomed over her, startled.

"Come with me," he said without any introduction, and he reached out and took her by the arm, gently but firmly. Contrary to his expectations, she did not protest, or even question his motives. She just quietly rose and let him lead her out the door toward the Gunny's office.

Lafeur knocked loudly on the Gunny's door and pushed it open without waiting for a reply. Besserman was sitting at his desk, doing some paperwork. He looked surprised when Lafeur guided Maripaz into the room and sat her down in the other chair.

"I want you to keep an eye on Miss Zuñiga for an hour or so, or until I come back and get her," Lafeur said firmly. "She is not to leave the room unescorted or to use the telephone. This is on my responsibility."

Besserman looked questioningly from Lafeur to Maripaz and back again, his mouth hanging slightly open. "Sure, Claude, but what's this all about?"

"I can't go into it right now. I can only say that it's very important that you do exactly as I say."

"Well," Besserman stammered, obviously embarrassed by the situation, "but what if she, you know, has to, you know?"

Lafeur paused for a moment. He hadn't thought about that, damnit. "Uh, just escort her to the bathroom and wait outside the door. Then bring her back here. She should also not talk to anyone in the halls."

Since Maripaz wasn't making any open protests to these arrangements, Besserman saw no reason to refuse.

"You got it, Claude," he said, "but you know we're stretched kind of thin right now. I was just about to relieve the man on Post One myself, 'cause we've got another man watching the walk-in."

Lafeur did a double-take. "What walk-in?" he asked.

"Don't you know? The santista guy. Mr. Stileforth and the General have been in with him for the past hour or two. I supposed that they had told you but you didn't want to expose yourself for some reason."

"A santista walk-in?" Lafeur stammered. "Right here in the embassy? Is he for real or some kind of nut case?"

Besserman picked up a sheet of yellow legal paper from his desk. "His name's Angel Santander, he says, although he's got real good-looking ID in half a dozen other names, including two American passports, but it's his photo on all of them with just little changes, you know, glasses, moustache, beard, and like that. I don't know what he might have told Stileforth in there. This is just the identification info the marine at Post One got when the guy turned up."

This was the guy, or one of them, that Quiroga and Arce had been following around. Lafeur was steaming with rage at Stileforth having usurped his authority. It was standard procedure for Lafeur to have full control of the debriefing of any walk-in, a loose term used to describe anyone who either walked, drove, flew, swam, wrote, or called in to any American facility overseas, offering some sort of information to the U.S. government, usually for a price. While such occurrences are fairly common, most of them turn out to be certifiable mental cases, or provocations either by individuals with an ax to grind against the Americans or a hostile foreign intelligence service. On the other hand, many of the Agency's biggest windfalls of intelligence had come from just this sort of walk-in, including more than one KGB Rezident in the old days. Agency operations against terrorism had been especially blessed with information from walk-ins looking for money or revenge against their former colleagues.

Lafeur wasn't so much concerned about his bureaucratic turf, at least this is what he told himself. His real concern was that he was experienced enough in dealing with walk-ins to tell a phoney from the real thing and to get the information needed out of the man, if he did turn out to be for real.

"No, I didn't know," Lafeur finally mumbled in a low voice. "I'll talk to Stileforth about it. Just get whatever extra help you need, and I'll be back as soon as I can." He glanced at Maripaz as he turned toward the door. She just sat in the chair, her hands folded in her lap and her head bent low. "And thanks, Gunny."

"No prob."

Lafeur dashed back to his office. He had to work the cipher lock on the door three times, as, in his haste, he fumbled it the first time. Then he didn't wait long enough for it to reset the second time. When he finally got through, he yanked open a safe drawer and pulled out a long brown file folder. He shuffled through the papers rapidly and finally pulled out a bunch of photographs held together with a rubber band. He leafed through the surveillance photos taken by Arce until he found one with a fairly clear face shot of a tall slender man with neatly combed, graying hair. He tossed the file back in the drawer and slammed the safe shut.

He was panting heavily now as he rushed back down the corridor to the reception area. There he found Lance Corporal Washington, a huge, muscular black marine standing at parade rest next to the door of the "walk-in room." This was a small office into which a walk-in could be shown for his interview after he had been thoroughly searched by the marines, without allowing him access to the rest of the embassy.

Lafeur nodded to Washington, who grinned broadly in return, and peeked through the eyehole in the door.

The walk-in room was simply furnished, just two metal chairs and a desk. Santander was sitting quietly in one of the chairs, staring at the door as if he could see Lafeur through it. Lafeur took a long look at him, then at the photo, then put his eye to the hole again. There was no doubt about it. It was the same man.

This could be a good thing, Lafeur kept telling himself as he hustled back toward the ambassador's office. He should keep his cool. If this guy was for real and gave them information which allowed the Delta Force to go in and save Ambassador Featherstone, and maybe gut the Guerra Santa movement while they're at it, then there would be credit enough to go around. It would be just like the Gulf War where every unit that took part along with every country that sent two medics and a bandaid, "made the victory possible," enabling them to roll their shoulders in a manly way and bask in the glory of the triumph of arms. He knew that Stileforth had cut him out of the walk-in on purpose, but don't get hung up on that, he kept saying. Let Stileforth do all the work, and you just take your share of the victory to the bank.

Then he paused. He suddenly felt very ashamed of himself. This is the way that people like Stileforth, and plenty in his own agency, thought. It was the way careers were made, but here a good man, the ambassador, was in danger, and all he could think of was scoring bureaucratic points. In that instant, Lafeur suddenly made a decision. He would do what was needed to save Featherstone and let the credit hounds scrabble for bones afterward.

As he stepped back into the ambassador's office, General Pennington, standing at parade rest at one end of the room, was apparently just finishing what looked to have been a Pattonesque introductory speech.

". . . and we hope to bring to this operation the same spirit of aggressiveness and precision which was the trademark of the Desert Storm campaign, which is the formula for total victory. 'One hundred per cent is the only acceptable grade.'"

Lafeur slipped into the room as quietly as he could, backing up against a bookcase to one side, but Stileforth locked him in a piercing stare as the General stopped talking.

"Thank you for joining us, Mr. Lafeur," Stileforth said with heavy sarcasm. "General, this is Claude Lafeur, the *acting* head of our one-man Agency presence here."

The General spun with parade ground precision and extended his hand. He glanced Lafeur up and down in a way Lafeur had long ago learned meant to say, 'oh, didn't expect a black man.' "Xavier Pennington," the General boomed as he locked Lafeur's beefy hand in a grip of iron which might have brought tears to his eyes had Lafeur not been expecting it. "Proud to have you on board." The General gave his hand one precise pump, wrenching Lafeur's shoulder only slightly out of joint and passed him on to the other officer.

"My exec, Colonel Linus Voorst," he said, as Lafeur shook hands with the younger, and rather more human-looking officer.

Lafeur was already burning at Stileforth's introduction. He had managed to get in not only the fact that Lafeur was only acting COS, but that the station was currently a one-man show.

"I apologize for missing your talk, General," Lafeur said. "I was just taking a quick peek at our guest. I'm afraid I hadn't been informed that he was in the embassy, or I would have gladly joined you for the initial debriefing."

"Yes," Stileforth interjected. "I'm very sorry about that, Claude, but you were out when he walked in, and this was obviously too important a matter to wait until you came back, so the General and I just took up the ball and ran with it."

Lafeur groaned inwardly at Stileforth's sports allusion. Stileforth never used sports allusions, and he was obviously tailoring his manner of speech to the General, probably assuming that all military men got off on that sort of thing.

"That's odd," Lafeur went on, talking directly to Stileforth now. "It seems that nobody in this room was aware of the presence of either the walk-in or of General Pennington in the Embassy, and we've been sitting here discussing the local scene for nearly an hour."

The General, taking quick command of the situation, raised a muscular arm and waved his hand from side to side. "No point in beating that particular horse, gentlemen," the General said in a patronizing tone. "Mr. Lafleur, what this terrorist had to tell us has been interesting and will undoubtedly be useful, but it merely served to confirm what we already knew. His detailed knowledge will help us plan our operation, but it won't be decisive. And, besides that, you can have all the time you like to talk to him right now."

"That's *Lafeur*, General. And that's just the point. I've had a good deal of experience dealing with walk-ins, some on the up and up and some not, and one of the first things I learned to question is someone who drops in out of the blue and confirms something you already believed. That's why it's important to give the man a thorough interrogation before we even begin to act on anything he's told us. He might be straight, but . . ."

"Point well taken, Mr. Lafleur," the General said, whacking Lafeur across the shoulders a little too hard. "We're running checks right now through our own people to try to establish the man's identity, and we expect you to chip in on that."

Now that his official protest had been filed, Lafeur felt a little better, even if he hadn't actually gotten much in the way of an apology, so he felt like getting down to business.

"Go ahead and check, General," Lafeur said. "But I can tell you right now that the man in the walk-in room *is* Angel Santander and that he has been involved with both the old MIR and the new Guerra Santa movement for some time. In fact, I've had him under surveillance since before the start of the street violence with the santistas." Lafeur paused a moment to let this little gem sink in. He noticed Jim Vernon's eyebrows rise measurably. For a brief moment, he thought about dropping the other shoe, about having discovered that Maripaz was working with the santistas, but something told him not to. He didn't exactly have a watertight case against Maripaz, although her attitude just now certainly tended to confirm his suspicions. He didn't want some pseudo-lawyer in the embassy insisting that he turn her loose before he had a chance to throw a scare into her and get her to tell him whatever she might know about the santistas' operations.

"With that knowledge," Lafeur went on, "and with the information I've been able to collect about the santistas and their personnel, I think I've got the kind of foundation I need to press Santander for everything he knows and to identify any areas he might be covering up. I can tell you right now that he's been involved in smuggling arms into this country. The same weapons that the santistas are using against the Army right now."

"Fantastic, Claude!" the General boomed, obviously giving up on Lafeur's last name. "Santander's all yours, son."

Lafeur didn't really like the "son" thing. He estimated that Pennington was perhaps five years older than he, to say nothing of genetic differences.

"Let us show you what Santander has given us so far," the General continued, crooking a finger at the major who unzipped his portfolio case with military precision and pulled out a wad of aerial photographs and street maps and laid them out on the coffee table along with several pages of scribbled notes on yellow legal paper. The General took up the notes and twisted one of the larger photographs around to face himself.

"He's confirmed that this building is the headquarters of the MIR-Guerra Santa group," he said, jabbing an index finger at a red grease pencil circle on the photograph. "Just where we thought it was. What's more important, he confirmed that Ambassador Featherstone is being held in the basement of the building and that he was alive as of about four hours ago, although he said that the group's leader Melgarejo has been going out of his head, drinking and taking cocaine, and has been talking frequently about just going downstairs and blowing the ambassador's brains out. Santander said that he had to stop the man once this very morning from doing that in a drunken fit, and that he didn't think many people in the group had the pull with Melgarejo to dare do that."

The General paused and pulled out some rough line drawings with notations in Spanish. "He's also given us a detailed diagram of the headquarters building and its guard setup." The General shook his head and smiled. "Those busy little bastards have turned this dump into a veritable fortress. They've reinforced the walls and doors, bricked up windows but in a way that you can't tell from the outside, and they've set it up so that the heart of the place is on the third floor of the four-story building, with guards living on the first, second, and fourth floors, providing them with a layer of protection from all directions. The basement can only be reached via an interior stairway which runs from the third floor straight to the basement, with no access from the other floors."

The General paused and turned to Lafeur. "Everything this man has told us, that we can check via the aerial photographs and such, has checked. Naturally, we'll go in with the assumption that we need to clear the whole building anyway, but we'll be looking for his information to check out what's inside as well. We'll put charges on the doors sufficient to deal with what he says is there, where we might have used insufficient charges on our own and had to hit the doors twice. I don't have to tell you how valuable each second is from the time you hit the target until you can get control of the hostage. If he's making all of this up, we'll move through the place even faster, but we'll be ready if all of these preparations are for real, and it could be a lifesaver. From *my* experience in dealing with intelligence work, Claude, that's not the kind of information the enemy just gives away."

Lafeur had to sigh and nod his head. "I have to agree with you on that, General. And I can't really see what good it would do them to send us a 'dangle' at this stage of the game. Now, if he were telling us that the ambassador was somewhere *else* from the place they probably figure we assume to be their headquarters, that would be different. Then he'd really have to prove his stuff, but when they've put this kind of effort into fortifying a place, you have to assume that they mean to defend it, and yet they must know that we can blast them out of anything they can build, if only we know where it is. No, this guy is looking more and more like the real thing."

Lafeur stood up. "Now, if you'll excuse me, I really should talk to Santander myself. One thing I need to ask him is whether his pals might miss him soon. If they will, they might figure out where he's gone and move the ambassador, . . . or worse."

"*We* asked him that question, Claude," Stileforth said, leaning back in the Ambassador's tall chair and rocking slightly. "He insists that he won't be missed until tomorrow morning."

"That's why we're planning to go in tonight," Pennington announced. The other men in the room collectively took a deep breath. "At precisely 0300 hours we'll hit that building like Omaha Beach, and by 0310 it should all be over. I have my team standing by in San Juan, Puerto Rico, and they're due to depart at 0130 hours by helicopter. After the ambassador has been secured in the target area, I have a reinforced company of the Puerto Rican National Guard on standby alert to chopper in and carve us a path right through the bad guys to safety, if the Dominicans can't do it for us. And don't let the National Guard title fool you, these guys are tough as nails and armed to the teeth. I've worked with them before and even trained them in airborne operations at Fort Benning."

Lafeur nodded and snapped a feeble salute as he headed for the door. It all sounded pretty good except that he had to ask himself, didn't they call it "Bloody Omaha?"

Lafeur paused when he came to the reception area. His first inclination was to talk to Maripaz immediately, but if things went according to the General's plan, it might all be over in less then 24 hours. Maripaz was effectively removed from any position in which she could pose a threat to the embassy, and she had probably already served the function the terrorists had had for her in any case. Meanwhile, Santander might still have some information that would be of use for tonight's operation, in which case he had better get at him first.

The Marine on Post One clicked him through the metal security door, and he went over to the walk-in room. Washington was about to work the cipher lock for him to enter, when Lafeur raised a finger, indicating that he should wait a moment. Lafeur ducked down the hall to the FSN lounge and rummaged in his pockets for some change. He got a couple of cans of soda out of the machine and then headed back to where Washington was waiting.

"Thirsty?" Lafeur asked as he entered the room, offering a can to Santander. Even with the air conditioning on, it was still warm and sticky in the windowless room, and the can was very cold, with drops of condensation clinging to its sides.

"No, thank you, Mr. Lafeur," Santander said, just glancing up.

Lafeur stood there a second with the can still extended toward the sitting man. It shouldn't have come as a big surprise that a group which had managed to penetrate the embassy would have compiled a mug book of the American officials. Being able to recognize all of the Americans coming and going from the embassy would have been of use in their surveillance of the ambassador. Still, it was a little disconcerting.

Lafeur sat down heavily and popped a soft drink for himself. He could never seem to get enough liquid in this climate. And he began his interrogation. An interrogation did not imply shining bright lights in the subject's eyes, but it was more than a simple debriefing of a cooperative source. Lafeur had already come up with a long list of questions for Santander. His goal at this point was less to obtain information than to attempt to determine whether Santander was providing all of the information that he had and whether he was being intentionally deceptive.

Lafeur had gained more experience at this tricky business than he would have chosen during his years of interrogating would-be Cuban defectors and others whose motives for cooperating with the sworn enemy of the Castro regime were murky to say the least. The method Lafeur used was to swamp the subject with a mass of detail, asking questions about everything under the sun, important or not, then going back over the same ground several times looking for inconsistencies.

He would then hold up those inconsistencies to the subject and force an explanation out of him. If the story became clearer, the case was probably good. If it only led to a more and more tangled web of deception, Lafeur would know what he was dealing with. Lafeur could then decide whether to try to "turn" the subject or pretend to accept the story and use the subject as a means of providing disinformation to the other side.

The entire process avoided open confrontation. He had seen enough interrogations where semi-trained interrogators would attempt to find obvious "handles" on their subject and use rather clumsy threats to get their cooperation, such as cutting off money or suggesting that the Agency would tell the subject's own government about his indiscretions. In Lafeur's mind such threats rarely worked. One could convince people to cooperate, or one could trick them into revealing more than they intended, but forced cooperation usually meant that the subject would find a way to get even sooner or later.

Lafeur did use a lot of pseudo-psychological tricks to gain the initiative in these "interviews," as he liked to call them. He would raise and lower his voice. He would study the subject's body language, something he had become quite good at, to determine points of vulnerability or topics which made him especially nervous. He would sit behind a desk to appear more authoritative or purposely sit on top of the desk, leaning over the subject, very close, or walk around the room, whatever seemed to work with the particular subject. Lafeur was proud of his ability to conduct this kind of interrogation and to get at what he wanted.

In this case, he assumed that the information itself was good, and that this would essentially be a cake walk. Normally, he would have had to spend half his time just determining whether the subject really had access to the information or whether he was making it up out of a vivid imagination and a quick reading of the newspaper headlines. That obviously wasn't the issue here.

"What do you want?" Lafeur asked. This was a good question to start with, since it let the subject open up and talk freely. The answer itself was less important than the category into which it fell. Did the subject claim to be selflessly altruistic? Then he was probably lying, and the skill with which he lied would signal how careful the interrogator would have to be on other matters. Did he just want money? That made things simpler. One could offer payment in line with the value of the information, but one also had to keep in mind that a flat-out mercenary would change sides as often as he thought he could turn a profit on the deal. Did he want revenge against his erstwhile colleagues? That was better, but one had to keep an eye out for intentionally distorted information. Or was it a combination of all the above?

"There are lots of things I want," Santander explained. "I want money. I want a green card to go live in the States. I want a new identity, because the *santistas* are not a very forgiving crowd, and they'll come looking for me when they figure out what I've done. I also want a world of peace and plenty for everyone. Whether I get any or all of those things is beyond my control now. You and your superiors will determine whether my information is valid and how much it is worth, and I can live with that. Whether the world will become a better place or not is beyond the control of all of us. The only thing I know now is that it's not going to be obtained by Padre Lazaro's methods."

During his little speech, Santander sat comfortably erect in his chair, not slouching and not rigid. His arms and legs and posture suggested openness and candor, or, Lafeur could not help but imagine, the posture someone who had also studied body language would assume if he were trying to convince someone else of his frankness. Santander's answer was, of course, the interrogator's dream, a mixture of idealism, pragmatism, and revenge. This was a man you could work with, Lafeur thought, but there was something in his eyes, something Lafeur could not identify, that frightened him just a little, even with the knowledge that this man was unarmed, while the rippling muscles and .38 revolver of Washington were just a shout away.

"And what brought you to that decision?" Lafeur continued.

"He's insane. At first I liked the idea of being part of a movement with the kind of purity of thought that Padre Lazaro talked about. We didn't want money. We didn't want power for ourselves. We just wanted to break the grip of the exploiting classes on society and give the common man a chance to make his own decisions. Maybe all those years of fighting for others, killing for others whose cause was not as pure as ours, just to earn the backing we needed to start our work here, finally eroded his own ideals. All that killing." Santander looked downward and shook his head, and Lafeur could feel the weight of guilt on his shoulders.

Lafeur let Santander talk. He talked about fighting in the hills of Nicaragua against the Contras, about burning a Miskito Indian village on the Atlantic coast, even about shooting up a jeep full of Swedish "internationalist" medical students and leaving evidence around to imply that the Contras had done it. Lafeur took copious notes, not wishing to rely on the tape recording, since machines have a habit of breaking down, but this was just historical background. He talked about the long years of fighting in Iran, both at the front in the Iran-Iraq War and against Iran's internal enemies. The level of brutality Santander described made Lafeur's skin crawl at the thought, and he had not the slightest doubt that this was all too true.

Santander acknowledged the responsibility of Lazaro and his followers for the assassination of the American naval officer in Madrid some months before. This was definitely new, and, although Santander himself had been sent ahead to Santo Domingo by that time, he had enough details about how the operation was conducted that Lafeur was certain that this was true as well. This was the kind of thing that would establish the man's *bona fides*.

Finally, he began to talk about Santo Domingo and the work with the MIR. It was as Lafeur had suspected Lazaro planned to use the MIR's infrastructure and membership as a springboard for his own movement and would discard Melgarejo as soon as he had fulfilled his purpose. Santander even mentioned the Palestinian businessman and the shipment of arms disguised as refrigerators. Lafeur was noting all this down, nodding occasionally or asking Santander to spell a name, and he barely caught himself before he asked about the second arms shipment, which would have tipped his hand. He held back, waiting for Santander to continue, but he then talked about the riots, the establishment of the "forbidden zone" and how they had conducted surveillance of the Ambassador for the kidnapping. Lafeur tuned out as Santander went into detail on how the security of the "zone" was set up.

Shit! Lafeur thought to himself, his pen still scratching away on the yellow pad, but mindlessly now. Lafeur had been buying the whole deal right up to that point, when the bottom had dropped out from under him. And he had almost missed it. It was what he was supposed to be looking for, the big gap, the part of the story that the interrogator knew, but the subject didn't know that he knew, the part that a "bad" subject wouldn't want to reveal.

He never mentioned the *second* arms shipment, the big one. It was just as Quiroga had said. They had been meant to spot the first one, not the second one. What was worse, Santander never mentioned Maripaz. His version of the kidnapping operation was that they had conducted careful surveillance of the ambassador's movements, and he had included such detail that one would have believed it really possible. The only trouble was that it would have been too risky for the santistas to conduct that kind of surveillance, to achieve the kind of certainty necessary to be in the right place at the right time. That was where most terrorist operations failed, when their pre-operational surveillance was spotted by casual observation. In this case, the surveillance hadn't been conducted, because they didn't need it.

Lafeur considered the possibility that Santander himself might not have been in on Maripaz' recruitment. In fact, he tried to convince himself that this would have been the case, a highly compartmented operation with only those who really needed to know being involved. But that wouldn't explain Santander's story of the massive surveillance effort that certainly was never conducted. No, there was no doubt about it. This man was concealing a big piece of the picture, a piece that someone in his position would definitely want to sell.

Lafeur considered that maybe Santander was holding back on these juicy tidbits, the location of a really big arms cache and the presence of a "mole" within the Embassy, to bargain up whatever kind of cash offer Lafeur would make him. Defectors were known to do that. But that didn't wash either. Santander's story, as he had laid it out, called for the Americans to take action immediately, to go in *now* to try to get the ambassador. If the ambassador were there, and were rescued, this other information would be of only marginal interest. It was right now that Santander should be trotting out this stuff to prove his value, but he wasn't doing it.

As Lafeur reached his conclusion, the door to the walk-in room swung open, and Stileforth and the General entered.

"Sorry to disturb you, Claude," Stileforth said in a tone which implied that he was not sorry in the slightest. "We've got the DAO plane laid on to take our guest here over to Puerto Rico for continued interrogation, and for his own safety," Stileforth added, with a pleasant smile and a nod in Santander's direction.

"Sure, Dane," Lafeur said, rising, "but could I have a word with both of you outside for just a moment first."

"Excuse us," Stileforth said to Santander, who nodded graciously in return, and the three men exited and closed the door firmly.

"What do you need, son?" the General asked, and Lafeur gritted his teeth again at the "son" appellation. "How is his information holding up?"

"Well, he gave me a ton of detail, all very interesting, including the fact that it was the santistas who murdered that Navy man in Madrid earlier this year," Lafeur began.

"The bastards!" the General growled. "Well, my boys will make them pay for that little job." He smashed his fist into his open palm, and the veins on his temples bulged slightly. "Great job, Claude. I talked to the scumbag for over an hour and never got a hint of that, but I guess that's what they pay you for." The General smiled broadly and patted Lafeur on the back, a little too hard.

"What they pay me for," Lafeur continued, "is to determine whether guys like this are on the up and up, and what I have to say is that this guy is bad."

Both Stileforth and the General reared back at this.

"What do you mean?" Stileforth spluttered. "I debriefed him in detail, and he had too much knowledge to be a fabricator, and he gave us too much information for him to be some kind of double agent." Lafeur could see that he was losing ground rapidly. Stileforth was taking the position that if Santander were proven to be lying, it would somehow make him a dupe for not having spotted it, and Stileforth was not a man to accept that lightly.

"You debriefed him, Dane," Lafeur continued, trying not to sound critical, "but I've spent years talking to this kind of man. You got as much information as anybody could have gotten in the limited time you had, but it was just the information he wanted you to have. The advantage I had was that I knew of some santista activities that you didn't and which Santander chose, for some reason, to conceal. *That* is the sign of a dangle."

"And what information is it, might I ask," Stileforth said, raising his prominent nose to an imposing angle, as if in reaction to an unpleasant odor, "that you didn't see fit to trust us with?"

Lafeur struggled with himself for a moment. If he revealed the information about Maripaz now, Stileforth would eat him alive, maybe even literally kick him out of the country, and would probably go on about his business in any case. And how sure was he, after all, about Maripaz and about Santander? Was it worth his career to stand up now, on a hunch, and duke it out with these two, who both obviously didn't want to hear any bad news?

"There was another arms shipment, a big one," Lafeur began, deciding to take the avenue of least resistance. "I never mentioned it before, because we were unable to track it after it came into the country. The thing is that Santander told us about the smaller one, the one that was easy to follow, and not about the other. Which makes me believe that he's intentionally concealing it because it's too important to his movement's plans to give us as bona fides. If you accept that, then you have to ask yourself whether he was sent in here intentionally. If you accept *that*, you have to ask *why*. The information he has given us clearly pushes us toward hitting the MIR headquarters right now, and it must be what they want us to do, which is why we shouldn't do it."

Stileforth just snorted in disgust, and the General took up the challenge. "Whoa up there, son," he began, shaking his head and chuckling slightly. "You've got a string of 'ifs' there long enough to choke a horse. Maybe he's just holding back on the other arms cache to bargain with. It happens all the time."

"I thought of that," Lafeur stammered as he tried to talk faster. "If he's smart, he would be telling us about it now to prove himself. Later, we're not going to care."

"*If* this second shipment ever existed," Stileforth interrupted. "Did you think of *that*? Maybe it's still sitting on a dock in North Korea, or wherever. Maybe the sellers skipped with the money and never delivered at all. Did you ever consider that that was why you couldn't track it here in country, and, consequently, why Mr. Santander did not mention it? Your whole argument rests on us accepting the fact that he is concealing something of great value, greater value than all of the very important information he has given us, much of which we can check, by the way. I, for one, don't accept that at all. I'm very sorry that you didn't get first crack at this defector because you were out stuffing your face with *watermelon* somewhere," Stileforth was turning a bright shade of red now, and his words were coming in a rapid but carefully enunciated torrent which dashed itself against Lafeur's lowering brow, "but that doesn't mean that you have the obligation to impugn the work of the General and myself and prove your own worth by 'discovering' that we had been made fools of."

Lafeur didn't miss the crack about watermelon, and he had always suspected that Stileforth was a closet racist. He was about to answer, and balling a fist to punctuate his remarks, but the General held up his hand. "What we have here is an honest difference of opinion," he said graciously. "Claude here has done his job by bringing these doubts to our attention. It is now *my* job to weigh the information and make my operational decision, and that decision is that we're going ahead with the rescue attempt. If these little assholes think they're setting a trap for us, we're ready for them, and your warning has raised our antennae even higher. They will definitely have bitten off more than they can chew if they try to screw with my team." He paused and turned directly to Lafeur like a benevolent teacher questioning an underachieving student about a late homework assignment. "Now, if you've got something more concrete to go on, let's hear it. If not, we'll go with what we have."

Lafeur was breathing hard, glancing back and forth between Stileforth and the General. If he told them about Maripaz now, Stileforth would demand proof, which the brief taped conversation really didn't provide, at least not to someone who was determined not to be convinced. He would also insist on talking to Maripaz himself, and she, of course, would deny the whole thing. What was worse, he would probably let Maripaz leave, to tell her friends the General's presence and the obvious plans to make an assault. As bad as the option appeared, Lafeur decided that it might well cost more lives for him to reveal this information now than to keep quiet about it. The attack would go in anyway, and the enemy would be thoroughly forewarned. Maybe the General was right. Maybe the Delta Force could handle whatever the santistas had in store for them. At least he had warned them that it might be a trap, which was all he really knew anyway. He let out a long sigh.

"No, General," he said at last. "That's all I have right now, but I still think that Santander was sent here for a reason. So, tell your boys to be extra careful."

"They always are," the General chuckled again. He whacked Lafeur on the back again, and he and Stileforth went back into the walk-in room. Lafeur saw no reason to accompany them and headed back down the hall.

Near the door to the Gunny's office, Lafeur looked up and saw Colonel Miller leaning against the wall. He had apparently overheard the entire conversation.

"Sorry about that," Miller said with a timid half smile. "Just how sure are you?"

Lafeur sighed again. "About as sure as I can be. This smells very, very bad, but they don't want to hear it."

"I could have told you to save your breath," Miller said, lowering his voice. "You have to understand something about the politics of the situation. America hasn't had a real great record in hostage rescue operations. The British have done it, so have the Israelis, the Germans, the French, even the Peruvians, just about everybody but us. What have we got? We had the fiasco with the hostages in Iran. There was the general cluster fuck of the Grenada operation. We had to sit on our hands for years with hostages stashed all around Lebanon. There was also the blood bath in Waco. Kind of depressing. Now here we have this beautifully trained, highly motivated, technological state-of-the-art team, and we've never really been able to use them. It hasn't been their fault either. We generally can't give them a viable target to hit, as your agency knows only too well. They're a very costly commodity and have a very high political profile, so when a scenario comes up where they stand even a remote chance of pulling it off, you'd have to have signed confessions on the table to call them off."

"Score another point for the bureaucracy," Lafeur mumbled dejectedly.

Miller smiled at him and lowered his voice still further. "Would your being certain about this guy's lying have anything to do with the fact that you've conducted a thoroughly illegal arrest of the ambassador's social secretary by any chance?"

Lafeur looked up in horror, but the expression of understanding on Miller's face reassured him immediately. "Yes, as a matter of fact, but I'm afraid I can't tell anybody about that just yet."

"You did the right thing," Miller said. "It wouldn't have helped, and I don't want to know any more about it. You tell me when you can and what you can." He gave Lafeur's bicep a comforting squeeze and headed out the door to reception.

When Miller opened the door, Lafeur caught a glimpse through the glass doorway to the street and noticed that it was pitch dark outside. He looked at his watch. It was already past eight o'clock. He hadn't realized it was so late. Now he had the problem of what to do with Maripaz until at least three o'clock the next morning, when the Delta commandos would have finished their assault. Then an idea occurred to him.

He entered the Gunny's office and found Maripaz sitting, just as he'd left her, her head slightly bowed and her eyes closed. In her hands she held a full styrofoam cup of coffee, which looked cold. The Gunny was leaning back in his chair, leafing through a field manual.

"It's about time, Claude," Besserman said, swinging his feet off his desk. "I don't suppose you'd care to tell me what this is all about. Maripaz certainly hasn't seen fit to tell me anything."

"You'll have to stand in line," Lafeur said, gently taking the cup from Maripaz and setting it on the desk and helping her out of the chair. "I'll tell you what I can, when I can, but for right now, we were never here, okay?"

"Who was never here?" Besserman asked, grinning.

Lafeur winked at the Gunny and escorted Maripaz toward the main entrance.

"Are you taking me to jail now?" she asked him in a barely audible voice without looking up.

"No, better than that," was all that Lafeur answered as he guided her around the side of the embassy toward the tennis courts. The look of total despair on her face and her lack of any kind of resistance tore at Lafeur's heart. He had never really dealt with an enemy before, not on this level. They had always been clever opponents, other intelligence officers, sparring verbally with him at diplomatic receptions, or unseen threats, such as hostile surveillance, which might or might not be there, against which he had to plan. But this was someone he had known and liked and who had betrayed him, personally, as she had betrayed the ambassador, and he had to remind himself of this as they walked around to the front of the residence.

Maripaz had been walking without raising her head, but as they stepped off the gravel driveway onto the brightly lit portico in front of the residence, she suddenly looked up, and her eyes went wide with fear.

"What are we doing here?" she almost screamed.

"There's someone inside I want you to talk to," Lafeur said flatly.

Maripaz clutched at her abdomen as if in excruciating pain and pulled back for the first time. "Oh, God! No, please! Take me to jail, lock me up, but I don't want to go in there, please!" She began to sob.

The noise of their approach had apparently alerted the butler, who now opened the door in his usual elegant way to receive them, but his normal impassive expression was quickly replaced by a look of total shock. Instead of the properly dressed Stileforth or some other Embassy official coming to call, here was the rumpled figure of Lafeur, half-dragging the near hysterical Maripaz through the door.

"Is Mrs. Featherstone at home?" Lafeur asked in a calm voice as Maripaz sobbed all the louder.

The butler couldn't quite make his mouth work, so he simply nodded and stumbled off to find her, leaving the door ajar.

A moment later, Anne appeared, followed at a safe distance by the butler and one of the maids, both of whom peered curiously around the corner after their mistress. Anne was wearing a simple but tasteful house dress, and she walked erect, but the dark rings under her eyes and the swollen redness around them told Lafeur that she had not slept lately and had probably been crying a moment before.

He could also see that she was still clutching in one hand a copy of the photograph of the ambassador holding the newspaper in front of himself. Of course, the technicians had insisted on taking the original photograph to run some sort of forensic tests on it, so all he had been able to do for Anne was to make a quick xerox. To his knowledge, she had not let it out of her hands since, and he could see from here that the paper was slightly buckled with moisture.

"Claude!" she said, startled. "Maripaz! What's the matter?" Then her eyes widened. "Is it something about Bill . . . the ambassador?"

"No news," Claude said quickly, hating himself for senselessly causing Anne even that moment of pain. Naturally, his unexpected appearance, given his job, and Maripaz' tears would suggest the worst. "We just need to talk to you. Maripaz needs to talk to you, that is."

Maripaz looked up for a moment at Anne's questioning face, then let out another wail and fell to her knees. "I-I'm so-so s-s-orry," she sobbed between gasps. Anne dropped down to her knees and hugged Maripaz to her breast. Maripaz struggled feebly to get away, but finally stayed, her shoulders heaving with each sniffling moan.

Anne looked up at Lafeur with anger in her face. "What the bloody hell is this all about, Claude?"

"I'm afraid Maripaz is going to have to tell you that herself, ma'am," Claude said quietly. "Go ahead, Maripaz. Mrs. Featherstone is waiting."

After a long moment, Maripaz finally raised her head and practically screamed between sobs, "It's the ambassador. I-I gave him to the santistas. I'm so-so sorry," and she collapsed to the floor again.

Anne's back stiffened when she heard this, and her mouth drew taut in a straight line.

"I wonder if you have any idea how much trouble you're in," Claude said offhandedly.

At this, Maripaz tore herself away from Anne and turned on Lafeur, shouting. "*Trouble*? Are you going to give me trouble? Are you going to cut off my baby's head or douse my mother in gasoline and set fire to her? That's what I call trouble, Claude. Are you going to do worse than that?"

Lafeur went cold, and Anne looked at him in horror as her eyes filled with tears. From what Santander had told him freely just a short time ago, this is exactly the kind of approach these "heroes of the common man" would have taken with Maripaz. What was she supposed to have done? Suddenly, he felt very small and very helpless.

Anne grasped Maripaz firmly by the shoulders and hugged her hard as both women broke down in tears.

"Where is your baby and the rest of your family now?" Lafeur asked quickly.

Maripaz wiped futilely at her nose and eyes with a soaked kleenex and tried to control herself. "They're all at my mother's house now," she said. "But I think they're safe. The santistas seem to have lost interest in me after the ambassador was kidnapped. I guess that was all they really wanted out of me."

Anne and Lafeur helped Maripaz to her feet and led her to a sofa in the living room. As Anne held her trembling shoulders, she told them of the first appearance of the santistas in her apartment and of their demands. Then she told of the rapes and the questions which she had had to answer. A small voice in the back of Lafeur's head carped at him that maybe Maripaz was just a very good actress, telling a carefully prepared story to distract him, but he doubted that. No one was that good an actress, he thought, and it would serve little purpose at this point anyway. The ambassador had been kidnapped, and the secret about Maripaz was out, so the santistas wouldn't care what happened to her.

Maripaz told them of how Luis had talked to her for hours about their movement, possibly trying to convince her of the rightness of their actions, possibly just to be able to brag about his horrible accomplishments. But she had not seen him now for days, and the last contact she had had with the santistas had been her phone call to advise them of the ambassador's departure. Lafeur had her write down the number she had called, and it corresponded to one of the numbers Quiroga had been checking out. She said that it seemed to be a private home, rather than a bar or office, from the lack of background noise. She also added that she was certain that the person she had spoken to was Padre Lazaro himself.

"I want you to stay here tonight, Maripaz," Lafeur said. "That is, if it's all right with you, Mrs. Featherstone."

"Of course," Anne answered quickly.

"This could all be over within 24 hours," Claude said, wondering how much he should reveal in front of Maripaz.

"I saw the General arrive," Maripaz said, mopping at her tears with a fresh kleenex from the box Anne had placed in front of her. "I know that they're going to do something soon, but I don't think you can beat these people."

This was exactly what Lafeur himself believed, but he didn't like hearing it from Maripaz, and certainly not in front of Anne.

"I think you're underestimating our people," he said without much conviction. "They're expecting a tough fight, but just because they were able to ambush some Dominican policemen doesn't mean that they can deal with the best the American military can provide. Most terrorists fail precisely because they start to believe their own press."

"I hope you're right," Maripaz said in a little voice, and she began nervously tearing her kleenex into little pieces in her lap.

†

Featherstone didn't have any idea whether it was day or night, but he had just finished what he assumed to have been his dinner, which was largely indistinguishable from what he assumed to be his breakfast. Both consisted of rice, beans, and a cooked banana, but the dinner also included a small piece of boiled fish, something he never would have eaten otherwise as the local fish was reported to be tainted by pollution and could cause a variety of dread infections. He was not, however, in a position to be picky.

They had never bothered to take away his newspaper, and Featherstone had now read it through several times, including the small print in the advertisements and all of the obituaries. He had even taken a stab at doing the crossword puzzle mentally since he had no writing material, but his Spanish wasn't quite up to that. To help pass the time, he had also begun a modest program of calisthenics, mostly push-up and bicycle kicks, since the floor was too hard on his bare back for sit-ups, and the roof of the cage too low for anything done standing upright. He even imagined that, with the enforced diet and exercise regime, his spare tire was starting to disappear. He had just finished cleaning his plate when the door opened, and Pedro walked in with an empty bucket and a fresh bottle of water. Under his arm was a small tape player.

"Do you like salsa music?" Pedro asked, a timid smile on his face.

"As a matter of fact I do," Featherstone lied. Actually, he thought it all sounded pretty much the same, and one tended to get rather tired of it after hearing nothing else for several months, but he sensed that Pedro was opening another chink in the wall of his prison.

Pedro set the tape player down on the floor and hit the "play" button, filling the room with the throbbing beat and tinny brass sound of one of the popular local bands. "I thought you might appreciate a little music, at least while I'm here."

Featherstone was about to thank Pedro, but he remembered his own silent vow never to do so while in this situation. "Yes, I would. Won't you get in trouble for that?"

"Things are only illegal if you get caught," Pedro said, and for a moment Featherstone could see the face of a mischievous Dominican street child who probably had been swiping fruit from open air markets as soon as he could walk. Around the eyes, however, was a hardness that didn't belong and which the smile softened slightly but did not erase.

Featherstone traded his half-full bucket for the empty one and his empty water bottle for the full one. Pedro didn't make him stand against the back wall anymore, not that he ever posed much of a threat anyway. He then passed out his plate with its plastic spoon, no metal with which to tunnel through the concrete floor, of course.

When they had finished, Pedro looked toward the door and reached inside his shirt quickly, pulling out a folded newspaper. "I'll trade you your old one for today's," he said.

Featherstone had stashed his newspaper in the corner, hoping no one would notice, but now he quickly retrieved it and swapped with Pedro, who slipped the old paper back inside his shirt.

"Why are you doing this?" Featherstone asked. "Not that I'm complaining, but you are running something of a risk."

Pedro just smiled again. "I think we've almost won. You aren't going anywhere, and I just don't see any point in making you suffer if it's not for the cause. Padre Lazaro is very strict, and he doesn't like people to argue with him, so sometimes we just have to do what we think best and not tell him about it."

Suddenly, the door of the room flew open and there stood Padre Lazaro and his two bodyguards. Featherstone shrank back against the far wall of his cage, but Pedro just turned calmly and stood facing him.

Featherstone expected screaming and shouting, but Lazaro simply strode up to the taller, lankier Pedro and stared at him with his burning eyes. Pedro stood stock still, like a soldier on parade, but Featherstone noticed his fingers trembling against the sides of his pants legs.

"You have disobeyed my instructions, Pedro," Lazaro said in a rumbling voice. "You know that I cannot tolerate that."

Pedro did not answer, and Featherstone didn't even see Lazaro's hand move, but it must have, for something struck Pedro a resounding blow on the side of the head which sent him staggering across the room, blood pouring from a gash at his temple. Lazaro followed him and kicked him hard in the midriff. When he doubled over, he kicked him full in the face, bouncing him hard against the cinder block wall of the cellar. Pedro collapsed to the floor, and Lazaro continued kicking him until he stopped moving.

Lazaro then turned and walked toward the door, not even breathing hard. As he reached the doorway, he stooped and picked up the tape player, which had been booming out another salsa hit the whole time, turned it off, and tucked it under his arm.

"You see, Mr. Featherstone," he said in a calm voice which belied the flush in his cheeks. "We are a very strict order." With that he left the room and disappeared.

The two bodyguards, still armed with their cattle prods, moved to opposite sides of the cage. One of them pointed at the newspaper on the floor, and Featherstone quickly rolled it up and passed it out through the wire mesh. The guard that took it made a lunge at Featherstone with his prod, causing Featherstone to jump back, only to be caught in the ribs by the prod of the man behind him. The jolt knocked the wind out of him and involuntarily drove him forward against the other prod, dropping him on the ground, his limbs jerking and his eyes rolling back in his head.

It took some time before the pain began to subside and Featherstone could see again. When he could, he raised himself agonizingly on one elbow to look around. Pedro's body was gone, but there was a dark stain of blood on the floor where he had lain. Featherstone flopped back on the floor and closed his eyes again.

SEVEN

Rain clouds had begun to gather along the southern coast of the Dominican Republic as a lone Hughes 500MD helicopter raced along only meters above the roiling waves, approaching the lights of the Malecon shorefront district. It was a small, roundish aircraft, the kind normally used by the military for observation. A bulky ball mounted above the central shaft of its main rotor, a sighting device which permitted the pilot to hover behind a hill, or trees, or buildings with only the tip of the sight exposed and observe from a position of safety. The helicopter was covered with a rubbery black radar-absorbent material, a product of "stealth" technology. It travelled well below the horizon of the standard commercial radar at Santo Domingo International Airport or the more sensitive sets employed by the military to identify drug trafficking aircraft heading north across the island from Colombia. Dominican President Selich had, in theory, authorized the American government to take whatever action it thought necessary, but General Pennington considered it necessary to the security of the operation not to advise him of the actual incursion.

The helicopter belonged to the United States Army 106th Aviation Group, the unit which provided for the unique transportation requirements of the Delta Force of the Joint Special Operations Command out of Fort Bragg, North Carolina. Equipped with a "black hole" infrared suppressor and mounting a 7.62mm minigun on one pylon and a pod of fourteen 2.75 inch rockets on the other, it carried "observers" in the persons of Colonels Voorst and Miller in addition to a two-man sniper team. Their mission was to take a final look at the target site and then take up position on top of the Banco Hispano-Americano, a ten-story structure just at the edge of the "forbidden zone" about 500 meters from the target complex. From this point Voorst would coordinate the operation and the snipers and the helicopter would provide fire support.

Precisely two minutes' flying time behind the first 500MD came another pair of the same craft, less the mast-mounted sight and external armament. Ten seconds behind those came another pair, and ten seconds behind those, another. Each of these carried a section of six heavily-armed Delta commandos. Ordinarily, the 500MD would have room for only two or three passengers, but these helicopters were equipped with seats attached to the skids outside the aircraft. The commandos sat, facing outward, three on a side, with their harnesses already connected to permit them to "fast rope" down to the ground as the aircraft hovered over the target. In their black suits and body armor and their camouflaged face paint, they were as invisible in the night sky as the darkened helicopters as they sped over the sea.

Most of the commandos were armed with a slightly modified Colt AR-15 assault rifle and the big 10mm magnum automatic pistol. In years of training and testing, the Deltas had opted for the unglamorous AR-15 of Vietnam fame for its ease of handling and the stopping power of its heavier 5.56mm round as opposed to more popular 9mm submachineguns. With its short nine inch barrel, it was only slightly less maneuverable in tight places than the MP5, while enjoying substantially better range and accuracy. Each weapon was loaded with a 100-round c-mag ammunition drum. They had also chosen the 10 mm magnum over the Beretta 9mm, for its powerful round for stopping opponents who might be wearing body armor or be hopped up on drugs.

The men also carried a variety of percussion and fragmentation grenades, and other explosive devices for blasting open doors, windows, and walls. Some carried bolt cutters and other tools for gaining entry to the building, and they were all equipped with individual radio sets with ear plugs and chin mikes for immediate, enciphered communication. They were all professionals who had undergone many hours of grueling, specialized training in Close Quarters Battle drill in their "shooting house," using live ammo, for just such an operation. A few had seen combat in the Persian Gulf, Grenada, or Panama, and all were pumped full of adrenalin for what promised to be the first successful overseas hostage rescue by the Deltas.

As the lead chopper crossed the beach at over 100 miles per hour, the few strollers who still dared to roam the Malecon at this hour of the morning glanced upward at the sudden gust of wind from the rotors but saw nothing. The helicopters were equipped with specially silenced engines and rotors designed to eliminate as much as 47 per cent of the normal "whop-whop" sound. Relying on speed and stealth, rather then firepower and armor, they would move quickly to the target and hit before their presence could be discovered. The first hint the enemy would have of their approach would be the sound of bullets thudding into his body at close range. At least that was the theory.

The lead chopper gained altitude slightly as it crossed the urban area and swung around the terrorist headquarters complex. The pilot scanned the scene with his night vision devices and infrared detectors and reported to Voorst through the headset intercom that the roof of the target building was clear as was the courtyard below. With a rainstorm fast approaching, the commandos had counted on any chance stragglers being driven indoors, although the snipers' role had been to eliminate them if necessary.

The chopper reached the roof of the Banco Hispano-Americano and rotated just inches above it as Voorst, Miller, and the snipers jumped off. It took up a position near another tall building about 200 meters away from which it could provide covering fire. As they hit the gravel covering of the roof, the four men made for the parapet in a crouching run, and the snipers took up their stance with their M21 rifles. These weapons were virtually identical to the old Army M14 rifle, but with a hand fitted and polished firing mechanism, gas cylinder and piston and specially gauged barrels. At this range, and with a freshening breeze from the sea toward the firers, and not across the line of fire, the expected hit ratio for the snipers was calculated at 97 percent within a six inch target circle.

Voorst had been explaining the general tactics for the assault to Miller, who, although a combat veteran from the Gulf, had not experienced anything like the Delta Force tactics. After reporting his arrival on station via the powerful radio set he wore on his back, Voorst continued his lesson.

"Although Santander told us that the third floor of the building is the key, with access to the basement where the Ambassador is being held, we'll go in on all four floors at once, both to clear the building of hostiles and to search for any other means of access to the basement. Then our task will be to gain control of the stairwell to the basement and hold it until the Ambassador can be located and secured."

Voorst and Miller took turns scanning the building with a hand-held starlight scope. There was no sign of activity in the target area, although the power in the neighborhood was on, and lights showed in some of the windows. If Lafeur did his job correctly, his penetration of the phone company would have cut telephone service to this sector, so that even if the commandos were spotted heading into the target, it would take time to pass the warning. An E2 Hawkeye electronic warfare plane staging out of San Juan was also aloft, circling in a racetrack pattern off the coast, jamming any radio transmissions the terrorists might attempt to make.

"If what Santander told us about the third floor windows actually being walled up is true," Voorst continued, "we'll have to go in through the door, which we can do even if it's a bank vault. On all of the other floors, our men will enter from the doors off the main landing and through windows on all sides of the building simultaneously."

"Isn't that awfully dangerous?" Miller asked. "You're going to have guys charging toward each other, firing like mad, maybe in the dark. How do you keep from hitting the friendlies?"

"That's what we train to do," Voorst said matter-of-factly. "It makes it a lot easier on the terrorists if they know that all the enemy are coming from one direction, and we're better prepared than they are to deal with this. Our men spend literally hundreds of hours in hand-eye coordination and target identification training, sorting out the good guys from the bad guys, and we're confident we can have men coming from every point of the compass, blazing away, and only the hostiles will get hit. You'll have to visit our 'shooting house' sometime. It's really an impressive show."

Miller's only experience with live fire training had been at Quantico and Camp Pendleton, where all kinds of precautions were taken to keep advancing infantry on line, so that no one was in front of anyone else's weapon. Chills went down his spine at the thought of his Marines actually firing at each other, picking out point targets to one side or another.

"Here they come," Voorst said in a low tone.

Miller had to take his word for it. Even though the wind was blowing toward them from the sea, he couldn't hear a thing over the subdued noise of the city at night. Finally, he saw what appeared to be two holes in the background, a little blacker than the deep blue of the night sky. Then there were two more. The first two hovered above the roof of the target building, and he peered through his starlight scope. He could see in the greenish image six figures from each chopper quickly slide down ropes to the roof. A second later, the two helicopters peeled off and disappeared. The second pair dropped their troops in the courtyard. Then the third pair arrived and did likewise. Still no indication that the enemy had noticed them.

The rappelling line hissed through Captain Patrick Ng's gloved hands as he fast-roped down to the roof of the headquarters building. His twelve-man squad had the most difficult assignment of the operation. It was their task to eliminate resistance on the fourth floor and seize control of the third floor, which was reported to be the center for the terrorists' operations, as well as the only point of access to the basement where the hostage was being held. According to intelligence reports provided by Major Voorst, there would be anywhere from one dozen to two dozen armed terrorists in the building, all presumed to be combat veterans and very tough. There would also be at least one hostage and an unknown number of unarmed civilians, dependents living in the building. His orders were to avoid unnecessary casualties among the civilians and to take one or more terrorists alive, if possible. Other than that, the building was essentially a free-fire zone, and he understood that the terrorists' dependents were not a major topic of concern.

Ng was the son of a Korean immigrant who had fought with distinction in the 1st ROK Division in the Korean War. Ng's father had been immensely proud to see his son join the American Army, go through airborne and ranger training, and rise to the rank of captain. Of course, Ng's membership in the Delta Force itself was classified, but his father knew that he was in an elite unit, and that was enough for him. Ng never stopped thanking his adopted country for the opportunity to command these crack troops in combat. An oriental immigrant's son like himself, giving orders to white and black soldiers whose families had been in the country for centuries, was a constant source of pride for him.

As soon as Ng cleared his line, he took a quick glance around the roof. His men were already taking their positions. Each was wearing night vision goggles. One of his men prepared to cut the city power cable, while another was already cutting the lines connecting the two large generators to the building's electrical system. If everything went black inside just as his men smashed in, the defenders would have no night vision, and it would take time to get any low light gear the defector had said that they had, and Ng and his men would see that they wouldn't live to accomplish it.

Four men would take out the fourth floor, and the other eight would join Ng for the assault on the key third floor. He peeked over the edge of the roof and saw the last members of the third squad roping into the courtyard below. The smaller second and third squads would clean out the first and second floors and provide rear security against possible enemy reinforcements. The second squad would be available to move up and reinforce Ng's men.

The men going for the fourth floor would each rope down a different face of the building and go in through the windows for maximum shock effect. Because there were no windows on the third floor, Ng and his men would use an explosive entry on the door off the exterior stairway and spread out through the apartment. One of his men had already cut the chain which held the gate to the stairway closed. Ng could see that the fourth floor men had hooked up their ropes and were in position.

Silently, but quickly, Ng led his men down the stairway, past the fourth floor to the third. He posted men on the open terrace which ran along the courtyard face of the building, and others on the stairway itself. He could see the men from the other squads taking position on the landing below. He made his way to the end of the terrace and leaned out to see that the rope man on that side was in position. He had an explosive device on a kind of T-bar stick which he would use to blow out the window. If only hostiles had been present inside, the charge would have been placed outside the window to turn the glass and its frame into shrapnel, shredding anything directly behind the window. Since civilians might be inside, the charge would be thrust through the glass and detonated manually by the commando, who would press himself against the wall and trust to his body armor to protect him from shards of glass blown outward instead.

He went back to the main door on his floor. In the time it had taken him to walk ten meters and back, one of his men had pressed a strip of explosive cutting tape all along the edge of the door where the latch was. He had also stuck another strip along the side with the hinges. Cutting tape is a long shaped charge, about one inch wide by one inch thick, designed to cut through steel the way an anti-tank rocket blasts through the steel of a tank. He connected a four-foot strip of Nonel initiator to the charge and pressed himself back against the wall with his detonator in one hand, his 10mm in the other.

†

In his fourth floor apartment, Carlos Aramayo, a recent graduate of the combined MIR-santista paramilitary training course had just poured himself another cup of coffee. A few moments before, he had been taking a turn around the rooftop as part of his normal guard duties, but the rising wind had told him that it would start to rain soon, and he thought it wise to come indoors. He had locked the gate to the stairs behind him and entered the apartment.

Aramayo and his wife, Cecilia, shared the duplex apartment with another guard, Tomas, and his wife and child. There was also a central guard room which connected the two small apartments in which two single guards slept. Although these rather cramped living arrangements were less than ideal, they were a step up from the cardboard and plywood hovel in which they had been living when Padre Lazaro had come along. He had been unemployed, gathering an occasional peso by selling shoelaces or razor blades or whatever else he could borrow the money to buy wholesale, but that hadn't been enough to put food on the table, if they had had a table. Now they had nice, clean rooms, a real bathroom, real furniture, and a large communal kitchen in which his wife and Tomas' worked together preparing meals for the whole crew.

Aramayo had never been very ideological, although the concept that his troubles were caused by the rich, either in his country or elsewhere, had always appealed to him. He had belonged to the MIR for some time, although he had never taken an active part until the santistas had kicked off their successful war against the establishment. He had fought the police in the streets with a club and had been selected for his bravery to take the training which had gotten him this job. He was honored at the thought that he was one of the key guards for MIR headquarters, but then he noticed that all of the men guarding the building were recent trainees like himself. The more experienced santistas and miristas who had massacred the police commandos the night before had come from somewhere else in the zone, but Aramayo assumed they would be close at hand if there were any further trouble, which he doubted, having seen the carnage in the street that morning.

No, it would be a long time before the police bothered to come back here.

As he reflected, he heard a heavy thump, quickly followed by another and another. Everyone else was asleep, and he wondered if maybe Tomas and his wife were having a little romantic interlude with the bedstead too close to the wall, but he was certain that the sound had come from the roof. He walked over to the window and opened the louvered glass slats. There was the sound of the wind, and nothing else until, suddenly, he saw a dark shadow appear overhead, then turn and disappear into the night.

Shit! he thought, they're here. He quickly went from bed to bed, waking the guards and Tomas. "Helicopters on the roof," he said in a half whisper as he unslung his G-3 automatic rifle from his shoulder and chambered a round. He raced to the telephone and picked up the receiver, but it was dead. Damn! He could feel the precious seconds ticking away as he tried to decide what to do. If he tried to go out the door, they would probably be waiting for him, so he ran to the intercom alarm and slapped the button with the heel of his hand. He hoped it worked. Cecilia and Tomas' wife and child had already crawled from their beds to the bathroom, the most protected room in the apartment, and all of the other men were up and armed, although only in their underwear. Aramayo could hear footsteps on the roof very clearly now.

The red light began to flash on the third floor, accompanied by an incessant but quiet buzzer, the signal that there was a serious security problem of some sort. Melgarejo came out of his bedroom rubbing his eyes, clad only in boxer shorts and a silk bath robe, one of the many luxuries he had allowed himself as leader of the movement. Through the half open doorway, one could see the very young girl who had been entertaining him this evening as she hastily pulled the sheets around her naked body.

"What the fuck is going on?" Melgarejo bellowed. "Where's Baca?" Then he remembered that Lazaro had called Pablo Baca away to some sort of tactical meeting earlier in the evening, and he hadn't come back. Melgarejo shook his head, trying to clear out the cobwebs, and now he remembered that the only santista in the headquarters at the moment was Diana, Lazaro's able female lieutenant. As he stumbled around the large living room looking for her, his half dozen bodyguards were rushing to and fro, handing out weapons and ammunition. The man on duty in the communications room called out, "The phone lines have been cut, and I can't raise anyone on the radio either. It sounds like some kind of jamming."

Melgarejo was getting scared now, and he made for the trap door to his escape tunnel. There he found Diana, kneeling on the rug which covered the trap door, her arms held out straight from her sides in the form of the cross. Her eyes were closed tight, and her lips were moving in silent prayer.

"Get the hell out of the way, dammit!" Melgarejo screamed shrilly, making a grab for Diana to pull her aside. "We've got to get out of here."

Without opening her eyes, Diana caught Melgarejo's hand in mid-air, twisting his thumb around in a direction it was not meant to bend, and bringing the fat man crashing to his knees with a whimper of pain. Her other hand had already drawn an automatic pistol from her shoulder holster, and she pointed it at the one bodyguard who was nearby.

"This way isn't safe, don Emilio," she said in a soft voice. "It's our duty to stay here and fight." Just then the lights in the room went out and the alarm was silenced.

†

Ng had each squad check in by radio. All were in position. He wedged himself back against the wall and said into his chin mike in a flat voice, to hide the mixture of fear and excitement he was feeling, "Execute, execute, execute."

Simultaneously, the power lines to the building were cut, the window charges and those on all of the doors blew, and the air was filled with dust, flying glass, wood splinters, and bits of jagged, hot metal. Even before the heavy steel door hit the floor inside the apartment, one of the men had tossed in a percussion grenade, which added its own flash-bang to the echoing thunder.

On the fourth floor, Aramayo saw something smash through the glass of the living room window and only had a second to hit the floor before it exploded. In the second it took him to lift his head again, something else bounced into the room and exploded as well. The clap of thunder shook his head like a rattle and left him disoriented, the room spinning around him. He saw a dark shadow pass in front of him, and he fired a burst at random, but he could see in that split second that the barrel of his weapon was pointed at the ceiling and only sent down a shower of plaster. The shadow had now materialized into the form of a black-suited man, but before Aramayo could bring his weapon level, he saw another flash and felt the pain as if several metal fists had smashed into his chest almost simultaneously. The last thing he felt in this world was his own body being thrown backward across the floor and up against the wall.

One of the bodyguards on the third floor had just made for the steel door to the outdoor stairway when the lights failed and the room was plunged into total darkness. At almost the same second, the door erupted from its frame, smashing the bodyguard beneath it even before he had a chance to scream.

The blast startled Diana and permitted Melgarejo to shove her aside before she could react. The percussion grenade, which was designed to affect the inner ear, and thus rob the victim of normal equilibrium, sent them both staggering. By instinct, Diana brought up her weapon to cover the door, while Melgarejo, screaming hysterically, pulled the rug aside and threw open the trap door.

Ng was the second man through the door. The first man had peeled off to the right and was engaging (a euphemism for killing) two men who were trying to bring their assault rifles to bear. Ng saw the woman kneeling to his left, taking a regulation two-handed aiming position with her pistol directly at his chest, but Ng was quicker. He fired a three-round burst which tore off the top of the woman's head, and she kicked over backward. Ng just had time to see a bulky figure disappear through a trap door in the floor. Ng fired another burst after him, but it just panged harmlessly off the metal of the trap door.

There were more terrorists coming in now from the back room, and a shot from their wildly blazing weapons caught the next commando through the door in the chest. Although his body armor would protect him from penetration by the bullets, the force threw him backward through the open door. Ng and the first man swung around simultaneously and cut down the terrorists in a vicious crossfire, as more commandos charged through the door to clear the back rooms. Unfortunately, the naked girl in Melgarejo's bedroom had pulled a pistol from the nightstand drawer, and she was virtually blown apart by 5.56mm rounds which spewed blood all over the white satin sheets on the giant bed.

With a silent hand signal, Ng directed four of his men to secure the apartment, while he and his own back-up yanked up the trap door and took off after Melgarejo. Ng had studied the photographs of the people he was likely to encounter, and he knew that this fat man was the guiding force behind this entire uprising. Killing him might save hundreds, if not thousands of lives, and he wasn't about to let him get away.

Melgarejo half ran, half fell, down the first half-flight of the sharply bending staircase. Once he rounded the first corner he felt a little safer, but he was still gasping for air, and there was a terrifying pounding in his chest as he stumbled onward, bracing himself against both walls of the narrow passageway. He heard the trap door clang open behind him, and he let out an involuntary whimper and hurried on. He had been so certain, just moments before, that victory was within his grasp. He had believed Lazaro's promises that his fortress was impregnable, and the bloody defeat of the Dominican commandos and armor had proved it to be true.

Where were all the damn santistas now? he asked himself. Even his one trusted fighter, Baca, hadn't been at his side, only that bitch, Diana, and she had even drawn a weapon on *him*. If it hadn't been for her, he could have had another precious five or ten seconds head start. He had no illusions about being able to outrun these athletic young soldiers he could already hear galloping down the steps after him, but he had a lead of nearly a floor and a half. If he could just make it to the basement level and through the steel reinforced door, Lazaro had shown him how to block it shut from the other side. In the time it would take them to blow it open, he could be into the maze of the sewer system and gone. And they would have to be watching out for ambushes around every corner. They didn't know that Melgarejo had no weapon, and that would slow them down a little. The stairs were pitch black, but Melgarejo felt his way, and there was no way to get lost. Eight steps to each landing, and he had only two more floors to go.

Voorst and Miller had watched the fireworks as the doors and windows of the building had been blown and could see an occasional flash of gunfire through the gutted windows. Now they were listening to each of the teams as they reported their areas secure. Miller could hear the shouted conversations between the team members as they indicated their current positions and directions of advance every few seconds. All the floors were cleared now, and one team was moving quickly down to the cellar where ambassador Featherstone was being held. Captain Ng and another man were in hot pursuit of a man who appeared to be Melgarejo. Miller found himself cheering each report like a fan at the Superbowl. After all the tension and questions, it really looked like they were going to wrap this up in one great blaze of glory. If Lafeur had been right about Santander having been sent at them, it seemed that the bad guys had sorely underestimated their opponents. Miller assumed that the santistas' easy victories against the Dominicans had given them a false sense of confidence.

Melgarejo stumbled as his foot searched for one more step, and found that there were none. He was finally on the basement level. He swung to his right and hustled down the narrow hall. It could only be a few more yards now. He would get through the door, block it, and be home free. He could hear someone bounding down the steps after him, but they were at least half a flight and two corners behind him. He was going to make it, and the thought added strength to his numb legs as he pounded on.

Ng had long since stopped worrying about ambushes. He had been cautious at the first few bends in the stairs, waiting for his back-up man to take up a covering position before thrusting himself around the corner, but there had been nothing there. From the sounds of the clumping steps and the heavy breathing from up ahead, it was apparent that the fat man was the only one on the stairs, and he was running for his life. Of course, Ng had to keep a sharp eye out for booby traps, but even doing so he could tell that they were gaining fast on the quarry. By Ng's calculations, he estimated that they had reached at least ground level, so there would likely be only one more level to go. Ng's grip on his weapon tightened as he rounded the last corner. In his night vision goggles he could see the faint outline of the fat man wedging himself through a narrow doorway. He brought his rifle up to take an aimed shot and squeezed the trigger just as he felt a sudden rumbling which turned immediately into a roar as the walls and roof of the passageway collapsed on top of him.

Miller did not understand what he was seeing at first. There was a flash, or maybe a rapid series of flashes, afterwards he could never be quite sure. The sides of the MIR building had seemed to bulge outward momentarily, like in a cartoon when something's about to explode, then the entire structure was engulfed in a massive cloud of dust and debris. It took another moment for the sound and shock wave to reach him, and it bowled him over like a giant hand. He could feel the heat, and as his head bounced off the gravel decking of the roof, he thought for a moment of when he would lean too close when opening the oven door to check on the Thanksgiving turkey. The thunderclap of the explosion hammered his ears and kept rolling over him with a physical force. Miller thought for a moment that the entire city had blown up.

When he had caught his breath again, he dragged himself back to his position at the parapet, and he could see that Voorst and the snipers were doing the same. Where the headquarters building had been standing was simply an immense cloud of reddish dust. He could hear things, chunks of brick, pieces of metal and glass, clattering down all around him. He was wise enough to duck and cover his head with his arms just as a section of pipe caromed off the wall a few inches from his head.

"What the fuck was that?" he screamed at Voorst.

"How the hell should I know?" the Major shouted back. "Maybe they had the building wired, or maybe something touched off all of the munitions they were supposed to have cached in the building. Whatever it was, I've never seen an explosion that big in all my life. For the love of God!"

The rain of wreckage appeared to have stopped, and both men now dared to raise their heads above the level of the parapet. The dust cloud was still there, although it had expanded greatly and had already begun to thin somewhat. Miller could see the red glare of small fires at a dozen points now, and the echoes of the explosion were only now beginning to die down. There was the continuing crackle of smaller explosions as the ammunition cached in the basement of the building cooked off. They could also hear a faint moaning, punctuated by an occasional high pitched scream, coming from the area surrounding the blast zone.

As the dust cloud gradually settled and drifted away with the stiff breeze which preceded the rain squall, Miller could see in the faint light of the fires that where the four story headquarters building had stood, there was only an immense crater, perhaps fifty feet across, surrounded by mounds of broken masonry and twisted steel reinforcing rods.

Miller, Voorst, and the snipers stood open-mouthed on the roof, looking at the destruction below them. Their helicopter had swung over the scene and played a powerful xenon searchlight over the area. Among the piles of rubble, they could now make out the limp, dark forms of human bodies, like discarded children's toys, scattered everywhere. Off to the left, on the adjacent street, where the neighboring apartment block had been smashed by flying debris, they could see the figure of a woman, at least Miller thought it might be a woman. Much of her skin and clothing had been blackened by the blast. The figure staggered about as if looking for something in the moonscape which had once been her home. After a moment, she stooped and pulled something out of the rubble which looked like a small pile of rags, but the way she cradled it in her arms, it was obviously more than that. The figure looked at the bundle for a moment, then threw back her head and let out a long, anguished, animal howl, followed by another and another.

Several blocks away, in an empty sixth floor office, just outside the "forbidden zone," Luis lowered a small device which looked like a hair dryer but was actually a laser device. He was panting with emotion, and had actually felt the surge of energy emanate from his body as he had activated the laser, shooting across the intervening space to the small receiver panel carefully located on the nearest corner of the headquarters building. The laser beam, hitting the panel had caused an electrical circuit to be completed, sending a charge through all of the detonators emplaced in the explosives distributed throughout the building. He had felt the answering jolt from the explosion, which had reached out to him and made him quiver with its raw power.

In their "remodelling" of the building for Melgarejo, the santistas had taken the opportunity to lace the structural columns with large amounts of Czech-made PE-2 plastic explosive, placed directly within cavities in the columns themselves and covered over with plaster and paint. There had been well over a thousand pounds of the highly efficient explosive in the upper levels of the building as well as nearly a ton in the basement, hidden within false bottoms and sides of the many weapons crates cached there. The entire structure had thus been turned into a massive fragmentation grenade, with all of the outer wall surface and much of the interior framework being instantly converted into lethal shrapnel, blanketing the entire neighborhood for hundreds of yards in all directions with deadly missiles which easily penetrated the flimsily constructed buildings around it. The placement of the explosives also allowed for the core of the building to fall, not vertically upon itself, but to topple, like a tree, smashing surrounding dwellings to the south. Of course, the munitions which had been stored in the basement had added to the blast, but this was almost an afterthought compared to the force of the PE-2, which was nearly twice the volume of explosive used in the destruction of the U.S. Marine barracks in Beirut by a truck bomb in 1982. The PE-2 also had a higher brissance factor than the older Semtex so popular with terrorists in the 1980's.

Luis had found the assault itself very impressive from his vantage point. If he had not known that the Yankees would have to do something tonight, and if he had not had a pretty good idea of how they would have to go about it, he never would have seen or heard the helicopters. Even if he had, had he been in the target area itself, judging from the speed and violence of the attack, he doubted that there would have been much he and all the rest of the santistas together could have done. At least they wouldn't have to worry about that particular group of commandos any more, and, if the overall plan worked as intended, there wouldn't be any more where they came from.

As it was, of course, the defenders had only been the partially trained new recruits, since the rest of the santistas and the more experienced mirista fighters had been carefully posted elsewhere during the preceeding day by himself and Padre Lazaro. Except for Diana, he recalled with something approaching sincere remorse, and he crossed himself mechanically. She had been a good soldier and had accepted the assignment to continue to lull Melgarejo into his false sense of security right up to the last minute.

Luis frowned slightly as he thought how the ranks of the "old guard" continued to shrink. There had been fewer than thirty of them when they had arrived in the Dominican Republic. Diana was now gone, and Angel was permanently lost to them. They had lost two santistas in the fight against the police commandos the other night, and another by pure chance when the kidnapping unit had been fired on by that police patrol as they entered the "zone." Luis winced at this, since the intentional provoking of the police to showcase their entry into the "zone" had been his idea, but who would have thought that these imbecilic cops would have gotten that lucky?

Still, he thought, Pablo Baca had turned out very promising, as had most of the veteran miristas, and the nearly two hundred men and women who were undergoing intensive training and battle-hardening in skirmishes with the police and Army, were coming along nicely. Even the gross Melgarejo had served his purpose well, providing the santistas with a ready-made network of recruits and informants and a political organization upon which to build, and, in his death, he would provide one of the first martyrs for the movement. Luis had become inured to the loss of friends over the years, and they were so much closer to their goal now than they had ever dreamed of being. He crossed himself again and offered up a silent prayer for the success of their mission as he pocketed the laser and casually walked out of the building and toward his waiting car.

†

Not having anywhere better to wait, Lafeur had returned to the residence. He was sitting around the kitchen table with Anne and Ramiro Escobar, the larger of the ambassadorial bodyguards, while Maripaz slept fitfully on a sofa in the next room. Lafeur had noticed that, while the other bodyguard who had been present when Featherstone was kidnapped, Lucho Ayala, had just shrugged his shoulders and gone off to another assignment, Escobar had apparently been very shaken up by the incident and ashamed at not having been able to do more. He had requested to remain with the embassy and had become a virtually a fixture around the residence, evidently hoping to be able to protect at least the ambassador's wife, even if he had failed his first test.

They had a small television tuned to CNN news. A CNN team had arrived in the country after the first outbreak of violence, not unlike sharks attracted by the smell of blood in the water, Lafeur thought. As the situation had worsened, the team had grown, along with contingents from other major news "manufacturers" as the embassy staff liked to call them. More prestigious television journalists arrived to make their in-depth, two minute analyses of the social, political, and economic situation of the country. They had been staring blankly at a story about a battle in the Pacific Northwest between directors of a major hydroelectric project and ecologists who argued that a species of water newt would face extinction if the project went forward, when the windows of the residence were rattled viciously by what sounded like the sonic boom of an aircraft.

Maripaz screamed and rolled off the sofa, and Anne rushed in to take care of her. Lafeur and Escobar went out onto the terrace. They could still hear the echoes of the explosion reverberating around the city, but they could see nothing in the darkness.

"Whatever that was," Escobar said quietly so the women inside wouldn't hear, "it didn't sound good."

Lafeur knew that Escobar had not been informed of the planned Delta Force intervention, but real secrets were virtually impossible to keep in a fishbowl like Santo Domingo. Escobar had known that the Dominican police had tried and failed to rescue Featherstone, and it stood to reason that the Americans would try, and soon. Lafeur just shrugged, and the two men went back inside where they found Maripaz back on the sofa with Anne holding her hand and stroking her hair as a mother would with a sick child. Anne was trembling and staring off into space.

A few moments later, there was a soft knock at the front door. Escobar answered and returned with General Pennington and Stileforth. Stileforth was his usual composed self, and Lafeur noticed that, no matter the situation, he always found time to shave and to change into an apparently inexhaustible supply of neatly pressed dark suits. The General, however, while still neat by any standard, did not have the crispness with which he had arrived. More notably, he had a downcast, nervous look totally at odds with his former "command presence."

"We need to talk with Mrs. Featherstone," Stileforth announced in a flat voice, and Lafeur noticed that he was actually guiding the General by the elbow as the latter moved with slow, halting steps.

Anne came forward and stood erect in front of the two men. She held her chin up and looked at the men unflinchingly, but her hands were clenched into tight fists at her sides, and the veins on the backs of her hands stood out, the knuckles white.

"I'm afraid we have some bad news," the General began after a long pause. "As you know, we sent a team in to rescue your husband less than an hour ago. We don't have a full report back yet, but from early indications, it would appear that the operation did not go off as planned, and we have reason to believe that unexpectedly heavy casualties and collateral damage may have resulted."

"What do you mean, General?" Anne asked, trying to control herself.

With an exasperated snort, Stileforth stepped in front of the General. Lafeur suspected that he was trying to exude warmth and heartfelt emotion, but it didn't come off well. "Anne," he began, "that explosion you just heard a few minutes ago. We think it was the building where William was being held. The terrorists may have wired it to blow up if attacked, and it looks like it was totally destroyed. The Dominican Army has moved into the "forbidden zone" all along the line, and they aren't meeting any appreciable resistance. We expect them to be in occupation of the site later this morning. We won't know anything for certain until then, but it appears that your husband, I am sorry to say," he added as an afterthought, "may have been killed in the explosion."

"Along with the entire Delta Force team," the General added, speaking to no one in particular.

Anne's hands flew to her mouth to stifle a gasp. Maripaz had come in from the living room, and now it was she who put her arms around Anne as the two women began to weep quietly. Stileforth watched the women cry, and it occurred to Lafeur that he had about the same level of pity in his eyes as had the snakes at the zoo.

"Under the circumstances," Stileforth went on, "I think it would be best if you returned to the States now, to be with your family."

Anne turned on Stileforth with a force which shocked Lafeur. "I'll accompany my husband's body back to the States, Mr. Stileforth. Until that can be done, I will remain here. I know that you're very eager to occupy this house, but you're just going to have to wait. My two children are due in from the States later today, so you needn't worry about my family."

"I don't think you appreciate the situation, Anne," Stileforth continued, unperturbed. "This residence is U.S. government property and is intended for the use of the ambassador and his immediate family during the period of his appointment, not for the housing of his relatives after that period."

Lafeur was about to say something, even if it meant the end of his own career, but Anne never gave him the chance.

Anne responded in a deceptively low tone. "I don't think *you* understand, you stupid little git. My husband *is* the ambassador until he is either withdrawn from that posting by Washington, or until he is legally proven to be dead. *If* my husband has been killed, I will leave this house and this island only too gladly and never look back, but until that time, this is *my* home, and I will thank you to keep out of it. And, if you try by some slimey maneuver to get me out of here before then, I have been with the Foreign Service long enough to have quite a circle of friends within the upper levels of the Department, and I will do your professional reputation such damage in ways you cannot even imagine that you'll be lucky to get posted to Ulan Bator. Is that quite clear?"

Stileforth's eyes narrowed to tiny slits, but he only snorted again, turned on his heel, and marched out the door. The butler had appeared and held the door open for him, but he pushed it closed just fast enough to slam into Stileforth's heel before he could get clear. The group heard a muffled curse from beyond the door, and Lafeur smiled grimly. The butler bowed and disappeared back into the servants' quarters.

Anne and Maripaz just turned and walked back into the living room, supporting each other, and Escobar withdrew to the kitchen.

"What happened, General?" Lafeur asked in a soft voice.

"Everything seemed to be going perfectly," he began, still staring at the floor and spreading his hands wide in a gesture of helplessness. "The assault team went in without drawing any fire. We were receiving regular radio reports as they cleared all the floors and took control of the stairwells. One section was just reaching the basement where we figured the Ambassador was located and another was just about to catch that Melgarejo character when the place just blew up! Maybe they triggered some booby trap or something, but from the reports of the size of the explosion, we're not just talking about a few crates of munitions. This must have been literally tons of explosives."

The General sighed and finally looked up. "If there is a positive side to this, it looks like we may have torn the guts out of the terrorist movement. When the blast occurred, the Dominicans rushed in from all sides. Apart from some scattered shooting, mostly between one Dominican unit and another by mistake, they're not seeing any resistance. They've got people on the blast site already, looking around, but there doesn't seem to be any hope for survivors from anywhere in the building. Maybe the war's all over now at least. General Tamayo is mad as hell that we went in without coordinating with them, even if we had the President's permission. There were apparently lots of civilian casualties in the blast, and now the government is blaming us for the whole thing. I've been ordered to get my sorry ass out of the country within two hours, along with all other military personnel apart from the Defense Attache himself. We offered them a forensic team to analyze the blast site, but they're not having any. Now that they don't need us any more to fight their battles for them, they're right back to Yankee bashing."

The General sighed again, shook Lafeur's hand in a distracted fashion and let himself out the door. Lafeur just flopped down in one of the uncomfortable ornamental chairs in the entry hall, not wanting to go back in and face Anne. Stileforth's pettiness and her bravery had only made him feel worse about the whole thing.

This was obviously what the santistas had wanted from their phoney defector. They had wanted the Delta Force to go in there too fast, expecting the ambassador to be killed at any minute, without trying to get additional intelligence about what they would be up against. Now the ambassador was gone, the Delta Force was gone, and the Dominican government was turning on the Americans. Of course, if the santistas were really done for, that wouldn't be so important. In time, the wound between the two governments would heal, but Lafeur had a sinking feeling that this was not the case. The santistas had done a lot in the past couple of months, but he couldn't think of a single serious mistake they had made. It seemed too easy for them to have been wiped out with a single commando raid, although he desperately wanted to believe it. No, he feared that something else was still in the works.

After sitting there, mulling things over for some time, Lafeur noticed that daylight was now streaming in through the windows which flanked the entry. He raised himself stiffly from the chair and stumbled back into the kitchen. Escobar was still there, staring at the CNN news, but the story was now about the Dominican Republic with a distinctive logo in the upper corner of the screen, a palm tree split by a lightning bolt with the words "Hell in the Tropics" tastefully emblazoned underneath it.

The balding correspondent was standing in front of an immense crater, surrounded by mounds of rubble, perhaps twenty feet high in places. Behind him one could see teams of soldiers carrying stretchers and searching through the debris in a haphazard manner. The wail of sirens could be heard plainly in the background. Lafeur speculated absently that, after he had made his name with this coverage, and written an insightful book on the politics of the Caribbean, he would probably be able to afford a decent hairpiece.

". . . . this tragedy," the correspondent was saying. "The cause of the blast has not been determined, but sources in the Dominican Army believe that it was a 'sympathetic explosion' caused by the charges used by the American commandos to force open the doors of the building. The military authorities here blame the explosion, and the massive loss in civilian life it caused, on the reckless use of these techniques by the Delta Force in a building known to have contained a large cache of munitions.

"The bodies of more than twenty American soldiers have been recovered so far, along with another twenty belonging to presumed terrorists. It is assumed that kidnapped American Ambassador William Featherstone is also among the dead. But it is what the military euphemistically refers to as collateral damage which has shocked the whole world." The correspondent pointed over his left shoulder, and the camera panned and zoomed in on another pile of rubble in that direction. "What you are now viewing was until hours ago an orphanage run by the Sisters of Mercy. It was located across the street from what was alleged to have been the headquarters of the 'Holy War' movement where the commando attack took place. When the explosion destroyed the headquarters building, one wall came crashing down here, smashing the orphanage and killing an estimated fifty children, aged six months to eight years, along with at least five nuns. The death toll in apartment buildings all around the blast site is similarly high, with a figure of over four hundred dead and at least as many injured thus far. Those numbers are expected to grow as the rescue teams comb through the wreckage in search of both bodies and survivors."

"The Dominican government has characterized the action by the American military as a brutal, irresponsible, and wholly unauthorized use of force within the territory of a sovereign nation, and American officials have been denied permission to visit the site. The bodies of the American servicemen will be turned over to the American embassy for identification and shipment home, but no further cooperation between the two governments appears to be in the offing. Meanwhile, there has been no sign of the dreaded santista terrorists, and it is hoped that the bulk of the group may also have perished in this terrible catastrophe. This is James Mensonge for CNN News, Santo Domingo."

Lafeur was shaking his head when he heard a small gasp coming from the door to the living room. Maripaz stood there with her hand clasped over her mouth. Her eyes were red and swollen from crying, but now they were wide with surprise.

"Did he say that this all happened at the santista headquarters, the building in the 'forbidden zone'?" she asked in a feeble voice.

"Yes, of course," Lafeur replied. "Where else would it have been?"

"But the ambassador wasn't there!" she almost shouted, and the corners of her mouth fought to form a smile.

"What?" Anne gasped, coming from behind her into the kitchen. "How do you know? Are you sure?"

"I'm sure that the place the ambassador was being held and the headquarters in the 'zone' were two different places, and not even close together," she answered, speaking more and more rapidly as she sorted out her jumbled thoughts.

Lafeur was mentally kicking himself for forgetting that he had been sitting around in the same house with his recently captured santista mole and had forgotten completely about questioning her.

"Tell me the details," Lafeur said, spinning around on his stool at the breakfast counter where he had been sitting. "Don't leave anything out."

Maripaz gathered her thoughts for a moment and then began, forcing herself to speak slowly and distinctly. "I remember Luis coming to my apartment one night, the first time since the kidnapping. He said he had just gotten away from the headquarters and out of the 'zone' before the curfew. He said that he only had time to get my reports, because he had to go and pay a visit to the Ambassador, and that was on the other side of town. He said he would pay me another visit the next day." She flushed and lowered her eyes as she said this but swallowed hard and went on. "I'm sure he was talking about two different places."

"But if the curfew was on," Lafeur asked, "how could he go across town, if that was a problem for him?" The curfew had been in force from midnight to dawn for some time, but it was mainly used to control individuals moving into and out of the "forbidden zone" and the surrounding area.

"He was only worried about crossing the line around the 'zone.' He joked about how he could go just about anywhere else in town, night or day, curfew or not."

"That means that Bill might really be alive!" Anne shouted and hugged Maripaz wildly around the neck. Lafeur let out a warwhoop, and he and Escobar laughed out loud and shook hands across the counter.

"Now all we have to do is find him and get him out," Lafeur said happily, as the thought sunk in that this was exactly where he had been the night before, and he hadn't had very much luck in that regard yet.

†

Several blocks away, at the headquarters of the Corps of Military Aides, a large, country club-like affair across the street from the now-closed American Consulate, an indifferently uniformed army sentry checked the documents of a delivery van from the Nacional grocery. The headquarters was justly famous for the quality of its officers' mess hall, and the van made the daily deliveries of fresh meats, bread, and vegetables. The driver was not the usual one, but his papers were in order, and the store had called ahead to advise of the change in drivers, so the sentry waved the van through after a cursory peek through the back window of the piles of bags and boxes from which stalks of celery and long loaves of bread jutted. The guard's mouth watered, as his Army rations consisted of a scanty serving of rice and beans with an occasional chunk of meat of questionable origin. He wished for just once to have the kind of meal these officers enjoyed.

The van pulled around the circular driveway which led past the front entrance of the building, where the main offices were located, heading toward the turnoff which would take him to the loading dock around back by the kitchen. However, instead of passing the entrance, the driver suddenly gunned the engine, swung the wheel hard to the right and bounced right up the low concrete steps, crashing through the large glass doors of the entry, scattering officers and other soldiers in all directions.

U.S. Marine Staff Sergeant Virgil Hood had been conducting a quick walk-through of the old consulate as the MSGs did twice a day, to make certain that neither outsiders nor the local hire guards were pilfering any of the office equipment still stored there. He happened to be looking out the third floor window facing the Corps of Military Aides when the van smashed into the lobby. Hood had been in the Marines since 1981, and his first assignment had been with the Marine force which went into Beirut the following year. He had lost a lot of friends in the truck bombing of the Marine barracks there, and he lost no time in hitting the deck when he saw the truck disappear into the building across the street.

The blast shattered the windows of the consulate and showered Hood with broken glass. When he got to his feet, he saw that the roof of the two story Aides' building had been collapsed by the explosion, and a fire was burning brightly on the ground floor. He could see the upper torso of an officer sandwiched between the ground and a fallen segment of the upper wall near the entrance. The surviving officers and soldiers were simply running away down the street for all they were worth.

Hood had been listening to music on a transistor radio as he made his rounds. As he surveyed the destruction, the music suddenly was cut off and replaced by a taped announcement:

"This is the voice of the Holy War movement. At this time the people will have struck again against the military oppressors of our nation. A truck bomb will have been driven into the Corps of Military Aides headquarters as an act of revenge for the massacre of men, women, and children in the intentional bombing of the working class districts of Santo Domingo by American warplanes last night. This brutal act of Yankee savagery had the full cooperation of the Dominican military, who are now cooperating with the Americans to fool the world into believing that the deaths were a result of some kind of commando action aimed at freeing the American ambassador. The people are not so easily fooled. The war continues. To demonstrate that we can act anywhere in the country at will, similar bombings have also occurred in San Isidro, Santiago, Haina, and Puerto Plata. Those who have cast their lot with the oppressors should realize that the time has come for them to run. We are coming for you."

Holy shit, Hood thought.

EIGHT

✝

Featherstone awoke, or to be more precise, he came to, rolled into a tight ball in the corner of his cage. He untangled himself painfully and sat up, attempting to clear his throbbing head. All the muscles in his body ached, and he noticed that there were ugly scrapes on his knees and elbows from when he had tumbled to the hard concrete floor. There were dark bruises on his ribs from the jabs of the electric prods as well.

He had totally lost track of time since his capture. He rubbed his hand across the stubble on his neck, the closest thing he had to a calendar, and estimated that it had been three, perhaps four days since he had shaved.

Featherstone also had begun to notice a very decided smell in his new world. As careful as he tried to be when using his bucket, there always seemed to remain something of the aroma when it was removed. He doubted whether it was cleaned out by his captors between uses. There was also a strong smell emanating from the floor drain, and the blood and vomit which remained from Pedro's beating had not been washed away. Lastly, of course, not having bathed in several days, Featherstone himself was aware that he was not exactly turning into a rosebud. He only hoped that he would become inured to the stench. He crawled over to the other corner and used his bucket, then took a long pull at his water bottle. At this rate, he pondered, a captivity of several years was going to seem like a very long time indeed.

He was not up to any calisthenics, so he lay back down on the ground and thought about his situation. He wondered whether any serious negotiations were underway for his release. To hear Padre Lazaro talk, it did not appear that there was much hope in that direction, since there was nothing in particular the santistas wanted short of the total seizure of power in the country. There was also the possibility of a rescue attempt, but he didn't even want to think about how long it would take the various authorities to negotiate among themselves over who would have what jurisdiction, much less actually do anything. He suspected that, at a minimum, a task force had been set up somewhere in Washington to "deal with" the crisis, a room crammed with desks and electric coffee makers in which harried men and women would rush back and forth with armloads of papers to no apparent purpose for sixteen hours a day until the crisis eventually resolved itself without them. He had been in government service too long to expect much else. He only hoped that the people responsible for the Branch Davidian crisis had retired by now.

As much as he tried to avoid it, his thoughts finally turned to Anne and the kids. His kids were grown now, and had not lived with them for years, but he could only picture them at the age of four or five, the age of nightmares, Santa Claus, and bedtime stories. He regretted every evening that he had worked late and every official trip which had caused him to miss even a short time of their growing up. He thought that he had been a good father, but now it seemed as if it would have been so easy for him to have done much better.

He thought of how happy Anne had been in the new house they had bought in Northern Virginia, after years of living in rented ones overseas. She had finally gotten one of those nice big, American kitchens, designed for women who did not have a maid to do the cooking and yet who wanted to turn out fine meals without spending all day doing it. The only thing he wanted out of life at the moment was to be in that home with his wife and family. He wanted to talk to her, to tell her that everything would be all right, as he had done many times over the years in hard times, mainly in order to convince himself that everything would be all right. Unfortunately, he was not at all sure of that himself.

As he sat there, legs crossed, with his head in his hands, he heard the latch of the door open. Pedro shuffled into the room with his food, water, and an empty bucket. Featherstone was surprised to see him at all, having assumed that he was dead, but at a second glance, it seemed that he had not been far off the mark. Pedro's shirt was unbuttoned, and he could see that his ribs were heavily taped. He dragged his right leg as he made his way painfully across the floor, and kept his face turned as far to the left as possible.

Featherstone got up and moved to the gate to receive his food and exchange buckets. Intentionally stepping to one side to get a better look at Pedro, Featherstone could see that the entire left side of his face was a puffy, blue mass of welts and scabs. His eye was swollen shut, and there was a ragged line of what appeared to be homemade stitches.

"Jesus Christ, Pedro!" was all Featherstone could think to say. He stared, open-mouthed, at the young man as he slowly completed his chores, exchanging the buckets and handing through the food and water. Finally, he felt obliged to say something more. "I'm sorry that you had to go through that for me."

Pedro raised his good eye to meet Featherstone's. Although he was in his late twenties, he had the look of a little boy.

"You mustn't think badly of him, you know," Pedro said carefully, wincing at the pain in his swollen jaw. "He did what he had to do. I was the one who disobeyed him, and he had no choice."

It took some time for Featherstone to appreciate what Pedro was saying. This was the sort of behavior that one got from a battered wife or child, the helpless victim who, against all reason, still loves the brutal husband or parent, who makes excuses for the violence, and who eventually ends up placing the blame on himself. Although Featherstone's own ribs still ached, and although he still identified Pedro with his captors as much as ever, still the anger welled up in him.

"Bullshit!" he shouted, grabbing the mesh of his cage in his fingers. "He had every choice in the world. You didn't harm anyone. You're his faithful follower, and this is how he treats you. He's just a little Napoleon who's gotten to think that he's God!"

Pedro's one eye flashed in anger. "Don't talk about him that way! What do you know? You don't live in our world. You live in a world of law and order. We live in a world of death and fear, and he has had to train us to survive in that world. I'm only alive now because of what he taught me. He has every right in the world to kill me, if he thinks for a minute that it would help the cause, and I'd bless his name for it."

Featherstone just shook his head. "Yeah, sure. Now just imagine how great a world it's going to be when he takes over and translates that attitude on a national scale."

Pedro hung his head for a moment. "I've seen him do worse for less, you know. I'm really one of his favorites. That's why he was so angry with me for betraying him. You have to understand. He's under tremendous pressure, and you have to forgive him if he over reacts sometimes."

Pedro dropped down onto his haunches and began tracing invisible drawings on the concrete floor with his finger. Featherstone sat down next to him and leaned his head against the mesh of the cage. "There was a woman in our group in Spain when we executed an American military officer for the Iranians. Her job was to walk a dog in front of the officer's house every morning and tell us when he left for work. When we had finished the operation, we all had to get out of the country as quickly as possible by different routes, and everything went very well. When we finally met up here in Santo Domingo, weeks later, we were all talking with Padre Lazaro about the operation, and he happened to ask the woman what she had done with the dog."

Pedro paused for a moment and gently touched his swollen cheek with his fingers, as if reminding himself of the pain. "It was just a dog we had taken from the local pound, you know. They would probably have killed it soon anyway. It wasn't a puppy, the kind that people would like to make a home for." The trace of a smile appeared on the half of Pedro's face which could move, and Featherstone wondered whether Pedro had ever had a dog of his own, or whether, maybe, he was casting himself in the role of the homeless puppy looking for a family. "Well, she said that, when she had received the radio message that the job was done, she had just dropped the dog's leash and run for the car to take her to the airport. Padre Lazaro went into a fury. He said that she had had no right to abandon that dog in the street. That the dog would never have done that to her. She said she was sorry, but he started beating her with his hands. Then he broke a chair on her back and started hitting her with one of the legs. I don't think he really meant to kill her. He just kind of lost control."

"And didn't anyone else try to do anything?" Featherstone asked softly.

Pedro's head jerked up, startled. "Oh, no! We would never do that. Padre Lazaro was right, actually. The woman should have taken the dog back to the pound, so he'd at least have had food and a chance that someone would pick him up. You see, Padre Lazaro has a heart this big," he extended both his arms to his sides, "when it comes to the helpless. That's why he was chosen for this work. He just can't stand it when someone or something suffers needlessly."

"Except when he's the one inflicting the suffering, of course," Featherstone said wryly.

Pedro shook his head, but winced again at the pain. "You just don't understand. He does what he has to do, and it breaks his heart to hurt us, but he has to make us strong for the struggle. If anyone should have done something to protect that woman, it was me. Her name was Carmen, and she was my sister."

"You mean your sister in the revolutionary sense?"

"No," Pedro said, sniffling a little. "When our mother died, when I was four, Carmen, who was about nine, took care of me. If I can forgive . . . no, if I can *understand* what Padre Lazaro did, then no one else should criticize him."

Just then the door opened again, and Pedro hurriedly grabbed up the bucket, spilling some of its evil-smelling contents in the process, and scuttled toward the door without looking up. Padre Lazaro held the door for him, and the two bodyguards stood aside as he hurried away. Lazaro wore his usual winning smile, and his two bodyguards took up their usual positions on either side of the cage.

"Things are going very well, Mr. Featherstone . . ., for us, that is," Lazaro said pleasantly. "I won't bore you with the details, but it seems that the American military blundered very badly last night in a vain attempt to rescue you. Just as we'd planned, their failure not only dispirited the American government regarding this little country, but it's knocked the props out from under the Dominican government at the same time. We've shown them that we're unstoppable, that we can reach any corner of the country, and any target we like. Our people have reported that more than half of the field grade and general officers in the military have abandoned their posts since we started our campaign. Desertions from the army have left most units at less than half strength, and you'd stand a better chance of getting an interview with the Pope than of getting a seat on a flight out of Santo Domingo nowadays. The middle and upper classes have decided to cut their losses and run for it. We've already won. The old society is already dead, and all it will take now is just a little pressure to stop it from running around like a chicken with its head cut off. You'll appreciate in time that this was actually a life saving method, far more humane than a civil war would have been. This is God's work, Mr. Featherstone." He smiled broadly again, his straight, white teeth shining brightly.

Featherstone looked him straight in the eye, purposely avoiding glances at the guards. "You asshole. Why did you have to beat him like that? If you wanted to punish someone, you should have punished me."

The smile froze on Lazaro's face and then faded completely. Even before he spoke, one of the guards took his cue and jabbed Featherstone with his cattle prod. Despite the pain, Featherstone mustered all his strength not to lurch against the far wall of the cage, partly from the knowledge that the other prod would be waiting for him there, and partly not to give Lazaro the satisfaction. He clutched the wire mesh and stood his ground, although his knees buckled, and he could not help gasping for breath.

"Now that you mention it," Lazaro said in a flat voice, "I think a little punishment would help cure you of the sin of false pride from which you suffer."

The second guard had now come around the front of the cage and reached through to give Featherstone another jolt with his prod. Featherstone collapsed to the floor, and he could hear the metallic sound of keys being worked in the locks of the cage. As he writhed on the floor, he felt strong hands grab hold of his ankles and drag him roughly across the floor, out into the open area of the room. He made a feeble effort to grab at the cage door as he passed through, but he lacked the strength. The rough concrete floor scraped his back raw, but he forced himself up to his knees when they let him go.

"You claim to be doing God's work?" he screamed at Lazaro, who stood facing him, his feet spread just over shoulder width apart, his weight resting lightly on the balls of his feet, like a fighter. "Did Jesus do this to his enemies, much less to his friends? You're just another dictator who's found a new gimmick . . ."

Lazaro's right foot swung in a graceful arc, first to his left, then back to the right sharply, catching Featherstone on the jaw with his heel. Featherstone went down on his hands and knees, and a trail of drool mixed with blood dangled down from his mouth onto the floor. The two guards moved in and began to use their prods like simple billy clubs, pounding his ribs until he fell prone, then kicking him in the stomach, in the kidneys, whichever part of his body his agonized contortions left exposed for a moment. All the while, he could hear Lazaro's voice droning on and on.

". . . the new Jesuits, the new crusaders. . . . Not in service to the wealthy or the powerful . . . to the common man . . . Our sacrifices will deliver the people from oppression. . . . Jesus died on the cross . . . take the lance from the soldier and turn it on him . . . God's word . . . a new tomorrow, a new beginning . . ."

Finally, mercifully, Featherstone passed out.

†

Lafeur made a snap decision. He leaned forward conspiratorially. "There's more than just hope," he said, leading Anne out onto the terrace, while Escobar stayed in the kitchen with Maripaz. "I really believe that I can find out where they're holding the ambassador, maybe within the next few hours. The only trouble is that I'm afraid that we couldn't convince either the Dominican or the American Army to go in and get him, not after the Delta Force disaster. I don't think they'd act on the kind of information I'm likely to be able to pull together. What we need, then, is a group of people with guns who can do the job. I'm not trained for that sort of thing, but from the looks of it, I'm the only game in town. Do you want me to try?"

Lafeur was thinking this out even as he explained it to Anne. He didn't want to get her hopes up unrealistically, but his thoughts started to jell, even as he spoke. He turned to her and found her absolutely beaming with joy.

"If there's one chance in a million, . . ." Anne said calmly. "Only I can't ask you to take that kind of risk. Bill is my husband, but I know he wouldn't want any more people to die trying to rescue him. The decision has to be yours.

Lafeur shook his head. "Then the decision's been made."

Anne gave him a bear hug. "So, what's your plan?"

"Well, I think I can piece together where he's being held, mainly because Maripaz was working with the terrorists, providing them with information . . . even under duress, and I think I may be able to use her as a conduit back to the terrorists." Lafeur swallowed hard. "If we can do that, then it will just be a question of pulling together people to go in and get him." As if that were easy, he thought to himself.

Lafeur pursed his lips. His plan, such as it was, was starting to look thinner all the time. "I'll do what I can, of course, and I have a couple of cops on my payroll . . ."

"How about the marine security guards?" Anne asked. "They've never let us down in the past."

"Yes, of course!" Lafeur said, brightening. "There are eight of them, and we could probably count on a couple of guys from DAO as well, and maybe DEA. They're not exactly commandos, but they know how to handle guns at least."

"My two children are due in here in a couple of hours," she said, raising one finger for attention. "Chris is an Army helicopter pilot, which might be useful, and I'm sure that Clare will do anything possible to help."

"The pilot could come in handy, since I'd feel better if we could get in and out fairly quickly. We'll also need a rough idea of what we're up against on the other side, but that should do for a start. You know, I think we might just have a chance after all."

"The one thing that concerns me, though, is Maripaz," Anne said in a low voice. "I'm afraid that she's betrayed us once. Mightn't she do it again?"

"You'll have to trust me, Anne," Lafeur said. "Besides, I don't think we have much choice. She's all we've got."

They walked back into the kitchen where Maripaz and Escobar were watching a local news broadcast. It dealt with the sinking of an overloaded fishing smack on the north coast of the island. The boats had always been used to smuggle illegal immigrants from the Dominican Republic over to Puerto Rico, for passage to the mainland United States. The story was tragic, but it had a new twist. In the past, only the poorest laborers would attempt this kind of passage, now even middle class people, terrified by the violence and unable to find any other form of transportation, were jamming the small boats, which frequently capsized in the shark infested waters. The screen showed one survivor being placed on a stretcher, clearly showing a large semicircular bite taken out of his thigh.

Escobar shook his head. "It's really starting to unravel fast, boss."

"Come with me, Maripaz," Lafeur said.

She got up without question, but she was clearly reluctant to go with him. Lafeur noticed this and took her firmly by the shoulders.

"Look," he said, staring her in the eyes. "I'm not going to force you to do this. I think that you can do something that would help Ambassador Featherstone. If you do, I'll make it my personal responsibility to get you, your baby, and any members of your family that you want over to the United States, permanently. You'll be safe there from these animals. Will you help me?"

Maripaz looked at Anne and then back at Lafeur. "I'll do it, but they said that they'd find us wherever we went, so don't try to tell me how you can protect me. You couldn't protect the ambassador, and they'll come for me whenever it suits their purpose."

Lafeur gave her a slight shake. "Bullshit! They can't hurt you if they're dead, and, if you help me, that's what's going to happen to them. They're not supermen. They're smart, and they've had everything their own way up until now, but I've got a feeling that we can blindside them if we move fast. We're out of their calculations at this point, and that's why we can take them. Now, will you help me or not?"

"I said I would," she said, raising her chin and looking Lafeur in the eye. "Let's worry about what comes after when we're done."

The two headed for the library, but Escobar quickly got up from the counter and called after Lafeur. "Boss! I don't know what you have in mind, but I would appreciate it if you'd include me. I figure that Ambassador Featherstone deserved more from me than he got, and I'd like a second chance."

Lafeur looked back. The large, beefy man looked out of character with a little boy's expression on his face, begging to go along. "Sure, Ramiro," Lafeur said, smiling. "Right now, I want you to take care of Mrs. Featherstone. Don't worry. There'll be enough trouble to go around when things start to happen."

Escobar gave him the thumbs up sign and rocked back and forth on his heels, his thumbs tucked into his belt, and the grip of his pistol protruding from his jacket.

Lafeur had some time to think as he mixed himself a drink at the ambassador's bar in the beautifully panelled library. Ordinarily he didn't drink hard liquor at all, much less in the morning, but these were not normal times. He knew that he didn't have the authority to promise her what amounted to resettlement in the States, but he figured that he'd answer for that when the time came. He did have access to the files and seals in the consulate, and he could at least issue non-immigrant visas to Maripaz and her family. He could also come up with some money for her out of his operational funds, but they would likely be stretched pretty thin by the other things he had planned. Actually, he figured, he really didn't owe Maripaz much of anything. She had a chance to make up for what she had done, at least that was what he was telling himself as he measured the liquor into his glass. He chuckled softly to himself, the old time careerist suddenly developing a set of ideals, putting it all on the line to save a friend. Who'd a thunk it?

He pulled a chair close to where Maripaz was sitting and sat facing her. "Now," he began, "I need you to tell me everything you can remember that this Luis character told you about the santistas. Even if it seems unimportant, it could provide a missing piece to the puzzle."

Maripaz looked down at the floor and talked rapidly, using her hands as Dominicans tend to do when they're nervous. He held his drink in one hand and took frequent notes with the other on a pad balanced on one knee. Luis had apparently been trying to recruit her, or impress her, or maybe he just liked to hear himself talk, Lafeur thought, but he had given out a surprising amount of detail during their "pillow talk" sessions. The details Maripaz provided confirmed her supposition that the ambassador's location and the headquarters within the "zone" were two separate places, the former definitely located outside the zone. She gave him the full phone number she had dialed on the day of the kidnapping, and Lafeur broke with normal security procedures and phoned Quiroga directly from the library extension. He calculated that if anyone had time to tap this phone nowadays, they certainly didn't have their priorities straight.

What interested Lafeur most was the implied timetable the santistas had. According to their schedule, they would first awaken the poor to the amount of violence and destruction they could inflict on their enemies, then terrify the upper classes with that violence. They would humiliate and defeat the Dominican police and armed forces in open battle, although in very carefully staged situations where the terrorists held all the cards. They would kidnap the ambassador to demonstrate the lack of protection for even the most important individuals in the country, and finally, they would defeat the Americans and engineer a rift between the American and Dominican governments to ensure that no further aid would be offered or accepted. When all of this had been accomplished, the santistas would move in and quickly seize the nerve centers of the government, and the security forces would be too demoralized to resist them. The terrorists had been intentionally left the transportation system unmolested, permitting as as possible many of their potential enemies to abandon the country. They had now achieved all of their goals except the final seizure of power, but Maripaz was convinced that they intended to act quickly to prevent the government from reorganizing its forces.

Lafeur was also interested in Luis' comments which had implied that there were relatively few hard core santistas, perhaps only a few dozen. Lafeur knew that even these had taken some losses in the past few days. Luis had talked about providing training for maybe another hundred former miristas, with more to follow, but these Luis considered of inferior capacity, worthy only of supporting roles or of use as cannon fodder. Lafeur jabbed his notepad with his pen. He didn't know quite what to do about it yet, but it seemed to him that knowing what the santistas planned to do, and when, and the fact that their major weakness was their lack of numbers should be usable in bringing about their defeat. Lafeur looked down at his notes for a long time before he raised his eyes.

"This information will help us a great deal," he began. "But there's something else that I have to ask you to do for us, and it will be a lot harder than just talking to me."

She didn't reply, but waited, watching him. Lafeur was asking himself all through his interrogation whether or not she was still working with the santistas. She had fooled him once already, after all, but that had been before it had ever occurred to him that the santistas would have actually recruited someone within the embassy staff. He had used all of his tricks, tested her information against the things he already knew, and it had consistently come up clean. He finally came to the conclusion that, either she had indeed been coerced into working with the santistas against her will as she said, and was now willing to do something to make amends, or she was the best actress he had ever seen.

"I want you to go back to your apartment and to get back into contact with Luis," he said quickly looking back down at his notes.

"No," she said quietly. "I can't."

"Then Ambassador Featherstone is a dead man," he said flatly, "and *you* killed him."

"Please don't say that," she said, her lower lip starting to quiver pitifully. "If I go back now, and Luis shows up, he'll see right through me. He'll know that I've confessed to you . . ., that you caught me," she added after a pause.

Lafeur looked her in the face now. He could see tears welling up in the corners of her eyes. "That's what you've got to get out of your head. These guys aren't supermen. They're just criminals, professional criminals. They've been careful, and they've been lucky so far, but they can't read minds. Luis wanted to recruit you to the movement all along, and you didn't resist, although you didn't accept. Now is the time to let him win."

He leaned closer and took both of her hands in his. "I know you're frightened and this whole thing isn't of your making, but there's no other way now. The Dominican government has written the ambassador off, and so have the Americans. Lots of men are dead, and women and children too, because of these people, and we can't just turn our backs. Mr. Featherstone is out there, and we're all he's got, and that, God help us, isn't very much. If we're going to win, we've got to know more about the santistas, get wind of just what they have planned, and short circuit them at the right moment. You're the only hope we have of that."

He sat back again, releasing her hands. "If you tell me that you're going to break down the minute you see him, that you just can't take it, then there's an end to it, and we'll have to do our best without you. I'm just asking you to try."

Maripaz was silent for a long while. Finally, she dabbed at her eyes with a kleenex and said, "What if he asks me where I've been all night?"

Lafeur smiled. "That's the girl! There's a good chance he didn't even go to your place yet. Those people have been busy lately, but you should tell him before he asks that you were tied up typing for the General. I can give you some papers of theirs for you to take to him, as if you had stolen them. They won't do any harm now, but they'll support your story." Of course, he had no authorization to release classified military documents to the enemy, a felony offense, but, in for a penny, in for a pound, he thought.

Maripaz just nodded and sighed.

†

Quiroga met Cuesta less than an hour later in a parked car not far from the telephone exchange.

"That's one problem solved," Cuesta had sighed when Quiroga handed him the number, "and I can give you an address for this number in fifteen minutes."

"I think we're going to have to do more than that," Quiroga said, calmly. "The bad guys gave this number to a spy, someone they forced to cooperate with them, but someone who almost certainly was not a trusted member of their group. They got this informant for her access, not for her commitment to their cause."

"So what?" Cuesta asked. "They still needed to give her someplace where she could contact them on short notice and where they could wait indefinitely for the call."

"These guys haven't made very many mistakes," Quiroga continued, "and I don't think that we can count on them making any now. What I'm afraid of is that this number belongs to a place they took just for that part of their operation, and now that they're done with it, they've dropped it. On the other hand, they can't have unlimited resources, so maybe they've used the number at a more permanent location, one they're still using, but they would have built in some kind of safeguard. How would you do that?"

"Hmmm." Cuesta scratched his upper lip with this index finger thoughtfully. "Probably the best way would be just to pirate a line. You know, take a line that, according to the billing records and the wiring charts, goes to one address, and tie it physically into another address entirely. It's not so very difficult. The only problem with that would be that the original owners would eventually report their line out of order, and you'd be found out. It's not something you'd want to rely on for any length of time."

"They would only have needed it for a couple of weeks," Quiroga said pensively. "Still that would have been a risk to them . . . unless they were pretty sure that the original owners wouldn't complain. Can you tell from the number what part of town it would be in?"

"Oh, yes, I knew that much before we identified the exact number. This would have to belong to Arroyo Hondo."

"Bingo!" Quiroga yelled. "You go get me that address, and I'll bet you a hundred pesos that it belongs to one of those big houses where the santistas massacred the entire family back when all this was just starting."

"Well, those families certainly aren't going to be complaining to anyone in a hurry," Cuesta grunted as he climbed out of the car and scurried off toward his office. He bent over as heavy raindrops started to fall. The weather had been getting progressively worse, and the scattered showers of the early morning had finally given way to a real downpour.

Lafeur let out a long sigh when his office phone rang. It was the receptionist who said that Yigael Gosher, the DCM of the Israeli Embassy, was out at the front gate with another gentleman and was asking to speak with him. Lafeur had the call patched through.

"Hello, Yigael. How are you?" Lafeur said as cheerfully as he could manage.

"Shalom, Claude," came the answer in heavily British-accented English. "Listen, I know that you must be very busy right now, but I'd like to have a word with you in your office, if that's at all possible. It *is* important."

"Sure. Come on in."

"Just one other thing, Claude," Gosher added. "I'm with someone, and I'd appreciate it if you could vouch for him without the local guards or your Marines checking his documents. I can only tell you that it's all right."

Lafeur paused for a moment. This was very strange, but Gosher seemed insistent. He only knew the Israeli, whom he had assumed to be the local Mossad rep, from an occasional chat at Diplomatic Association luncheons, but Gosher didn't have a reputation as a practical joker. "Fine, put the guard on, and I'll clear it."

When Lafeur entered the embassy reception area, Gosher and his guest were just coming in the front door, shaking the water from their umbrellas. Gosher was a tall, carrot-haired man in his early fifties. Lafeur always thought that he looked more Irish than Jewish, but then white folks tended to look a little bit alike to him. The other man was short, stocky, and dark. He had a thick beard which climbed unusually high on his cheeks and disappeared down to his shirt collar. He had on a black suit and a clean white shirt buttoned all the way to his neck without tie or collar.

Gosher and Lafeur shook hands. "This is Majid Ansari-Kermani, an old colleague of mine, and I think he has something to tell you that you'll be interested to hear."

Lafeur didn't have a clue as to what this man might have to say, but he was reasonably certain that it wasn't something that should be discussed in the lobby, so he escorted the two men into the walk-in room.

After they had sat down and politely refused Lafeur's offer of coffee, Gosher explained their presence.

"Majid is a colonel in the Iranian Ministry of Intelligence and Security, the MOIS or Vezarat Etala'at. He's been sent here very discreetly by his government to try to . . . to rectify a situation which has developed. I have worked with Majid on several projects in the past, and I can confirm that he is who he says he is. Other than that, there is nothing in writing, just our word as to what he is here to do."

"I've heard of the MOIS," Lafeur said, raising his eyebrows, "or at least I've read of their exploits. Such as the assassination of Bakhtiar in Paris in '90 or '91? I'm not certain that we have anything to talk about."

Majid nodded solemnly and folded his hands in his lap. "I do not pretend that your service and mine have ever been on the same side of any question. Too many of my colleagues suffered in the prisons of the Savak, at the hands of men you trained and advised, and I assure you that I find this meeting as distasteful as you do, but I have my orders."

Lafeur just spread his hands and waited for the Iranian to continue.

"I'm not sure how much you know about my country or my government, but I should explain a couple of things first," Majid began in correct but heavily accented English. "We really have two governments, the secular one, and the religious one. The MOIS is the intelligence arm of the secular government, and we are responsible for the same sort of things you are."

Lafeur didn't much like the idea that this Iranian knew, that he was CIA. He had never worked in a liaison capacity with Gosher, who had never openly admitted his own Mossad affiliation either. Since the pro-Iranian Hizballah groups in Lebanon were responsible for the kidnapping, torture, and murder of former CIA Beirut Station Chief Bill Buckley, the thought that this kind of person knew about Lafeur's job was unsettling, to say the least.

Majid evidently read Lafeur's thoughts and continued. "My service has been involved in what the Soviets call 'wet operations' beyond our own borders, generally the elimination of violent opponents of our government, and I make no excuses for that. We live in a violent world, and we must defend ourselves. However, things are changing in Iran. My government has been pursuing better relations with the Americans for years, since before the Gulf War. Negotiations have been going on, and we recognize that we need to engage in trade and diplomacy with the West. We have differences of politics and religion, but there is every reason to believe that we can learn to live together without conflict if we each learn to respect each other's sovereignty."

Yeah, yeah, Lafeur thought to himself. Enough commercial time. Let's get to the point.

"Unfortunately," Majid said, "ours is still a revolutionary society, and my government does not enjoy undisputed authority. While we in the MOIS are faithful Shi'a, we do not agree with the political rule of the ayatollahs. That ended with the death of the great Ayatollah Khomeini. But the religious leaders have created a shadow government within Iran, complete with their own intelligence service. This is called the Sepah, the intelligence arm of the Iranian Revolutionary Guard Corps. They are less professionally competent than we are, and are selected and promoted solely on the basis of their religious fanaticism. Those are the people who have most of the dealings with foreign terrorist groups like the Hizballah. We in the MOIS have our contacts, of course, but it's the Sepah that relies on them heavily for its work.

"How does this affect you in the Dominican Republic, you ask," Majid said. "We have information that the Sepah has financed and trained a group of Dominican terrorists. They have worked with them within Iran for some years and have now agreed to fund their effort to overthrow the Dominican government."

"I hate to disappoint you, after your big build-up," Lafeur said with a wave of his hand, "but we know this. The group is the santistas, and this is old news. I'm not certain that I believe in this clear distinction between the good Iranians and the bad Iranians, both of whom deal with terrorists. It seems that my organization already got itself in enough trouble not so long ago by trying to play to the 'moderates' in your government. I might add that one possible explanation for why you've come here to talk to me, rather than having more senior people on your side talk to more senior people in Washington is that you might be hoping to hoodwink this poor old boy who doesn't know diddly about the Middle East, where in Washington we have experts who could ask you all sorts of embarrassing questions."

Gosher bridled, his face starting to turn red, but Majid held up his hand and smiled for the first time. "You're absolutely right, Mr. Lafeur, at least in having your doubts, although I do not understand this 'hoodwink.' However, the reason that I'm here is that our two governments really have no formal relations as yet, and things have gotten only worse with the assassination of your military attache in Spain."

"In which you were not involved, of course," Lafeur interjected. "We know very well that the santistas did that job for the Iranians, and it's relatively academic to us which group actually signed the checks for them."

"It shouldn't be," Majid went on, unperturbed. "If I were here asking you to do something, you would have every reason to be suspicious of my motives. The MOIS was not behind the killing of the American officer, although as Iranians, we did not shed any tears over the death of a man who was involved in the deaths of so many Iranian men, women, and children. I am only here to tell you what I know about the santistas, and you may then use the information as you see fit."

Lafeur sighed. "I'm all ears."

Majid frowned a little and moved his head slightly from side to side, checking Lafeur's auditory equipment, then shrugged and continued. "The contact for the santistas is a man called Abdol Reza Hashem-Zai-Nehbandan. I believe you will find some reference to him in your files." Majid pulled a white envelope from his inside coat pocket. "Here is a photograph of him, along with a complete list of the war materiel he supplied to the santistas and the account numbers of two Swiss bank accounts the Sepah have been using to funnel monies to them."

Lafeur raised his eyebrows at this. Now this was the kind of information that could be checked out. "So why are you telling me all this?" Lafeur asked. "These Sepah characters may belong to a different office, but they are on your team, after all."

"We come from the same country," Majid explained, "but we work for different governments within it. The goal of the Sepah in this operation is to aid the santistas in the bloody overthrow of the government here. They will then make it very well known that Iran helped them to do it. The purpose of the Sepah is to permanently derail any efforts of the government of Iran to improve relations with the U.S. and to open up economic ties with the rest of the world. Basically, the problem is that our government has learned that we cannot provide for the welfare of our people without ensuring some kind of economic progress. The religious leaders have learned that, if there is economic progress, if Iranian students start going back to study in universities to support that progress, if we break out of our international isolation, more and more people will question the domination of our society by a group of semi-literate mullahs who want to keep Iran in the twelfth century. If they can show the world that Iran is still dedicated to terrorism across the globe, they can accomplish this. Perhaps, if I can help you defeat the santistas, not only will this one attempt of the

Sepah fail, but we will have earned a little respect as a rational force in the world."

"I should add," Gosher said, raising a finger, "that my government does not know that I'm conducting this interview. Majid contacted me here personally, and asked this favor. I can only say that I believe what he's saying. He's put what he has up front and isn't asking anything in return."

"I appreciate that," Lafeur said.

"One other thing," Majid added. "We believe that the santistas have completed their preparatory work and will be making their move soon, perhaps within the next two or three days. That is all we know at the moment, but I have my own means of communication with my headquarters and will advise you of any new information which comes in."

"Thank you, Majid," Lafeur finally said. "And thank you, Yigael. I have to admit that this all looks very real and ties in with other information we have obtained. My only question now is what we can do about it."

"It seems to me," Majid said off-handedly, "that you have two tasks. First, you must defeat the bid of the santistas for power, and second, you must effect the rescue of your Ambassador."

Gosher turned in surprise to Majid. "But the American ambassador was killed in the bomb blast last night, Majid."

Lafeur looked from one man to the other.

"Of course he wasn't," Majid said, shrugging his shoulders. "The explosion was the intentional work of the santistas to drive a wedge between the American and Dominican governments. That was part of their original plan from months back. That was why you'll find such a large quantity of PE-2 explosive on that list of munitions the santistas received," he said, gesturing at the envelope in Lafeur's hand. "I had assumed you knew that. No, the ambassador was being kept elsewhere. I don't know precisely where, but I can assure you that he was not in the location of the explosion."

Lafeur's mind was racing. Could this be another carefully laid trap by this same group of villains? What if they only wanted him to believe that the ambassador was still alive in order to get him to mount another rescue operation which would also result in disaster? So far, his only indications that Featherstone hadn't died in the explosion had come from this Iranian, a self-confessed sponsor of international terrorism, and from Maripaz, who had already betrayed the embassy once to the santistas, not very much to go on.

"The only other thing I can offer you at the moment," Majid added, "is that, if you do manage to arrange some kind of action against the santistas and need an extra gun, I have had considerable combat experience. And I have a personal matter to discuss with Abdol Reza, if we can locate him."

"Count me in, too," Gosher said. "This would have to be very unofficial, but I like Bill Featherstone, and I don't like the idea of him being held hostage."

"I'll keep you in mind," Lafeur said. He wondered if Giorgissimo's was open. The situation definitely called for some ice cream.

†

Early the next morning, Padre Lazaro knelt in the center of the room, his arms outstretched and his head bent in prayer. Luis was next to him in a similar pose, along with three other santista team leaders, two men and a woman. Pablo Baca and Abdol Reza stood respectfully against one wall, waiting for them to finish. Baca had made it known to Lazaro that he was committed enough to the movement to take part in their religious activities as well, but Lazaro had calmly told him that a lifetime of atheism couldn't be undone overnight and had patiently advised him to start attending mass regularly, adding that he should only make his confessions to Padre Lazaro himself, for security's sake. After some fifteen minutes of this silent worship, Lazaro and the others raised their heads, as if on cue, and smoothly got to their feet. Baca wondered that they were able to move at all.

"The time has come, my friends," Lazaro announced, "to begin to make our final plans. We have been a long time in reaching this point, and we should make certain that we do not let anything slip because of eagerness for the final victory."

"The news from the street is very good," Baca said as the group collected around a dinner table at one end of the room over which maps of the city had been laid. "I would estimate that two thirds of the businesses in town have been closed. At least half of the homes in the rich neighborhoods are empty. The airport is a continuing mob scene for departing flights to anywhere, the same with the dockyards.

All the private boats are gone from the yacht marinas, and people are offering up to $10,000 a seat on private planes to fly them out to Puerto Rico, anywhere. Even the roads into Haiti are jammed.

"Our sources in the police and in the military report that barely fifty per cent of the soldiers remain in the First Brigade and less than a third of the officers are reporting for duty," Luis added. "In the police the numbers are even lower, and the Army has stripped units everywhere else in the country just to reach those levels here in Santo Domingo. They moved through the 'zone' after the explosion, but, of course, they only rolled up a dozen or so of the raw mirista recruits we left for them to find, in addition to killing maybe a hundred innocent people. That just antagonized the other people all the more, and the troops quickly pulled out again when some of their men started getting chopped up with machetes on the side streets. They've mostly gone back to their barracks now, but the bombings at the Corps of Military Aides and other barracks scared the daylights out of them. They've dug in around their bases and are afraid to set foot outside. We estimate that, from a strength of 20,000 men for the military and 10,000 for the police, there are not more than 6,000 men under arms in the military and maybe 4,000 with the police, between casualties and desertions, and losses have been heaviest in the combat formations."

"And how are things going with our people?" Lazaro asked, still studying the maps.

"Pretty well, all things considered," Baca continued. "We still have about twenty-five of your original santistas and ten of my mirista veterans, but we have another hundred fighters who have completed the basic training course and another thousand who have just begun training. Add to that maybe twenty army and police deserters who have come over and whom we think we can trust, and we've got quite a force, or will have within another month."

"We can't wait a month," Lazaro said flatly. "We'll pull our cadre out of the training schools at the last moment, but we can't count on the new recruits for much. We also can't count on the deserters. If they betrayed their former employers, they'll turn on us if they feel the wind blowing the other way. We'll use them on missions where they are likely to get themselves killed to save our own people for other things. Even so, things are in order. For what we have planned a hundred fighters should prove adequate. Then we'll have time to finish training and equipping the new troops."

"We have a Liberian-registered freighter off the coast with more than enough weapons to equip your new army," Abdol Reza said.

Lazaro reached across the table and shook Abdol Reza's hand warmly. "We thank you and the Iranian people for their solidarity."

"The trick will still be to gain power without having to fight a stand-up battle with what remains of the military. As badly as they've done to date, they could still swamp us by sheer force of numbers if they ever got organized and found us out in the open," Luis said.

"That is the purpose of our plan," Lazaro said.

He spread the city map of Santo Domingo flatter on the table and took the top off a red marking pen. "Our assault groups will seize control of the three television stations, here, here, and here, the telephone central, and the two large radio stations, here and here. They will also blow the southern bridge over the Ozama and set up a roadblock, backed with anti-tank missiles on the northern one, in case the military decides to try to come across from where they're holed up in San Isidro.

"Jaime's demolition team," he said, nodding to a pale, nervous, older man in the group, "will wire the bridge and the other radio stations around the city, to knock them off the air and avoid any competition. They'll also blow the microwave tower to cut off international and long distance telephone communications. We'll have small ambush parties near the two main police barracks in the city and on the roads leading into town from the west and from the north, just in case some military units decide to take an active part in events."

"Our big weakness," Luis interjected, "is manpower, at least manpower that we can count on."

"It's also our strength," Lazaro objected. "We may not have many men and women, but those that we have are very good, and we can trust them implicitly. That's more than the enemy can say. In this plan, we'll only need experienced troops to man the ambush positions and the roadblock on the bridge for any length of time. The demolitions will be placed beforehand and can be blown at any time. The radio, television, and telephone sites will not be defended, except maybe by a stray security man, and once they are seized and our instructions have been given, security at those places can be entrusted to new recruits. That way we can collect the bulk of our forces after the initial assault and be in a position to strike back at any reaction by government troops."

"But the government forces will still have a considerable superiority," Abdol Reza warned.

"That's assuming their men stick with them, and that's just what we're planning that they will not do," Lazaro answered. "When our message is broadcast on all television and radio stations continuously, and when it is apparent that the government cannot reply, the enemy soldiers will leave their units in droves. The few officers remaining will take advantage of our generous offer to let them leave the country unmolested . . . within a 24-hour time limit.

"It's like fighting with a giant," Lazaro explained. "We can't just stand up to him and fight, or we'd be crushed. We've already blinded him in the city and deprived him of his friends. We interdict the transportation network in the critical area, so the troops can't move freely, like cutting his tendons so he can't make use of the powerful muscles he still has. Then, we take advantage of his blindness and growing fear to convince him that the battle is over, before it's even been joined. We convince him that we have won, and when it appears to him that we have, then the lie becomes the reality. We don't need to be able to defeat the army in battle, because the battle will never be joined. All the evidence of their senses will tell them that we have seized power and the soldiers will then look out for themselves, leaving us in power by default."

"But you don't make any provision for capturing the presidential palace or the legislature," Majid commented.

"The power here is not in those places," Lazaro said. "It's drifted from them out into the streets, and we rule the streets. In this country the government only counted for anything because it could deliver on specific promises to interest groups. We have shown that it cannot even do that anymore. We have defended our territory, provided food for the hungry, medical aid, and even education. We have shown ourselves to be scrupulously honest and brave, something neither the current government nor any of its predecessors has done, and the people will not hesitate to choose us. The government needed a large army to keep the mass of the people down. We only need to strike at the head of the giant, and its forces will disappear. The people will support us."

"When will you be ready to move?" Abdol Reza asked.

"The demolition charges will be placed tonight," Lazaro answered. "We will conduct our final rehearsals tomorrow, and the operation itself will be scheduled for that evening. That will give us time to seize our objectives before the city awakens, and they will get our message with their breakfast." Lazaro raised his head from the map and graced the room with a smile of saintly goodness.

"By the way," Luis said. "What are we going to do about the American ambassador. He's already served his purpose. Right now he's only tying up several good men who could be put to better use elsewhere."

"Oh, he's still got some value for us, Luis," Lazaro said. "If we let it be known, after we seize power, that the ambassador was saved, by our intervention, from the clutches of the evil Melgarejo and his bloodthirsty thugs, and then we release him, our stock with the Americans will go sky high. This will work especially well if we can find some publicity-hungry American politician to work through. Our Shi'a colleagues in Lebanon have played this game with great success for years. Now, my brothers, let's get on with our jobs."

Luis was pleased to get the meeting out of the way. He was eager to get the meeting over with and get back over to Maripaz' house. He had a feeling that he might finally be wearing down her resistance to becoming a full member of the movement.

†

The reduced staff at the embassy was just going through the motions of the morning country team meeting. Virtually all official activities had been suspended, and no one within the government was even speaking with anyone from the embassy. USAID had packed its bags and gone home. The Dominican military had completely frozen out Colonel Miller after the Delta Force raid fiasco. Even the international press sensed that the world-class news was largely over and had been drifting out of the country as quickly as they had gathered.

The only regular business of the embassy nowadays was its own limited administration and the monitoring of local political events for reports to Washington. Stileforth had been drafting a series of "think pieces," a phrase Lafeur never really liked, since it implied that they didn't think about the other pieces, focusing on the political situation and predicting optimistically that a little professional diplomacy, meaning directed by Mr. Stileforth, and a heavy dose of economic aid, could still make things right, save the Selich government from disintegration, and win back the hearts and minds of the Dominicans. None of these bore any relation to reality but even Lafeur had to admit that reality was not in much demand in Washington.

Lafeur slumped in his chair at the conference table. Stileforth had decided that the seriousness of the meetings required that they be held in the formal conference room, even though the more comfortable venue of the ambassador's office would easily hold the reduced group. Although Lafeur had decided to attempt to rescue Ambassador Featherstone through "extra-official" channels, he felt he at least owed it to the system, if not to Stileforth, to attempt to gain support for one more try based on his new information.

The difficult part was that he still couldn't reveal the source of his information. He couldn't tell them about Maripaz, since he still hoped to use her clandestinely. He was already very worried that he had made the wrong decision in sending her back to seek out the santistas. Escobar and at least a couple of the domestic staff at the residence had heard enough to understand that she had been caught doing something wrong, and if the santistas had happened to have recruited one of them as well, she would be walking into a deathtrap. While Lafeur felt he could trust this kind of information to Miller or Fiore, or even Vernon, he had his doubts about Stileforth. Not, of course, that the man might be working for the santistas, but because he was enough of a political animal that, if he saw a moment's personal advantage in "leaking" the information to enhance his own image, he wouldn't hesitate to do it. That was the trouble with dealing with some State Department types. They understood the importance of discretion in handling their own sources of information, but some of them couldn't make the leap of imagination to the level of absolute secrecy necessary for clandestine work.

Stileforth had just finished with his evaluation of the situation, with himself in a starring role, and he was "going around the table," asking each person to make their contributions to the general fund of knowledge, although there was always an implication that Stileforth really didn't want much in the way of contributions from others.

Miller gave a very depressing account of the state of the Dominican military, that part of it which hadn't already fled the country, and Vernon gave an equally dismal review of the condition of the rest of the government, also operating with a skeleton crew. When it came to Lafeur's turn, he decided to shoot for shock factor and hope his momentum would carry him through.

"I have information to the effect that Ambassador Featherstone is still alive," he began. There was an outburst of murmuring and shifting of bodies from positions of near coma to rapt attention.

"I suppose you have a good reason to have kept this little tidbit from us until now, Lafeur," Stileforth said coldly, fixing Lafeur in one of his patented freezing gazes.

"I only just received the information," Lafeur continued. "It's from technical sources which I cannot discuss, and it's far from certain, but there is a chance that the ambassador is alive and that the information we were given prior to the assault by the Delta Force was planted, designed to lead us to the wrong location and to lead our troops into a trap."

"Ah," Stileforth said, a little too loudly, "so this is a replay of your feeble effort to undermine the validity of the statements of a bona fide defector, and the only thing you can come up with is some mysterious source which you cannot discuss." Stileforth leaned way forward, placing both of his palms flat on the table, as if about to do some kind of push-up. He dropped his voice to a low register, and Lafeur thought that the sound he made when he hit an "s" reminded him rather too much of a snake. "I don't suppose you could tell us where the ambassador is located at this moment, what?"

"No, not yet," Lafeur stammered, "but I'm working on it."

"You're working on it," Stileforth mimicked, dripping venom. "How very reassuring."

"Well," Miller interrupted, "we do know that whatever was destroyed in the explosion in the 'zone,' wasn't the real headquarters of the santistas. They're apparently still alive and well and running operations from another location, so there's some reason to believe that maybe the ambassador was being held at the second headquarters and not the one that was destroyed."

"Maybe and perhaps are just not going to do it, gentlemen," Stileforth screamed shrilly, slapping both palms on the table for added emphasis. "Lafeur, unless you can give us some information to support this theory or unless you can shed some light on the nature of your sources, there certainly isn't much we can do, is there? Do you have this information for us at this time?"

"No, not yet."

"Have you conveyed any of these conjectures to Washington, behind my back, by any chance?"

"No, I . . ."

"Very wise of you," Stileforth cut him off. "It's bad enough that you have destroyed your credibility with us in this room without damaging the reputation of this embassy as a whole with Washington. I will be drafting a cable later this afternoon, when I have a moment, asking for your immediate recall to Washington and requesting a replacement ASAP." Stileforth obviously didn't want any additional discussion, and he leapt to his feet, and marched to the door. "Thank you for your time, gentlemen. Now let's get to work."

He paused in the doorway a moment, with one hand resting on the door frame and a strange, coy smile on his lips. "Oh, and one other thing, Lafeur. As your last official act here, you may inform Mrs. Featherstone that *I* have been in communication with Washington, and they have authorized her withdrawal from the country. An embassy driver will be at her door at 0900 hours tomorrow morning to take her to the airport. There will be no further discussion on this matter, and you may tell her, since you apparently have become quite close since her husband's 'disappearance,' that she may complain to her heart's content in Washington. The orders have come from there, in writing."

Lafeur's arms tensed and he almost came out of his chair at the tone in which Stileforth put the word "close," but Fiore gave him a discreet but painful kick in the ankle before he moved. It was then that Lafeur realized that Stileforth not only didn't believe that Featherstone was alive, he didn't *want* it to be true. Stileforth was in charge now, and that was the way he wanted it to stay, at any price.

When the room had emptied except for Lafeur, Fiore, Miller, and Vernon, Miller was the first to speak.

"Now that that's over, what's all this about? Are you sure that the ambassador's alive?"

"About as sure as I can be," Lafeur answered, "and I'm putting together something to go and get him out. I had really expected pretty much what we just got from Stileforth, although I'll admit that he outdid himself. I just wanted to touch base and give him the chance to offer to help."

"Well," Fiore chuckled, "at least you got your ticket home. That's not a bad day's work in this place."

"I've got all the time I need," Lafeur answered. "If things work out, this little incident won't count for shit. If they don't, well, I'll be going home pretty soon, one way or another."

"Looking for company on this little excursion?" Miller asked.

"All I can get," Lafeur admitted.

"Count me in," Fiore said. "It's a shame that I've had to send everyone else home during the crisis, but I've got a .357 to chip in."

"And me," said Miller. "I suppose you'll be going after the MSGs next."

Lafeur nodded.

"In that case," Miller continued, "having another marine along won't hurt any."

Vernon shifted uncomfortably in his chair. "I'm all for what you're doing, but I don't really know what I can do to help."

"That's okay, Jim," Lafeur said. "I'm only in this from an intelligence angle. I'm no soldier myself. If you could just sort of cover our backsides here in the embassy, maybe keep tabs on what Dane is up to, that would be help enough."

Vernon smiled, and Lafeur could sense his relief. He was a family man, already on edge at having to remain in what was essentially a combat zone. He had perked up considerably when Featherstone had moved his family out to safety, but then there had come the nagging doubts that he might never see them again. The fact that he didn't have to shame himself in front of his peers, made a notable improvement in his mood.

"Thanks," Lafeur said. "I'll be in touch with you soon about what I'm going to want you to do, and then we'll see just how crazy you all are."

NINE

†

Maripaz was sitting on her sofa, her face buried in her hands, when Luis came through the door. When he entered, she immediately jumped to her feet but remained standing there, looking at the floor, trembling.

"Where have you been?" she asked in a tiny voice. "I didn't know what happened to you. I saw that building downtown destroyed, and I didn't know if you were in it or not."

Luis smiled slyly. "And which would you have preferred, my love?" He walked up to her and took her in his arms, pulling her close.

Maripaz didn't answer the question directly. She kept avoiding his eyes, leaning her forehead on his shoulder. "They're saying in the streets that it might have been an American atom bomb that destroyed the building or that the *santistas* blew the building up to kill the Americans and themselves along with it, or that the Americans just decided to blast the middle of Santo Domingo because they were frustrated at not being able to find you. They showed all those dead people on the television . . ." She began to weep quietly and finally raised her eyes to his. "I didn't want anything to happen to you."

She kissed him full on the lips. He had been grasping her upper arms at her sides, but now she twisted free and threw her arms around his neck. At first Luis was taken aback, and he pulled away. He could taste the salt of her tears on his lips. He held her a few inches away from him while she sniffled softly, then he pulled her to him again, holding her tight.

This had been the first time that she had actually kissed *him* voluntarily, and Luis wondered what she was up to. Certainly, he had been working on her, since the very beginning, establishing his domination over her, and he had been rewarded with just the kind of subservience and obedience he liked so well, but he had never expected it to blossom into anything like this. As he held her, his hands roughly roaming her body, a grim smile slowly spread across his face. He knew that he had become a master of delivering both pleasure and pain, at his discretion, and his dominance of this poor creature had obviously become such that the only stimulus in her life that mattered now was what he provided her. Whether that was pleasure or pain was his decision, but she could no longer live without either one or the other, and it didn't matter, to her numbed mind which it was. That was it.

Luis experimented with this newfound sense of power, fondling her roughly or caressing her gently and being equally rewarded with a sensuous moan. When he had taken charge of her, Luis had vaguely hoped to be able to "recruit" her to the cause in a more conventional sense. She certainly had enough reason to resent the affluent Americans she had been serving as a lackey, but she had resisted all of his attempts, passively, but resisted nonetheless. Now he realized that he had achieved by himself, with his body or with the power of his will, he didn't know which, the kind of domination that Padre Lazaro enjoyed over the members of the movement, the *other* members of the movement, Luis had to admit frankly. Although he was dedicated to the movement and would sacrifice his life for it, he was not the same kind of sheep as so many of the others. He knew he would not be Padre Lazaro's equal, as long as Padre Lazaro was alive, but he was only just below his level.

As they sank slowly onto the sofa, Luis began to realize what it was that gave Padre Lazaro the kind of energy and staying power which had so impressed him all these years. It was this kind of blind obedience, the total power, albeit over one helpless creature. Luis realized now that what he had been relishing before, the sheer physical terror of his victims, had been a mere echo, a cheap copy, of this feeling of power. Now he had his own "follower" who would not only obey his every whim, simple fear can produce that kind of obedience, but who would do anything she even suspected he might want, whether he was there to force her to comply or not. This was different and infinitely better.

"The American soldiers have all gone," Maripaz whispered, as Luis continued stroking her body as she stretched luxuriously next to him on the couch. "The Dominican government will have nothing more to do with them. They both blame each other for the explosion."

"We know," Luis said, reinforcing his image as the omniscient being. "This was all part of the plan. The rotten Dominican government must stand alone to face us now."

"But they still have an army," Maripaz continued, whining just slightly, "and the Americans say that your people are so few."

"They're right about that," Luis admitted, "but there are enough of us, and the army won't be able to stop us. Within the next 48 hours it will all be over, and *we* will be the rulers of this country. There will be nothing more for you to fear, ever." Except me, he added to himself.

"But there are still so many soldiers," Maripaz insisted, "and they frighten me. After the explosion, I had to work at the embassy all night, and I saw some papers from the Defense Attache Office, I managed to make some copies for you. I didn't know if you needed them, but I wanted to do something to help." She pointed to a small pile of papers and envelopes on the coffee table. Without opening her eyes, she rolled her head back and forth invitingly over Luis' shoulder.

Luis reluctantly sat up and picked up several of the sheets. Although Lafeur had stamped them liberally with various classifications, from "Limited Official Use" to confidential and secret, the information they contained about the deployments of the Dominican armed forces had all been obtained from overt sources, readily available to the santistas, journalists, or anyone else with enough interest to ask a few questions and do some legwork. Luis chuckled out loud as he glanced over them.

"Here, you see?" he said, waving the papers. "It doesn't matter how many soldiers they have, although you can see that our campaign to terrorize them into running away has driven their numbers way down as well, because they're all in the wrong places. They're dug in at their barracks, at the Presidential Palace, the legislature, the Ministry of Defense, and those aren't the places that count anymore." Luis explained in simple terms to his new pet how easy it would be seize control of the nerve centers of society, leaving the soldiers holding meaningless symbols without substance. "Believe me," he continued. "When we've done our work, the soldiers will lay down their arms or come over with them, cheering, while their officers run for the boats."

"I just want it to be all over," Maripaz groaned seductively.

"Don't worry," Luis said, as he began to take off his shirt. "Tonight we begin our final preparations, and tomorrow night we strike! Within three days we will be the new government, and no one will be able to touch us. And that's just the start. Haiti will fall whenever we want it, then Jamaica, Puerto Rico, Mexico, who knows? We intend to start a brushfire that will engulf the entire hemisphere, even the poor of the

United States itself. This time we won't depend on any foreign ideology that none of us really understood anyway. This will be a simple movement of the poor against the rich, walking in the light of God, and we cannot be defeated.''

"Then you will be very busy for the next few days," Maripaz giggled softly.

"Yes, so we must make the most of the little time we have now."

†

Quiroga drove slowly along a hillside road which bordered the Arroyo Hondo area as the heat and humidity seemed to fuse the hot plastic seat of the pick-up truck to the bare skin of his back. Even having the windows open only moved the hot air more quickly without cooling it. As he leaned well out the window on his side, he could clearly hear the buzzing din raised by the horde of unseen insects in the roadside brush. Quiroga scanned the sky. The rain clouds which had been dumping occasional showers on the city for the past couple of days really looked serious now. The wind was picking up, and when it died down again, the rain would come. The radio was even talking about this storm gathering enough force to be classified as a full-fledged hurricane. He wondered if that was good or bad for their plans.

He finally reached a convenient vantage point and pulled the truck over to the left shoulder of the road. From the slight rise on which he had stopped, he had a view of the rear approach to the houses of the unfortunate wealthy who had been massacred by the santistas, how long ago? It seemed like ages to Quiroga, who had been averaging less than four hours of sleep a night. The houses were arranged in a neat "U" pattern converging along the cul de sac they shared. They all had swimming pools and large, shaded patios. Some had tennis courts, and one even had a large flat grassy area on which the chalk lines of a soccer field, now gone to seed, could be faintly discerned. Quiroga pulled a crumpled sheet of paper off the dashboard and consulted a diagram which Cuesta had provided him. The house at which the telephone line had been installed was the one to the left of the house with the soccer field. He took a small black cylinder from next to him on the seat, palmed it in his fist, and looked through it at the house. It was a small telescope, ideal for discreet surveillance work.

Like all the others, this house had been badly damaged in the raid, and while the structure still stood, its blackened windows stared out of the whitewashed façade like the empty eye sockets of a skull. Like the others, it had been abandoned. Quiroga could see no sign of life in the place, but then he hardly expected to. These places were big enough that the santistas could easily have set up shop in a basement or interior rooms. Of the eight houses, only the one with the soccer field seemed to have attracted a family of migrant Haitian workers who were camped out on the patio. He could see a fat black woman washing clothes by hand on the steps of the swimming pool, her skirt hiked up above her knees as she stood in the now greenish, dirty water. He decided he would have to come back after dark to see if any lights betrayed the presence of any other inhabitants.

The ancient lawn mower and other gardening implements which filled the back of the truck scraped and slid around the bed as he pulled back out onto the road. Quiroga rubbed the stubble on his chin with a grimace. He had always been very conscientious about his appearance, but lately he had been taking on the aspect of a vagrant, even when surveillance work didn't call for it.

This was the most difficult assignment he had ever had. If the American ambassador was still alive, as Lafeur seemed convinced he was, he could easily be hidden in one of those houses. That would certainly help explain why his and Arce's surveillance work had gone so easily before. They had been fed disinformation, like a couple of babies, leading them to the wrong location. It still rankled Quiroga that the enemy had won that round.

†

When Lafeur walked through the front door of the residence, he found several suitcases standing in the entryway. At least Anne had decided not to fight Stileforth on the issue of remaining in the country, he thought. Although he hated to give the creep the satisfaction, Lafeur would feel more at ease when Anne was safely out of the country. Then he would be free to pull out all the stops, find the ambassador, and get the hell out of Dodge himself. His own official departure was now set for three days hence, but he estimated that he would either be successful in that timeframe, or not, in either case the matter would be out of his hands. Then it occurred to him that the two unmatched suitcases and two carry-on bags did not look at all like the amount of luggage a woman would normally take when departing a country.

Just as this thought occurred to him, Anne stuck her head around the door to the living room.

"Oh, Claude, come in. There are some people I want you to meet."

He entered the room and was greeted by two tall young people. There was a young woman, who must have been the picture of Anne herself some 25 years before, with a pert nose, bright blue eyes, and stylishly short blonde hair. There was also a tall, well-built young man, who would have been a couple of years older than his sister. He had Featherstone's dark eyes and a bushy moustache.

"My children, Chris and Clare," Anne said, "Mr. Lafeur, our CIA station chief, and a good friend of the family."

They shook hands all around, and the young man held onto Claude's hand for a moment. "I want to thank you for the support you've given my mother through all of this."

"No thanks needed," Lafeur said. "I really couldn't have done any less, or any more. That's just the way things are." He put a meaty hand on the young man's shoulder. "But I'm very glad you're here. I suppose your mother told you that we may have to do something ourselves if we want to get your father out of this, and you're the only pilot we've got."

The young man frowned amusedly. "If I'm the only pilot we've got, we're in deep trouble, Mr. Lafeur."

Lafeur noticed that the young woman had her mouth set in a determined line, her fists balled on her hips. Anne was seated comfortably on the sofa, smiling benignly.

"That's Claude, by the way," he went on. "This is no time for false modesty, Chris. I'm sure if you can pilot those fancy Army Blackhawk helicopters on search and rescue missions, you can fly something else if we can find it." He put his arm around the young man's shoulder and started to lead him off to the library. "If you ladies will excuse us for just a minute, we really need to get some preliminary planning done. I've taken the liberty of asking Colonel Miller, the Gunny, Fiore, and a friend from the Israeli embassy over here for a quick skull session starting in about half an hour."

"That's quite all right, Claude," Anne said, "but . . ."

"We'll be right back," Lafeur interrupted, "but I want to get some of Chris' ideas about what kind of flying machine we should try to beg, borrow, or steal . . ."

"Then why the hell don't you ask me, since I'm Chris?" the young woman snapped, still in the same aggressive pose.

Lafeur spun around, hitting his forehead with the palm of his hand. "Oh, I'm sorry. My mistake. I just got mixed up, not having met you. I just assumed that Chris was the boy, and Clare the girl."

"That's short for Clarence," the young man said, grinning. Lafeur suspected that they had had this problem before.

"Well, then," Lafeur went on, turning Clare back toward the library, "if you'll excuse *Clare* and me, I need to get a pilot's advice on how best to proceed . . ."

"Then why the hell don't you ask me?" the young woman asked again.

"Uh-oh," Lafeur mumbled.

Clare just wiggled his eyebrows. "I do have an MBA, if that's any help."

"I think we might have an EEO problem here," Anne sighed.

Lafeur froze for a second, then spun around, grabbed Chris by the arm and started escorting her to the library.

"You know," Chris started in a heated tone, "I've had it up to about here with you macho jerks who automatically assume that only men know how to fly big silver birds. It used to be funny when I'd pick up some dumbshit pilot who'd been shot down over Iraq, and we'd be tooling over the desert, dodging Triple-A fire, having a fine time, when he'd almost have a heart attack when he realized that his pilot for the evening was this skinny little girl . . ."

"We're really going to have to sit down and have a long talk about prejudice and things, over drinks perhaps with your folks," Lafeur broke in, "but right now, what do you say we limit our discussion to how to save your father's life?"

That caused Chris to stop in mid-breath. "Right!" she nodded as they sat down. "Now what options have we got."

"Well, it looks like we're going in to an area of big mansions. Lots of open ground, but it's mostly rolling hills broken up with garden walls and some trees."

"In that case," she said, "a helicopter would probably be the thing. I can fly just about anything you're likely to find, but what kind of carrying capacity are we talking about? I assume that this is going to be a hot LZ and we're going to need some people to go in and convince the bad people to let my father go."

"Exactly. The problem is that just about everything that can fly on this island has already flown. The big exodus caused by the terrorists has driven just about everything with wings and rotors over to Puerto Rico for the duration. I've been out to the airport, and the only thing there, other than the big commercial jets that are still flying in and out, are a couple of real small helicopters, I don't know what they're called, but not big enough for more than two or three passengers, and a some equally small prop planes, like Piper Cubs. I don't think either of those will do, since we want room for at least ten to twelve men, people, plus your father."

Lafeur noticed that Chris straightened up a bit and raised her chin slightly when he referred to her as their only pilot. "Any chance of getting someone with a bigger chopper to fly over here from Puerto Rico, maybe sucker him in with an offer of big money, and then just take the damn thing away at gunpoint?" Chris asked.

Lafeur smiled. This young lady thought like a case officer. But he shook his head. "I'm afraid too many people have tried that already. There was even a shootout at the airport when someone tried it, and the incoming pilot had brought a couple of heavily armed cousins with him to ride shotgun. One round hit the gas tank, and they all turned into crispy critters. Things have gotten very ugly around here very fast."

"What other option have we got? Could the grunts, no offense, go in and get out on foot and let us just use one of the small choppers to pull Dad out of there?"

"The chances of detection are much greater," Lafeur said. "We've seen here how good these folks are at establishing this kind of living warning system all around them in the shantytowns. I wouldn't want to bet on our being able to get close to them on the ground without them being tipped off by people we never even see."

"So what can we do?" she asked, a note of frustration entering her voice.

"That's what I wanted to ask you," Lafeur said. "I've got this friend, well, actually he's an asset of mine, a rich guy who rents apartments, buys cars, and stuff like that for us to use, discreetly. He's got several ranches, and he's got this plane he's told me about that sounds like it might be useful to us, and it's here in country. I said that he's rich, but almost all of his wealth is tied up in land, which might be worth zippo here in a couple of days. So, I think I can get him at least to lend us the plane. He says it has a carrying capacity of about 20 people, including the pilot, which is plenty for our purposes."

"But unless these mansions are a hell of a lot bigger than I had imagined," Chris countered, "how are we going to land a plane on one, and take off again? What kind of plane is it?"

"That's just it. I remember him telling me all about it when he bought it last year. It's called a Skytrader, a special airplane built by a Canadian company for use on very short runways."

"A STOL aircraft?"

"If that's what you call a plane that he says can take off within maybe 150 yards and land in less, yes."

"That's Short Take-Off and Landing," she explained. "I saw it once, a twin-engine prop with the wing on top and a long pointy nose. Do you think you can fly it?"

"I'm cross-trained on aircraft not very different from it, in fact, that's the kind I originally learned to fly on, but I'd want to practice as much as possible beforehand on the actual machine. I also noticed that the weather outside is starting to look real ugly. How soon are we planning to go in?"

"That's what this next meeting's about, but I'd say we have to go tomorrow night. Can you do it?"

"I can die trying." She looked at him unblinkingly, and he suspected that this young woman didn't have much of a sense of humor.

Lafeur heard the buzz of voices coming from the entry hall, and he jerked his thumb toward the door. "Let's go and make some plans."

When they entered the living room, Fiore, Miller, and Besserman were seated, talking with Clare and Anne. Lafeur noticed that Gosher was serving himself a drink from a decanter near the patio door.

They made their introductions quickly, with Lafeur taking pains to make certain that everyone knew that Chris was their pilot. No point in going through all that again. They pulled some extra chairs into a rough circle around the coffee table, and Colonel Miller laid out a foggy overhead photo of the northern section of Santo Domingo.

"This is the best photo I could find which included the area we're interested in," he apologized. "I'm afraid that, once things really got organized for overhead coverage, we were already just focusing on the downtown area, but this at least gives us something to work from."

Lafeur jabbed his finger at one of the large houses on the cul de sac. "This is where my people tell me the ambassador is most likely being held. I have someone going out there tonight to conduct a more detailed reconnaissance, but this is our best bet." He paused. "In fact, it's our only bet. It's the only lead we have." He looked up and saw that tightness around Anne's eyes.

"Now this is what I figure we've got in terms of manpower," Miller chimed in. "We've got ourselves in this room, plus six of the Marines. We want to leave two on duty as usual in the embassy, both to provide a minimum of security there, and to throw Mr. Stileforth off the scent." Miller raised his head, and everyone nodded.

"I've got two more men who won't actually go in with the assault group," Lafeur added, "but they'll recon the place right up to our landing and be in a position to give us covering fire and help pull us out if we run into trouble."

"That gives us ten on the ground, plus the pilot, and two doing overwatch on the ground," Miller said.

"Make that eleven," Clare said, raising his hand. "I may not be a soldier, but I can fire a gun if I have to, and this is my father we're talking about remember."

Lafeur saw Anne stiffen at that, and he interposed. "We've got to provide security for Anne as well. Stileforth's kicking her out of here today, and I would think it prudent that she leave the country, but I kind of doubt that she plans to do so."

"Bloody hell!" Anne said pleasantly. "I will not set one foot outside the bloody little country without my husband, thank you. End of discussion."

"That's what I thought," Lafeur continued. "So we're faced with a choice. I can find a place for Anne to stay, but someone's got to protect her, or we might have to through this whole thing again next week. We have Escobar, the ambassador's bodyguard. He's a good man, and I think we can trust him. It's a question of whether you think it's more important for you to go along on the operation, or to let us take Escobar, who does have rather more experience in this sort of thing than you do. I'll leave it to you."

Lafeur knew that it was hardly fair, to put Clare in that position, and he watched him rubbing his hands, his head hung low.

"I suppose you're right," Clare admitted. "But where can we stay, if this Stileforth character kicks us out of here?"

"Here's an option," Gosher announced brightly. "Tell me, Mrs. Featherstone. Do you like falafel?"

"What?" she asked, puzzled.

"I just thought that, if you were to stay at my home, with my wife, you'd be conveniently out of the way but handy to monitor events. Both of my daughters are away doing their military service in the Negev," he said, nodding at Chris, "so we have plenty of room."

Anne nodded. "Just tell me where to go and what to do, and I'll do it." She strode out of the room but stopped at the door and turned. "You just get Bill back." Then she left. They heard the click of her heels on the tile floor pick up from a determined march to a rapid run as she headed for her bedroom.

"Well, that's settled," Lafeur said, after a moment. "That gives us eleven then."

"Make it twelve," Gosher said. He turned to Lafeur. "My colleague, the one you met, wanted to come. He says he expects to find a compatriot of his there, and has something to discuss with him. It's your decision, but he's an experienced soldier, and he doesn't know the meaning of the word 'fear'."

"Hell," the Gunny interrupted, "there's lots of words I don't know the meaning of, but all that ever got me was 'D's' in English."

Lafeur laughed. "I suppose so. We won't tell him anything. Just have him sit around with his gun in his lap until tomorrow, and you pick him up when we're ready to roll."

"Speaking of guns," Fiore put in, "I don't know if it's really a good idea for us to go up against these terrorists with their machine-guns and anti-tank rockets with just my .357 and the Marines' .38s and shotguns."

"As it so happens," Gosher answered, "we just had a mission here attempting to interest the Dominican military in the world famous Galil assault rifle. Although the sale didn't take place, primarily because our German competitors seemed more amenable to very large bribes in the right places, I happen to have in my Embassy a case with twelve of these wonders of modern military technology and a goodly supply of ammunition. Not to suggest that *all* of the weapons produced by Israel are not top quality, but, since these were samples, I suspect that these particular ones enjoyed an even higher level of attention to technical detail at the factory."

"I've heard that the Galil isn't nearly as accurate as the M16," the Gunny argued.

"Perhaps you have a stock of M16s around that you'd prefer to use," Gosher answered.

"Thank you, Yigael," Lafeur said. "We'll take you up on your offer. Now, what we need to do is get down to brass tacks on the actual operation." He noticed Chris studying the photograph closely, twisting it this way and that. "How does it look to you?"

"It's hard to say," she replied. "I see some shadows here on the soccer area that could be depressions, or maybe they're just clouds overhead. If the net and poles from this grass tennis court are down, and you can't tell that from the photo, there should be room enough. The tricky part is that takeoff is tougher than landing one of these birds, takes more room, so the simple fact that we can fly in might not mean that we can fly out. I'm going to want to get ahold of that plane ASAP and practice as much as possible, maybe do at least one fly-by of the site itself tomorrow, high enough not to tip them off, of course."

"Hopefully, if we get in and get your Dad all right, we'll have pretty much gutted the opposition in the process, so it might not be necessary to fly out, but that would be the preferred method," Lafeur said. "I'll work on a back-up, just in case."

"Do we have any idea how many people we're facing?" Miller asked.

"We have a good idea of how many they've got all together," Lafeur answered. "Unfortunately, that's more than we can handle, which is why we have to go tomorrow night. We have information that they're going to make their play to seize the government itself then, so there would be a skeleton crew at this place, and probably not their best people either. The way I see it, we've got three advantages. We know their weakness in numbers; we know that they plan to make their big move tomorrow night, and we know that the Ambassador is alive. The main thing is that they don't know that we know any of this. Since they assume that *we* assume the ambassador's dead, there's no reason for them to expect us to try to rescue him. They're probably focused totally on the Dominican Army and any opposition they face to their takeover plan. As far as they're concerned, the Americans don't count any more, and that might be the one mistake they've made in this whole campaign."

"If they're making a bid to seize the whole damn country," Miller said, "it might not be a bad idea to pick up all of our toys and go home tomorrow. I mean, what if we rescue the Ambassador, and then the bad guys take over two hours later, they could take the whole embassy and everybody in it in reprisal. I don't know if any of us would lose sleep over Stileforth sitting out four or five years as a hostage, but we do still have other people here, including God only knows how many other Americans not connected with the embassy, all of whom would be in danger."

"It sounds like we're trying to talk ourselves out of this whole thing," Fiore said angrily. "We can't keep them from taking over the country, dammit. We'll be real damn lucky if we can just get one man away from them and live to tell the tale. Let's just take this one step at a time."

"Actually," Lafeur spoke up, "the Colonel's right. I've given this some thought, and I think I can gin up something that might throw a monkey wrench into the santistas' whole plan, which might even indirectly help us in our work. Just leave that to me."

"Well, I want to get out and see that airplane," Chris said.

"Give me an hour to set it up with the owner," Lafeur said. "With some money and a visa or two, mountains can be moved. He moved his family out to Jamaica a few days ago, but he stayed here to keep an eye on his property. He can't get a visa to the States, because he used to be a communist, and he's still blacklisted. If I fix that little problem for him and promise to get his plane back to him in a day or two, I think he'll go for it. I'll give you a call with the directions, and you can take Escobar with you for security."

"I want to get those Galils issued to the Marines who are going to use them," the Gunny said. "My biggest problem will be deciding who *doesn't* go. Mr. Featherstone was, I mean is, popular with the boys."

"You can bring them over to our Embassy two at a time during the course of the day," Gosher said. "We don't want to draw attention, and they can practice on the small range we have set up in our basement, get the feel of the weapons, and learn to field strip them. They're really very rugged, forgiving weapons, and, I assure you, quite adequate for our purposes."

"Count me in on that," Fiore said.

"You all know what you need to do," Lafeur said. "I've got some very important meetings to attend to, so I'll be on my way."

†

Featherstone had never known such pain to exist. He lay on his side on the hard concrete floor, his body one large, throbbing ache. He had tried to move to a more comfortable position, but the slightest motion sent new waves of pain, above the level he thought could not be surpassed.

He finally forced himself to roll over onto his back with a groan. He slowly felt himself from head to foot with his right arm, his left being numb and lifeless from his apparently having lay on top of it for some hours. At least he hoped that was all it was. His face was a sticky mess, coated with half-dried blood and mucus. Inside his mouth he could feel with his tongue that at least two of his teeth were missing. Only his right eye would open at all, and that only a narrow slit. He could only breathe through his mouth, and he suspected that his nose was broken. His hand passed down over his ribs gingerly, and he could feel the welts and bruises. With some effort he bent his head enough to look downward and saw that his legs were pretty much untouched.

He was relieved to find some feeling coming back into his left arm, although that feeling was mostly pain, so it was a mixed blessing. He groped awkwardly for his water bottle and splashed a little of the cool liquid over his face before taking a drink. It even hurt to swallow. He found that his left eye, while swollen, was only sealed shut with dried blood, which a little water and gentle rubbing removed, giving him slightly improved vision.

He could see the plate of food from his last meal, which he had not eaten, now covered with a horde of large cockroaches, not that he was in the mood to eat anyway. He just sat there, drank a little more water and felt around inside his mouth, his tongue exploring the new gaps between his teeth.

He had sat there a long time, taking a vague interest in the battle among the cockroaches for his food, occasionally flicking an adventurous one away from himself in the direction of the plate, when the door finally opened and Pedro entered. He noticed that Pedro was walking a little more easily now, and he wondered how long he had been unconscious.

Pedro reached through the opening in the gate and handed him a warm, damp towel. "Here," he said. "You can wipe off some of the blood with that. It will make me feel better."

If Featherstone could have smiled, he would have. "You mean it will make *me* feel better?" It was like trying to talk right after leaving the dentist's with a mouth full of novocaine. "That's what we call a Freudian slip."

"That's what I meant. It will make you feel better."

Pedro quickly reached through the opening and lifted out the plate, cockroaches and all and scurried with it to the door, apparently dumping the whole thing into a garbage can outside. Featherstone gently wiped his face and torso with the towel, and it did help a bit.

"I'm sorry they beat you," Pedro said after a long pause. "I was listening at the door. You shouldn't have talked to Padre Lazaro like that. He was right to beat you."

"Give me a break, Pedro," Featherstone said, more in weariness than in anger. "That kind of attitude is fine for you, but all I see in Lazaro is a megalomaniac and a sadist. I didn't do anything wrong. You didn't do anything wrong. He's the only one around here who is doing something wrong."

"Do you want your food?" Pedro asked shyly.

"No."

"Is there anything I can do to help you?"

"Let me out of here," Featherstone said, turning his head slowly and carefully to look Pedro in the face.

"They won't give me the keys."

"By which you mean that, if they did give you the keys, you would let me out?" Featherstone asked, sarcastically.

"Yes, I believe I would," Pedro said, turning away and heading toward the door.

"Wait, Pedro," Featherstone called after him. "I'm sorry. I know that none of this is your fault. You've treated me as well as they've let you, and I thank you for that." So much for *that* resolution, Featherstone thought.

Pedro stayed near the door, but he didn't leave. "You're the first American I've ever really met. I went with Padre Lazaro to Nicaragua when I was seventeen. I'd seen Americans, tourists, on the streets here when I was little, and I even stole from them or begged from them, but I never really spoke with one before. You're really not bad at all, not like the Sandinistas, or the Iranians, or like Padre Lazaro said."

"Most people turn out that way when you get to know them," Featherstone said. "At least, they turn out not to be like what you'd thought. You have to see things for yourself." He paused a moment and looked at the shy, sad little boy, in the body of a man, who stood by the door, his lower lip protruding slightly. "You go on your way now. I don't want you to get in trouble again." Featherstone refolded the towel to put a clean side out and lay back down, placing the towel over his eyes.

†

Lafeur wasn't really surprised that Quiroga had so little trouble setting up a meeting for him with Colonel Palacios early that evening. He had long suspected that Quiroga had much closer contact with the Colonel than he had ever let on, and it certainly was no surprise that the Colonel's house arrest was honored more in the breach than in the observance. Lafeur was a little nervous about using the same safehouse that he always used with Quiroga, but, like so many other things in this operation, this would be a one-time arrangement.

"Captain Quiroga tells me that you have some important information that you wish to pass to the Dominican government but that the current tense relations between our two countries prevent this kind of official contact," the Colonel began.

"That's right, Colonel," Lafeur responded. "Actually, it's more than that. It's not only that we lack an official channel for liaison these days, but I wanted to make certain that the information goes to someone who will recognize its value and put it to some practical use."

"You're aware, I assume that I am not currently on active duty?" the Colonel commented, delicately wording the fact that he had been removed from government service altogether and was facing the possibility of a criminal investigation for his insubordination in launching the ill-fated commando attack on the 'zone.'

"I have worked in Latin America, and in this country in particular, too long to believe that such official obstacles pose much of a problem to determined men who have earned the respect of their subordinates." Quiroga had briefed Lafeur thoroughly on Palacios, advising him to take advantage of the Colonel's self-image, not to call it vanity.

"Just precisely what is it that you want me to do for you?" the Colonel asked with a suspicious grin.

"It's not so much for me that I want you to do it," Lafeur explained, "but by serving your own country, the action I have in mind for you would tend to help us in our own efforts. The situation is that we have reason to believe that the American ambassador is alive and still being held hostage."

"That is no longer a concern of mine," Palacios interrupted quickly. "I think I have done as much as can reasonably be expected of me in that regard."

"You certainly have, Colonel," Lafeur went on. "That is why my colleagues and I will be taking care of that ourselves. I'm afraid that we cannot even count on the support of our own government. What I have to tell you is that the santistas are planning to seize control of Santo Domingo, and thereby, of the country, tomorrow night. They are counting on being able to capture such 'soft' targets as the communications and transportation centers of the city and controlling television and radio transmissions. They are also counting on this so demoralizing the armed forces that there will no longer be any organized resistance and they will establish their own government by default."

Palacios rubbed his chin pensively. "That makes a certain amount of sense," he said. "But why come to me? Why not just pass this information to the government, to the army, and let them surround these positions with their troops? I don't have official command over anything anymore."

"For one thing," Lafeur said, "I doubt that I could get anyone in your government even to listen to me, relations being what they are. More importantly, if a platoon of soldiers shows up at the telephone central and sets up sandbagged machinegun nests, the santistas will see it and just postpone their operation. The government will figure it was all a hoax, pull the troops off after a couple of days, and then the santistas will strike later."

"If we can't put troops out to protect these places, what good is it for you to tell me about it?" Palacios asked.

"I don't pretend to be an expert on this sort of thing," Lafeur admitted, "but I have seen a coup or two in my time, and it seems to me that the best way to defeat a conspiracy like this, a clandestine attack, is by a clandestine defense."

"What the hell is a clandestine defense?"

"If the santistas have designed their strategy around Mao's doctrine of guerrilla warfare of striking where the government forces are weak, then the only way you can sucker them in is to make them think that these targets are still weak. Leave the army troops in their barracks, guarding buildings that don't really matter in terms of ruling the country, but if you could put even a couple of men, well-trained, well-armed and ready for anything, inside these soft targets, you could catch the santistas flat-footed when they strike. They're not expecting any resistance at all. They plan to seize these places, immediately turn them to their own use and then set them up for local defense. The only counterattack they're prepared to deal with is a large-scale one from across the river, from the base at San Isidro.

"We know they're short of experienced fighters," Lafeur crossed his fingers as he said this. He prayed that the information that Maripaz had been able to provide him wasn't part of a larger trap being set by the santistas. "If our men can get off the first shots, drop one or two of their scarce troops in each of these places and prevent them from seizing them, we'll be ahead of the game. They'll have to pull back and regroup, while the army troops will be duking it out with their covering forces at the bridges. If we're very lucky, we might be able to inflict losses on their experienced cadre that they'll never be able to replace, between your men at these target sites, the troops on the periphery of the city, and my people striking to rescue the ambassador. We could gut the whole movement and certainly set their plans way back."

Palacios was rubbing his chin so hard now that Lafeur imagined that he could actually see erosion at work. "There is certainly nothing I'd like better than to get a couple of those scumbags in my sights again."

Lafeur calculated that this was the time for another dose of vanity medicine. "My sources tell me that your commandos did them some serious damage," he lied. "They say that they had expected to bag all of you, like they did the Army troops in the armored column and were taken by surprise by how quickly your men recovered from their surprise and fought back. If you've got any more men around like those, those are the kind we're looking for to do tomorrow night's job." Lafeur could see that Palacios was tasting victory and hoped to push him over.

"I may not be on active duty," Palacios said after a long pause, "but my men from the cascos negros still look up to me. I suppose I could convince perhaps thirty or forty of my best men to take the night off and do a little moonlighting with me."

"I was hoping you'd say that," Lafeur said with a sigh of relief. "Remember, they have to be men who can work independently, in small groups, taking the initiative in a fast-moving situation."

"Don't worry," Palacios said expansively. "That's the way I trained my men, not like the little sheep in the regular infantry. My big question is how we're going to slip these men into the target areas without attracting attention."

"Well, first of all, they'll have to go in civilian clothes, concealing their weapons. I have contacts who can get them 'jobs' in the telephone central and at one of the television studios. My theory is that we don't really have to cover all of the targets, just a couple of them. Here are some notes I've drafted. You tell me if you think it will work."

The two men huddled over Lafeur's yellow legal pad. Palacios read for a moment as Quiroga stretched to look over his shoulder. Palacios began nodding his head, first slowly, then rapidly and firmly.

"I like it!" he said, slapping the pad with his strong hand and almost knocking it out of Lafeur's grip. "He who would defend everything, defends nothing, I always say. Your plan has a certain elegance of economy in it, Mr. Lafeur."

"Then I can count on you to have your men ready, say by six o'clock tomorrow afternoon?" Lafeur asked tentatively.

"They will be armed, briefed, and ready," he answered. "Would it be too risky for a couple of the officers to make a preliminary reconnaissance?"

"If they can do it discreetly," Lafeur said. "Say, if one of them had a phone bill to pay anyway, that would be pretext enough, or if another pretended to have a small business that wanted to place an ad on one of the radio stations, that might be another."

"We'll give it a try," Palacios said, slapping Lafeur on the back with bone-crunching enthusiasm. "Until tomorrow then."

†

It was well past midnight when Arce and Quiroga made their way through the roadside shrubbery from the hills behind the cul de sac where the gutted mansions stood. They had already taken nearly an hour to move down from the dirt road where they had left their truck, moving silently and hiding whenever the rare passing car shone its headlights along the road. The two men took advantage of a spot of dead ground to hoist themselves over the garden wall of the house they had identified from the telephone number. They were fortunate that the owner had not bothered to have broken glass embedded in the top of the wall as was common practice, and someone apparently had come by and stolen the razor wire installed above the wall.

Quiroga wasn't at all certain what kind of security he would have to face, so he and Arce took every precaution. Quiroga had done a break-in a couple of years before, a private job designed to place a microphone in the bedroom of one local politician on behalf of another local politician. He had dealt with all kinds of technical security devices, video cameras, motion detectors, pressure plates, and more, in addition to a pair of very nasty dobermans, but he had done it. Now he led the way, crawling inch by inch along the edge of ornamental shrubbery which was already beginning to revert to the wild state. He could hear lizards and other small creatures scurrying for safety as he approached, but there was, as yet, no sign of life from the house.

A steady, light rain was falling as the two men slithered along through the yard. In the hills to the west of the city, lightning occasionally flashed, and the brief glare illuminated the white walls of the house with its cavernous, empty windows. As uncomfortable as the weather might have made Quiroga normally, he was grateful for it now. It provided a welcome level of noise to cover his own movements and increased the likelihood that anyone in the house would remain indoors. All he and Arce had to do was ensure that the santistas were actually there. They didn't hope to be able to catch a glimpse of the ambassador himself, and Quiroga was too experienced a man to expect that, like in the movies, he would stick his head out of the bushes at the precise moment when some key official would be getting into a Mercedes in front of the house, permitting him to overhear some vital snippet of conversation. This was just a preliminary reconnaissance, and they didn't expect to answer all of the questions. The rescue force would still be taking a large risk when it came in, as to the kind of resistance they would meet, and whether the ambassador was present at all.

The two men had reached the main house, and they could see in through the blasted plate glass windows of what must have been some kind of recreation room. There had been a fire here, and the remnants of blackened furniture were still scattered around the room. Strands of the colored tape the police had used to cordon off the scene were still stuck to the door frames, flapping wildly in the freshening breeze. In one corner of the room, the high ceiling had collapsed, revealing a patch of sky illuminated by the lightning flashes. The two men lay still for a long while, just watching. When they saw no other movement, they stepped inside the room.

Quiroga could see a couple of dim lights glowing from across the garden wall in the next house, the one the vagrant family had squatted in, but there was no way they could see into this building. He set down a large shopping bag and removed a large black cloth tool bag. They both stood up and unzipped the soaking wet coveralls they wore, depositing them, along with their overshoes, in a pile just inside the door. Quiroga had anticipated the rain, and didn't want wet footprints giving away the fact of their visit

Quiroga swung his tool bag over his head and cinched it tightly to his back by a strap. Both he and Arce had their service revolvers drawn, and both carried small pen flashlights to guide their way. Quiroga was looking for either a large interior room, without windows, or a basement, either of which could be used to house the terrorists or their captive without showing lights to the outside. He took time to find the circuit breaker box to check if there appeared to be any wiring for an alarm system. There wasn't, and the power to the house was turned off.

They stepped carefully over the fallen ceiling beams and the broken bits of furniture. Quiroga was grateful that most of the broken glass had been by the doors and windows and not spread around the room to crunch underfoot and give them away. They proceeded to the kitchen, the servants' quarters, and the other rooms of the first floor without discovering any evidence that anyone had been in the house since the terrorist attack and the subsequent police investigation. Quiroga found the stairs to the basement, but discovered that it was only a small cellar used for storing the owner's wine collection, or what was now a collection of broken bottles and thick, sweet-smelling sludge several inches deep across the floor of the room.

As they moved upstairs, Quiroga led the way, watching for booby-traps or alarms while Arce covered him from below. Quiroga had just about concluded that they had reached a dead end, that their hunch about the terrorists having given Maripaz the telephone number of their real headquarters had simply been a long shot. He paused to listen as he reached the top of the long, sweeping stairway when his eye caught a reflection from a lightning flash on something stretched across the top step. He turned on his pen light and discovered a taut piano wire, about four inches above the top step. At one end it was affixed to a screw in the wall, at the other, to the bannister, and attached to that, the pin of a fragmentation grenade.

Quiroga made a clicking noise in his throat, the signal for Arce to join him. The younger man's eyes went wide as Quiroga played the light along the wire to the grenade. They both tightened their grips on their pistols, and Quiroga moved ahead, carefully stepping over the wire. He hoped that, if things got hectic farther on, he wouldn't forget this wire as he made his getaway.

They moved along the upstairs hallway, listening at each door. Most of them stood open, and it became more and more confusing for Quiroga, since it appeared that no one had been up here either for some time. Obviously, the tripwire had been set *after* the police inspection, but why? If they had hoped simply to kill off a few more policemen, they had certainly acted too late. Otherwise, what point was there? If the trap were there to protect something, what? There was not a soul in the house, and nothing of apparent value to anyone.

The two men finally reached the last room and its closed door. Quiroga carefully checked around the door jamb but could see no alarm wires or any other traps. He turned the knob, pressing his body far to one side of the door as Arce flattened himself against the wall on the other side. When the latch came free, he pushed the door open, gently but firmly. As it swung wide, Quiroga heard a faint but unmistakable metallic click. He swore under his breath and awaited the explosion, but none followed. The door swung all the way to its little rubber stop, bounced slightly, and stayed ajar.

Quiroga took a quick peek into the room, jerking his head back behind the protection of the wall after a split second, but his glimpse only told him that this was another empty room. He looked again, this time flicking on his pen light and shining it around to the four corners of the room. It had apparently been a girl's bedroom. The fire had reached here as well, but the furniture which remained was only singed. Thieves had been in and taken the mattress from the ‟bed, and the dresser drawers were tossed about the room. The door to the closet stood open with a few pieces of clothing still on their hangers.

The beam of light angled downward as Quiroga relaxed his tense muscles, and he saw a wide arc of white on the tile floor. At first he assumed that this was just some more mess created by the looters, a dropped box of body powder or something, but then he noticed that the semicircle of white was rather carefully arranged, without a trace appearing outside the doorway. It was just the sort of thing that one might put down to see if anyone had entered the room.

Quiroga remembered the click, and he looked around the inside of the door jamb. There, above the frame, was a small black box, smaller than a box of matches, with a metal arm on a spring which reached down to below the frame itself. There was a row of numbers visible on the front of the box, as on an odometer. Quiroga recognized at once that it was a SED (Surreptitious Entry Detection) counter, a simple device which would tell the owner, if he kept careful track of the reading whenever he opened the door himself, whether someone else had been in the room. The counter now read 67.

Quiroga would figure out what to do about that later, but first he had to determine what it was in this room, in this otherwise vacant house, that needed so much protection. Perhaps the santistas had been using the place but had abandoned it, but these devices were, unmonitored devices to tell whether someone had been there in your absence, not something which would protect you while you were there. No, it had to be something else.

He let the beam of light wander around the room again, looking for something out of place, out of the ordinary. This was particularly hard to do in a house which had been ransacked, since *everything* was out of place to a certain degree. Perhaps, then, something that *wasn't* out of place, something that hadn't been half-destroyed, he thought.

The only thing which fit that description was a large bureau set against the far wall. While what was left of the other furniture was made of light wood, this was rather dark and heavy, not the sort of thing you'd expect to find in a girl's room. Quiroga had noticed it at first, thinking it odd that someone would place a piece of furniture so that the upper left corner overlapped the room's one large window, taking a bite about eight inches square out of the lower corner of the window. He had assumed that the cabinet had been shoved there during the attack or subsequent looting, but then noticed that the legs of the cabinet were bolted to the floor. A heavy metal frame encased each leg of the cabinet, which in turn were fastened to the solid tile floor with large hexagonal bolts. Aha! Quiroga thought to himself, smiling in the darkness.

He signalled Arce to remain where he was, and took a long step into the room, standing on tiptoe in the center of the circle of white powder. His second step reached beyond, and he balanced on one foot as he carefully wiped off the powder which had adhered to his shoe. He gingerly approached the cabinet, looking at it from all sides.

It had two large doors, both of which stood wide open, revealing an empty interior. What attracted Quiroga's attention was that, unlike the drawers or the closet, which still held scattered items which the thieves, in their haste, hadn't bothered to remove, the cabinet was absolutely empty. He looked inside, on top, and underneath, but nothing. He stood up straight, one hand on his hip, the other scratching his head furiously with the pen light, when he noticed something.

The upper corner of the cabinet, the one which overlapped the window, happened to be just at eye level for Quiroga. As he stared ahead, blankly, trying to figure out the importance of this piece of furniture, his eye happened to focus, not on the cabinet, but out the window, to the neighboring house, perhaps 300 meters distant.

"Aha!" he said out loud this time, causing Arce to flinch at the sound.

Quiroga stepped up to the cabinet and sighted along the upper edge, as along a rifle. His line of sight passed through the window, across the garden, and to an upper story window of the house opposite. He looked again at the cabinet. The doors took up the entire front, except for a space about eight inches high from the top of the doors to the top of the cabinet itself. He looked inside, and the roof of the interior space was flush with the top of the doors, leaving a convenient, enclosed cavity, eight inches high, running the length of the cabinet.

He pressed himself against the wall, next to the window. He didn't dare use the light this close to the window, but, by waiting patiently for flashes of lightning, he saw what he was looking for. In the small square area of the cabinet which overlapped the window, although appearing to be made of the same fiberboard, covered by a thin sheet of black material, Quiroga could barely discern that a small circle was a slightly different shade of black from the rest. He touched it lightly with his fingertips, and found that, under the material, the circular area was not backed by the wood of the cabinet. He smiled again. He had seen all he needed to see.

He walked back to the circle of powder and carefully stepped in his own footprint as he exited. In the hallway, he took off his tool bag and opened it on the floor.

"What is it?" Arce asked in an excited whisper.

"It's the answer to my question," Quiroga hissed, as he took a paint brush with soft bristles and a small plastic container of talcum powder from the bag. "I was wondering why these clever people would be so stupid as to give an unwilling recruit the number to their real headquarters, even for convenience sake. That implies a level of laziness that these people haven't displayed in anything else. Now I understand it."

"Well, I sure as hell don't," Arce said in exasperation.

"It's really quite simple," Quiroga said as he reached out and lightly brushed away his footprint. Then he sprinkled talcum powder from the can on the bald spot. He always carried some to help him put on surgical gloves, which he used when he didn't want to leave fingerprints. He could only hope that the powder on the floor was, indeed, white, and not pink or beige or some other color. "The phone number the girl at the embassy called, does actually belong to this house, and the line runs in here. However, the phone which rings isn't here at all."

"And how did they accomplish that?" Arce asked.

Quiroga now turned his attention to the SED counter. If it was properly made, which it appeared to be, there would be no way simply to reset it. There were four digits on the face of the counter, which read 0067. When all four reached 9999, the mechanism would freeze, and the counter would have to be replaced. There was no backward movement possible.

"I can't move that cabinet to prove it, but I'll bet the telephone line runs into the back of it, straight from inside the wall. In there, in that closed space between the top of the doors and the top of the cabinet itself, is a device which works with a laser beam, making the beam simply an extension of the telephone line, shooting it directly and into a similar device inside the window of the house across the way." Quiroga scratched his head again for awhile then began to move the trigger arm on the SED rapidly back and forth.

"As far as anyone outside can tell," he went on, "the telephone line belongs in this house, but the telephone instrument is in the next one, with no visible link between the two. So, if our people had come storming in here, looking for the bad guys, the santistas would have been sitting comfortably next door, watching the whole thing, maybe laying a trap of their own, or maybe just quietly walking away in the other direction. My guess is that they were reasonably confident the woman wouldn't reveal the number or that we wouldn't find it out, but this was their last little trick to make sure of it. I suspect they come in here frequently to check to see if anyone's fiddled with their set-up, but, they must feel pretty secure."

"So they're in that other house?" Arce asked. "But that's the one with the vagrant family living in it."

"Don't forget the situation they had at their other headquarters in the 'zone,'" Quiroga cautioned. "They relied heavily on what you might call human alarm systems, layers of non-combatant informers surrounding them to warn them of the approach of the police. I suspect that family serves the same function over there. Besides, the family's living there would go a long way to cover the movement of the santistas in and out, much better than could be done in a supposedly abandoned house."

"So what are we going to do about it?"

"Nothing. This is what we came here to find out. Our target is next door, and we were very lucky to have discovered it in time. Now we know where to go. There's no point in trying to sneak into the other place."

"What are you doing now?"

"Maybe the santistas will be getting lax in their security now that they figure no one's looking for an Ambassador who's supposed to be dead and since they plan to make their big move in about 24 hours, but just in case, we don't want them to know that someone was in here. It might make them pull in their horns and maybe even move to another location.

"Our problem is this little counter. I can't set it back, but I can run it forward. It'll stop when all of the tumblers hit the 9 position, but if I move it to read 9965, maybe we can convince the next person in here that it was just a little mechanical failure. When I finish clicking this damn thing, and we shut the door, when the next bad guy comes in, it will read 9967. Since the 9 and the 0 are right next to each other on the tumbler, he'll probably figure that something jostled the device a bit and twitched the first two tumblers the wrong way. That's what I'm hoping, anyway, and that's all we can do in the time we've got, so this will have to do."

Quiroga switched hands and kept moving the little arm. After what seemed to both men like an eternity, he stopped moving it rapidly and began to go much more slowly. Finally, he stopped, swung his tool bag back onto his back, and the two men retraced their steps, being careful to avoid the tripwire on the stairs.

The donned their soggy coveralls near the doorway and slipped out into the yard. Quiroga resisted the temptation to peer over the wall which divided the gardens of the two houses, knowing that it was as likely that someone over there would spot him as it was that he would see something useful. By the time they reached their truck again, it appeared as if they had swum all the way.

†

Lafeur sat on the edge of his bed, watching a cable TV movie and downing the last of a large can of chicken chow mein. He knew that he should be trying to get some sleep, since it was past four in the morning before what promised to be a very busy day, but he had tried and failed. The one nice thing about being on the verge of what he was confident would be a violent death, was that there was no point in worrying about his diet, such as it was. He had a one pound bag of M&Ms with peanuts sitting by for when he finished his dinner, and he saw no point in leaving any of those for posterity either.

Lafeur had known just what was expected of him in his job, what it took to get promoted on time, and what it took to impress the right people to get the assignments he wanted. Even the subtle prejudice which existed in the Agency was a known quantity for him, and he could deal with it. Now he was involved in something completely beyond his experience.

In all his years of service he had never carried a gun, and now his life would depend upon his being able to handle one effectively against enemies he knew to be combat veterans. He had taken Gosher up on his offer of a little familiarization with the Galil and had fired off a couple of magazines on the little firing range, with marginal results. Then Gosher's security man had shown him and a couple of the marines around the Israeli Embassy, really just a converted house, which he had transformed into a mini-version of the Delta Force's shooting house for the occasion, as he explained he did every summer when most of the staff was on vacation. The security man and Gosher had a number of electrically controlled pop-up targets which they placed around the building and practiced firing against, using blanks, of course, in case they should ever have to recapture their embassy some day. Lafeur had run through the little course a couple of times, since Gosher said that it would help his hand and eye coordination. By the end of the second run, Lafeur had indeed noticed a marked improvement, and he was certain that, if he had only another six months of intensive training, it might have lifted his skills up to "below average."

What made matters worse was that this dangerous and unfamiliar activity was actually torpedoing his career. He had passed about fifty thousand dollars to Maripaz when she had met with him earlier to provide the information she had gleaned from Luis. And he had done it all very much "off budget," as he did not want anyone coming along later to take the money back from her. He hadn't asked her what she did to obtain the information. He didn't really want to know, but he was convinced that she had earned the money many times over, and this feeling was only reinforced by her reluctance to take it at all. He wasn't in a position even to try to get authorization for these expenditures, or for the money he had passed his contact for use of the airplane. The steps he had taken to get the man's record cleared to issue him a multiple entry visa to the States were well within the bounds of "visa fraud," a felony offense.

Of course, Lafeur had the vague hope that, if everything worked out, and Ambassador Featherstone was rescued, he would be forgiven all of his transgressions, but he knew that this was unlikely to be the case. The Agency might find it inconvenient to prosecute a hero, but he doubted whether this level of insubordination would be totally forgotten by his superiors, who were likely to be around for a long time.

Still, he knew that he didn't really have a choice. All of the intel reports he had written and the agents he had recruited over the years had been little more than fluff in the final analysis. He supposed that someone had cared whether or not the Peruvians had decided to buy MiG 29s over the Mirage 2000, or was it the other way around? Or maybe it had been really important to someone that the Ecuadorean Communist Party was about to split again, but he doubted it. He merely provided grist for a mill which just produced more grist for some other mill. What he was doing now would make a difference, in a very real way, in the lives of people he knew and cared about, and that made it all worthwhile. He'd take his chances and pay the price later, whatever it might be.

His main worry now was not about his career but about whether he had done his job properly. He had been as objective as he knew how to be in evaluating Maripaz' information, and it all seemed to make sense. Yet, he was stuck with trusting his life, and the lives of others, to the word of a woman who had already betrayed them once. On top of that, he had made assumptions which might prove totally off the mark.

Things seemed to have fallen into place. Maripaz had given them fairly detailed information about the santista plans, which radio and television stations they planned to incapacitate and which they would take over. She told them how they planned to defend the bridges and seize the telephone exchange, and Lafeur and Palacios had come up with what seemed like a good plan given their limited resources, but he couldn't be sure.

When Quiroga had told him about the true location of the santista headquarters, or at least what appeared to be the true location, Lafeur had almost had a heart attack. Of course, he had been glad to get the correct location, but he couldn't help thinking how close they had come to launching their attack in the wrong place. The terrorists would have been watching, and laughing at them in safety, killing the ambassador at their leisure, and maybe swooping down to massacre them for good measure.

Lafeur felt that he was out of his depth, and the faith others were placing in him made him feel the pressure all the more. He looked up at the television. The credits for the movie were running, and he realized that he hadn't noticed how it came out. Just great, he thought, the last movie I might ever get to see, and I don't know how it ended. He also noticed that the M&Ms were gone. It was after five o'clock now. He turned off the TV with his remote, flopped back down on his bed, turned off the light, and fell asleep almost immediately.

TEN

$\dagger$

Padre Lazaro was very pleased with how smoothnly Jaime and his teams had completed the placement of their charges around the city during the night. There had been no incidents with security forces as the police and army had pretty much surrendered the night streets to the santistas and were concentrating on defending their barracks and major government buildings from potential mad truck bombers. They had failed to realize the true value of the mundane communications and media services to the semblance of authority which was fast drifting away from the government and would soon be within the grasp of the movement. Things were going very well indeed.

Lazaro was still very nervous. He was used to taking a more direct role in the actions of his group, but this time he would essentially be sitting back and letting Luis and Pablo Baca handle most of the fighting. Lazaro, his bodyguards, and a few other fighters, would form a central reserve at the headquarters in Arroyo Hondo, connected to each detachment by radio, and ready to move to any point where the success of the mission appeared to be in doubt. Lazaro prepared himself for a long night of nail biting and prayer.

By stretching their resources to the maximum, the santistas had amassed a force of nearly one hundred and fifty fighters. They were all well armed with automatic rifles, grenades, ample ammunition, and special weapons and explosives as their particular mission demanded. Only about forty of those, however, were combat veterans. The rest had received rudimentary training and some had seen action in the early fighting in Santo Domingo, but well over half had never fired a shot in anger. The essence of planning the assault had been to divide the experienced troops among the green to give them a certain "stiffening" and proper leadership at the tactical level.

To avoid tipping off the scattered government security forces still about, Lazaro had had to deny himself the luxury of supervising the final preparations of the troops. With him in the Arroyo Hondo house, apart from the dozen or so men who would remain to provide security for the headquarters, were only Luis and his teams which would seize the targets within the city proper. About sixty fighters, half of them veterans, would split into four teams of ten, one each to capture the radio and television stations they would put to use, one to the telephone central, one to blockade the police barracks near the American embassy. The remaining twenty fighters would serve as a floating reserve to reinforce any of the others. They were scattered between the two large basement rooms they were using as the command post, cleaning weapons, checking ammunition, and going over their individual assignments again.

Baca would be in charge of the defense of the main highway bridge over the Ozama River against any counterattack the army might launch from San Isidro. This group consisted of fifty fighters, provided with Armbrust anti-tank weapons and a number of machineguns concentrated in the deserted dockside area near the bridge. The remainder of the santista force was divided into two smaller groups secreted near their posts of assignment, one each on the highways heading north and west out of the city. They were to protect against the off chance that one of the weakened government garrisons elsewhere on the island might muster a force to thrust through to the capital.

The tactical plans had been laid, and Lazaro now spent his time praying and passing among the troops, giving a word of encouragement and quizzing them on the role they were to play. They had already had a hearty dinner, and he would soon insist that they all get a few hours rest, if possible, before they moved into action at about nine o'clock that night.

†

"So how was the airplane?" Fiore asked Chris as she and her brother entered the doorway of the residence. She shook the rainwater from her hair and dropped her army poncho unceremoniously in a soggy pile in a corner of the foyer before she answered. The assembled group, including Lafeur, Miller, Gosher, Besserman and the five other marines all looked up from cleaning their weapons with nervous expectation. Chris could see what appeared to be a shadow on the wall of the hallway beyond and the toe of one of her mother's shoes peeping out from the edge of the door jamb.

"It handles like a school bus," she said, grabbing a coke from a cooler near the couch, "and it isn't as well maintained as I'd like, but it flies. I've looked over the new landing site, and it's actually better than the other place. It's got a regular football field laid out, which we can assume is quite flat. That in itself isn't quite big enough, but it looks like a good margin around the edges is also clear and firm, so I think we're okay from that standpoint. We did a lot of take-offs and landings, and, depending on the weather, I think we can do it."

"How *is* the weather out there?" one of the marines asked, casting a worried glance at the sheets of rain lashing the windows.

"I've seen worse," Chris said, "but I can't remember when. This aircraft is built to work in Canadian weather, so it's pretty stable in chop. Our big problem is that we're not exactly coming into Dulles International, you know, so there's nothing like airfield recognition. I'm used to that sort of thing, but with a helicopter it's different, you can hang around and look for your spot, and the birds I usually fly also have all sorts of snazzy navigational equipment and night vision devices on board, which this hog just doesn't have. I've checked the weather for tonight, and it looks pretty grim. What we're going to need is some kind of beacon I can home in on near the strip."

"Well," Fiore chuckled, "we've got their phone number. Why not call them up and ask them to flick on the playing field lights for us?"

Chris shot Fiore an impatient glare through narrowed eyes and ignored his comment. "Look at this," she said, clomping her combat booted foot onto the edge of the delicate antique coffee table in front of Lafeur, revealing a map of the area which was still taped to her right thigh.

"There's a rise here, just south of the LZ, on the approach route I plan to take. Just south of that, maybe half a click from the LZ itself, is a gas station. It looked abandoned, but if someone could torch it for us, say five minutes before showtime, I could line up on that and mark my distance to the LZ. The rise should shield it from view from the house, but there seem to be half a dozen fires burning out of control in the city at any given time anyway, so that shouldn't tip them off."

Lafeur canted his head to one side. "Sounds good to me. I'm sure that my police friend can handle that. What do you think, Colonel?"

The group hadn't really elected a leader, but Lafeur made a point of deferring to Miller on all matters of tactics.

"I concur," he nodded. "It sounds like Captain Featherstone knows her stuff. I'm just a ground pounding jarhead and know when to listen to sound advice."

"Well," Lafeur said. "If that's settled, I think it best if we were all on our way. I'll meet you out by the airplane. I've got to check and see if there's any last minute information to be had, and I have to get to my man to see about that gas station. We've got about six hours until we go in, at about ten o'clock, and you should take time to go over your instructions again and try to get some rest."

There was nervous chuckling in the room, as each person imagined how easy it would be to take a quick nap at a time like this.

"I left Escobar to supervise the refueling of the aircraft," Chris said, "but I'm going to have to go over the engines with a fine tooth comb, just to be sure. We don't want a bad spark plug to screw things up for us now."

Lafeur waved goodbye and disappeared out the back door to the terrace. They had planned to leave in small groups to avoid attracting attention. Anne had dismissed the domestic staff earlier that day, claiming that she wanted time alone with her children before leaving the residence for good. They had borrowed two large vans from the embassy motor pool, ostensibly to transfer the Featherstones' luggage to the airport, but they would serve to carry most of the assault group out to the airstrip, while Chris followed in a separate car after a brief interval. Anne and Clare would leave later for Gosher's home.

The assault people gathered up their weapons, body armor, and other equipment, stashing them in an assortment of dufflebags and suitcases, and headed for the door. The vans pulled out of the driveway with a marine driving each. The other passengers tried to scrunch down inside as much as possible except for Miller and Fiore, who rode shotgun in their respective vehicles. As they passed through the gates to the street, Fiore was surprised to see a small crowd clustered on the sidewalk just outside the gate, taking indifferent shelter under an array of broad umbrellas from the pouring rain. He rolled down his window to attempt to see better and recognized the old gardener from the residence smiling benignly, the butler, standing ramrod straight, several of the maids and the char ladies from the embassy, and over a dozen other FSNs. Some of them were crossing themselves solemnly, others were giving the thumbs up signal.

The old gardener pulled out a much-used machete and waved it over his head. "Kill them for us, boss!" he shouted as the vans bumped down the driveway and into the street. Fiore just waved and smiled.

"So much for security," he sighed.

"Do you suppose any of those folks are talking to the other side?" the marine driver asked.

"If they are, son," Fiore answered, "we'll know soon enough."

The residence seemed eerily silent after the vans had gone. Some-one had left a television on somewhere, tuned to CNN, some report about the continuing drought in California, but the rest of the house echoed to the footsteps of the two young Featherstones as they gathered up their own things.

Suddenly Chris looked up and saw her mother standing in the doorway to the living room. She was neatly combed and dressed, and a small overnight bag lay at her feet. She stood erect, but Chris could see that her right hand had a death grip on her left, and she was trembling all over.

"Good luck," Anne said in a tiny voice.

The trembling got worse, and Chris and Clare tied as they leapt to their mother's side, the three of them locking each other in a frenzied embrace.

"Don't worry, Mom," Clare said. "We'll get Dad back all right."

"Why do you think we had you?" she asked between sobs.

They stood that way for a long time. Eventually, they separated, each sniffling and wiping away at nose and eyes with whatever came to hand.

"Be careful, Chris," Anne said, and broke out in a laugh. "It seems I've been saying that for decades now, but you're not just going out to play on the swings this time."

They each hugged again, and Clare punched his sister lightly on the shoulder. Chris then hurried out the door.

†

Jim Vernon sat in his office, blankly staring at that morning's newspaper. He had read the article about another police patrol being ambushed in the southern part of the city, apparently part of the continuing santista effort which was working pretty well, to keep the streets for themselves. In fact, he had read the article at least nine times, but none of the words seemed to stick with him. He owed Washington another sitrep, but he doubted very much if he would be able to write it today. He looked up at the clock over his desk, one of the typical government sort, large and round with a black border, which he had to reset every two or three days as it had a tendency to lose ten minutes every 24 hours. He had already reset this one four times since lunch.

At forty-five, he was too old to start a new career. He didn't have a PhD, so he couldn't even get a decent teaching position in international relations, the only subject about which he had more than a passing knowledge. In fact, there was no career, other than teaching, which Vernon could even imagine himself doing.

He was due for promotion to the rank of FS-1, the highest on the Foreign Service scale before one passed to the senior levels, but he was still short of "capping out" in terms of salary. This was a point of concern for him, because, one could make ends meet on a single salary at his level in the Washington area, but just barely. He had been counting on a promotion in Santo Domingo to make life affordable in D.C. on his return so that his wife wouldn't have to go back to work just yet. For that reason alone he had swallowed all of the little snubs and insults Stileforth had tossed his way for the past year and a half. This could be the key year if he were to get promoted or become "terminal," i.e., unpromotable, at his current level.

Stileforth strode into Vernon's office without even the pretense of a knock and dropped a packet of papers on his desk. "Take these over to the DAO shop, and get them to coordinate. I want this to go out before six o'clock."

"I don't think anyone's there right now," Vernon said, and immediately bit his tongue. He realized that he should have taken the papers and disappeared for half an hour before reporting back to Stileforth.

"Well, where the devil are they?" Stileforth shrieked. "And where are Lafeur and Fiore? I don't like this."

Stileforth picked up the phone and punched the extension for Marine Post One.

"Let me speak to the Gunny," he snapped.

Vernon couldn't hear the reply, but Stileforth slammed the receiver down on its cradle with a grunt.

"I knew it!" he growled. "They're all off together doing something insane, with no authorization from Washington."

Vernon made a clucking noise in his throat. "That's awful. I think we should always have authorization before we do anything insane." He smiled, hoping to calm Stileforth down, but the latter obviously wasn't having any.

"Shut up!" he hissed. "So, the Marines are doing some kind of 'training,' are they? And everyone else is conveniently out of the office. They've gotten it into their heads that they can do something about Featherstone or I'm very much mistaken. Well, they're not going to get away with it. I'm going to call Dominican Army General Headquarters and report them, insist that they get some troops out looking for them."

"But, if they *are* doing something like that," Vernon said in a voice that came out at a higher pitch than he had intended, "won't that ruin any chance they might have of pulling it off?"

"Oh, please," Stileforth said, pacing back and forth frantically. "The only thing they're likely to do is to get themselves killed, and then I'll look the fool for supposedly being in charge when they did it, and even if they do get lucky, I'll still look like an idiot for not having been part of it. No, my friend, this just can't be."

"You sound like you're more concerned about your own image than you are about their lives."

"What do I care about their lives?" Stileforth asked, coming to an abrupt stop in front of Vernon's desk. "If they want to die, let them do it, but they have no right to place a stain on my record while they're about it. I have an even better idea. I'll call a couple of radio and television journalists I know with a little 'deep background' information about this. If we can get it on the air in the next couple of hours, maybe they'll hear it and cancel whatever they've got planned, and I can tailor the information to cover myself in any case."

"And what if the terrorists hear the news and our people don't? Are you crazy?" Vernon shouted, coming to his feet. "They'd all be killed, and you would have done it."

"Nonsense!" he answered, reaching for the telephone. "They did it to themselves."

Vernon surprised himself when he clamped his hand down hard on top of Stileforth's, smashing the receiver back into its cradle. "No!" Vernon shouted.

"You're fired!" Stileforth screamed, yanking his hand back in horror. "Get out of my embassy! You are relieved of all duties, and I want your security badge left with the marine on your way out." He shouted this last over his shoulder as he raced back into his own office.

Vernon stood for a moment at his desk, his fists balled at his sides and his whole body shaking. He'd finally done it. Nearly twenty years of work down the drain. He wasn't old enough to qualify for retirement, even at a reduced pension. He was certain that Stileforth would word any message he wrote in such a way that his own actions would appear the product of the purest reason and logic, while Vernon's were a clear act of insubordination, if not derangement. He heard Stileforth fumbling with the receiver of his phone down the hall.

Vernon rushed into Stileforth's office and saw him frantically punching the buttons. Vernon ran directly to the phone jack and ripped the wire out of the wall.

"You're insane!" Stileforth shrieked. "I'll have your retirement account seized as well, you bastard!"

But Vernon had made his choice, and it felt great. Stileforth danced back and forth nervously behind his large desk, but Vernon lunged over to the huge marble fireplace against one wall. The fireplace was an anachronism, evidently someone's idea of style in a country where the temperature never justified blazing logs on the hearth, but it did have a convenient set of utensils, and Vernon grabbed the brass-plated poker.

"You want to get out of this office?" Vernon yelled. "Then you'll have to get past me you slimy little twerp!" He waved the poker over his head and tossed it deftly back and forth from hand to hand. "Come on! What are you waiting for? Let's do it, Dane!"

"You're absolutely mad!" Stileforth screamed, but he retreated behind the high-backed swivel chair, still hopping from one foot to the other in terror. "Listen," he stammered, "I know that you're under a lot of pressure, and I know that none of this was your fault any more than it was mine. We could draft a message together, right now. I could recommend that you be withdrawn, for medical reasons, no bad mark on your record there, what? You'd be back with your family and could get out of this hell hole."

"I like that, Stileforth. Let's hear some more," Vernon shouted, smashing the desk lamp with a swipe of the poker. "Maybe you could see your way clear to get me an early promotion, maybe an exceptional performance cash award too!"

"Certainly," Stileforth said, tears beginning to well up in his eyes. "Lord knows you've earned it. Maybe I haven't made it clear to you how much I've relied on your hard work and good judgement in these past few weeks. You've been a real brick, Jim, a brick!"

"You know, Dane?" Vernon said, dancing to match Stileforth's own frightened movements. "I was just thinking. If I were to smash your skull in, then *I* could write that cable all by myself, tell them pretty much whatever I wanted, couldn't I? Tell them how you went bonkers and attacked me and everything. I'd see that you got a decent burial though, don't worry about that."

Stileforth had now moved back into the very corner of the room, where he dropped down to the floor, his pale, thin hands fluttering in front of his face like tethered birds.

"That's more like it," Vernon said, taking another vicious swing at a floor lamp, shattering the bulb and knocking the shade across the room. "Now you just stay there and be a good boy, and we'll get along just fine." He began to bounce around the open area in front of the desk in a kind of primitive warrior's victory dance.

†

Baca knelt on the roof of a two-story warehouse overlooking the highway bridge over the Ozama River. To his right some men were setting up a tripod on which they mounted an American M60 machine-gun and a Sagger anti-tank missile. Across the street he could see another team setting up a .50 calibre. On the floor below him, other men had Armbrust anti-tank rockets. There was a small plaza to his front, at the center of a traffic circle leading to the bridge. Other fighters, in pairs or singly, were making their way toward positions from which they would cover this end of the bridge. There was a small army outpost, manned by four sleepy soldiers, at each end of the bridge, supposedly checking the cargos and papers of buses and trucks which continued to cross in both directions, but, because of the rain, the soldiers were staying inside their small sheds and just watching the vehicles pass by.

When he could see that all his fighters were in position, Baca picked up a small radio transmitter and keyed the mike twice. Several blocks behind him, up the main avenue leading through the city, the motor of a large diesel truck roared to life, and the vehicle lurched out into the sparse traffic. The flat-fronted tractor was pulling a long trailer on which was loaded an immense preformed concrete beam, which had originally been intended to be part of a bridge somewhere. Baca thought it particularly appropriate that it now be used to close off a bridge.

The truck picked up speed as it moved around the traffic circle, although still only going about ten miles per hour. It passed the guard shack, and the bridge shook with the vibration of its weight and speed. When the truck reached the midway point on the bridge, the driver suddenly jerked the wheel sharply to the left, sending the cab bouncing over the low divider strip and across the oncoming lanes. The trailer jackknifed at the abrupt turn, wobbled a moment, and then tipped over, the concrete beam firmly blocking three of the four lanes of traffic, while the cab blocked the remaining one. The driver and his assistant leaped from the cab, carrying their automatic rifles and quickly took cover among the steel girders supporting the bridge superstructure. Baca clapped his hands. Even through the curtain of rain he could see that the placement of the block had been perfect, enough to stop any immediate movement and yet easy enough to open up to limited traffic when the time came.

One of the soldiers stepped out cautiously into the rain to see what had happened. He peered at the wreck, one hand shading his eyes, as if from a bright sun, as cars and trucks coming from both directions began to back up, their horns honking furiously. It would be curfew time in less than an hour, and everyone wanted to get to their destination in a hurry.

The soldier appeared to have finally made the decision to walk down to the wreck and investigate personally, when the sound of automatic weapons fire cut through the din of the car horns. A muzzle flash appeared from the shadows next to the bridge, and the soldier doubled over as bullets tore through him. The other soldiers in the guard shack never had time to get up from their card game as .50 calibre rounds tore through the thin plywood walls and shredded them where they sat. A couple of shots rang out from the guards at the far end of the bridge, but the fire of the truck driver and his aide quickly silenced them as the guards turned and fled into the night.

The drivers of the other vehicles immediately forgot their rage at having their way blocked, and made frantic maneuvers trying to escape the firing. A small red Datsun bounced over the median strip, and the driver floored the accelerator, but an old green pick-up truck had had the same idea and smashed into the Datsun broadside as he made his turn. In a moment there had been a dozen similar collisions, and the surviving drivers and passengers abandoned their vehicles and ran screaming from the scene. Baca smiled as he radioed in his "mission accomplished" signal.

Luis had opted to accompany the team which would seize the television station. Although it was arguably the radio station which would really reach the most people with the santistas' message, the television station was a much bigger place physically, and needed to be secured before they could begin transmission. While the radio stations probably had no security, this television station was known to have a private guard force of perhaps a dozen men. Of course, they wouldn't be much of a challenge to Luis' command, but there was no point in taking any chances.

The complex was surrounded by a tall wrought iron fence and had its own massive generators around back for a power supply. Since its equipment was the newest in the city, Lazaro had chosen it as the one which the terrorists would capture, rather than disable.

Luis had a total of ten fighters with him. One of them had had considerable training in television equipment in Iran, but they were counting on "convincing" as many technicians as necessary of the wisdom of cooperating with the new government, getting in on the ground floor, as it were. He had ambushed a news crew from this station earlier in the evening as it roved the city, killing its four members in a brief, but for Luis, satisfying action. He now rode in the front passenger seat of the small yellow and blue van with the station's logo on the doors as they pulled up to the gate. The guard, from the dry comfort of his control booth, waved at them and opened the electric gate. As they pulled through, one of the men in the back of the van opened the door, hopped out, and dispatched the guard with a burst from his silenced Uzi. The gate stood open now, and another van followed the first up to the main building of the compound. A lone terrorist took the dead guard's position, pressing a button to close the gate behind them.

Luis' van pulled up to the front entrance, while the other sped up and drove around to the loading docks in the rear. Several of the terrorists bailed out of the other van and spread out around the artfully landscaped grounds, searching out any other security men, eliminating them, and then setting up their own defensive positions in the shrubbery.

Luis had three people with him now, two men and a woman. Luis wore a reporter's trenchcoat, which he had picked up from the ambushed news crew. He found it fine camouflage, in addition to conveniently concealing his Uzi with its long silencer under its folds. The others looked like typical news crew support team, except that the battery belt one of the men wore actually contained fragmentation grenades, and the various satchels the others lugged did not have sound equipment but rather munitions and explosives.

There were two uniformed security men at the information desk to the right of the broad entry hall. They tried to wave Luis over as he strode past, the woman member of the team walked up to them with a welcoming smile. She placed her shoulder bag on the counter and fished inside, apparently for the group's identification, but came out with a Beretta automatic with silencer, and killed both men with a single shot each.

The receptionist and other people in the lobby area now realized that something was terribly wrong, and one woman screamed. Luis threw back the flap of his trenchcoat and fired a burst from his Uzi at a row of wall lights, shattering the bulbs and sending a shower of plaster chips across the floor.

"Everyone be quiet and obey instructions, and you won't be hurt," he shouted.

One of his men who had gone around to the back entrance then appeared in the lobby. He gave Luis a hand signal to indicate that they had found and killed two security men and that all was well. While one of the terrorists rounded up the hysterical people in the lobby and another herded forward another group that had been rousted out of offices in the back, Luis quickly led two others to the studio set up for the news broadcast. He knew exactly where to go.

They burst through the double doors into the studio to the accompaniment of screams and shouts of protest from the crew. One soundman lunged at Luis with some kind of wrench, but Luis cut him down with a burst of gunfire in the chest. Luis just shook his head at the thought that this man, who was essentially a worker, would have so distorted an idea of the society in which he lived and was exploited, that he would actually attack someone who had dedicated his life to freeing him.

The newscaster was already sitting behind the long table on which his notes rested with a little paper bib around his neck, the kind the dentist uses, while a young woman worked on his makeup. The woman ducked under the table, while the newscaster sat bolt upright, scattering his script across the set. One of the terrorists stormed into the control booth, holding the technicians at gunpoint, while the other took up a position at the back of the studio from which he could cover the rest of the workers.

Luis walked casually forward, his submachinegun now openly displayed. He stopped in front of the news desk and swept the pages of the script onto the floor. With his free hand he reached into his inside coat pocket and pulled out some neatly folded sheets of paper, which he lay in front of the anchorman.

"This will be your text for this evening's broadcast," he said in a quiet voice. "I see that we still have a few minutes until the end of that Brazilian soap opera, and I wouldn't want to interrupt that, so we'll just wait patiently. By the way, I'm a big fan. I really am," he added, patting the trembling journalist on the shoulder.

†

Quiroga hauled back on the handbrake of the tanker truck as he parked in front of the gas station. He had learned that the underground tanks of the service station were virtually empty, which was why the place had been abandoned. However, the driver of the gasoline tanker had been only too willing to cooperate with Quiroga when the latter had explained to him the alternatives. The driver had given Quiroga the keys, shown him how to open the valves at the back of the truck, and had gratefully run off into the stormy night to seek another line of employment.

Quiroga had stopped the truck directly between the idle pumps and the station building itself. Arce had been waiting for him and had opened up the access panels to the underground tanks. Quiroga calculated that there must be enough fumes in the tanks, in addition to oil and other combustibles stored in the building to contribute something to a fire. He raised his wrist, twisting his watch to read the hour in the dim light. It was time.

He hopped down from the cab, instinctively ducking his head as large raindrops pelted him and quickly soaked through his thin, dark blue police fatigue uniform and plastered his hair to his skull. He ran around the back of the truck, lifted the lever the driver had indicated, then spun open a valve. Gallon after gallon of gasoline gushed from the drain under the truck as Quiroga sprinted over to where Arce stood next to a large yellow school bus he had commandeered for the evening.

When he had escaped the reach of the spreading fuel, he stopped and freed a large, cylindrical white phosphorus grenade from his belt. He spread his feet, cocked his right arm, and pulled the safety pin from the grenade with his left. He hurled the grenade in the general direction of the truck with all his might, then roughly slapped Arce on the shoulder, shoving him toward the bus door and scrambled in after him.

The grenade tumbled end over end as it arced through the air and clattered to the pavement. A moment later, an intense white flame and billowing smoke erupted from it, but only for a fraction of a second, as the entire scene was almost immediately engulfed in an immense ball of fire. The force of the blast blew out the plate glass windows of the station, and the flames licked into the structure, igniting piles of oily rags, sticks of furniture, and oil-soaked cardboard boxes, adding to the conflagration. The two men crouched behind the windshield of the bus, watching the flames settle down into a roaring, steady blaze for a moment. Then Arce put the bus in gear and pulled slowly out onto the highway.

†

Chris was desperately battling with the controls of the Skytrader as winds buffeted the craft up and down and from side to side. Colonel Miller was at her side in the co-pilot's seat, attempting to help her handle the aircraft. He was a qualified private pilot, although he didn't have nearly the experience of the young army captain.

"There it is!" Miller called out, pointing to a miniature mushroom cloud of flame and smoke which suddenly appeared almost dead ahead of the bouncing plane's nose.

"Right on time, too," Chris added. "So far, so good." She bent forward and checked her instruments again and adjusted the heading of the plane slightly. She touched the transmit switch on her intercom headset. "Touchdown in two minutes, gentlemen. The captain has turned on the seat belt sign," she purred over the intercom. "For your safety and comfort, do NOT wait until the aircraft comes to a complete halt, but get your butts out of the plane anyway you can as soon as you feel something under the wheels that's thicker than fog. And thank you for flying Air Terror."

Lafeur was too sick to smile. The men in the back of the plane were packed in tightly with their weapons and munitions. Every jolt of turbulence sent Lafeur jamming into the shoulder of the Marine next to him, or vice versa, crushed him down into the seat, or sent him straining upward against the protective restraint of the seat belt. Every item of food he had eaten in the past forty-eight hours seemed to be doing a pass in review up his throat as he struggled to keep it down, a struggle from which not all of the passengers had emerged victorious. He had never enjoyed flying in small airplanes, and it seemed to him now that he had had larger ones than this hanging from the ceiling of his room when he was a boy. At this rate, he thought, dealing with the terrorists would come as a distinct relief, anything so long as he did it on solid ground.

Chris pulled back on the controls at the same time as she eased the throttle forward. She would need to "push" power a lot to stay aloft while slowing her forward speed sufficiently to let her land within the limited space available. The knoll behind the burning gas station rushed by scant meters beneath the belly of the plane.

"Thirty seconds!" she shouted into the intercom. "Here we come, ready or not!" She let out a shrill rebel yell. Miller stole a glance at her and shook his head. Chris was hunched over the controls, her eyes squinting slightly as she tried to see through the darkness, rain, and low clouds to pick out the white garden wall of the house, which would be their last landmark. A mildly insane smile turned up the corners of her mouth.

†

A pickup truck scraped to a halt in the gravel driveway of the telephone central. Two men climbed out of the cab, and another eight hopped out the back. All were carrying automatic rifles. They took a hurried look around them, and then four of them rushed through the front door of the building, while the others ran around back.

At this hour of the evening, there were no customers in the building and none of the regular office workers or cashiers, but there would be a full staff of technicians to handle possible breakdowns. The terrorists had also been warned to expect at least one security guard, although he would only be a typical rent-a-cop, perhaps armed with a shotgun.

The leader of the group was first through the door. He quickly scanned the reception area and saw only empty cashiers' booths and desks, as expected. He left one man to watch the door and led the way through another doorway which led to the technicians' offices and the rack rooms which occupied the rear two-thirds of the building.

He cleared the doorway and jumped to one side, allowing the men behind him a clear field of fire. There were two technicians in blue coveralls hunched over some machinery in the corner of the room. To get their attention, the leader fired a burst from his G3 automatic rifle toward the ceiling.

The two men spun around, but, they did not have the pliers and screw drivers in their hands as the terrorists had expected. The leader of the attackers was virtually cut in half by the first burst of the policeman's Uzi, before he even had a chance to bring the barrel of his weapon back down level. The next man through the door caught two or three rounds from the same burst, but, hit in the legs, he managed to get off a shot which killed one of the policemen in turn. The surviving policeman flattened himself against the wall and hurled a concussion grenade into the hall. After the resulting flash and bang, he spun away from the wall again, braced himself in the doorway, and let loose a long burst of fire, sweeping the hall from side to side. The stunned terrorists were cut down without being able to fire a shot in their own defense.

The terrorists in back of the telephone were bounding up the steps to the small loading dock when they first heard the sound of firing. Most of them assumed that this was from their own men, scaring the workers inside into quiescence or perhaps dealing with an unusually intransigent employee. Only one of the men, one of the original santistas, recognized the reports as belonging to Uzis, not the G3s of the attackers, but this only caused him to move all the faster to take any defenders in the rear.

When the knot of men had almost reached the door at the end of the loading dock, they were startled by the sound of scraping metal and running chains as the steel shutters which covered one of the large loading bays to their left suddenly was lifted about two feet from the ground. Most of the attackers were directly in front of this bay when the M60 machinegun hidden within simultaneously began coughing fire at them, tearing the legs out from under three of them in a matter of seconds and sending the others diving for cover in the gravel driveway below the dock.

Two of the survivors cowered against the bumper guards of the dock, and only the lone santista had the presence of mind to fumble in the shoulder bag he carried for a hand grenade.

"Freeze!" a deep voice thundered from the shadows at the edge of the driveway.

"For the Lord!" the *santista* screamed as he cocked his arm and tried to pull the safety pin from the grenade with his rain-slick fingers. A single shot rang out, and he crumpled to the ground, a dark stream of blood gushing from what had been his right eye. The other two men quickly dropped their weapons and thrust their hands skyward.

†

From his position on the rooftop near the bridge, Pablo could see the sites where several of the santistas' bombs had been planted. They would knock out the radio and television stations that the santistas themselves would not be controlling. Those bomb sites which were not in view were still within easy range of the powerful radio transmitter that the demolitions man, Jaime, had set up under cover of a roof of corrugated tin to protect the equipment from the rain. Jaime knelt before a square black box with a large silver antenna and rows of dials, knobs and a digital number pad on its face.

Pablo nodded to Jaime. "Hit number one," he said, and raised his binoculars as he scanned the horizon on the far side of the bridge for the radio tower that was located there. Jaime punched in a number code on the transmitter, then pressed a red-lighted button at the bottom. There was a flash in the distance which revealed the tower that Pablo had been unable to pick out in the gloom. In the light of a small fire that the explosion started at its base, Pablo could see the tower first lean drunkenly to one side, then topple over. It was too far away to hear more than a dull thump from the small but carefully placed charge, but the job had been done.

"We'd better do the other bridge now, before the army gets organized," Pablo said, gesturing with his chin to the smaller highway bridge about half a mile downstream. He shifted the angle of his binoculars and waited while Jaime punched in the next number code and pressed the red button. He could see the row of headlights coming west across the bridge and the red tail lights of those headed the other way. He braced himself for the blast, since this involved a much larger quantity of explosives, designed to drop the center span into the river. He waited, but nothing happened.

Pablo turned quickly toward Jaime. Jaime was frantically punching the code buttons again, and again hit the red button. Pablo turned back toward the bridge, but nothing.

"Could the problem be in the transmitter?" Pablo asked, a note of nervousness betraying itself in his voice.

"I don't think so," Jaime answered, as he tried to detonate the charge twice more. "If that had been the problem, the first charge wouldn't have blown either. No, it has to be with the charge itself."

"Well, get the hell down there and check it out," he shouted. "Take the jeep and a few men to cover you, and hurry."

Jaime was already disappearing down the stairs before Pablo had time to finish his sentence. He turned his binoculars back to the bridge. It was difficult to tell from this distance, but it still looked as though it was only civilian traffic crossing. It would take the army some time yet to get on the road, but he didn't have enough men or firepower to hold both bridges against a serious assault. Of course, he tried to reassure himself, the odds were that the army troops wouldn't even budge from their bases, if Padre Lazaro's plans went right. Then a nagging little voice inside his head mentioned to him that they were already starting to go wrong, weren't they?

He raced over to the transmitter and knelt beside it. He fished in his soaked shirt pocket for the slip of paper with the number codes for the other charges. While Jaime was gone, at least he could take care of this. He found the paper and carefully unfolded the soggy note. He pulled a flashlight from his belt and shone it on the somewhat runny numbers, breathing a sigh of relief when he saw that he could still read them.

Pablo punched in the first code. It was for another radio transmitter on this side of the river. It would be out of his line of sight, but he should be able to hear the explosion. He hit the red button, and a few moments later he was rewarded with the dull crump which he felt as much as heard. He punched in the code for one of the television transmitters next.

†

Jaime's jeep careened through the streets where rainwater was often up over the curbs due to the poor drainage system. He pulled to a stop about two hundred yards from the bridge. There was a small guard shack at this bridge as well, and the guards might have been alerted by the sound of firing a few minutes earlier, but they might also have taken the opportunity to end unilaterally their periods of enlistment. There was no sign of them now, but two of the men in the back of the jeep took up positions from which they could provide covering fire if necessary. Jaime grabbed a bag of tools and a pistol and raced for the river's edge. The charges were placed at the point where the bridge itself left the abutments, one at either end. He would check this side first. Then they would drive across and check the other, hoping only that Pablo didn't decide to test the circuit once more in the meantime.

Jaime gave a quick hand signal to the man who accompanied him, pointing to a pile of rubbish from which he would be able to cover the last ten meters of his approach. He then dashed to the bridge itself and flattened his body against the concrete supports. He took a moment to catch his breath and to listen for danger. The only sound was the rumble of passing trucks and cars overhead and the constant drumming of the rain.

He pulled a flashlight from his bag and edged out onto the narrow walkway between the bridge supports and the water. He flicked on the light and played it along the top of the bridge support where he had placed the explosives the previous night. There was nothing there.

"Looking for this, asshole?" a harsh voice came from somewhere behind him.

Jaime spun around and saw the silhouette of a man standing by the water's edge. He was casually tossing up and catching something that looked like a block of PE-2 plastic explosive. Jaime dropped the flashlight and tried to raise his gun, but he heard the muffled cough of a silenced pistol. He felt the bullet smack into his forehead, fought for his balance for a second, and then tumbled into the murky brown water of the sluggish Ozama.

†

Luis glanced up at the large clock on the back wall of the television control room. The news program was scheduled to start in about one minute, at ten o'clock. The technicians were sitting like statues at their work stations, with a grim-faced terrorist braced against the back wall, covering them with his G3. The newscaster was gripping the edge of his desk with both hands, unable to move, but a couple of the stage crew had recovered enough to gather up his copy and arrange it, to remove his make-up bib and straighten his tie. On top of the news copy was now a single sheet of typescript with the announcement of the coup by the santista movement, declaring it as the only legitimate government of the country and giving officials of the former government twelve hours to leave the country voluntarily. Otherwise, "revolutionary justice tribunals" would investigate everything from nepotism to graft to "atrocities against the Dominican people," and justice would be "swift and final." After the reading of the declaration, the television would broadcast a videotape made by Padre Lazaro himself, explaining in more detail the philosophy of the revolution and naming the new government's ministers. Luis had already seen the tape placed in the video machines by the technician awaiting his cue to play it. This would be followed by a series of revolutionary propaganda tapes in Spanish, obtained from various sources, such as the Peruvian Sendero Luminoso and the Colombian M-19 movements, which would play for hours, interspersed with repeats of the original announcement of the revolution. The purpose of this would be to demonstrate the control of the Guerra Santa movement over the country and the inability of the former government to silence them. Meanwhile, the same message would be broadcast over the one radio station controlled by the *santistas*, while the other television and radio stations would have been silenced by Jaime's explosives.

The second hand on the large wall clock swept around toward twelve. Luis nodded to the control room technicians, who pressed their buttons and cued the newscaster. Just then, there was a loud noise, like a very close clap of thunder from just outside the building, and the lights in the station went out. The only illumination was now provided by a few battery-powered emergency lights in the hallways.

"What the hell?" Luis shouted.

A woman in the studio screamed, and everyone began ducking for cover and dashing for the exits. Luis fired off a long burst in the direction of the news set, but he couldn't be certain that he had hit anyone. He saw a burst of fire tear into the ceiling of the control room, and he realized that the shadowy figures were the technicians, struggling with the terrorist there for his weapon. Luis loosed another burst which shattered the windows on the front of the booth in a cascade of broken glass, hoping that the technicians would shield his man.

Another terrorist backed up against Luis, firing indiscriminately.

"What happened?" the man shouted over the din of screams, moans of pain, and falling equipment.

"How the hell should I know? Maybe that idiot Jaime made a mistake and placed his charges on the generators here instead of one of the other stations."

"No way, boss," the man replied. "I was with him as an escort when he placed them last night. He didn't come within a block of here."

"Shit!" Luis hissed. "Pull back to the main entrance. This place is no good to us now. We've got to link up with the reserve team. I've got a feeling that this is all going to hell very fast, and we've got to be ready to move in a different direction."

The two men moved quickly for the door, shouting to their comrades to join them. Luis dropped his empty magazine and loaded a fresh one, firing at moving shadows as they moved toward the entrance. After a moment, the terrified television personnel, those who survived, realized that their safest bet was not to try to escape, but to lay low and let the terrorists leave on their own. When the tight group of attackers had congregated in the lobby, Luis found that the terrorist from the control room had apparently not survived, and he heard from one of the women fighters that another had been killed by a janitor who crushed his skull with a fire extinguisher before she had done for the janitor. Amid a stream of curses in Spanish and Farsi, the group dashed out into the rain and piled into their vehicles.

†

Padre Lazaro sat next to Abdol Reza on the tattered couch in his headquarters. Several of his men had been monitoring radio stations and had heard them go off the air, one by one. In the storm, reception from the tactical radios of the various teams had been poor. He had heard Pablo's initial report of his success in blocking the main bridge and of Luis' seizure of the television station, but later messages had been broken up and difficult to understand. There was some kind of trouble at the bridges, but that could well prove secondary as long as the rest of the plan worked, Lazaro consoled himself. There had also been a report from the team assigned to screen the National Police headquarters, something about heavy fighting and some losses, but then the transmission had been cut off, probably by interference from the storm, Lazaro thought. Since the role of this team had mainly been to tie up possible police reinforcements going out to the primary targets, this unit was apparently fulfilling its mission, and some casualties had been expected, after all.

A small television set had been placed on a table facing the sofa, with the sound turned way down, while the soap opera played out the final minutes of today's episode. Lazaro and Abdol Reza stared blankly at the screen, listening to several radios, all tuned to different frequencies, and waiting for the picture on the screen to change. There was some sort of tragic confrontation taking place in the waiting room of a hospital, and an elderly woman was obviously not taking well some news that a heavily moussed young man was providing. Finally, the credits began to roll, and Lazaro leaned forward a bit further.

Suddenly, one of the women fighters came into the room and whispered to Lazaro. "The radio station we were going to use for our broadcast has gone off the air, Padre."

Lazaro was silent for a moment, and he caught Abdol Reza casting him a sidelong glance with one eyebrow raised. "It's not important," Lazaro said. "They probably had to make some adjustments to the equipment before making our announcement. It's still about thirty seconds before the time. Keep monitoring."

The woman nodded and quietly slipped from the room.

"Trouble?" Abdol Reza asked, being careful to keep his eyes on the television screen, which was now in the midst of a commercial which involved a walking tube of toothpaste defeating hordes of bouncy green things which were trying to attack a row of sparkling white teeth.

"Nothing really," Lazaro replied with a wave of the hand. "In an operation this complicated, one doesn't expect everything to work out exactly as planned. 'Man proposes, and God disposes,' you know. Still, we are well ahead of the game and have seized all of the important objectives without much trouble. Our main problem right now is the poor communications caused by the storm, which only magnify our own worries and blow them out of proportion."

Just then, there was a moment of static on the screen as the victorious tube of toothpaste was about to receive the adulation of his toothy proteges, followed for a moment by a scrambled image.

"Here it comes," Lazaro said, bouncing slightly in his seat and clasping his hands firmly together.

The screen went to the dark snowy image which signified "dead air" in television parlance.

"What?" Lazaro said, under his breath. "Just wait a minute. They must be shifting connections of some sort at the studio." But the image remained unchanged as the seconds ticked off. The veins on Lazaro's temples began to stand out from his head in sharp relief, and he impatiently grabbed for the remote control which lay on an end table next to him. He first turned up the volume, but the only sound was the rushing noise of static. Then he tried changing channels. The American ones were also dead, indicating that the satellite reception facility had been destroyed, but as Lazaro rapidly flicked through the channels, there was the brief shadow of a seated man on the screen and he had to pause and go back. Finally, the image returned, but it was not the newscaster Lazaro had expected to see, nor his own videotape. It was on another channel entirely.

The image was of a man in a police uniform, seated at a desk and reading from a sheet of paper in front of him. Lazaro turned up the volume further.

". . . inability of the former government to deal with the acts of terrorism which have covered our nation in blood or to withstand the pressure from foreign powers and defend the national sovereignty, the National Police and Armed Forces have removed President Selich from office and have formed a triumvirate to head a provisional government formed of Army Commander, Major General Aurelio Tamayo, Colonel Leon Calvo, Commander of the First Brigade, and myself, Colonel Antonio Palacios of the National Police. All citizens are advised to remain in their homes, and all security forces will henceforth take their orders directly from the triumvirate . . ."

"What?" Lazaro screamed, hurling the remote control against the wall, where it shattered into hundreds of pieces. "They've stolen our coup! Where is Luis? Where is Baca? What have they done?"

†

At that moment Baca was huddled behind the scant protection of the parapet of the roof on which he had his command post. Several large calibre rounds had already penetrated the parapet in places, one of them disemboweling the gunner of the Sagger missile before he had a chance to fire. Baca had been trying to raise Lazaro or Luis or the reserve team on the radio, but evidently there was enemy jamming of the airwaves. When he managed to sneak a peek over the low wall, he could see that a column of Army halftracks had crossed the other highway bridge with strong infantry support and were pressing back the squad he had sent to contain them when he had realized that Jaime wasn't having any success in blowing the bridge. Another infantry force, at least a company in strength, was working its way across the main bridge in front of him, fighting from girder to girder against the fanatical resistance of the handful of fighters facing them. And now a Navy ship, the gunboat *Separacion*, sister ship to the *Cambiasco* which the santistas had sunk earlier in the war, had chugged upriver and was raking Baca's positions with fire from her two 3-inch and three 20mm guns. A force of Dominican marines had apparently landed upriver from Baca's location and was working down to put pressure on him from three sides.

†

The fixed landing gear of Skytrader dug deep into the soggy grass of the football field, rudely throwing the passengers forward in their seats and nearly tipping the plane up on its nose, but Chris had enough of an angle on the flaps to maintain control, and the aircraft fishtailed to a stop within inches of the house.

Miller was out of his seat well before the plane stopped moving, shouting "Go! Go! Go!" as he bodily shoved the men out the rear loading ramp. Just as they had rehearsed, the men peeled off into two separate squads, one to each side of the plane, the first fanning out to clear the grounds, and the other rushing into the building to look for Featherstone. The inside team was led by Miller himself and included Lafeur, Gosher, Majid, and two marines. The outside team was led by Gunny Besserman and Escobar, Fiore, and three other marines, with Chris leaping out of the cockpit door with a .45 automatic to cover the plane.

Fiore ran around one side of the house with one of the marines hard on his heels, and almost ran headlong into a woman running hard in the other direction. The woman wore Army fatigues and had a mop of straggly, soaking black hair. She screamed when she saw Fiore and started firing her Uzi long before she had brought the barrel around, but Fiore, who had opted to use his own snub-nosed .38 had the advantage of her and placed two rounds in the base of her throat, about an inch apart. The woman skidded in the mud, coming to a stop against a cement planter near the pool.

Fiore heard firing coming from the far side of the house and desperately tried to determine who was shooting at whom, and who had come out on top. He and the marines took up positions behind some decorative shrubs near the front entrance, trying to make out something through the sheets of rain which lashed the ground. Finally, they saw the familiar shape of Gunny Besserman emerge from around the corner and wave to them. The outside perimeter was secure.

Besserman posted his guards and returned to where Chris was inspecting the aircraft.

"Can't you get this thing turned around in case we have to get the hell out of here in a hurry . . ., sir?" he added after an embarrassed pause.

"I'd love to, Gunny," Chris answered, "but look at this." She walked him around to the left side of the airplane. The strut for the left landing gear had snapped off when the plane had swerved, burying the jagged stump deep in the soft ground. "The only way this baby is getting out of here is on the back of a trailer."

"Shit!" the Gunny said, taking a gratuitous kick at the crippled machine. "I guess we'll have to walk home after all."

Miller led the way into the house through the broken sliding glass doors off the patio. A tall black man, clad only in gym shorts, but carrying a G-3 assault rifle, emerged from what was probably the kitchen area, firing wildly. His first burst missed Miller, who had dived into the adjacent hallway, but it caught a marine, the next man through the door, full in the chest. His body armor absorbed most of the rounds, although the impact knocked him back against the wall, and one bullet tore through his upper arm, sending his rifle clattering across the floor.

Majid came in next, doing a neat tuck and roll across the floor as bullets chewed up the sofa behind him. He sprang to his feet in one smooth motion, and stitched a half dozen rounds from his Galil horizontally across the doorway, cutting the black man nearly in two.

"*Allah u akbar*!" he shouted as he raced up the stairs to check out that part of the house.

Lafeur charged in behind Majid carrying a Remington pump shotgun he had borrowed from the Marines. He hadn't been confident enough of his marksmanship to accept one of the Galils, and he speculated that, within the confines of a house, even he couldn't miss with a shotgun. He took a quick glance at the marine, who was obviously hurt, but had already struggled to his feet and was going to retrieve his weapon.

Lafeur continued on his way, looking for an entrance to a basement. He finally found a narrow staircase leading downward and was about to descend when DeSoto shoved him brusquely out of the way.

"Excuse me, sir," DeSoto said flatly, the edge of the bandage around his head just visible under his "Fritz" helmet. "This is my job." And he charged down the stairs.

Featherstone had been aware of a great deal of activity in the house all night. Although the door to the cellar room was thick and tight in its frame, he could hear the thud of doors slamming, and the tromping of footsteps on the floor overhead. Things had seemed to quiet down an hour or two earlier, but now they had picked up again.

While he didn't regret not having a mirror to see what he might look like, it seemed to him that his injuries hadn't been as bad as all that. The swelling in his face and body had gone down, although he suspected that at least one of his ribs might be broken, due to the knife-like pain which jabbed into his side every time he turned his torso. Still, he could see out of both eyes now, and could move his jaw almost normally. He had just finished off the water in his bottle and was wondering whether that had been a wise idea, never knowing when they might bring a refill, when Pedro burst through the door, slamming it shut behind him and leaning up against it, panting.

"It's started!" Pedro whispered unnecessarily.

"What's started?" Featherstone asked, coming to his knees painfully and hanging on the wire mesh of the cage.

"They're here!" was the ambiguous reply.

"Who's here, Pedro?" Featherstone asked in a dull tone, trying to hide the terror in his heart.

"Your people. They've come for you!" Pedro said.

Featherstone's heart almost jumped out of his throat, and then he noticed that Pedro had an automatic pistol in his hand.

Lafeur could hear more firing and an occasional scream coming from elsewhere in the house as he followed DeSoto down the stairs at breakneck speed. The stairway had a right turn, halfway down, and DeSoto paused when he reached it. When Lafeur had caught up, DeSoto nodded, and the two of them leaped around the corner together, DeSoto erect and Lafeur on his knees.

A burly man in a tank top shirt was standing at the bottom of the stairs, holding an automatic rifle. He fired, but too high, and Lafeur squeezed his trigger before the man could adjust. Lafeur had to shoot lefthanded because of the angle of the turn, but at that range the buckshot tore off the man's face, and the shotgun kicked viciously. His scream was lost in a gurgle of blood as he collapsed to the floor.

Lafeur jacked another round into the chamber as he got to his feet, but DeSoto was already at the bottom of the stairs, blazing away into the room which opened off to his left. Lafeur followed as quickly as he could, but he reached the bottom just in time to see DeSoto hit, just above the top of his flak jacket. He turned slowly toward Lafeur clutching weakly at the jagged hole in his throat, his mouth agape. Then his knees buckled, and he fell.

Lafeur let out an animal yell of rage and fear and stuck the barrel of his shotgun around the corner and fired. He loaded another round and dove into the room, twisting in the air to land on his back, his gun pointed in the direction of the unseen enemy. He fired again, blindly, but no one was there. There was one body sprawled backwards across a table loaded with what looked like radio gear and another atop an overturned chair, probably cut down by DeSoto. An open door led into another room beyond.

Lafeur scrambled to his feet, but a dark form raced past him to the door. It was Majid, running low to the ground, his Galil pointed in the same direction as his fiery dark eyes. He charged through the doorway without stopping, and Lafeur rushed to catch up. There was a flurry of firing in the next room, and Lafeur spun around the doorframe, his shotgun levelled.

Majid was lying face down on the floor in a pool of blood. Opposite him, in a sitting position against the far wall, was another man, bearded and swarthy like Majid, wearing a dark suit with a white shirt, buttoned to the neck with no tie. The shirt below the breastbone was now stained a rich red color, and the man's dark eyes stared at Lafeur unblinkingly. Another doorway led to a short flight of steps leading farther down.

Pedro had walked slowly across the room toward the cage. He

didn't speak. He stopped and stood there. Featherstone thought to close his eyes, but then he reasoned that it wouldn't make it hurt any less, and since he would only see this sort of thing once in his lifetime, it would be foolish to miss it. Indeed, the weapon in Pedro's hand now held Featherstone's total attention. He had never seen anything quite so interesting in his entire life.

Suddenly, the door flew open again, and Padre Lazaro charged in, an Uzi in his hand, the barrel still smoking.

"Kill him, you idiot!" he screamed at Pedro. "What are you waiting for?" He stormed up closer, so that both Pedro and Lazaro were within a foot of the cage, facing each other.

"No," Pedro said, quietly but firmly. "I won't."

"Traitor!" Lazaro shouted, raising his weapon and pointing it at Pedro. "Do as I command!"

"No," he said, simply, dropping his weapon to the floor and going down on his knees, his arms outstretched to his sides and his head bowed.

"Don't you dare pretend to be a believer, you scum!" Lazaro screamed shrilly, placing the muzzle of his Uzi against Pedro's forehead. "The Lord has commanded you, and you have rejected him, Judas!"

"You are not the Lord," Pedro said calmly, and his lips began to move softly in mumbled prayer.

"No!" someone screamed, and Featherstone realized that it was himself screaming. He lunged forward, ignoring the stab of pain in his side, and thrust his arm through the opening in the cage gate. He grasped Lazaro's crotch with all his might and squeezed. Lazaro's weapon fired, but the barrel jerked up, the rounds tearing into the ceiling, sending ricochets twanging around the tiny room.

Lafeur burst through the door at that moment. His mouth open in shock, he threw his shotgun to his shoulder and fired, collapsing the side of Lazaro's head and finally jerking his body out of Featherstone's desperate grasp.

Featherstone's arm was still extended through the gate, but his shoulders were now heaving with uncontrolled panting and sobbing. Lafeur was panting as well, as he stood and stared at the ambassador, kneeling in a cage in his underwear, his face and body a mass of bruises, with two teeth missing from his gaping mouth. Pedro remained in his kneeling position, as if nothing had happened.

"Jesus Christ, sir," Lafeur breathed. Then he shook himself and moved over to the gate to examine the locks, keeping his shotgun pointed warily at Pedro.

"Stand aside, Claude," Gosher said. Lafeur turned and saw the Israeli, limping badly from a leg wound, as he approached the cage. "You'd better move back, too, Mr. Ambassador," he said. "We'll have you out of there in a moment."

Featherstone slowly withdrew his arm and crawled on all fours to the far corner of the cage. Gosher aimed his weapon at the hasp of the first lock and fired, blowing it apart, then did the same with the second. He yanked the gate open and then got down on all fours himself, moving halfway inside the cage. He extended his hand to Featherstone.

"Come with us, sir. We're going to take you home."

Tears were streaming down Featherstone's face as he reached out and took Gosher's hand.

"Th-thank you," he forced himself to say. "I thought a moment ago that it was all over." He got stiffly to his feet, even though he had virtually to duckwalk out the small gate. He decided he had crawled enough for one lifetime. As soon as he was outside, he stood erect, slowly, using both Gosher and Lafeur for support. Then he pulled free and helped Pedro to his feet and the two of them supported each other as they headed toward the door.

"This boy tried to help me, you know," he said softly. He looked from Gosher to Lafeur. "I don't want anything to happen to him."

Gosher took the lead heading upstairs, as Lafeur took Featherstone's free arm over his shoulders. When they reached the room where Majid had died, Featherstone pulled away from them.

"Wait a minute," he said. "I'm not going outside looking like this."

"We're really not in a position to worry about appearances, Mr. Ambassador," Lafeur said. "We may have taken care of all of the terrorists here, but there are dozens more loose in the city, and they could be coming any minute."

"Too bad," Featherstone said, looking around. "This guy's about my size," he commented, pointing to Abdol Reza's body. "Help me get his pants off."

Lafeur shrugged and stooped to pull the pants off the dead man. Then he braced Featherstone's shoulders as he stiffly eased his legs into them.

"A little tight in the waist," Featherstone said, "but a week ago I couldn't have gotten them past my knees. So this whole thing hasn't been a total loss." He smiled weakly. "Get me his jacket too." It had some splotches of blood on the lapels, but Featherstone figured that it was dark, and no one would notice.

They reached the next room where two of the marines were preparing to carry DeSoto's body upstairs.

"Oh, God," Featherstone said, kneeling next to the body. He laid his hand gently on the young marine's chest. "If this is the price, you should never have come. We didn't come out ahead on the trade."

"He wanted to come, Mr. Featherstone," Lafeur answered. "We all did. We had to."

"Thank you, my friends," Featherstone sobbed, choking back more tears. He patted DeSoto's chest again, and they continued outside.

"Daddy!" Chris yelled when the group emerged from the building. She ran up to Featherstone but stopped short. "Jesus, you look awful!"

"I'm glad to see you too," Featherstone replied, wrapping his arms around his daughter's neck. "It's nothing that a shave, a shower, and a few weeks in traction won't fix."

"Let's get out of here, please," Lafeur whined a little.

"Sorry about that, Claude," Chris said. "I seem to have bent your friend's bird a little bit when we landed, and it isn't going anywhere. We've looked around, and the only car on the grounds got shot up pretty bad in a firefight between the guards and one of the Marines. I'm afraid we're stuck."

Lafeur smiled and raised a finger in the air, cocking his head to one side, as the sound of a claxon tore through the rushing of the windswept rain.

"There's something going on down by the front gate," one of the marines shouted from the front of the house.

Lafeur ran around to the entrance where Miller was eying a large yellow school bus stopped at the entrance gate. A white flag of some sort was waving frantically from the driver's window. Lafeur moved up to the cover of some low bushes and took a closer look just as Quiroga's face appeared in the driver's window.

"Don't shoot! It's only me," he shouted.

"Let him in," Lafeur yelled to Besserman, who was sighting along his Galil at the bus. "He's one of ours."

Quiroga jumped down from the bus and shook hands with Lafeur. "I hope you really need us after all, and we didn't come all this way for nothing."

"It turns out we were right, landing is easier than taking off," Lafeur laughed. "How goes the war?" Miller, Besserman and Fiore crowded around as Quiroga explained.

"I've got a police band radio, and I've been following the action. As near as I can figure, the army has a large group of terrorists surrounded by the Ozama river bridges, and they've driven them into a single building. There have been heavy casualties on both sides, but the terrorists are outnumbered and outgunned. The police massacred the groups that were supposed to take the telephone central and the radio station and who attacked the National Police barracks. Another group from the television station got away, although they've had at least one shootout with a roving police patrol. I can see that you all did your job here pretty well, so my guess would be that the Guerra Santa movement is history."

"Well, that's good news," Miller said. "We didn't know whether we were going to have to face another hundred of those bastards or not."

"What you probably haven't heard," Quiroga went on, "is that Palacios pulled a little trick of his own."

"I kind of figured he'd step in to settle the score with the santistas with the information we gave him," Lafeur said, "and from the sound of it, I guess he did."

"That's only half of it," Quiroga laughed. "I guess he thought the santistas' plan to seize control of the country sounded so good, that he did it himself."

"What?" Miller and Lafeur asked in unison.

"Well, instead of just setting up ambushes for the santistas and screwing up their plans, he adopted the plans himself. He just pulled the explosives off one each of the television and radio stations the santistas had planned to disable and put them on the ones the santistas were going to use themselves and knocked them off the air. Then he took over the stations he had saved himself and broadcast his own message. They've installed a military government and kicked old Selich out on his butt. So the military gets the best of both worlds. They boot out the old government for not being able to deal with the terrorists, which they couldn't deal with either, and at the same time we hand them the terrorists on a plate and they grease them, so they can start out with a clean slate."

"Stranger things have happened in Latin America, I suppose," Lafeur said.

The marines and the others had already started to load up the bus, which Arce had pulled up the broad circular driveway. Three of them gently carried DeSoto's body, which they placed across the back seat of the bus. Then they went back in and brought out Majid, placing him next to DeSoto. The rain continued to pour down, and the last stragglers were quickly gathered up, and Arce pulled the handle slamming the doors shut.

Inside the bus, the dripping, laughing people had already begun to jabber away excitedly, recounting their experiences, their fear, and the close calls. They gathered in little groups, the Featherstones together near the back, each lounging across a full bench seat, since there was plenty of room. Lafeur, Miller, and Gosher were animatedly discussing the political developments with Quiroga, and the marines were solemnly talking in low voices about their missing comrade. Escobar braced himself in the stepwell at the front of the bus, next to Arce, with Fiore leaning over the railing between them, while Pedro sat silently staring out the window just behind Escobar. Arce tooted the horn happily, and the bus lurched forward, down the driveway.

Suddenly, a white VW minivan screeched to a halt in the gateway, blocking the exit. Arce slammed on the brakes and leaned on his horn, his first reaction as an experienced Dominican driver. As he did so, a man popped up through the open sun roof, while another leaned out the passenger's window, and both sprayed the front of the bus with automatic weapons fire. The windshield of the bus first seemed to turn a milky white color as a million tiny fractures spread across it in all directions, and an instant later, it disintegrated. Arce, Pedro, and Escobar were killed instantly. Fiore was hit twice in the chest, but managed to drag himself out into the aisle, only to receive another round in the back which felled him.

"Quick, out the back!" Miller shouted, and a marine jumped out of his seat and kicked open the emergency escape door at the rear of the bus. He leaped to the ground and helped Featherstone and Chris clamber down. The Marines were firing wildly through the shattered windshield and out the windows. They had dropped the man in the sunroof, but Lafeur could see other vehicles outside the gate, all discharging armed men.

"Get up to the house," he yelled.

"We'll cover you. Go!" Besserman called back as he loosed another burst out his window. He grinned in a vicious way as he saw a dark figure collapse as it had tried to dash through the gate into the garden.

The two Featherstones had reached the small terrace at the entrance to the house, and Chris was firing furiously from behind the dubious protection afforded by the low shrubs. Lafeur and Quiroga joined them there.

"It must be that group that got away from the television station," Quiroga said, firing his service revolver with two hands at a figure that had scaled the garden wall to his left. "Damn!" he added as the figure dropped to the ground and moved away through the bushes.

"Don't you have some way to call for help?" Lafeur asked.

"What with? That wasn't a patrol car I was driving, you know."

"Wait a minute," Lafeur said, slapping his forehead with the heel of his hand. "They've got a whole room full of radio gear downstairs. If you know what frequencies to use, maybe you can get ahold of someone."

"It's worth a try," Quiroga said heading off in a running crouch for the front door with Lafeur hard on his heels.

Miller and Gosher had reached the terrace now, helping a wounded marine. Besserman and Washington were out of the bus, one firing around each side of it.

"Grenade!" screamed one of the Marines still in the bus, but a second later the cab of the bus erupted in a ball of flame, knocking Besserman and Washington to the ground. The shrieks of the two men still inside could be heard plainly over the clatter of gunfire, the roar of the flames, and the continuing drumming of the rain.

Besserman and the tall black Marine scrambled to their feet and raced for the terrace, vaulting over the shrubs.

"Jesus!" Besserman gasped as he tried to catch his breath. "I counted a dozen or more. We've scragged a few, but they're still coming. We've got to get inside and set up some kind of defense. These guys really seem to know what they're doing."

"I want a gun, dammit," Featherstone said. "I'm pretty fucking tired of being a victim here."

"There's plenty inside, Mr. Ambassador," Besserman said and they scuttled toward the large double doors of the house. "Help yourself."

Inside the house, the defenders formed a tight perimeter around the stairways both to the upper level and down to the basement since they didn't have enough people to cover the entire expanse of the ground level adequately. Featherstone scooped up an Uzi next to a body near the kitchen and found a couple of magazines already loaded nearby. They pulled furniture together to form makeshift breastworks and huddled behind them. They could hear the rush of the wind and the rain as it gusted through the glassless windows, causing the shredded drapes to wave like battle standards through the living room. They could also hear an occasional shouted command from outside.

"They must be regrouping, getting ready to hit us for real," Besserman said. "I think we hurt them pretty bad, and they'll need a minute to get organized."

Featherstone looked down at his weapon and worked the bolt back and forth. When he looked up, he saw Chris smiling at him from behind an overturned sofa, holding her .45 in front of her with both hands.

"Daddy's little girl," Featherstone said, returning her smile. "Thanks for coming."

"It's just my way of saying thanks for sitting up with me that night that I had an earache when I was six," she said.

"You remember that? I often wondered if you and Clare noticed that your mother and I were around."

"We probably noticed more when you weren't, but that wasn't very often. I remember that night, though. You let me watch TV with you very late and then read me stories to take my mind off it while the medicine had a chance to work. At some point I fell asleep."

"And here you are, covering your old Dad with a .45." He shook his head, then winced slightly, touching his hand to his side.

"Does it hurt?" she asked.

He shook his head again. "I can honestly say that I've never felt better in my life."

"You know," Besserman whispered. "A thought just occurred to me. Do you suppose that they've got this place wired to explode the way they did their other headquarters downtown?"

Miller stuck his head through the doorway from the kitchen. "Shit! You know you might be right! That would certainly explain why they haven't stormed the place. Maybe they just wanted to drive us in here to get rid of us in one big bunch."

"Well, what are we going to do about it?" Featherstone asked.

"It just occured to me that we might actually stand a better chance out in the open," Besserman said, jerking his chin toward the yard where the tail section of the Skytrader could be seen through the falling rain.

"I doubt that they'd be expecting it, in any case," Miller agreed. "That might give us the time we need to get some help here, if that cop can raise anybody on the radio."

"It's done," Lafeur said, emerging from the basement stairway. "Quiroga got ahold of Palacios personally, and it looks like they'd love the chance to nail a few more of these assholes in a stand-up fight. They've got an armored column heading our way from the bridge, where they just mopped up the last resistance."

"Get them back on the horn," Miller said. "Captain, come over here," he motioned to Chris. She sprinted to his side and knelt next to him, flattening out the map which was still taped to her thigh. "Tell them that we're breaking out of here, heading due north to the open country, toward elevation 309 on the military grid map of Santo Domingo. They'll know the place."

"We're leaving?" Lafeur asked, raising his eyebrows.

"Just do it, and quick," Miller snapped. "We don't know how much time we've got."

Luis was cursing precisely because there were no explosives wired in the headquarters. He had advised Padre Lazaro to do it for just such a situation, but he had been over-ruled. It hadn't conformed to the great strategic plan, which, he added to himself, had all gone to shit right in front of his eyes. Luis had linked up with the reserve group only to learn that every other team in the city had already been wiped out or, like Baca's group, was in the process of being exterminated. He had hoped to join up with Lazaro here, and together they could have moved the survivors off under cover of the storm into the hills north- west of the city, heading toward the Haitian border, or northeast into the rough country leading toward Punta Cana on the eastern tip of the island. When he had seen the bus pulling out of the driveway, he had known that the place had already been taken and Lazaro probably killed.

He had let his rage overcome his common sense. It would have been better just to let these people go and slip off quietly with his reduced force. But he knew these people had killed Lazaro, and he couldn't let them get away with that. Now he had to plan a way to storm this mansion, which was built like a fortress anyway, with thick stone walls surrounded by open lawns, perfect fields of fire, with barely a dozen fighters against what looked like at least as many of the enemy. And all of this he must accomplish before the police and army finished off the remnants of the movement in the city and decided to investigate the battle taking place in this northern suburb.

He had enough combat experience to know the value of concentration of force. That was the one major advantage the attacker had over the defender, the ability to mass his forces at the point of his own choosing, while the defender would have to disperse his forces to cover every eventuality. Luis sent two lightly wounded men to the far corners of the grounds behind the house, to cut off any possible escape by the defenders or to give warning of the arrival of reinforcements from outside. He sent another man up the road to the entry to the cul de sac on which the house stood to provide rear security. The remaining terrorists were now massed near the gardener's shed in a corner of the grounds where the shrubbery came closest to the house itself and where several ground floor windows and a sliding glass door offered ready access. One of his men had set up an M60 machinegun off to his left to provide covering fire for the assault. Luis could see the weary faces of the men and women crouching in the bushes around him as they looked to him for the sign. He raised his arm, when he heard the rattle of small arms fire coming from the rear of the house.

Two of the marines led the charge out through the patio area, past the pool. They raced twenty yards or so and then threw themselves to earth behind whatever cover they could find. Besserman and Gosher followed, rushing past them to the next covered position, while the first pair and those still in the house watched for any enemy reaction. There was a muzzle flash off to the right, near the base of the garden wall, and bullets kicked up tiny geysers of mud around Besserman's feet as he ran and dove behind a cement planter. Miller spotted the firing, and he and several others let rip on full automatic in the general direction.

Another muzzle flash appeared to the left of the garden, and Gosher, who had a 40mm grenade launcher mounted under the barrel of his Galil, popped a round at the tree behind which the firer appeared to be hiding, followed by several rounds of 7.62 calibre fire even before the grenade landed. There was a flash followed by a loud bang, and they heard a scream.

The first two marines were now maneuvering to get a shot at the

first firer, while Besserman and Gosher swung around the left side of
the house. This would secure a corridor for the others, with Quiroga
and Lafeur serving as rear guard to prevent the enemy from following
them through the house itself.

Chris flanked Featherstone as they went pounding across the patio
to the small cabana near the pool with Miller in close pursuit. a sudden
flurry of firing and several loud explosions came from the front of the
house.

"Here they come!" yelled Miller.

The M60 stitched a long burst along the side of the house where
the assault would go in, just above the level of the window sills. Luis
jumped up and charged forward, using the "silent run" technique
favored by the Israelis, no yelling or cheering, no firing by the attackers,
just trying to cover as much ground as possible until they could get
within killing range. As the ragged line of attackers neared the house,
several of them paused and hurled grenades through the windows. Luis
dove through his window even before the debris from the exploding
grenades had settled, spraying the room with bullets.

Lafeur had been about to rush out the back of the house, and
Quiroga had tarried a moment by the stairs when the attack went in.

"Go!" Quiroga shouted to Lafeur. "Don't stop!" He waved Lafeur
on frantically, then disappeared into the dark hallway.

Lafeur took his advice and ran for the cabana.

Quiroga heard heavy footsteps in the next room, took a firm, two-
handed grip on his revolver, and popped around the edge of the doorway. His first round caught a wild-haired woman full in the face, but
there was a man behind her who fired even before she had fallen out
of the way. The bullets chewed up the doorframe and sprayed plaster
and bits of concrete in Quiroga's face, and one of them creased his
forehead, just above the right eye.

Quiroga staggered back, then quickly turned and raced up the
stairs, diving into one of the bedrooms. He could hear people storming
through the ground floor, firing into each room. He suspected that they
hadn't realized that the defenders had moved out. He lay flat on his
stomach in the doorway of the bedroom, his pistol pointed directly at
the top of the stairs. Then he heard the bannister creak. He fired even
before he could identify the dark shape which appeared above the top
step. For a moment he feared that he had merely shot off someone's

hat, but then he heard a heavy tumbling noise. He smiled and raised himself, jumped to his feet and began racing toward a rear window, but then glanced back over his shoulder and saw several egg-shaped objects appear in the air, arching up from the ground floor. Each step seemed to take an hour, and he heard the grenades hit the floor just as he heaved himself through the window. The blast tore at his legs and propelled him through the air. He was only just able to remain conscious long enough to tuck his shoulder under and roll as he hit the grass outside after dropping ten feet, followed by a cascade of broken glass and bits of window frame.

Lafeur rolled to a stop next to the cabana. The first thing he realized was that the rain had suddenly stopped. Fat drops of water were plopping down from the trees, and he could hear the gurgle of water draining from the roof of the cabana through a broken piece of rainspout. In the distance, the clouds had begun to part, letting through the feeble rays of a full moon, giving the scene a slight bluish tinge. He looked back at the house and saw Quiroga land in a heap on the lawn and lay motionless.

"Run for the garden wall," Miller hissed at him from nearby. "We've probably got a minute before they realize that we're not in the house anymore. Then they'll come looking for us."

Lafeur didn't need to be told twice, and he ran as fast as his wobbly legs would carry him over the slippery, muddy lawn, but not toward the wall. He slung his shotgun over his shoulder and scooped Quiroga up in his arms as if he were a baby. Sometimes bulk paid off. He turned and lumbered quickly toward where Washington and Miller had braced themselves at the base of the eight-foot whitewashed wall and made a step using a Galil held between them.

Chris hit the step at the run, and they boosted her smoothly to the top of the wall, where she sat, straddling it. Featherstone came next, and it took all three of them to help the weakened man over the wall, where he tumbled unceremoniously into the tall grass on the other side.

There were shouts and firing coming from the house now, and they seemed to be getting closer. A wounded marine went next, followed by Gosher, and Lafeur found himself again in the role of rear guard.

Besserman had taken Chris' place on top of the wall and helped Miller over.

"Come on, Claude," Besserman shouted. "Run for it."

Lafeur hustled as fast as he could and heaved Quiroga's inert body up to Washington and the Gunny who were now both atop the wall. Then Lafeur took a jump and grabbed the top of the wall.

Although both men grabbed his arms and heaved, Lafeur couldn't quite pull his bulk over the top, his feet scraped desperately at the smooth face of the wall, but he dropped back heavily.

"Forget the damn shotgun, Claude," Besserman said. "Use it as a step."

Lafeur was panting hard as he jammed the barrel of the shotgun into the ground and braced the butt against the wall. There was more shouting now, and a bullet pinged off the wall nearby. Lafeur stepped on the butt of the weapon and was able to hoist himself up. Now, with his center of gravity over the top, he bent forward and flopped, head first, to the other side.

"This way," Miller called hoarsely from the shadows.

Washington and Besserman hit the ground almost at the same time as Lafeur, helped him to his feet, and all three scrambled off through the bush. A few yards farther on, they paused for breath. Lafeur turned in time to see a dark silhouette appear above the wall. A short burst of fire from Gosher made it disappear, and they heard a scream followed by a dull thud.

Luis had found Lazaro's body in the basement and let out a piercing animal yell which sent chills down the spines of the other fighters. He charged back upstairs. They had found only one man in the house, and he had gotten away, which meant that the firing he had heard was caused by a breakout attempt through the back.

He gathered his remaining troops, only seven or eight now, and formed them into a skirmish line across the yard, moving quickly, past the airplane, past the soccer field. There was some firing, but it was apparent that his prey had escaped.

He was just about to call in his men and pull back to the vehicles for their own escape when he was suddenly blinded by a searing bright light from above. He hadn't heard the whopping sound of the helicopter's rotors because of a stiff wind which carried the sound away, but now he could see the form of several American-made Hueys hovering over the house.

He tried to shout a warning, but his voice was drowned out in the snarling, ripping noise of the minigun from the lead helicopter as it plowed up the turf, a finger of fire which lashed out and cut down two of his men in an instant. There was nowhere to run or hide now, and Luis and his fighters fought back like cornered wolves, blazing away at the helicopters with their automatic weapons.

Luis could see that at least one helicopter had landed and disgorged infantry near the pool, and there were now gun flashes coming from the ground as well as from above. A woman fighting to his left groaned and doubled over, followed quickly by a husky black man to his right. His own Uzi clicked empty as he blasted away at the treacherous spotlight. He fumbled with another magazine, and a metallic voice called out from the darkness for him to surrender. Luis cursed and slapped another magazine into his weapon and brought it up to take better aim. He suddenly felt a burning sensation in his stomach and a cold one in his legs, and he realized that he was on his back now. There were more and more lights around and the sound of men walking nearby. Several men stooped over him, and he recognized one of them as being the man who had led the Cascos Negros back when the santista campaign had begun. The man smiled warmly, pulled an automatic from his holster and placed the barrel against Luis' forehead.

EPILOGUE

†

It was just turning light out when the army truck pulled up to the gate of the residence. Miller was sitting in the cab with the driver, and he was surprised to see that the same crowd of FSNs who had seen them off the night before were still there. The dark circles under their eyes implied that they had not gone home. They cheered as the truck moved through the gate, but he saw more than one person cross himself when they saw how few of those who had left were returning.

Featherstone was lying on a blanket in the truckbed, his head cradled in Chris' lap. He had refused to be taken to an army hospital until he had had a chance to return home. Miller had telephoned the embassy after their rescue, by the Dominican Marines, he was pleased to note, expecting Stileforth to object, but Jim Vernon had answered and explained that he was acting charg d'affaires since Stileforth had apparently suffered a nervous breakdown due to the strain, adding that he had restored Mrs. Featherstone to the residence as soon as the curfew had lifted earlier that morning.

The tailgate of the truck clanged down, and Washington and Besserman hopped off to help the others, but they were quickly though gently shoved aside by some of the burlier FSNs who insisted on the honor. Besserman accepted the fait accompli gracefully, and drifted off through the crowd, around the corner of the residence, where he leaned up against the wall, covered his face, and cried softly for the men he had left behind.

The crowd parted, permitting Anne, followed closely by Clare, to approach the truck just as Featherstone alighted. He gritted his teeth as she enveloped him in a bear hug, but the pain from his ribs was soon forgotten. Chris and Clare, in turn, wrapped their arms around their parents, and the assembled crowd clapped warmly. Not wanting to let go, the entire package then moved as a unit up the front steps of the residence, where Featherstone finally disentangled himself. He straightened up, wiped his eyes with a very nice silk handkerchief he had found in Abdol's coat pocket, and cleared his throat.

"My friends," Featherstone began, "I cannot tell you how happy I am to be back here, and how full my heart is to know what you all have done for me and for my family while I was in captivity. The most terrible thing about what I have just been through was the thought that I was all alone, but now I know that I never was, and the memory of your courage and faithfulness will remain with me long after the scars of my wounds have healed and disappeared." His voice cracked, and he could only wave in response to the frenzied cheering as Anne herded him into the house.

They sat in a circle in the living room as the teary-eyed butler and maids brought in trays of coffee and pastries. Featherstone noticed one tray heaped with dozens of his favorite chocolate chip cookies, which the cook personally brought in and set by his side. Anne, Chris, and Clare all squeezed in next to him on the couch, while Miller and Lafeur flopped in easy chairs. Gosher, Quiroga, and at least one of the marines had been taken to an Army hospital, where they were all reported in reasonably good condition. Besserman and Washington had headed for the marine house, to gather up the effects of the other marines. Vernon appeared at the terrace door and rushed inside.

"I'm glad to see you back, safe and sound," he said.

"I'm even gladder to be back, although I'm not as sound as I used to be," Featherstone replied, smiling.

"I'm afraid we had a little trouble in the office while you were out," Vernon said breezily. "Dane went bonkers, smashed up some of your office furniture, and now he's hiding in a closet in the embassy and won't come out. I've got one of the marines watching him."

"That's too bad," Featherstone said, shaking his head. "I'll authorize a med-evac for him immediately. He's been under enough pressure to break any man."

Anne just sighed, and Vernon grinned broadly, winking at Miller.

"I've also got a little problem, sir," Lafeur mumbled. "I think I have to turn myself in."

Featherstone raised his eyebrows. "Can't I leave the office for a minute without everything going to hell? NOW what's the problem, Claude?"

"Well," he began, stirring aimlessly at his coffee. "I seem to have appropriated large sums of U.S. taxpayers' money which I used to obtain information regarding your whereabouts and also to get the use of that airplane, and some other things."

"That doesn't sound too bad to me," Featherstone answered.

"It's just that we've got some rather strict rules about disbursing funds, incumbent upon us due to the great flexibility we have for conducting clandestine operations, and I'm afraid I didn't bother to get any of the appropriate authorizations. I can prove where all of the money went," he added hastily. "I got receipts for everything, but I don't think that will be enough to satisfy the auditors."

"Would this have anything to do with Maripaz?" Anne asked.

"Yes, in part," said Lafeur. "She's safe in San Juan by now with her family and a rather generous nest egg to get her started again, along with a U.S. green card and other documentation in a new name, which I also didn't have any authorization to give her."

Miller had told Featherstone about Maripaz' role in both the kidnapping and in the later rescue on the way back from the countryside, and now Featherstone hung his head. "I only wish I could have seen her before she left," he said sadly. "Still, Claude, I suspect that, since things turned out rather well, if I were to get on the secure line to Washington and explain things, we should be able to get some post hoc approvals for all of this. The only possible heartburn there would be that the bureaucrats in Washington didn't think of any of this themselves. Especially when I explain that, if there is any trouble with this, I would be more than happy to take the matter to the press, and I imagine that no one at Langley is going to want to go on record as having chastised you for using your initiative and saving your Ambassador simply because you didn't fill out all the forms first."

Lafeur smiled and sank back gratefully in his chair.

"I don't suppose you'll be ready for work for awhile," Vernon said, "but President Palacios has also been on the phone wanting to pay you an official visit at your earliest convenience. I think he wants to see about getting your approval for renewed American economic aid, even though he did overthrow a democratically elected government."

"He's a smart man," Featherstone chuckled. "He took the santistas' own plan and, instead of just short circuiting it, he turned it to his own use. I have to give him that. I also have to agree that I'm probably more favorably inclined toward him personally than any other ambassador is likely to be, seeing as he saved our bacon more than once in the last twenty-four hours. Tell him I'll see him this evening and that

I'll go to bat for him, for whatever it will be worth. You should also tell him that I'm retiring and will probably be out of here in short order. By the way, I'll be recommending that you move up to the DCM slot permanently and serve as charge until they find a permanent replacement, Jim."

Vernon smiled, and Anne squeezed Featherstone's hand and leaned her head on his shoulder.

"Let's go home, Bill," Anne said shyly.

"I never want to go anywhere else."

GLOSSARY

†

The following is a brief glossary of terms and acronyms found in the text. Although the author has made an effort to explain each term when first introduced, readers should find this glossary a convenient means of refreshing their memories. Please note that, while most of the terms are actual ones used in the *real* world, some of the terms, particularly those referring to fictional Dominican political parties, are not.

Armbrust (crossbow): A German-made anti-tank weapon. This is a disposable, single-shot weapon, and the firing tube is discarded after use. With an effective range of about 300 meters, its HEAT (high explosive anti-tank) round can penetrate most kinds of conventional armor. The unique feature of this weapon is that, unlike traditional recoilless weapons, it does not have a tremendous backblast of hot gases, relying instead on a countermass (of harmless plastic flakes) to absorb the normal recoil of firing the projectile. This permits the weapon to be fired from within a confined space, such as a room or bunker. It also lacks a significant flash when fired, and the report is no louder than a pistol shot.

COS: CIA Chief of Station. DCOS and ACOS would be the deputy chief and the acting chief respectively.

Country Team: This is essentially a committee within an embassy comprised of the heads of the different sections. This would include Political, Economic, Commercial, DAO, DEA, Administration, USAID, and others depending upon the size of the mission.

Dangle: Sometimes referred to as a double agent. To be precise, a dangle is an individual who is intentionally but clandestinely offered up by one intelligence service, terrorist group, or other organization, to another intelligence service with the purpose of passing false information or obtaining information on the target service's personnel and modus operandi.

DAO: Defense Attache Office. The office of military attaches in an American embassy. The senior military or naval officer assigned at the post is known as the DAO. This position normally remains with a particular armed service for a given country, usually depending upon which military service seems to have the greatest interest in the host country's affairs.

DCM: Deputy Chief of Mission. The second in command of an embassy. He or she becomes charge d'affaires in the absence of the Ambassador.

EPS: Ejercito Popular Sandinista (The Sandinista People's Army). The official name of the Armed Forces of Nicaragua under the Sandinista government.

FSN: Foreign Service National. These are the individuals hired locally by virtually every American embassy overseas. While they are generally citizens of the country in which the embassy in located, this need not be the case. In most American embassies, FSNs make up the majority of the people working there. While they do not have access to classified information, and thus do not work in the Political Section, Defense Attache's Office, DEA, or communications, they perform many other necessary functions as secretaries, maintenance, personnel, and in management positions, particularly in dealing with the local government on administrative matters. Many FSNs make working for the embassy a lifelong career, including full retirement benefits. After 15 years continuous service, an FSN is entitled to an immigrant visa to the United States. Also, because FSNs are necessarily paid based on local pay scales, a long-serving FSN will occasionally have a gross salary higher than that of the Ambassador himself, in countries with especially high costs of living.

Liberation Theology: That element of both Catholic and Protestant churches which adopted the premise that it is not possible to profess the Christian faith and, at the same time, accept gross inequities in social justice. The more energetic proponents of this movement, such as the radical priest Camilo Torres in Colombia in the 1960's, actually joined or even organized armed guerrilla movements. Another aspect of the movement was the unquestioning support of "progressive" (i.e., leftist) political organizations or governments, such as that of the Sandinistas in Nicaragua, despite questionable human rights records and the open opposition of the more traditional Church. While very fashionable in the 1960's and 1970's, it has lost much of its attraction with the collapse of communism in much of the world.

LP: Listening Post. This term is borrowed from the military expression for a small outpost tasked with discreetly monitoring enemy activity. In the espionage sense, it usually refers to any place at which the "take" from telephone taps or audio penetrations are received and recorded. Often it is an apartment or office in which the receiving equipment is installed, but it could also be a mobile LP, located in a van or other conveyance equipped with the necessary electronic gear. In the case of a telephone tap LP, the only requirement is a working phone line, to which the technicians connect the target line (or lines), making that phone essentially another extension for the target line. Likewise, the term OP (observation post), is another military term adapted to espionage purposes to designate a static surveillance position for observing activity.

MIR: Movement of the Revolutionary Left. While this name has been adopted by a number of parties in different Latin American countries, there does not appear to be any particular connection between them. In this case, it is a fictional group.

MOIS: Iranian Ministry of Intelligence and Security (Vezarat Etala'at). The official security arm of the Iranian government. It works extensively both within Iran and abroad to provide intelligence, pursue opponents of the regime, and to help export the Islamic fundamentalist revolution.

Mujaheddin-e Khalq: A pro-communist guerrilla group within Iran which has been largely eliminated by the efforts of the Sepah and MOIS.

NOD: Night Observation Device: A sighting device which magnifies ambient light, sometimes needing as little as star light, to provide visibility. This is a passive system that emits no energy to function.

PCD: Christian Democratic Party. There is such a party in most Latin

American and European countries, and there are some international ties between them. In this case, it is another fictional organization.

PE-2: A new generation of plastic explosive replacing the popular (among terrorists) Czech Semtex and the American C4. Like Semtex and C4, PE-2 is a soft, pliable material but with an even higher *brissance* (explosive) rating.

Sagger: A Soviet-made, man-portable anti-armor missile which made its spectacular battlefield debut in the Arab-Israeli October War of 1973. Although somewhat obsolescent by today's standards, it has a range of 2,000 meters, and its HEAT (High Explosive Anti-Tank) warhead can penetrate 500mm of standard armor plate. Its major drawback is that it must be "flown" by the firer manually, by using a small joystick, to the target, which means that, if the firer can be distracted by counterfire, the missile will likely swerve and miss.

Sepah: Short for the Etelaat-e Sepah-e Pasdaran, the intelligence arm of the Iranian Revolutionary Guard Corps. In organization and mission it parallels the MOIS, but concentrates its efforts within Iran, generally speaking. This group has been more involved in sponsoring outright terrorism and the assassination of individuals hostile to the fundamentalist regime in Iran than has the MOIS.

Thermal Imager: Similar to a NOD in purpose but using infrared to identify heat sources, generally living organisms or vehicle engines. The advantage of this system is that it can "see through" smoke and other obstructions and pick out likely targets against colder backgrounds, as in the urban environment.

Tudeh Party: The outlawed communist party in Iran.

Walk-in: A generic term used to describe anyone who offers information or services at an American facility overseas. While this usually involves someone actually "walking" into an embassy, he or she could call or write first, and might do this at some facility other than an embassy, such as the residence of an American official. A price is frequently demanded in return for the cooperation, such as resettlement in the States or money. While most of these cases involve mentally unbalanced people or those who are merely harassing the Americans, there is an occasional windfall of vital intelligence when the walk-in proves to be a foreign intelligence officer or terrorist or someone else with valuable information to offer. The walk-in is first screened by the local hire guards at the entrance and then passed on the Marine security guard. If his case appears to merit further interview, he will be searched for weapons and escorted to the "walk-in room" where an embassy officer will check his identification and discuss the case.